THE CRUSADER'S VOW

A Medieval Romance

Claire Delacroix

Books by Claire Delacroix

Time Travel Romances
ONCE UPON A KISS
THE LAST HIGHLANDER
THE MOONSTONE
LOVE POTION #9

Medieval Romances
ROMANCE OF THE ROSE
HONEYED LIES
UNICORN BRIDE
THE SORCERESS
ROARKE'S FOLLY
PEARL BEYOND PRICE
THE MAGICIAN'S QUEST
UNICORN VENGEANCE
MY LADY'S CHAMPION
ENCHANTED
MY LADY'S DESIRE

The Bride Quest
THE PRINCESS
THE DAMSEL
THE HEIRESS
THE COUNTESS
THE BEAUTY
THE TEMPTRESS

The Rogues of Ravensmuir
THE ROGUE
THE SCOUNDREL
THE WARRIOR

The Jewels of Kinfairlie
THE BEAUTY BRIDE
THE ROSE RED BRIDE
THE SNOW WHITE BRIDE
The Ballad of Rosamunde

The True Love Brides
THE RENEGADE'S HEART
THE HIGHLANDER'S CURSE
THE FROST MAIDEN'S KISS

THE WARRIOR'S PRIZE

The Brides of Inverfyre
THE MERCENARY'S BRIDE
THE RUNAWAY BRIDE

The Champions of St. Euphemia
THE CRUSADER'S BRIDE
THE CRUSADER'S HEART
THE CRUSADER'S KISS
THE CRUSADER'S VOW
THE CRUSADER'S HANDFAST

Rogues & Angels
ONE KNIGHT ENCHANTED
ONE KNIGHT'S RETURN

The Brides of North Barrows
SOMETHING WICKED THIS WAY COMES
A DUKE BY ANY OTHER NAME

Short Stories and Novellas
An Elegy for Melusine
BEGUILED

Dear Reader;

In **The Crusader's Vow**, the quest of the *Champions of St. Euphemia* continues to Scotland, as Fergus returns home—with Duncan, his squire Hamish, Leila, two Templars, and the hidden reliquary. It's been four years since his departure and he has been plagued by a sense of foreboding since the party left Jerusalem, even though he is eager to see his betrothed again. What will he find at Killairic? Has Isobel waited for him, as Fergus expects, or was Duncan right about her nature? And what about the fiery kiss that Leila and Fergus shared at Haynesdale? Was it an impulse or a sign of the future? Danger seems to follow the reliquary—will it be safe at Killairic? All of these questions and more come to the fore in this book, which was a lot of fun to write.

One of the elements I wanted to explore in **The Crusader's Vow** was the notion of home—where you find it, what it's like to return there, and how changes in your home affect your perspective. Fergus is due for a surprise or two on his homecoming, while Leila has left the home she knew far behind. They're both confronted with choices in this story, choices that maybe neither of them anticipated—but their decisions will influence their chances for a happily-ever-after. I like Fergus' resolve to keep his promises, as well as Leila's determination to make her life what she wants it to be. I particularly like how these two help and change each other. It's only when they begin to work together that their chance of a happy marriage improves.

Like most grand adventures, the writing of *The Champions of St. Euphemia* series has brought its share of surprises, most notably in the addition of Radegunde and Duncan's story to the saga. **The Crusader's Handfast** includes the final epilogue on the treasure entrusted to the party that left Jerusalem, as well as the romance of Radegunde and Duncan. This book is available now and there's an excerpt in the back of this one for you to read. It's very satisfying for me to have the saga complete, and I hope you enjoy all five books.

As always, please follow my blog or subscribe to my monthly newsletter, **Knights & Rogues**, to keep up to date on all the news about my medieval romances. The newsletter contains advance notice of most sales on my books, as well as chances to win audiobooks, cover reveals, and updated news of releases.

Thank you for reading my books! I hope you enjoy Fergus and Leila's story!

All my best
Claire
http://delacroix.net

The Crusader's Vow

SATURDAY, APRIL 23, 1188

Feast Day of Saint George

Claire Delacroix

PROLOGUE

Haynesdale

It seemed that all was right with his fellows. Fergus would never have anticipated such a happy conclusion to events when they had left Jerusalem the previous summer. But on this fine spring evening, Bartholomew and Anna were returned, the signet ring of Haynesdale placed upon Bartholomew's finger by King Henry himself and the seal in Bartholomew's purse. The new couple had a license to hold an annual fair and—thanks to the efforts led by Fergus—had returned to find the old keep of Haynesdale taking shape once more. Bartholomew had brought grain in York and the mill was turning even now, grinding flour from some of it while the rest would be sown in the fields that had already been plowed.

Fergus was glad that his friend and comrade had found happiness, and also that he had been able to help while Bartholomew and Anna sought the king's favor.

His thoughts inevitably turned to his own future. Now, Fergus could return home to Isobel. It had been four years since his departure, and he was eager to see his beloved again. He left the festivities in the great hall when the dancing began and stepped out into the night. The moon was full and the sky was clear.

Fergus smiled as he stared up at the glittering stars. Killairic—home—was so close, and there, every dream he yearned to fulfill. He wished, not for the first time, that his gift for foresight included his own future. He saw happiness for Bartholomew and Anna, just as he had seen it for Wulfe and Christina, and Gaston and Ysmaine. He saw babies in the futures of each of the couples, a number of children, their eyes filled with joy and mischief. He even could see his companion Duncan cradling a dark-haired child. But for himself? There was no glimmer of what the future held for him.

There was only that persistent sense of foreboding, the one that had plagued him since their departure from Jerusalem. He had assumed thus far that the shadow had been about the future of his companions or the fate of the reliquary they secretly carried, but on this night, Fergus wondered what he would find when he arrived home. He hoped his father was well as yet, for he wanted days by the fire to tell the older man of all he had seen. He could not imagine his welcome from Isobel, who surely had been as impatient for his return as he had been. He wondered how Killairic itself had changed, if it had changed at all. There would have been births and deaths in the village during such a long time, but he hoped that those he wished most to see were hale. Had there been battles? He imagined as much, for there was often strife in Galloway, and hoped that Killairic had fared well.

The sense of dread persisted, though. Fergus decided it was impatience, no more than that, and strode toward the village. If he walked, he might sleep. Perhaps he would ride forth the next morning, since Bartholomew was returned.

His heart fluttered at the promise of that, and he resolved it would be so. He would see his fellows again at his own nuptials, to be sure, for they had pledged to come to Scotland. It could not be long before he and Isobel exchanged their vows.

A slight movement caught his eye, and Fergus realized that he was not the only one to have left the celebration. Leila sat by the river, staring up at the sky. It still surprised him to see her in women's garb, though on this night, she wore no veil. Her dark hair gleamed in the moonlight. Her face was tipped up to the moon, and its light touched her features with silver. His heart contracted at the sight of her, for he had missed her as much as any of the party who had ridden to France. She did not seem to be aware of his presence, so he cleared his throat as he approached.

"You are missing the dancing," he said when she glanced his way.

Leila smiled and moved along the log where she was seated, making room for him. "I do not know your dances."

"You could learn. I could teach you."

She chuckled. "And what will your betrothed think, if you arrive home not only with a Saracen woman in your company but one you have taught to dance?"

Fergus was startled. "I had not thought of it."

"She will believe you have brought home your whore," Leila said with conviction. "There is no need to reinforce that conclusion."

Fergus leaned forward, bracing his elbows on his knees, and looked at her. "You have been thinking of this."

"I have been thinking of many things." She gestured to the moon. "It is full, the tenth full moon since we left Jerusalem."

"I suppose it is."

"I know it is. I have counted them."

He eyed her, hearing the sadness in her tone. "What does that mean, Leila?"

"It means that my cousin's son is a year old." She fell silent then.

"You miss your cousin?"

"Of course! We grew up together. She was the one whose hair I learned to braid and arrange." Leila sighed. "I grew up in my uncle's home after the death of my parents. We might have been sisters, almost twin sisters, for we were born the same month."

As he listened, Fergus realized how little he knew about the woman who had joined their company in Jerusalem. "When did your parents die?"

"When I was an infant."

He saw the tear glisten on her cheek and wished he had the right to brush it away. "I would take you back to Outremer, if you wish it," he found himself saying. The offer was impulsive, but as soon as the words were uttered, Fergus knew it was true. What if Leila did return to the east? He would regret the lost opportunity to learn more about her, to be sure. He could not imagine a future in which he never saw her again, yet realized in this moment, that it might well come to be.

Fergus had assumed she would stay, but had never thought of what she would do.

Leila wiped her tears and touched the back of his hand with her fingertips. "I thank you for that, for you know the price of what you offer. But I cannot go back."

"Not even to see your cousin?"

"Especially not. It was my uncle who arranged my marriage."

Fergus dared to acknowledge his own relief, even as he realized it was selfish. How would he feel when she wed another man? It was strange to admit that a possessiveness lurked within him, for he had no right to make any claim upon her. Perhaps it was only that he wished to see her happy, and he doubted that a match Leila had fled had any power to make her so.

The notion that others would see her as his whore was both troubling and titillating. It was all too easy to imagine a night of exploring Leila's charms. He liked her throaty laughter and found her smile to be both shy and knowing.

Clearly, he had been too long without Isobel's sweet touch.

He cleared his throat again. "Bartholomew said you were to be wed against your will, and that was why you wanted to leave Jerusalem."

Leila nodded and spoke mildly. "A marriage had been arranged."

"That happens to many."

"It does, and if I had known naught of the man, I would have accepted my uncle's word. But I had heard rumors of his violence."

That she might have been wed to a man who might treat her with less than adoration sent fire through Fergus. "You should have told your uncle," he said, hearing his outrage.

"I did! But the alliance from the marriage was good for both families. Like a good comrade, my uncle dismissed the rumors that he believed to be malicious."

"You did not."

She turned to face him, her dark eyes filled with conviction. "Women do not lie to each other about such matters. All the same, I could not prove what I had heard."

This was intriguing. Leila had pretended to be a boy in order to tend horses at the Templar stables. It seemed that she had defied expectation in other ways. Fergus wanted to know more. "Who told you?"

"It does not matter now. I believed her, and so I fled."

"Did your cousin know of your plan?"

Leila smiled. "Aziza suggested it. She knew I went to the Temple to help with the horses, because my uncle would not have approved and she helped to disguise my absences. She told me to find a knight there to aid me, preferably one who was leaving Jerusalem soon." She watched her own fingers as she pleated the fabric of her kirtle, and he knew she was reliving her fears in that moment. He wanted to draw her close and console her, but fought the urge for it was inappropriate. "But I only knew Bartholomew. He was not inclined to help me."

"But fortunately, I overheard you."

"You did." Leila met his gaze once more. "Thank you." She smiled at him and flushed a little, her eyes seeming to glow. Her lips parted and he found himself desiring a kiss.

Just one.

Though it was not his to take.

Leila did not avert her gaze and the air seemed to heat between them. Fergus felt keenly aware of Leila as a woman. He noted the ripe curve of her lips, the thick waves of her dark hair, the luminosity of her eyes, the sweet curve of her throat. She was tiny compared to him and delicately wrought, but achingly feminine. He had an urge to protect her, even as he was aware of her strength and resolve. It was a marvel what strong bonds grew between fellow travelers on a journey such as theirs had been.

Fergus recognized that it had not been impulse alone, or even a need to do what was right, that had prompted his offer in Jerusalem to hide Leila in their party. She was both resilient and vulnerable, beautiful and strong, mysterious yet forthright. He had been intrigued with her when he had overheard that conversation, and more so when first he had glimpsed her. She had proven to be an asset to their party more than once, gave much and asked for little, yet as her hair lifted in the breeze, he wanted more for her.

Far more.

It was not good enough for her to be considered any man's whore.

She should be a queen.

"Any regrets?" Fergus asked, his own voice husky.

"Only for what can never be," Leila admitted softly. "I would see my cousin again, but not return to Palestine. I would play with her son, but not risk my own future. I would wed, with my uncle's blessing, but not to the man he chose." She blinked quickly and shook her head once more. "I want the impossible, and so I fear that there is only disappointment ahead for me."

"Nay, not that." Fergus had his arm around her waist before he realized what he did, and once her soft warmth was against him, he could not pull away.

"What do you see in my future days?" she asked. "Duncan says you can see what will come."

"Not on command. Only in dreams and glimpses."

She cast him a quick smile. "Do you lie because you have seen sorrow in my future, or is my future veiled?"

"I would never lie to you, Leila." He spoke with conviction, because it was true.

"Not even out of kindness?"

"Not even then." Fergus took a breath and confessed the truth. "I have not had any glimpse of your future." He did not admit that he believed that might be because she would return to the east.

He would not consider that she had no future, only that it was not within his world.

"No future for me," she echoed, a bit of sadness in her voice.

"Just because I cannot see it does not mean as much. I never see my own."

"Then perhaps our future days are bound together," she whispered, making the opposite conclusion to his own.

Fergus did not know what to say.

Leila looked up at him, then, and her gaze lingered on his mouth. She ran the tip of her own tongue across her bottom lip, as if she hungered for more than he had any right to give, then she took a deep breath and dropped her gaze, hiding her thoughts from him.

Fergus felt immediately bereft. "What will you do?" He lifted one hand when she did not reply. "Will you stay here at Haynesdale with Bartholomew and Anna? I know they would welcome you."

Leila shook her head.

"Will you continue to Killairic with Duncan and me?"

"And face the wrath of your betrothed?" she suggested, a smile in her voice.

"Isobel might not make the conclusion you expect."

"Then she is a fool," she said hotly and straightened beside him. "For any woman with blood in her veins would desire a man so loyal of heart as you, even if he were not wrought so tall and fine, nor possessed of such valor."

"Leila!" Fergus protested, surprised by her endorsement. "You know little of me..."

"After eleven months in each other's company, I know much of you, and all of it has merit." She looked up at him, her eyes flashing. "I admire you, Fergus. You are the manner of man to whom I should like to pledge my troth." Her gaze clung to his, her desire so easily read that Fergus was shocked.

Indeed, her confession made his heart leap, and he wished it had not.

Leila must have seen his expression change, for she smiled ruefully. "You need not fear that I will act upon this, or that I will be more than your faithful companion," she continued more quietly. "But if the lady Isobel fails to see your merit, or dares to doubt your integrity, she will answer to me."

Fergus's answering smile faded when Leila's hand landed on his thigh and any words died on his lips. His entire body went taut as an unruly desire rolled through him.

He had been chaste too long, to be sure.

Leila's eyes were so dark as to be fathomless. Fergus could not tear his gaze away from her. When she spoke, her voice dropped low with intent. "And if there is ever any deed you would desire of me, Fergus, you have only to ask."

Fergus was honored and might have admitted as much, but he had no chance. For Leila caught her breath, then stretched up and touched her lips to his. He knew it was intended to be a chaste kiss, perhaps the sole one they would ever exchange, but her caress fed that newfound fire within him.

He found himself bending closer, unable to resist what she offered so freely. He cupped her nape in his hand and deepened their kiss, tasting her sweetness and wanting more.

When she opened her mouth to him, surrendering to their embrace, Fergus realized that Leila was not the only one who wished for the impossible.

WEDNESDAY, APRIL 27, 1188

Feast Day of Saint Anastasius

CHAPTER ONE

Dumfries, Scotland

eila regretted that impulsive kiss.

She should never have touched Fergus. She should never have kissed him. She should never have indulged her secret yearning. Now, her desire for him burned like a flame. It was distracting. It was inappropriate. And worse, that one kiss had changed the way Fergus looked at her, forevermore.

She had sacrificed his friendship for a single kiss, and while she could not regret the wondrous taste of pleasure itself, she did mourn the loss of his companionship. He had left her that night and avoided her ever since. He no longer spoke directly to her and did not even meet her gaze.

Fergus was clearly disgusted with her. Did he think she had behaved like a whore?

Leila realized quickly that the kiss that she had desired beyond all else had come at a very high price.

She was lonely as a result of his lost companionship. Hamish, Fergus' squire, had not even been able to look her in the eye since the revelation at Haynesdale that she was not a boy. The two

Templars who had accompanied them from Châmont-sur-Maine and thence from Haynesdale had seldom addressed her when they believed her to be a squire. They regarded her with something akin to horror now that they knew the truth. She was an infidel to them in more ways than one. Leila could not help but think that their brethren in Palestine would not have been quite so distant. Gaston had always spoken to her, for example, as had Fergus until that kiss.

The Templars' squires contented themselves with whispering to each other like young girls, and Leila did not deign to give them even a glance. The warrior Duncan was the only person who had talked to her since leaving Haynesdale the morning after that fateful kiss. Mostly she spoke to him of his beloved Radegunde. He wanted to know every detail of what Leila had observed of Radegunde while at Châmont-sur-Maine, and recognizing that his curiosity was born of affection, she indulged him. Repeatedly.

Duncan was not the only one to miss Radegunde and her merry nature. Leila missed her friend as well as the company of women, even those far above her station. She rode out from Haynesdale in a company entirely male, except for herself. She chose not to disguise herself as a boy again, for she did not want to enter Fergus' home under a pretense. At the same time, she knew that she would be assumed to be a whore.

Some notions had no borders.

What was she to do? Her plan had been to escape the marriage arranged for her by her uncle, and little more than that. The party of knights leaving Jerusalem had offered the perfect cover, especially when she was given the role of Fergus' third squire. But now the quest reached its completion. All of the knights were home, save Fergus, and his home was just ahead.

She could have remained at Châmont-sur-Maine or even Haynesdale, but she could not bear the possibility of parting forever from Fergus. She had not lied to Fergus before that kiss— in fact, she had not told him the fullness of the truth. Leila knew she loved Fergus and that he was the sole man she wished to wed. She had no expectation that her love would be returned, but could not abandon his company that readily.

What would she do once she arrived at Killairic? She was curious to see his home, of course, and would like to meet those he held in affection. She even wanted a glimpse of Isobel, but what then?

Her hope that she might make a future there, perhaps even with Fergus himself, was a foolish dream. He adored Isobel. She would love no other than him. Yet in this land, she could not disappear into the crowd. Each day that they rode north, Leila was more obviously a foreigner and the curious stares were more open. Yet she was resolved not to return to the east.

Would she be compelled to become a whore? Without a man to defend her, Leila could see no other choices. Plus she was resolved to wed only for love, since her departure had been a protest against an arranged match. It made no sense to come so far and compromise her hopes for her future.

Was there any chance she might win Fergus' heart? Leila could not be certain until Fergus and Isobel exchanged their vows. She would decide what to do when that marriage was celebrated, and not before.

When they departed Haynesdale, Leila refused to delay the party and declined any concessions the men would have made to her gender. She rode long and hard, just as they did, and slept on the ground, just as they did, and washed quickly in cold rivers, just as they did. In a way, she admired Fergus' haste to reach home and his beloved.

She knew she would come to love Scotland as much as her birthplace. The winter had been longer and colder than any season Leila had ever endured but that made the arrival of spring seem even sweeter. She took note of the greenery crowning the hills, the activity of birds, the appearance of flowers by the road. The air warmed each afternoon, smelling rich with new growth and possibility, though it was still chilly in the morning and evening. The land was fertile and lush, the wind was crisp, and the streams were clear.

The land was a veritable paradise.

Leila knew she was not the only one who was relieved when Fergus chose to halt at Lincluden Abbey on what was to be their last night before reaching Killairic. The monks and nuns welcomed them kindly, although with many glances at Leila. The Templars, Enguerrand and Yvan, were visibly gladdened by the choice, though Duncan was less impressed with their accommodations. He grumbled that he had enough of monks but Fergus only smiled at him. Leila welcomed the opportunity to both bathe and sleep on a straw pallet. She feigned incomprehension when she was asked a few questions and was glad of the imposition of the establishment's vows of silence.

She awakened to a sunny day, filled with anticipation to see Fergus' home.

They rode through Dumfries early in the morning, when the fishermen were selling their wares, and the bustle of commerce was keenly familiar. Leila could have spent a day there easily, examining the wares, but Fergus was intent upon reaching Killairic by noon. It was not long before they took a road leading to the west. The land grew even more beautiful, though Leila would not have believed it possible. The wind was crisp and smelled of the salt of the sea, and the sun was warm on their shoulders. The company rode in veritable silence, but she felt the anticipation of both Fergus and Duncan.

When they crested a rise, Leila caught her breath at the hilly expanse of land spread before her with the sea sparkling beyond it. The forest was so richly green that she thought her eyes deceived her. The water, beginning at the base of the hill and stretching into the distance, shone silver in the morning light. Mist was gathered near the water and obscured the view to the left and in the distance. The wind lifted her hair, though, and she imagined the mist would soon disperse.

Perched on a hill several miles ahead of them was a keep ringed with walls. The square tower was built of stone, though it was much smaller than those she had seen further south. The tower was surrounded by a fence of timber with a moat, and there was a village nestled within the walls. A pennant waved from the high tower of the keep, though Leila could not discern its insignia at this distance.

She saw a profusion of white within the walls on the south side, moving in the breeze, and reasoned that there was an orchard in bloom sheltered there. Smoke rose in the morning air from fires both inside the walls and in the village. Two men worked furrows into a field to the far right, pushing a plow, birds swooping around them as they worked. A stream sparkled as it ran past the keep, some of it diverted to fill the moat, then continued to the left. Upstream of the keep there was a mill and a millpond, too. Part of the millpond looked to be divided from the rest with nets and she wondered what manner of fish they raised.

What a prosperous and peaceful holding!

"Home," Fergus said beside her, his satisfaction clear. Leila glanced toward him quickly, her heart thumping that he spoke to her again. She seized the chance to admire his rugged good looks. His hair was auburn and curled on his collar. His eyes were an enticing green, and he was both tall and broad-shouldered. He had changed his garb when they left Haynesdale, packing his mail away and dressing instead as Duncan had for months. A length of plaid was wrapped around his waist, its hues echoing that of the wild land around her. He wore a white chemise, open at the throat, a boiled leather jerkin and dark boots. His cloak was wool, like her own, but lined with fur. He looked vital and masculine, so alluring that her lips burned in memory of that kiss.

He had come to ride beside her, which was a welcome change, but still avoided her gaze. Leila would take all improvements, however small. She blamed her own impetuous kiss for the change and was greedy for more of him than even this.

"Beautiful," she said, ensuring that her admiration showed.

Fergus smiled, obviously pleased. "You can perhaps see how the promise of returning here gave me strength and hope."

"I can, indeed. What a dream to return to a land of abundance, a good home and a loving betrothed." Leila swallowed. "I am certain that you and Isobel will have many happy years together."

Fergus opened his mouth as if to speak, then closed it again. After a moment, he pointed down the water. "This is the Solway Firth. The far shore is Cumbria, sworn to the English king, but this shore is Galloway and Scotland. You can see Henry II's realm on a clear day." His tone was cool, as if she were a visiting acquaintance, and Leila supposed that she was.

She also supposed she should not have mentioned Isobel. But was the prospect of seeing his beloved not the main reason for his pleasure? How she wished a man might wait for her with such ardor!

Nay, she wanted Fergus to speak of her with such ardor.

She was a fool, to be sure.

"And that keep ahead is Killairic," he continued.

Leila nodded in understanding. "I should have guessed as much."

"How so?"

"The horses have quickened their pace, at least yours and Duncan's have done so. They recognized the road when we left Dumfries." She smiled. "Every creature's step is lightened at the prospect of returning home. After four years away, you must be glad to see this place again."

"I am." Fergus spared her another intent but quick glance. "Does that mean your step will never be lightened again?"

Leila shook her head. "No. It means I will make myself a new home." She let Fergus see her resolve.

"You did not care so much for your own?"

"I loved it dearly. I would never have left, save that the one thing of greater import to me was at risk."

"Your chance to choose your spouse?"

"And thus my happiness. I did not believe I needed to choose my husband before a bad one was chosen for me. I would not condemn myself to a life of woe, even to please my uncle." She shrugged. "I had to choose."

"You miss Outremer."

"Of course. But the choice is made, and now my future must be made."

Fergus studied her, his curiosity clear. "Where?"

"Here, if I am welcome to linger," she said, holding his gaze for a long moment.

"But it is so different!"

Leila noted that he did not give her any reassurance, but refused to be insulted. The choice of welcoming a guest might not be his to make. Fergus was honest, and she admired that trait. He never promised what he could not ensure was given.

And every vow he made was kept.

"It is, and I like that difference," she said instead. "The earth is fertile and so green that it defies belief. I like the mist and the rain, and the confidence that there will not only be water but enough of it." Leila smiled. "And I like the wildness of the hills. It seems that I could ride away from the party and be utterly alone within moments."

"You could be."

"What a beguiling notion." She shook her head, looking around herself with wonder. "I have lived in cities all my life. I have known dust and sun and crowded markets. I like that there is this tranquility and yet the town is so very close." She smiled at him again. "This could be an earthly paradise. Do you know anyone named Adam or Eve?"

Fergus laughed. "Be warned, Leila. Scotland is much colder than your home, without olives or so many fruits."

"Each land has its own fruit. I see that orchard within the walls of Killairic. What kind of trees are those that bloom?"

"Apples, mostly, though there are a few others."

"A fine and versatile fruit." She nodded approval. "And so there must be bees, and so there must be honey."

"You seek familiarity in the differences," he noted.

"I have made my choice, Fergus, and I must ensure its success," Leila replied. "There is much I left behind, to be sure, but it is better to admire in the road ahead. Yearning for the past is of no merit."

His gaze was thoughtful and he was silent for a moment.

"Can you not envision any situation that would compel you to surrender Killairic?" she asked, knowing full well that it was different for a man and heir, but wanting him to understand.

"Nay," he said without hesitation.

"Truly?"

Fergus frowned but did not reply. "It will be easier for you to remain in Scotland if you take a husband."

"No doubt," Leila agreed, her words tight. She supposed that wedding another man was one way to give herself some security. It was a notion of some merit. Perhaps she would find love in an arranged match, as Gaston and Ysmaine had. It might be a compromise that would lead to the happiness she sought.

In this land, though, Leila was at a disadvantage, in language, custom, and the knowledge of men's reputations. She wondered if Fergus would grant her advice as to suitable candidates. Were there more men like him in this land? Leila could only hope so. A tall and handsome man of honor with a valiant nature would suit her well, even if that man could not be Fergus.

He said naught, though, so she decided to ask. Fergus would be a good judge of character, particularly of his fellows.

She cleared her throat. "Perhaps you might be so kind as to suggest men of merit to me. I will not have my old sources of gossip available to me, after all, and I would prefer not to put myself in a similar situation to the one I left."

Fergus seemed startled, then he nodded. "Of course." He pointed again and changed the subject, though Leila could not imagine why. Perhaps he had never been a matchmaker before. Perhaps it was not the occupation of men in this land. "There is an herb garden beyond the orchard, also within the walls, which is where the bees are kept."

"I will be delighted to see it all."

"My father will be glad to show you. He takes great pride in Killairic. He has overseen much of its construction, since it was a simple timber keep when he took command of it."

Leila gestured to the water glistening in the distance. "And what lies out of view? Is it the ocean itself?" It amazed her that she could ride further west, then sail south and eventually back to the Mediterranean again, then onward to Palestine. Would it take longer by sea or not? It would be much farther, to be sure.

"Eventually, but first a traveler must sail around the Rhinns of Galloway, then between Ireland and the western Isles." Her confusion must have shown because he smiled. "The western islands are the realm of the Kings of the Isles, laid bare to both wind and sea."

Leila wanted immediately to see them. Fergus' affection for his homeland was more than clear and she could understand his feelings. This journey had awakened her taste to see even more of the world than she had. "I thought there was a king of Scotland. Duncan mentioned as much when we left Haynesdale."

"And so there is, but the isles have always been reluctant to bow to authority from afar. They were claimed by the Irish from across the sea, and thence by the Vikings, crossing another sea. The highlanders would claim them and the English would claim them, and the Scottish kings try to contain them as well. In the northern islands, the Norwegian king makes claims. Alliances are uneasy in these parts and always shifting."

"That sounds familiar," Leila said wryly and Fergus smiled.

"I imagine that situation is familiar to more people than not."

"And your home?"

"Is a small holding, as you see, but sits at a junction of a kind. That river is a border between Galloway and Scotland, although sometimes this side of the river is pledged to England. From the southwest and northwest, the Kings of the Isles have their lands and often dispute who holds what. Up Solway Firth and on this shore, much news and many warriors travel. My father is trusted to ensure a careful alliance between kings and lords, and Killairic has prospered as a result of his efforts." He spared Leila a fleeting smile. "My marriage will secure his responsibility for the future."

Leila did not ask about Isobel this time. "Tell me of Galloway," she invited instead.

"To the immediate west of Killairic are the lands of the Lords of Galloway, my cousins. They are much inclined to warfare. I was named for Fergus, Lord of Galloway, who died just before I was born. His sons, Uchtred and Gille Brigte, battled over his territories until Gille Brigte killed his own brother and claimed his lands." Fergus' lips tightened to a grim line. "It was a barbaric end for a savage warrior." He paused, then added with care. "They are unpredictable allies despite our blood bond."

"Or perhaps because of it," Leila suggested. She considered the gently rolling hills and wondered at them being scarred by warfare.

Fergus nodded. "Perhaps."

"And Killairic?"

"Granted to my father by the English king upon the surrender of Fergus, to defend the border between his lands to the east and south, and those claimed by Fergus' sons to the west. The Scottish king agreed to the grant, and marriage to my mother secured my father's alliance with the Scottish king."

"She was related to him?"

"His niece."

"So, your father is of Galloway and your mother of Scotland."

"Aye."

Leila had to ask. "And the lady Isobel?"

"Her kin are of the Kingdom of the Isles but have no claim to that throne. She has Norwegian blood, as do many on the islands. They are tall and fair, with golden hair and eyes of blue."

Leila could not help but think that she, small and dark, would compare badly to a woman of such queenly stature. She had already noted that the Franj had great preference for women with blond hair and wondered if her hope of finding a husband who cared for her might be doomed.

She straightened in her saddle. She would not expect failure, not before she had tried to succeed.

"Her father fought for Fergus and was granted a holding to the west of here, closer to the sea. Dunnisbrae it is called. We knew each other as children, and it was decided early that our nuptials would balance the ambitions of the English king to expand north and west from Carlisle."

"And so your marriage will have you torn between loyalties?" Leila asked, trying to keep her tone as dispassionate as his. In truth, she was fiercely interested in this Isobel who had claimed Fergus' heart so securely and hoped the lady deserved Fergus' regard. She had already divined that Duncan did not think Isobel trustworthy, which made her doubly intent upon making her own assessment.

She supposed she would have that opportunity soon.

Perhaps Isobel awaited Fergus' return at Killairic. Leila had never asked the whereabouts of his betrothed. Her innards clenched at the prospect of seeing Fergus wed his beloved in the next few days. No doubt the celebration would not be delayed any longer after his return.

Would Isobel tolerate Leila's presence at Killairic?

While her thoughts spun, Fergus laughed. "It is an established way to ensure that a man best keeps his obligations."

"I suppose as much," Leila had to concede. "I thought yours was a love match."

"It is, but that is a fortunate coincidence. Even if Isobel and I were not in love, we might be fated to wed all the same. The alliance is a good one for both families and both kings."

And if Isobel had not possessed a lineage that would offer a strategic alliance, then Fergus might not have been permitted to wed his beloved. Leila's lips thinned that some matters remained the same in all lands.

That was the moment she realized how little advantage there could be to any man in wedding her. She had no family connections, fortune, or powerful alliance to offer. And she was not blond. It might well be that no man would find her alluring in this land where women were so much more fair, much less come to love her. The prospect was sobering. Would she even be able to ensure her survival as a whore?

Perhaps that explained Fergus' silence. Perhaps he understood the challenge that faced her better than Leila did.

Nay, she would not lose hope. Not now. Somehow, Leila had to find a future for herself and she was determined that it should be in Scotland. The adventure, she reminded herself, had only just begun.

The forest closed around the road ahead as it dipped down to a river, and Fergus halted his destrier.

"Enguerrand, will you take the lead?" he asked the more senior Templar. Fergus was more cautious than Leila might have expected upon entering a copse so close to his home. "And Yvan, I would have you at the rear. I will follow Enguerrand with Duncan behind me, then Leila, the squires and the baggage."

"Do you suspect an attack?" Enguerrand asked.

Fergus' eyes narrowed. "Perhaps I have become too cautious."

"Better safe than sorry, lad," Duncan said heartily, and Leila remembered his assertion that Fergus could glimpse the future. Had Fergus not said that he spied a shadow ahead? Would he be cheated of his homecoming on the very threshold of Killairic? Her heart beat a little more quickly and she glanced around them.

They organized as instructed and rode onward at a steady pace, all of them scanning the forest on either side as they progressed. Leila thought of the assault upon their party at Haynesdale and listened keenly for any indication that they were being watched. She heard none, but that did not mean they were unobserved.

It was not a great distance through the forest, but it seemed longer because of their concern. The trees parted abruptly, granting a closer view of the keep they had glimpsed earlier and it looked even more prosperous at close proximity. The insignia was of a golden stag leaping on a green field. Leila felt the tension ease in both Duncan and Fergus.

"He lives," Fergus whispered, then gave his destrier his heels.

Leila understood immediately. He feared that his father might have passed away in his absence. Her heart clenched that his concern had been unfounded.

Meanwhile, Fergus raced his stallion to the gates, hollering with joy as he rode. Tempest tossed his head and ran with abandon, clearly sharing his knight's joy. It was also clear that Fergus felt safe within sight of the keep. The gates did stand open, though Leila had to believe they were secured at night. A few villagers left their tasks to see who approached, and Leila heard them shout in greeting. Duncan had been teaching her Gaelic in the evenings, and she was pleased that she could understand some of what was said.

It helped that they said what she anticipated they might say.

"'Tis my lord Fergus! He is home!"

"The laird's son is returned!"

"All hail, the return of my lord Fergus!"

People spilled out of the cottages, the mill, and the keep itself, surrounding Fergus. Their happiness was as evident as his own. He leaped from the saddle and shook hands, accepted kisses, was hugged and clapped upon the back repeatedly. He might have been greeting family instead of those pledged to his father's service. Leila approved of this warm relationship between laird and villein. Children ran through the delighted crowd, geese honked, dogs barked, and goats bleated. Leila heard Fergus laughing and smiled herself at such merriment.

The rest of the party were similarly surrounded once Fergus had been welcomed. The Templars were regarded with wonder. A bearded man with dark eyes and a leather apron stepped forward to run his hands over the flanks of the horses, and Leila guessed he was the village smith. Hamish was plucked from his saddle and hugged by a great bear of a man with an enthusiasm that made the boy blush crimson.

"Uncle Rodney," the boy protested but without much vigor.

"And a kiss for your aunt Mhairi, if you please," a buxom woman said, seizing Hamish to kiss his cheeks. Hamish was surrounded by this pair, who spoke to him quickly. Leila watched the woman tousle the boy's hair and guessed that they were talking about how much he had grown.

"You are one less than before," the blacksmith noted, his gaze flicking over the party. He had a low resonant voice that commanded attention and the villagers fell silent after his words. Leila saw several count the party, pointing fingers as they did so, and the word 'Kerr' rose like a whisper though their ranks.

Fergus nodded and bowed his head. "Alas, Kerr was killed on our return home. He is buried in the mountains west of Venice." This Leila did not understand completely, but she heard 'Kerr' and 'Venice' and guessed what tidings Fergus had shared.

Murmurs slipped through the company at these sad tidings and most people crossed themselves. One who was clearly a priest— for he wore a crucifix on a cord around his neck and his hair was tonsured—said something and gestured to a small building downriver. There was a cross on the roof, indicating that it was a chapel. Leila guessed that he invited the others to attend a mass for Kerr. Fergus spoke to him and the priest nodded, then hastened to the chapel.

Leila doubted she would be welcome there. In some parts of Palestine, holy places were shared between faiths, but it seemed unlikely that there would be similar tolerance here. She was probably the first Saracen these people had ever seen.

Duncan was greeted warmly and embraced another tall warrior

tightly. That man looked to be of an age with Duncan or even older, and his long hair was mingled silver and gold. He wore a patch over one eye, and he alone wore a chain mail hauberk in the company. His gaze flicked to her and he smiled. Leila dropped her gaze, her heart racing at his obvious appreciation. Was he a man whose attention she should cultivate? She had spent so long in the company of men yet disguised as a boy that she had forgotten any feminine arts and allures.

It might be timely to recall them.

She noticed that Duncan hefted his saddlebag to his shoulder when he dismounted, keeping the precious relic close by his side when his horse was led away. He came to help her from the saddle and she knew that the villagers—and that warrior—were watching her closely.

"And so we reach our destination," Duncan murmured to her in French as he offered his hand. There was understanding in his eyes as he held her gaze.

"I must find a husband, Duncan," Leila whispered. "Have you any advice?"

"That rogue will not suit," Duncan said. "He has not a *denier* to his name, though I do not doubt that he will attempt to charm you."

Leila smiled. "Thank you, Duncan."

"You can do better." Duncan winked and led her toward the open portal. "Come and meet Calum, Laird of Killairic."

"And your patron," Leila said, recalling Duncan's pledge to serve the man who had once saved his life.

"Indeed."

"I hope he will release you from his service, now that Fergus is safely returned."

"We shall see. We shall see."

"What of your friend?"

"Murdoch Olafson." Duncan nodded with approval. "There is a warrior to have at one's back, but not one to speak for the likes of you. I am glad he remained with Calum while we were gone and do not doubt he will demand a full accounting from me at earliest opportunity." Duncan gave her a look. "I will tell him to leave you be, for you are lady not whore."

Leila nodded, well aware that Murdoch watched her still.

An older man with white hair had come to the portal and stood there, leaning on a cane, his eyes alight as he regarded Fergus. He was dressed in the style of French nobles, in a long robe of heavy cloth but with a length of plaid cloth hanging from his shoulder like a cape. The pin holding the cloth shone in the sun, for it was set with a purple stone. He embraced Fergus with such obvious affection and pleasure that tears rose to Leila's eyes. Father and son spoke quickly, so quickly that Leila found their words incomprehensible.

Duncan squeezed Leila's fingers, evidently noting her reaction. "You do well with Gaelic. Soon you will speak as quickly as they do."

"I hope as much."

Duncan sobered, his gaze assessing. "Do not wed against your instincts, Leila, simply to see the matter resolved."

"You know I will not, Duncan. That is why I fled, after all."

"Aye, that is true enough." He held her gaze, his own filled with conviction. "Know this, lass. If ever I have a home, you are welcome within it, be you wedded or not, for so long as you should choose to stay."

A lump rose in Leila's throat at his unexpected offer and relief flooded through her. "Thank you, Duncan. I do not know what my fate will be, so your generous offer is most welcome."

"None of us know our fate, lass, none of us." Duncan took a deep breath. "But I will do all that I can to make a home for Radegunde. I know that she would welcome your company as much as I would be honored to have you as a guest."

Leila blinked back unexpected tears. "Thank you. You are a good friend, Duncan."

"For a Franj," he teased, a merry glint in his eye.

Leila laughed. "For a Franj," she ceded, for she had learned that there was much more diversity in Christians from the west than she had once believed. "I hope I am a good friend for a Saracen."

"The best I have ever known," he agreed promptly.

"And how many Saracens do you call friend?" Leila teased, her mood lightened by his offer.

"Only one, but she is worth a thousand others." Duncan grinned. "Why, we crossed the breadth of Christendom to find such a friend."

"That was not the sole reason you journeyed so far."

"True enough." Duncan dropped his gaze quickly to his saddlebag. "But few need know the truth of it."

Leila nodded without looking at the bag. What would happen to the reliquary now that they had reached their destination? Could it truly be hidden in this keep forever? Or would the Templars take it to another sanctuary?

Would she be entrusted with the truth?

If naught else, she would do her part to see the prize defended, as she had before.

The change in Leila's appearance was most troubling.

Fergus had known that she was a maiden all along, of course, ever since that first day in Jerusalem. He had caught glimpses of her hidden truth on their journey. A quick smile that was unabashedly feminine. A flash of a wrist too delicate to be that of a boy. But seeing her in women's garb had been a revelation.

She was a beauty.

And that kiss.

That kiss.

It had been wholly unexpected, yet not unwelcome. His powerful reaction to it had been a surprise. The memory tormented Fergus. His lips burned in recollection of it in the middle of the night. His pulse leaped at the sight of her. His dreams were filled with the possibilities of what would have come next, if he had not stepped away and returned to the festivities in Bartholomew's new hall. He would have sworn that each time he licked his lips, he tasted Leila's sweetness, though it was impossible.

It had been a fortnight and still he thought about that kiss at all hours.

He had even dreamed of Leila, holding a babe with golden skin and eyes of blue. The child's hair was dark and wet, as if it had only just been born, and Leila appeared to be tired but radiant all the same. Curiously, Fergus knew it was a boy.

The boy had to have a father from the west for his eyes to be of that hue. That should have reassured Fergus that Leila would have her desire fulfilled, but the vision had troubled him greatly. He had awakened on the night it had come to him and wondered at her future. Would she be happy in Scotland? Who was the father? Would that man treat her with honor? Leila looked delighted in his vision.

That beguiling sight, coupled with the memory of that kiss and his questions, meant that Fergus found Leila dominating his thoughts more than he thought she should.

It was clear he had been chaste too long. His marriage to Isobel could not be celebrated soon enough.

And what of Leila? He had to find her a good husband, with all speed.

As Fergus approached his father's keep for the first time in four long years, he was surprised to find himself wondering what Leila would think of his home. Nay, he had wanted her approval. It was impossible to keep himself from riding alongside her, telling her about it, watching for her reaction. Leila's admiration of Killairic gave him enormous pleasure—more pleasure than was reasonable. He should be concerned with how soon he would see Isobel or even what she would think of his gifts for her.

But it was Leila who claimed his attention.

Given the duration of his absence and his chastity, Fergus supposed it was inevitable that he had begun to notice other women, particularly one in whose company he had journeyed so far. Four years was a long time, almost an eternity. Was it not reasonable that his memories of Isobel faded?

Fergus was glad to be home. He told himself that he was glad of his pending nuptials, and of the promise of soon seeing Isobel again.

But the truth was he dreaded Leila's inevitable departure.

Or worse, her need to become a whore to survive. He could not let that happen. He must find her a spouse, a man of honor who would treat her well. He owed her that much, to be sure, but he would have to decide quickly.

As Fergus strode through the village, his chest was tight at the familiarity of it all. He had been glad when the villagers spilled forth to welcome him home, and greeted them, each and every one. The sight of his father at the portal to the keep had been a more profound relief than Fergus could have believed possible.

He had feared that the shadow he sensed might have been his father's death. To see Calum hale and laughing, if a little more white of hair than silver, if leaning a little more on his cane than before, was the most welcome sight in all the world.

"Father!" Fergus embraced his father, feeling a new frailty in the older man. It made him feel protective of his father and doubly determined to never leave home again.

"My boy," Calum said with obvious pleasure. "My boy, home again, just as promised." He shook his head, then surveyed Fergus with pleasure. "A boy no longer, but still one to keep his every promise." He ruffled Fergus' hair as if he were a small boy, though he had to stretch upward to do it.

"Of course!" Fergus agreed. "And I have brought you gifts..."

"The only gift I need is you by my side," his father declared. His eyes lit as he glanced over the company. "And with such a noble escort." Calum greeted the Templars in careful French as they bowed deeply before him.

"It was the command of our grand master that our comrade Fergus be escorted to his home, after his exemplary service," Enguerrand said, using the tale they had agreed upon.

"Indeed?" Calum lifted a brow. "You shall have to tell me of your exploits, my son."

"Of course, Father."

"Did I hear correctly about Kerr?" his father asked in a murmur.

"You did," Fergus agreed, recounting another tale they had agreed upon. "We were beset by thieves outside of Venice and Kerr paid the price." He did not like lying to his father, but he and Duncan had resolved that there was nothing to be gained by revealing Kerr's deceptive nature after the boy's demise.

Calum's lips thinned. "Someone will have to deliver that news," he said beneath his breath and Fergus nodded.

"I will tell Isobel, of course." In truth, Fergus was more concerned with the sight before him. Duncan was approaching with Leila, and Fergus could not look away from her. His heart leaped to see her eyes sparkling as she jested with Duncan and her laughter was merry. She wore the dark green kirtle that Radegunde had given to her and a cloak of wool in a deep golden hue. Her boots were plain and sturdy, and she had not a gem to her name, but she was radiant all the same.

Surely, he could find a husband who would treat her with the honor she deserved?

"And Duncan returned with you, as well." Calum embraced Duncan like another son and not like the hired man-at-arms he was.

"I pledged to return him hale to you, my lord, and so it is done," Duncan said.

"And so you did, and so you did. Never did a laird have a more honorable warrior sworn to his cause. I thank you, Duncan."

The back of Duncan's neck turned ruddy at this praise, but Calum gave him no opportunity to reply. The older man gave his cane to Fergus and clasped Duncan's shoulders in his hands. "I welcome you to Killairic as a guest on this occasion, Duncan, for I do not doubt our wager has been repaid time and again between here and Outremer." Calum smiled. "Indeed, I am now obligated to you. I owe you much, Duncan, for taking this ruffian into your custody and bringing him home again."

"The honor was mine, my lord," Duncan said, apparently unable to keep himself from bowing. "I am as pleased as you to see him safely returned home."

Fergus was aware that Leila could not understand what his father and Duncan were saying, but did not know how to gracefully translate for her without drawing attention to the fact that she was Saracen.

But then, he supposed that was no secret, with her golden skin and dark hair. She looked exotic and had been increasingly the focus of attention since their departure from Paris. The villagers eyed her with wonder, and he guessed there was speculation in their whispers.

Was her inevitable departure at root of his portent?

His father was hale, which was a relief, but the shadow had not dissipated.

"And who is this flower of the east?" Calum asked, switching from Gaelic to French. He gestured to Leila. "Is this your companion, Duncan? Dare I hope that you have lost your heart and mean to plan a future as a wedded man?"

Leila flushed and lowered her gaze, her dark lashes sweeping over her cheeks in a gesture so feminine that it stole Fergus' breath away.

"I am not so fortunate a man as to have won this beauty," Duncan said with a rare flourish. "This is Leila…"

Leila interrupted him smoothly. "I am Leila binte Qadir lufti al-Ramm, sir," she said, bowing low before Fergus' father. "I am honored to meet you."

Fergus knew he was not the only one astonished by her full name. Why had he never asked her what it was before? Murdoch Olafson stepped forward, perhaps to ensure he had a better view of Leila, and Fergus granted that old warrior a hard look.

Murdoch seemed to be amused, but if he had any notions about Leila, Fergus would ensure they were dismissed along with that predatory smile.

"And I am delighted to welcome you to my home," Calum said to Leila. "How did you come to be in this party?"

"I sought the protection of this company in Jerusalem and my lord Fergus was kind enough to honor my request." Leila's French was quick and smooth, so much better than Calum's that it took the older man a moment to understand her meaning.

"A damsel in distress," his father said then with satisfaction.

Leila smiled, her gaze flicking to Fergus. "One might say as much, sir." She was beguiling when her eyes sparkled so. Because they were so dark, Fergus thought of stars in the midnight sky when they twinkled.

"And who better to defend you than Knights of the Temple?" Calum continued. Enguerrand and Yvan said nothing, but stood a little straighter. "I am honored for your presence to grace my home, Lady Leila, for so long as you would choose to be my guest." He gestured to the hall even as his words reminded Fergus that Leila would visit for a short time only. "Please, come and restore yourself from your journey. I warn you that I will pester you for tales of distant lands."

"I thank you, sir, for the kindness of your hospitality." Leila bowed again.

"The honor will be all mine, for you will help me with my French. I forget it in these hills, and the practice will be welcome." Calum chuckled and reclaimed his cane. He winked at Fergus, then offered his arm to Leila. "Have you journeyed west before, my lady?"

"This is my first such trip, sir." She took Calum's arm as if she needed his support. Fergus saw the way she slipped her hand beneath his father's elbow, letting him lean upon her a little without anyone being the wiser. She was kind and he liked that well.

"Then you knew only Outremer before that departure from Jerusalem?"

"Indeed, sir."

"You must find Scotland vastly different from your home."

"The weather is considerably different, sir, and so is the food, but people, it seems are much the same wherever one travels."

"And that has long been my thinking as well," Calum agreed, leading Leila into the great hall. Fergus and Duncan followed, the Templars behind them. The fires had been stoked to blazing and the high table was already set up. Iain, his father's steward, was straightening a length of embroidered linen atop it and directing the placement of candles. He spared Fergus a warm smile and welcomed him home before calling to the cook that there had best be enough bread for the evening meal.

That launched a typical and friendly dispute between Iain and Xavier the cook, both of them defending their skills and domains, and taking offense at the meddling of the other. In truth, they both were similar in nature, being older, unmarried men devoted to Fergus' father's service and comfort. He found himself smiling at the familiarity of it all as they bickered.

"You had best mind your labor instead of mine," Xavier concluded, indicating the arriving party. "*You* have not set enough benches in the hall for all of the company."

"I know best how to see the hall prepared." Iain sniffed the air delicately. "Is that burning venison I smell?"

Xavier swore with gusto and stalked back to the kitchen. Iain shook his head, then turned upon the man rolling a cask of wine into the hall.

"Not here, not here," the steward complained. "It must be mulled, for it is the last of the wine. Take it to the kitchen and see if that *fiend* will spare you a place on his fire to ensure his laird's pleasure."

"If you mean to mull the wine, I have brought some spices for the kitchens," Fergus raised his voice to interject and Iain's eyes lit with pleasure.

"Indeed, sir? They would be most welcome." The older man came closer, bowing before Fergus. "Do you have a list of them, sir? I would add them to the inventory of the spice box before they can be dispersed without regard for their expense—as *some* people are wont to do."

Fergus bit back a smile, for it was easy to guess who Iain thought might be guilty of that crime. "I regret that I did not list them fully, Iain, but Hamish has been learning his sums." He beckoned to his squire, giving that boy the means to escape the affectionate welcome of his aunt and uncle. "Hamish can record them in the ledger for you accurately, if you will lend him a scale. It will be good practice for him, and you, I know, must be too busy for such tasks on this day."

"An excellent notion, sir." Iain nodded at Hamish. "You can use my counting room."

Hamish bowed and followed the older man, standing much taller than he had on their departure. Of course, he was four years older and much grown.

His aunt and uncle beamed with pride as Hamish left the hall. The boy would see them again at the board this night, for Fergus would ensure as much.

Fergus supposed he should consult with Hamish about his

desire for the future. Did the boy wish to continue his training and be knighted? He had begged to accompany Fergus for the adventure and Fergus had taken him and Kerr as he had no squires before his departure. Perhaps Hamish could train at Haynesdale.

"I will need peppercorns and cloves first," Iain said to Hamish. "Dare I hope that there is cinnamon? For that would be a fine addition as well."

"There is, Iain, as well as star anise," Hamish replied and Iain's delight was clear. "I negotiated for it myself."

"Did you? I scarce remember the taste of that spice for it has been so long. What an adventure you must have had..."

Meanwhile, boys were dispatched from the hall to bring the baggage and Calum headed for a seat set close to the fire. Leila helped him to take a seat and he granted her a smile of gratitude. She sat beside him at his invitation and visibly shivered. "You will need a man to warm you on our nights here, my lady," Calum teased and Leila blushed again. "Have you chosen one yet?"

"Not I, sir. I would not be so bold."

"Then we will find you one," Calum said, giving her hand a pat. "A robust warrior with a tender heart, one who will defend you and honor you, as all men of merit should do for their wives. Do you like a song, my lady?"

"Indeed, I do."

"You have come to the right land to find a husband. We have poets aplenty in these parts, and men whose songs charm the birds from the trees."

Leila seemed to be fighting a smile. "Indeed, sir?"

"You sound skeptical, my lady."

"She has heard me sing, sir," Duncan interjected.

Calum laughed, his gaze flicking between Duncan and Leila with such delight that his conclusions were clear. "Perhaps we shall have a wedding at Killairic, after all," he said with pleasure, then caught himself. His gaze darted to Fergus and the entire company fell ominously silent.

Fergus' heart stopped.

It was clear that something *was* amiss.

CHAPTER TWO

fter all?" Fergus echoed, knowing that every gaze was locked upon him. The hair pricked on the back of his neck, and he found it remarkable that no one explained his father's comment. Indeed, the hall was filled with a fearsome silence. "Surely, Isobel and I will be married at Killairic, Father." The words were as dust in his mouth, for he was watching Leila. Her interest in the conversation was most clear.

As clear as Murdoch's interest in her.

His father grimaced. "Surely not," he said quietly. "I am sorry, Fergus."

Fergus thought he must have misunderstood. "Has Isobel fallen ill?"

"Nay," Calum said, his frown deepening.

Iain had paused in the portal to the kitchens and looked back. He was ashen and motionless, as if he had been struck to stone. Hamish frowned in confusion as he looked between them all. Duncan was grim. Murdoch folded his arms across his chest and watched the exchange as if entertained. Leila's eyes were wide and she clearly strove to follow the conversation.

Fergus asked the inescapable question. "Is she dead?"

His father winced. "Isobel is married, Fergus."

Married?

Fergus was outraged and he felt betrayed. How could his beloved be wed to another? It could not be true! "But how can this be? Isobel is *my* betrothed."

"No longer," Murdoch noted in his gravelly voice.

Fergus spun to face that man. "She pledged to wait for me!"

"It seems the lady changed her thinking," Duncan noted.

"But we love each other," Fergus protested.

"I would wager that your admiration was not returned in equal measure, lad," Duncan said quietly.

Fergus realized from Duncan's tone that he, of all those who had just returned, was not surprised. Duncan shrugged, then dropped his gaze to his boots. Leila inhaled sharply, her eyes flashing in his defense.

Still Fergus could not believe it.

"But we are betrothed!" he protested again. "We are *pledged* to each other..."

His father shook his head. "All the same, she exchanged vows with Stewart MacEwan..."

"*Stewart MacEwan?*" Fergus paced the hall, astonished twice in rapid succession. He knew he had experienced doubt, but he had not broken his vow. Isobel should not have done as much, either. She had *promised.* And Stewart? How could she love Stewart? "But he is twenty years her senior!"

Calum shrugged. "That does not appear to be an issue. She has borne him a son in your absence. She ripened with a second child, but I heard that something went awry." Calum shook his head and most of the company crossed themselves.

Two pregnancies? So quickly as that? Fergus had been gone almost exactly four years. He felt his eyes narrow as he turned to face his father again. He found Leila's eyes snapping, her arms folded across her chest, and appreciated that she was insulted on his behalf.

Something in him stirred at the sight of her fury, something he did not wish to consider in this moment.

There had to be an explanation, and he immediately thought of one.

"Did her father compel her choice?" Fergus asked tightly.

His father shook his head. "Not as I heard it."

Fergus exhaled. He paced. He was livid that a sworn word would mean so little to Isobel, that his trust had been so badly misplaced, that her love for him had been so fleeting. He was devastated that his loyalty had been so rewarded. How could she have done this? What would his life be without Isobel by his side? Fergus shoved a hand through his hair and did not wish to consider it.

"When did they wed?" he asked, disliking that his father winced and dropped his gaze to his hands.

"Three months after you left," Murdoch supplied.

Three months? Only *three* months? Had she thought so little of Fergus as that? His pride was pricked, to be sure, which did not add to his composure. If Isobel had waited a year or two, he could have understood her choice, at least to some extent. She might have believed him dead, or unlikely to return.

Three months made him wonder whether she ever meant to wed him at all.

That shook him to his marrow. He loved Isobel and had been faithful to her, yet she had forgotten him so quickly as that. He felt sickened and empty.

Fergus could not look at Leila, for fear that she would guess the depth of his despair.

The boys were bringing in the many boxes of gifts he had brought for Isobel and the sight of them made him feel like a fool. All the time that he had been shopping for her, she had been married to Stewart. All that coin he had wasted, buying gifts that would never be granted to the recipient. He had been chaste. He had been true. He had kept his vow. Was that of no merit to the woman who had said she loved him and promised to wait for him?

And Stewart MacEwan. To be cast aside for such a man—a rough warrior of little scruple and much older than himself—was galling.

Could Isobel have been compelled to wed Stewart, despite his own father's view?

The possibility made perfect sense. Her father's keep of Dunnisbrae was moderately prosperous and Isobel was both her father's only surviving child and a beauty. He could readily understand that Stewart might be attracted to both woman and holding—and that a man of Stewart's nature might not have accepted the lady's refusal as a reply.

He could believe that Isobel's father might have forced her to marry, and that she, out of loyalty to her father, would not have made that fact evident. Her father might have been under duress of Stewart's making. Aye, that made sense!

Fergus had to know for certain. He had to see Isobel and hear the truth from her own lips. He had to hear her say either that she had no love for him or that she had been forced to wed against her own will.

He had to visit Dunnisbrae as soon as possible.

Fergus spared a glance at the company watching him with such avidity and knew he could not leave immediately, though it might be his impulse. Isobel was married. He would not bring suspicion upon her or launch rumors. His horse deserved a rest, and he would not ride another when he rode to Dunnisbrae. He also would not insult his father by abandoning the meal being prepared to celebrate his return.

He would depart at the dawn.

Even though he itched to ride out immediately.

"Fergus, she did not see your merit and so she does not deserve your regard," his father said with forced cheer. He patted the seat on his other side. "Come and let me tell you all of the news, for there is more than this to be shared."

"Of course," Fergus said, hearing the heat that still lingered in his words. He was stung by Isobel's betrayal and the destruction of his own hopes, even if the marriage had not been her choice. He had a thought at that and spun to face his father. "Was it a handfast?"

"Nay, nay," his father said. "The bishop himself came to witness the exchange of their vows. It was no small event."

Fergus' gaze collided with that of Leila, who watched him with evident concern. Was Isobel's choice the reason he had felt a portent of doom?

Or was there more bad news to come?

He could not deny that his sense that something would go awry still lingered.

"Come, Fergus, and tell me how you came to be of aid to this damsel in distress," Calum encouraged again. "I would hear it all, and if she tells me in her wondrous French, I might well miss a detail."

"I would give the spices to Iain and Hamish first, Father," Fergus said, bowing deeply. He needed a moment to collect his thoughts and to accept the disappointment. "And then, my steed must be tended. I must see Tempest settled before I take my leisure with you, if you will so allow it."

"Of course, of course. Was I not the one who taught you to tend your responsibilities before taking your pleasure?" Calum chuckled as those in the hall returned to their duties and chatter. "Now, Lady Leila, tell me of your home in Outremer. Slowly, if you please."

"I should be delighted to do as much. I lived in Jerusalem, although I was born in a small village outside of its walls," Leila began.

"Al-Ramm," Calum contributed and her eyes lit.

"You know something of Outremer!"

"Aye, I do, though it is many years since I was there. Continue, if you please, my lady."

"My uncle is a blacksmith..."

Fergus strode from the hall to the bailey, feeling torn. He wanted to listen to Leila's story as much as he wanted a moment to himself. Duncan followed behind, bringing the saddlebag with its precious burden, and Fergus recalled that it had to be secured, too.

It seemed he had only obligations at Killairic, instead of the joy he had anticipated for so long!

Duncan was not surprised by Isobel's choice.

He was more concerned by Fergus' reaction to the news of her faithlessness. The younger man was distraught, and rightly so, but Duncan was troubled on his behalf. He hoped that Fergus would not act on impulse and put himself in peril.

Duncan was glad that Calum had released him from service to Killairic and yearned to ride north immediately. The matter of his family had to be resolved before he could offer Radegunde a future. He would speak to his father and end their dispute somehow, rather than risk having his father send another assassin after him. At the same time, Duncan did not want to leave Fergus in such a mood. They had been companions too long for him to dismiss concern for the man who had become his friend.

To Duncan's surprise, they had scarce stepped into the shadow of the stables when Fergus turned upon him. "Where shall we secure it?" he demanded in an undertone.

Duncan flicked a glance down the length of the stables. The ostler was at the far end, several boys helping him to remove the saddles from the horses that had recently arrived. That man gave instruction in a booming voice that would disguise the sound of their own conversation.

Duncan kept his voice low. "Would your father's treasury be too obvious?"

"It has the stoutest lock, though it is also the first place any soul would seek it," Fergus acknowledged. "I will need to find a better sanctuary for it in time, but the treasury will have to suffice for the moment."

Duncan nodded agreement. "Perhaps the Templars will demand its return shortly."

"I can only hope as much," Fergus agreed. "I fear it will be difficult to keep it safe for a long period of time."

"And your repute is at risk if it disappears."

Fergus nodded and frowned. "It could be easily moved to the treasury today along with the gifts intended for Isobel. I will say that I am concerned about the cloth, for it was expensive."

"Will you tell your father?"

"I would prefer to tell no one," Fergus admitted with a grimace. "I suppose at some point I will confide in him. But not yet. Let us secure it first."

"A fine notion."

"Perhaps you would supervise the delivery of the gifts to the solar," Fergus suggested.

"Of course." Duncan hesitated before following the suggestion, wanting to say something of encouragement to the younger man about his broken betrothal. "Every end is a beginning, lad. Remember that."

Fergus smiled but there was no joy in his eyes. "That is one way to consider the matter, Duncan. I cannot make sense of it." He shook his head. "I must see her and soon."

"Why soon? If you hasten then, others will think you smitten yet."

"I do not care what others think!"

"But you should. You sound smitten yet. Give it time, lad."

"You do not understand, Duncan. I must *know* why she did it."

Duncan snorted. "And you believe a woman who did not keep her word to you will confess the truth of her choice? You had best remain at Killairic and find a new beginning first."

"It matters!"

"It does not. She is wed now—by the bishop, no less!—whatever her reasons for so doing. She will remain thus so long as Stewart draws breath." Duncan tapped Fergus on the shoulder. "Do not even think of shortening that man's days, lad."

"Nay, nay, I would never do that!" Fergus was horrified, as Duncan had hoped. The younger man frowned. "But I must see her and hear her explanation. I must go on the morrow." Duncan made to argue but Fergus held up a hand. "I do not care what others think, Duncan."

"You might give a care as to what Stewart MacEwan thinks," he retorted. "I would not be in haste to convince him that I coveted his wife."

"And so I will not." Fergus' expression set. "But I must look her in the eye." He sighed. "And I must give her the tidings of Kerr, of course."

Duncan grimaced, for he knew an excuse when he heard it. "You might seize the moment and make your beginning before you depart," he said, not surprised that his words claimed Fergus' attention so quickly.

"How?"

"Your father falters in his strength and another winter may see him stumble. I would not wish for it, but I would see you prepare for the moment that comes to us all."

Fergus leaned against a stall, his expression grim. "You noticed his frailty as well. I hoped I was the only one."

"He is much less vigorous than when we departed," Duncan said and Fergus nodded agreement. He was relieved that Fergus had noticed the change in Calum so they could discuss it. "I suspect he feared for you, for he of all men knew the challenge before us, and that may have aged him more quickly. At any rate, there is a chance to make good of your situation."

"How so?"

Duncan took a breath, wondering how the younger man would respond to his suggestion. "If I were Stewart MacEwan, I would be much more welcoming to another married man at my portal than to a spurned suitor, even if both came to give tidings to my wife."

Fergus shook his head. "But I am not married and will not be by the morrow."

"You could be," Duncan said. "Here is an opportunity to see your father reassured as well as Leila's situation improved."

"Leila?" Fergus blinked. "What has Leila to do with this?"

"She has need of a husband to remain in Scotland. You have need of a wife, because Killairic has need of a son. Your father would be much encouraged to see you settled and the next heir born, and it is clear that he admires Leila already. Stewart, as I noted, would likely be more welcoming if you came to Isobel as a married man yourself."

"Leila!" Fergus repeated and turned to pace the width of the stables.

"There is friendship between you," Duncan noted. "Successful marriages have begun on less promise than this."

"But she wishes to wed for love. A marriage of convenience would be too much like the arranged marriage she abandoned."

"Would it? I understood the chosen man was violent, as you are not."

Fergus shook his head. "She must have the opportunity to find the love she seeks above all else. I will defend her right to choose. A marriage will not do."

"Then a handfast," Duncan suggested. "A year and a day together. It will give her security and you companionship, perhaps even a son. Your father will be pleased, as well."

"A handfast," Fergus echoed. "It is an excellent notion and a good compromise." He straightened with purpose. "But she must know all of the truth. It can be a match of convenience and no more."

Duncan hid his approval, guessing that his preference for Leila as Fergus' bride would not be welcome. "Then wed her on this day, without delay, the better to ensure that your motives are not doubted when you ride to Dunnisbrae, and that Leila herself is safe from those who might prey upon her."

Fergus' eyes narrowed. "Murdoch," he said with a bitterness that Duncan found encouraging.

"He eyes her, to be sure, and you know as well as me that Murdoch will bed a woman but not wed her. If she is unwed in this hall, he might take advantage of her."

Fergus fairly growled at that notion, a most welcome sign to Duncan.

He continued. "If Leila is your wife, though, he will defend her to his dying breath. I have always said that Murdoch made a better ally than foe."

"It must be today, though." Fergus glanced toward the ostler and his boys. "But I need to speak to Leila alone first, in case the suggestion is not pleasing." He indicated the ostler and his helpers, then arched a brow, inviting Duncan to create a tale.

Duncan cleared his throat and raised his voice a little, knowing that those men had taken note of their arrival. "All the same, sir, I am sorry that you arrived home to such news of your betrothed."

"If she did not wish to wait, perhaps it is better that she wed another," Fergus said with a sigh. "Indeed, I will send her congratulations and a nuptial gift."

"Of course, sir."

"Will you see all my purchases and belongings placed in the solar, Duncan? I will come to make a choice shortly." Fergus dropped his voice to a whisper, his gaze locking with Duncan's. "Send Leila to me, please. I do not care what excuse you use."

"Of course," Duncan had time to say before Fergus strode the length of the stables. He admired, as ever, that once the younger man had resolved upon a course, he did not delay in fulfilling it.

"You have a gift with steeds, Stephen, it is most clear," Fergus said and that man smiled at this praise. "And such speed with brushing them down. It must be because you have such enthusiastic assistance."

"Aye, sir, the boys do very well."

"I would complete the grooming of Tempest myself, Stephen." Fergus patted the rump of his dark destrier. "We have become quite accustomed to each other these past years."

"Aye, sir."

"I see that Duncan's mount, Caledon, is groomed already, which is admirable." Stephen bowed and Fergus continued. "I did want also to speak to you about the stabling."

"Sir?"

Fergus shook his head in apparent dismay. "We have found the stallions to be most amorous in recent days."

The ostler chuckled. "Spring is in the air, my lord."

"Indeed. Perhaps the palfreys could be stabled in the village and temptation thus put at a distance."

Duncan was intrigued by this tale, for he had noticed no change in the horses' manner. He lingered to listen.

"Of course, sir."

"Could you find accommodation for the Templars' destriers elsewhere, as well? We have found it best of late to divide the stallions from each other and from the mares, though I hope their inclination will soon pass."

"Of course, sir. Tempest can have the most distant stall from Caledon, and the palfreys can be stabled in the smith's barn. I would imagine that one of the Templar's destriers could be stabled in the plowman's small barn and the other housed by the miller's abode."

"That would be excellent, Stephen. Duncan will depart in the morning, and I expect the Templars will leave shortly, as well."

"Then all will be returned to normal soon enough, sir. It is no trouble to make a change or two to accommodate guests such as these fine steeds."

Duncan watched as the ostler and his boys led the horses out of the stables, leaving the knight alone with the two destriers. Duncan strode into the bailey to do his part in giving Fergus the opportunity he needed to speak to Leila alone.

The warrior smiled as he approached the hall, convinced as he was that Fergus would find precisely the partner he needed if he took Leila's hand within his own. It was all the encouragement Duncan needed to ride north with all haste and ensure that he could invite Radegunde to join him by the anniversary of their handfast.

He had but four months remaining to see his own future secured.

It was painful to witness Fergus' shock and dismay.

Leila wished she could console him, but feared that any gesture on her part would restore the strained silence of the past days. She watched, furious, as the boys brought in trunk after trunk, each one laden with gifts for Isobel. What kind of woman would break her vow within months of her betrothed's departure? Certainly not one who deserved the regard of *this* man.

It seemed to her that Fergus could not even bear to look at the trunks. That only added to Leila's sense of injustice. She remembered all too well how delighted he had been after visiting the markets in Venice, how he had clearly anticipated seeing his gifts adorn his beloved.

Faithless shrew! Had Isobel forgotten the man who held her at the forefront of his thoughts? Home was of the greatest import to Fergus and he had admitted himself that it was the prospect of his return that had given him strength in the face of adversity. It seemed Isobel had cared little for him. Leila might not have followed all of the conversation, but she had understood that.

Did Isobel ever consider that anticipation of their future, that his love for her, might have helped Fergus to survive? He and Duncan never spoke of whatever battles they had joined in

Palestine, but Fergus had served with the Templars and those knights rode to battle regularly. Leila did not doubt that the two men were close because they had each saved the other's life, and probably more than once.

Did Isobel think of *that?* Nay, it seemed that beautiful Isobel cared only for her own comfort and satisfaction. A son! Her match was not a mere formality, to be sure.

Leila's hands balled into fists in her lap as she sat beside Calum, and she hoped that no one noticed her indignation. The older man was charming and asked questions about Outremer that showed he had journeyed there. His French was slow, but he was good-natured about it, and Leila found that she liked him well. She could see that Calum had been a warrior himself, for he shared Duncan's alert manner and quick gaze, and there were scars upon his hands and one upon his cheek. Doubtless there were more scars she could not see. She admired that warfare had not made him bitter and suspected that he was more tolerant than many she had known.

She was well aware of Murdoch watching her, but avoided the warrior's gaze. His interest was clear but without knowing its precise nature, Leila would not encourage him.

Even so, her thoughts were with Fergus.

When Duncan returned to the hall alone, Leila's gaze flew to him. To her relief, he came to her side.

"I beg your pardon, Leila, but Fergus asks if you might look at the hoof of his destrier," Duncan said. "He fears Tempest has stepped upon something this morning, for the beast favors one foot."

Leila stood immediately, knowing the value of the destrier and the importance of prompt attention. "Of course!"

"Do I misunderstand?" Calum asked, looking between them. "Do you know much of horses, Lady Leila?"

"She would challenge the knowledge of the best ostler, my lord," Duncan said. "We have come to rely heavily upon her counsel."

"What a marvel," Calum said. "The Saracens have much knowledge about medical matters, I know, and it makes good sense that such expertise extends to horses. And you did mention that your uncle was a blacksmith. Do not keep an injured destrier waiting, much less his devoted knight, Lady Leila. Not upon my account." He winked at her. "There are males not worth the trouble of vexing, but I am no longer one of them."

"I thank you for your courtesy," Leila said with a smile and bowed to him. She hastened out of the hall, both concerned for the horse and glad of the opportunity to see Fergus again.

Duncan accompanied her to the bailey, then indicated the entry to the stables. "I believe my lord Fergus would speak to you alone," he said to Leila's confusion.

About his horse?

Leila picked up her skirts and hurried to the stables. She had no sooner stepped inside and blinked at the relative darkness, than the door was closed behind her. She spun to find Fergus leaning against it, his arms folded across his chest and his eyes gleaming. "Marry me, Leila," he said.

Leila blinked. She took a step back. She was certain her ears had deceived her.

But she could not have misunderstood because he had spoken in French. "I beg your pardon?" she asked all the same.

"I am asking you to marry me," Fergus repeated, his manner more resolute. "You have need of a husband. I have need of a wife, as the woman I intended to wed has married another. If you would only consider the option, I am certain you will see that it offers much merit."

Leila looked down the length of the stables, only to see Fergus' dark destrier grazing contentedly in his bucket of feed. Duncan's destrier was in a nearby stall, chewing as he regarded her.

"Your horse is not injured," she said with relief.

"Not at all. I wanted only to speak to you and soon." Fergus pushed a hand through his hair and looked suddenly rueful. "I have even concocted a tale about the stallions being amorous this spring to ensure that I could be alone with you here."

Leila sat down on a bench between the stalls. She could not make sense of Fergus' offer, as much as she yearned to accept it. She wanted to know why he would propose such an arrangement.

He could not love her, not so suddenly as this.

What detail did she not know?

"Why is the matter urgent?"

"Because you must wed to remain here, and I would not have you thought a whore." Fergus shrugged. "In fact, I would halt such speculation before it begins."

Leila did not tell him that it was probably too late.

He surveyed the stable, as if more concerned with his thoughts. "As Duncan reminds me, my father grows older. Indeed, I am a little surprised by the change in him in just four years. I know he would be glad to see the succession ensured before his own passing. He has but one son, so it is left to me to wed and have a son myself, for the future of Killairic."

Leila nodded understanding. It was not a romantic confession, but it was a truthful one. Given the choice, she preferred honesty over sweet lies.

Killairic, his home, was of the greatest import to Fergus. He would see it secured, and he offered to ensure her safety with his scheme.

Leila would be glad to be part of such an agreement.

"And, as Duncan notes, Stewart is less likely to take issue with my visiting Isobel on the morrow if I arrive as a married man myself."

Leila chose not to comment on that, for she knew naught of Stewart.

Fergus evidently took her silence as an indication that she might refuse. "You would have the protection you need to remain in Scotland," he reminded her. "And my defense in case there are those who would be intolerant."

It seemed too good an offer to be true.

Surely there was a chance of their match becoming one of love and passion?

Still, Leila hesitated. She wished he might have made some sweet confession, even just expressed some admiration.

Or given her a kiss. That might have reassured her of her future hope coming true.

She feared a match proposed so lightly could be put aside just as lightly, but her maidenhead would be gone all the same.

Fergus sat down beside her, his manner intent. "I had not expected you to be so surprised. Not after our kiss last Saturday at Haynesdale."

"After which you ignored me, as if I were a harlot coming to your home," Leila felt obliged to note.

Fergus smiled. "As if you were a temptation I dared not indulge. I fear I have been chaste too long."

Was it more than that? Leila desperately hoped it might be. Their gazes locked for a moment and she could not take a full breath when he watched her so closely. "You seek a match of convenience."

"Perhaps it would be so at first. Perhaps it would ripen to more. Who can say? Think of Gaston and Ysmaine." He smiled but she guessed that he did not have any expectation of surrendering to love again. His sadness tore at her own heart and she put her hand over his own.

"I do."

"As Duncan notes, a match would serve both of us for this moment." His implication was clear. Perhaps it would *not* ripen to more. Perhaps they would live as friends and companions, but not true loves.

Convenience had never seemed so unpalatable to Leila as it did now, and that only because she wished for more.

She chided herself silently for being greedy. The suggestion had much merit.

"They will assume you are wedding your whore," she noted.

Fergus was dismissive. "Let them believe what they will. Marry me, Leila, for the sake of both our goals."

She shook her head. "It is not so simple. Our faiths are different..."

"Not so different as that. There is common ground between them, as we saw in Outremer."

"But the differences are of import and have immediate implications. I do not mean to make obstacles, but how should we be wed? Who will officiate—a priest of your faith? I do not doubt that any such would insist upon my being baptized first, and I am not prepared to do so."

Fergus studied her with curiosity. "Not ever?"

"Not yet, if ever. I do not know enough of your doctrine to make an informed choice." She smiled at him. "When one talks of the immortal soul, only an informed choice will suffice."

"True enough." He frowned at the floor. "But I would suggest a handfast to you, not a marriage."

Leila took a breath. "A pledge of a year and a day, as Radegunde and Duncan have made?" She instinctively disliked the casual nature of this bond, but it was a custom in this land and would not be the first such that she might need to embrace. It seemed an arrangement that would appeal to men, especially those who liked to have different partners, but perhaps she was too critical.

Radegunde had chosen it with Duncan, and done so wholeheartedly. Perhaps Leila should let her friend be her guide.

Fergus nodded. "We would live as husband and wife for that term, then decide how best to proceed. It would give you an opportunity to find a man to claim your heart truly and make the kind of match you desire." He nodded with satisfaction. "It might be a good compromise."

Leila knew it was unfair to be irked. Was she to simply be his consolation?

And that for only a year? She wanted so much more!

"Is Isobel wedded or does she have a handfast?" she asked, keeping her tone light.

"My father said the bishop wedded her to Stewart." He met her gaze. "What difference?"

Leila resolved in that moment that she would be utterly honest with him, in all matters. To her thinking, that was the sole chance of gaining the future she desired. "I thought you might hope for her return."

His gaze hardened then, and she understood that Isobel had hurt his pride as well as his heart. "If so, it is of no import. Isobel has chosen to be my past. I ask you to be my future."

His words sent a thrill through her, even though there was no passion in his tone. Still she had questions. "What if there is a child?"

"I will take full responsibility for him or her," Fergus vowed. "Upon that you can rely."

Leila folded her arms across her chest. "While I should be compelled to leave you, your home, and our child as an unchaste woman with neither kin nor allies? That will leave me with no prospects at all!" She shook her head. "Nay, that will not do."

"It is not so different to your situation now."

"I am a maiden. That is always of import. Is it not so here?"

"Not so much as you might think," he said so earnestly that she believed him. "A handfast is an honorable arrangement, and if I am the one to introduce you to your future partner, there will be no stain upon your nature. It is like a marriage, but one of the highlands and not the church."

"Is that what all the men who offer a handfast say to their intended?" she asked with a smile.

Fergus smiled back at her. "Perhaps so, but the fact remains chastity is of less import here than further south."

"You were chaste."

"I felt it fitting. It is clear that Isobel did not share my view." He sobered and she wished his honorable choice had been reciprocated. "What would you do otherwise? If you do not handfast with me, how can I protect you? How will you live in this land?"

His concern made Leila's heart clench. "And how will you provide an heir to your father if you do not take a woman to wife?"

"Exactly. I know he would see the succession ensured, and I think sooner would be better." Fergus held her gaze, hope in his eyes. The warmth of his thigh was close to her own, making Leila wonder if she accepted a fool's wager. She knew she would only fall more deeply in love with Fergus over that year and a day. Indeed, it might destroy her to have him put her aside, especially if she had borne him a son.

Fergus took her hand in his and appealed to her, his voice husky. "I would give my father this gift, Leila, even if the match is only one of convenience."

That he appealed to her for the sake of his father's contentment could not be resisted. Fear was like a stone in her gut, but Leila knew naught was ever gained without taking a risk. That kiss hinted to Leila that they might find love in this match, regardless of Fergus' expectation. She did not doubt that physical intimacy could lead to an emotional bond—indeed, if she declined to meet Fergus abed, he might seek pleasure elsewhere and she might lose the chance to win his heart. Could she help him to heal from Isobel's betrayal?

Leila chose to take the risk.

"You think your father would accept a child with Saracen blood as his heir?" she asked, already guessing the answer.

"I do," Fergus said with a nod. "You saw his greeting of you. He rode to the east when I was young, though I will let him tell you of it. As you can see, he harbors no ill will as a result of his experience."

Leila nodded. "I look forward to that tale." She dared to put her hand over his. Fergus turned his hand, capturing her fingers with the warmth of his own, and her heart leaped for her throat. His gaze warmed and his thumb slid across the back of her hand in a smooth caress. Desire unfurled within her, a need so potent that she could not believe he was immune to the spell he cast. Leila's pulse raced and she watched Fergus swallow. He fixed a hot look upon her, one so ardent that she flushed to her toes.

He did desire her! That was a start.

"A year and a day it will be then," Fergus murmured, his voice so low that Leila's blood nigh boiled. He lifted her hand to his lips and kissed it, his sweet caress sending a welcome fire through her. "We shall tell them now and celebrate the handfast at the feast tonight."

And she would begin her conquest immediately.

"Surely such an agreement demands more than a kiss on the hand," Leila whispered boldly. She watched as Fergus paused, then smiled when his eyes darkened. His gaze dropped to her lips, then she saw his pulse at his throat. Leila took encouragement where she found it.

She would wager that his reaction was not entirely because he had been chaste.

But she would have to prove that to him.

One night at a time, she would conquer his heart.

Leila dared to believe it could be done. She reached to touch her lips to his, just as she had before, and felt satisfaction when Fergus slanted his mouth over hers and drew her close.

Just as he had before.

Nay, he kissed her even more thoroughly, which made her heart pound with satisfaction.

She had a year and a day to claim Fergus completely.

Let her quest begin.

It might have been a balm to Fergus' pride if Leila had readily agreed to his offer, but he admired that she had sensible concerns and wished to know his answers before making her choice. He had made one betrothal impulsively, following his heart and his father's timely suggestion, and had to believe that a thoughtful choice might be a better one.

Truth be told, it could not be worse.

What he could not fully explain was his sense of triumph in her final agreement. It must be a question of pride. And his heated reaction to her kiss was surely fed by his long bout of chastity. By the morning, such physical distractions would be dismissed. It would be better for him to confront Isobel then, for his thinking would be clear.

As he led Leila back to the hall, Fergus was already wondering where he could find a suitable husband for her. Not in his father's hall, to be sure, for there was only Iain, Xavier and Murdoch. He would have to find occasion to take her to another keep or a meeting. He had time to make her a good match, and that was no small thing.

He was certain that he would not love again, and he knew she wanted a loving match. Theirs might evolve into affection, but Fergus was determined to make Leila's dream come true. She had left everything to begin anew, after all.

He had a year and a day to find her the husband she deserved.

His father looked up, eyes bright with curiosity, when they

stepped into the hall and Fergus called to him "Father! I am a fortunate man this day indeed."

"Are you?" Calum asked with a knowing smile.

"Leila has agreed to pledge a handfast with me."

Those in the hall turned to listen, then murmured to each other.

Fergus smiled at Leila, who gazed at him as if theirs was a love match. The sight made his heart pound. "We shall pledge to each other this very day, before the feast."

"That is most excellent news!" Calum declared, then rose to cross the floor to them. He seized Leila's hands in his and kissed her cheeks, evidence that he already admired her. "I am delighted, Lady Leila, to welcome you to our family."

"And I am pleased to join it, my lord," Leila said, bending to kiss his hand.

Calum chuckled with satisfaction, then raised his voice. "Iain! I have more labor for you, but it is a joyous task. Fergus and Leila are to pledge a handfast this very day, and the solar must be made ready for the bride."

"But Father, you do not need to surrender the solar," Fergus protested. "You are Laird of Killairic."

"Of course, I do! I have long thought that I should pass the lairdship to you upon your return, and this day will be the perfect time to do so." His father lowered his voice. "Let your new wife be lady of her own hall, Fergus. Killairic has been without a woman's guidance for too long, and I welcome the surrender of my responsibilities."

"But, sir, I would not oust you from the comfort of your chamber," Leila protested.

"But you must, Lady Leila," Calum insisted. "The heir to Killairic should be conceived in the great bed in the solar, if you will forgive my blunt speech, just as Fergus was." He winked. "Indeed, you cannot begin too soon upon that endeavor."

Leila blushed and smiled, even as Calum turned to Iain. "Move my belongings into the chamber at the south side of the tower. I have thought often of how the morning sun warms that small chamber more than it can heat the solar. There is space enough for a good bed and several braziers. I have only the two trunks that will need to be moved."

"Of course, my lord," Iain said, a thread of dismay in his tone. Fergus guessed the reason immediately. This new task would add to his already-full schedule for the day.

"We will all help," Fergus said and Iain's relief was visible. "The boys can move my baggage to the solar, and Duncan and I will help move Father's trunks. Every man in the hall is already occupied with preparations for the feast, so let the newly arrived take on this task."

"Indeed, sir," Iain said.

"In fact, leave the matter to me, Iain," Fergus continued. "You have much to manage this day, and my bride and I can decide how best to arrange the chamber for her tastes."

"Thank you, my lord!" Iain declared, glancing at the state of the hall.

"When Hamish is done with the spice inventory, send him to me," Fergus said. "I will ask the Templars if their squires might share the task."

"You will need this," Calum said in an undertone, revealing a pair of keys that hung from a lace around his neck. They had been hidden beneath his chemise, where once they had hung from Calum's belt. He removed the lace and gave it to Fergus. The larger was the key to the solar, which was seldom locked, and the smaller to the treasury, which was accessed from the solar. "There is an inventory in a ledger just inside the door. Be certain that all is as it should be."

"Thank you, Father. I will." Fergus offered his arm to Leila. "And now, let us see to the solar."

CHAPTER THREE

hat are you going to do with the gifts?" Leila asked quietly when they were on the stairs. Several boys had already scampered ahead of them with small trunks of purchases intended for Isobel and there were many more following them. "It would be a shame to waste such fine goods."

"True. You should choose what you like from them," Fergus suggested. "I would like to send one item to Isobel as a wedding gift, but not any one item in particular." He glanced down at her. "There must be a length of cloth that will not suit your coloring."

She slanted a glance at him but said nothing. He found her mysterious when she was silent, for it was difficult to guess her thoughts. That intrigued him.

"Tell me," he urged.

"In private, perhaps," she agreed softly, then entered the busy solar. "You will have to send word that your marriage is not to be celebrated, after all," she continued mildly. "I think Lord Gaston will be relieved to remain at home with Lady Ysmaine so close to her time. Though, of course, they will be disappointed to hear your news."

Fergus wondered whether they would be so disappointed as that. He knew they both liked Leila.

"I will send a missive to Bartholomew," he said, glad that Leila thought so sensibly. "I believe he intended to write to Gaston with some regularity." He halted to admire the chamber, trying to see it through Leila's eyes.

The solar filled the top floor of the tower of Killairic, and the windows offered views in all directions. The solar was of goodly size, with a large pillared bed in its very midst. Thick curtains hung around the bed and the mattress was plump with goose down. There were wolf pelts cast across the bed as well as woven wool blankets and a large brazier on the south side of the bed. On the eastern wall was a small altar with a beeswax candle upon it, and there was a crucifix hung on the wall above it. Leila's gaze lingered on it for only a moment, but she did not seem to be troubled by it, to his relief. Fergus was not ardent at his prayers but he had fond memories of his mother praying there. The shutters on the north and west windows were closed against the wind, but Fergus opened them to show Leila the view.

"Beautiful," she said, coming to stand beside him and taking a deep breath. "And such a crisp wind."

"You will not find it so admirable in winter," he noted and Leila laughed.

She slanted a glance at him. "I shall have you to keep me warm, will I not?"

Their gazes locked for a heady moment and Fergus could not summon a word to his lips. He thought of Leila's kisses and could not wait to hold her against him, to explore her delicate figure, to couple with her. She held his gaze unflinchingly, her lips curved in a welcoming smile that made him anticipate the night ahead.

"Hold this safe for me, if you please, Lady Leila," Duncan said from beside them, startling them both. He offered Leila his saddlebag and she put the strap over her shoulder.

"Of course," she agreed easily, then touched a fingertip to the braid of Radegunde's hair tied around his wrist. "How long will you stay?" she asked.

"I will ride north in the morning, lass, now that you are cared for."

"Then you will not ride with me?" Fergus asked in surprise.

Duncan spared him a glance. "You have my opinion already on that scheme."

Leila turned a questioning glance on Fergus and he felt his neck heat. Duncan granted her a gruff smile, then turned to direct the boys. Even when they were alone again, Fergus could not bring himself to explain his desire to see Isobel to Leila. He thought it obvious and felt awkward to even consider expressing his intent to visit his former betrothed to the woman he would wed this night.

"The floor is cold even in this season," Leila noted after a long silence.

"I brought some rugs," Fergus said, seizing upon the change of topic. "Perhaps we should put them on either side of the bed, so that floor is not a shock in the morning."

Leila laughed so easily that he was relieved. "That is a good notion." She surveyed the chamber with a critical eye. "I am put in mind of Radegunde's scouring of the chamber at Châmont-sur-Maine."

"It is a bit dusty," Fergus agreed, seeing the cobwebs in the corners. "I wonder if it has had a thorough cleaning since my mother's death."

Leila arched a brow.

"Eight years ago," Fergus supplied.

A gleam of purpose lit in her dark eyes. "If that is the case, it shall have one this day. Is there a maid or two who might assist me?"

"You do not have to do the labor yourself!"

"I do," Leila insisted. "They must know that I do not put myself above them and that I am prepared to do my share." When he might have protested, she placed her fingertips on his arm. "I am from afar, Fergus, and they know it well. They must learn that we have more commonalities than differences, and I must begin immediately to build alliances in your home."

Fergus could scarce argue with such good sense.

Iain came into the solar then, doubtless checking on all activities in what he saw as his domain.

"Ask him to recommend a maid for me," Leila advised. "It would be fitting to seek his counsel in such a matter. Ensure that he is not insulted by my desire to clean the chamber, if you please."

Fergus nodded agreement. "Iain, Lady Leila will have need of a maid. Is there a young woman in the hall or village you would recommend for such service?"

Iain considered the matter for only a moment. "We have a young girl assisting in the kitchens, my lord, but she has a fine eye for women's garb. Her skills might be better put to use in the service of Lady Leila."

Fergus smiled, for Leila had been right. He was amused that she already gave him good advice in his own home. "I knew you would have a recommendation. There is no one who understands the nature of each soul at Killairic better, Iain."

The steward bowed. "I thank you, my lord, though truly, this is simply my responsibility."

Fergus grimaced and lowered his voice, flicking a glance at Leila where she stood at the window, seemingly oblivious to their conversation. "My intended is most fastidious, Iain, as many Saracens are known to be."

"Indeed, sir." The steward cast a disapproving eye over the solar. "Then perhaps she might be more inclined to see the chamber cleaned than your father has been. It is past due for a scrub, but I have not wanted to disturb your father's comfort." The steward sniffed. "He insists that he *likes* older rushes."

Fergus guessed that his father had been trying to save the steward from extra labor. "I assure you that Lady Leila does not share that view."

"Excellent, my lord." Iain bowed to Leila, his approval clear. "I shall send Agnes to her immediately, although she is the only one who can be spared from the kitchens on this day. Perhaps some of the cleaning could wait until tomorrow."

"Perhaps. I will suggest as much." Fergus cleared his throat. "She may insist upon helping with the task herself to see it done more promptly."

"I would not wish to give offense..."

"Nay, Iain," Fergus protested. "It is my lady who does not wish to give offense. She told me already that you must be nigh overwhelmed with duties this day, and that she seeks to contribute."

Iain considered Leila who smiled at him warmly.

He blushed and bowed, so clearly pleased by her attention that Fergus found his own smile. "Of course, sir. Please give the lady my regrets that we have so few staff to serve her will."

"Of course."

"Tell her that I look forward to a woman's administering hand. And please tell her, sir, that I, like your father, will be glad of the opportunity to improve my French."

"Then let us do as much now," Fergus said, recalling Leila's desire to make alliances. The steward would be a good place to begin. He beckoned to her and introduced the pair, standing back to watch as Iain made his greetings in careful French. Leila was patient and listened to him completely before replying, giving no sign that she noticed two errors.

She was diplomatic and gracious, as a laird's wife should be, and he watched with pride as she put the older man quickly at ease. They agreed that one maid's services would be sufficient on this day and disagreed politely upon Leila's determination to help in the cleaning. Leila laughed at Iain's protests and teased him just a little, just enough to charm the steward completely.

"You have made a quick conquest," Fergus commented when Iain left the solar, his step filled with purpose.

"I expect he misses having a lady to consult about the administration of the household," Leila said. A smile played over her lips. "I like him very much. He reminds me of a man who spent most of his life in my uncle's service. Karayan might have been one of the family after such long association."

Fergus glanced around, noting that they were alone in the solar. "And what were you thinking earlier, that you said you would only confide in private?"

Leila sobered. "It is not for me to grant you advice..."

"But it is, for you are to be my wife."

"So, the role is perceived to be the same?"

Fergus nodded. "In these lands, yes."

"Then, you must think about the appearance of all you do, Fergus. There will be those who assume you wed your whore as a matter of simplicity because your betrothed has chosen another. Those people will think me a second choice, and not unfairly so. But if you would have me treated as wife and not as courtesan, then your regard for me must be clear. Even if I am not first in your esteem, you should make it appear so."

"This seems reasonable."

"Your sole gifts to me cannot be what was intended first for Isobel," Leila said with quiet heat. "This is not greed on my part or any criticism of what you have brought, but to grant your new bride the leavings from your betrothed is..."

"A poor choice," Fergus concluded. He spread his hands and raised his voice, just as Duncan and the boys returned. "Tell me, Leila, what nuptial gift would make your heart sing?"

She smiled, so well pleased that his heart thundered. "Two mating pairs of pigeons," she said, to his surprise, but speaking with such resolve that he could not doubt the honesty of her reply.

Perhaps they were a delicacy often eaten in the east. Fergus remembered seeing them for sale in the souks, but not ever having tasted one. Of course, if they were an indulgence, they would not have been served at the Temple, where austerity was the rule.

"And a means of keeping them," she added.

"A cage?" Fergus suggested.

Her smile turned mischievous. "They will breed, and quickly, Fergus. A cage will not contain their numbers for long."

He thought about the garden and nodded. "Perhaps it is time we added a dovecote to the garden."

Leila's features lit with delight. "That would be a most welcome gift, indeed."

"Then it shall be done." Fergus turned to the others and switched to Gaelic, discovering quickly that there were often pigeons for sale in Carlisle, and that a man who knew best how to build a dovecote could be found in Dumfries. He made sure it was understood that this was to be Leila's wedding gift, then divided his father's keys. The key to the solar, he put in his purse, but the smaller one he kept in his hand, the lace hanging from it.

"Before I depart for Dunnisbrae, let us see the valuables secured," he said to Leila. "When I return, I will have the silversmith copy the keys so that both you and I shall have a set."

"No more copies than that, though," Leila said darkly.

Fergus nodded agreement, knowing that she was thinking of Châmont-sur-Maine and the plentitude of keys to the solar there. He unlocked the treasury and glanced inside it, noting the small chest where his father had always kept his coin and the second larger one that contained deeds and legal documents. He fetched his trunk that had gems within it and placed it in the small chamber. Leila was placing the saddlebag in the treasury when someone rapped on the door to the solar. It proved to be Iain.

Fergus locked the door once the treasure was secured, then gave the key to Leila, still on its cord. She put it around her neck and dropped the key into her chemise, just as his father had done, but this time, Fergus watched the path with greater interest.

When Leila smiled, he realized what he had done and cleared his throat. "I will ask Iain how soon we can arrange for your gift," he said, then turned to find a young girl waiting on the threshold. She was young and would be considered pretty, but he had no interest himself in her charms.

She curtsied. "I am Agnes, my lord, sent to be maid to your lady."

Fergus introduced the pair and left Leila to manage Agnes.

As he left the solar, he was thinking of golden skin and dark eyes, of a mysterious smile and woman both finely built and strong. He was thinking of good sense and loyalty, and the merit of having a partner whose word could be relied upon.

And Fergus was thinking, with far more anticipation than he might have expected an hour before, of his wedding night ahead.

Agnes was no fool.

Every soul she knew commented upon her ability to see the truth of a situation—and her gift for calculating how best to use that information to her own advantage. She had been likened to a cat in many places, given her talent for landing upon her feet.

Agnes knew it was less about the landing than in assessing when to jump.

She made good choices. Going to Stewart MacEwan had been a good choice, for her brother had found labor there. Accepting Laird Stewart's request that she go to Killairic and await the return of Fergus had been a good one, too. Laird Stewart wanted to know when the son of Killairic returned home, which was only reasonable, in Agnes' view, given that his wife had been betrothed to Laird Fergus first.

The old Laird of Killairic liked her, which meant she gained special favors. Those in the village were foolish in their trust, a trait that Agnes hoped to use to advantage when necessary. Stephen, the ostler, was a competent lover but more importantly, a collector of gossip and rumor. People confided in him, which gave Agnes fodder to gather in anticipation of a generous reward—from the right laird at the right time.

It served Stephen as well as Agnes to have no one know what they did together in the stables at night, which was another advantage. His unhappy marriage, in truth, was why Agnes had chosen him. She had learned young that men wedded to shrews were the most discreet lovers and often the best trained ones.

On the day of Laird Fergus' return, though, Agnes was stymied by her choices.

Of course, she owed a report to Laird Stewart of the return of the son of Killairic. Old debts should be paid first.

But then, there was the question of how to proceed to see her own advantage best served.

At first, Agnes thought it might be beneficial to charm one of the Templar knights. To be sure, both were tall and handsome, with dark hair and dark eyes. Their manner was stern, but Agnes had been certain she could tempt at least one of them to smile—if not more. Perhaps her destiny was in London or even Paris, larger cities with greater opportunities for the ambitious—and even access to royal courts. Her first effort, though, earned her a stare from one that was cold enough to freeze her marrow and disdainful, too.

As if she was a mere whore.

She would not sully herself with a man who did not appreciate her.

The village priest then told her that the Templars were sworn to poverty, chastity, and obedience, like other monks. Agnes had not realized that detail, since Fergus had joined their ranks. Apparently, there were distinctions between those who joined for a specific term of service and those who joined for life, as well as between lay brothers and knights, but Agnes was quickly bored with the details.

She had more interest in her own fate.

Agnes did not know any of the returning party, for she had not been at Killairic before their departure. She recognized this Duncan by his friendship with Murdoch. They were of a kind, to be sure. Duncan would be honorable and feel compelled to report any misdeed he witnessed, just like Murdoch. It was best for Agnes to avoid them both.

The laird's son, Fergus, was as handsome and charming as Agnes had heard over the years. It was to his credit that she could find naught about him that disappointed, and she wondered if he could truly see the future. Although he might provide an excellent opportunity for her ambitions, she was leery of his rumored talents. It might be wise to avoid him until she knew the extent of his abilities better.

They brought a whore with them, an infidel so shameless that she rode openly in the party, as if she were a lady. Her skin was so dark that it looked to be filthy, and Agnes thought that all the indication of her nature that was needed.

She peeled onions in the kitchen, weighing the merit of the boy Hamish, the squire of Laird Fergus who had journeyed all the way to Outremer and back. He was slightly younger than her fifteen years but so much more innocent in the ways of the world—and this, despite his travels! Agnes thought that there might be amusement in introducing him to the pleasures of the flesh. He might have secrets of his lord's to share, as well. In fact, she was certain she could coax any tale from him, given his sidelong glances of interest, but that would cut both ways.

Hamish was likely incapable of keeping any secret, and Agnes could not afford such a liability.

What of the squires of the Templars? They looked as grim as their knights.

She was curious about the trunks of gifts brought for Lady Isobel and wondered if she might be able to assess their contents at some point. Perhaps theft would be the sum of the opportunities available to her. Laird Stewart would be curious about Laird Fergus' generosity, she was certain. The hall was too busy for her to have a look as yet, and Agnes did not want to steal some trinket that would be missed too soon. Impatient with the prospects offered by the arriving company, Agnes watched them closely, intent upon gathering tidings for Laird Stewart. Her sole reward might lie there.

And that was when she noticed how the Templars watched Duncan.

Why?

Perhaps they distrusted him, but their expressions were not judgmental. The more she watched, the more Agnes wondered. Why *were* there two Templars in the party in the first place? If they always accompanied those who left their service for home, why had she never seen one before? Or heard of one venturing this far north and west before? Agnes was certain that at least one of the sons of the Campbell clan had taken the cross and returned from Outremer. Even the old laird himself had seemed to be surprised by their presence.

Could there be another reason for them to accompany the laird's son?

Why did Duncan hold so fast to that one saddlebag? He did not look to be a man who had many worldly possessions, let alone those he would fear to see stolen in his companion's home.

The Templars, too, kept an eye upon that saddlebag, as did the infidel whore.

Agnes wanted very much to see what was in that bag.

It was not long before Fergus announced to all that he would make a handfast with his whore. Agnes was not surprised. If he wanted to continue to savor the infidel's charms, he would need a tale for his father. The old man had a firm moral code, and Agnes had been careful to let him believe that she shared his views.

She had thought all along that it might prove advantageous to do so, and on this day, it did. The steward came directly to her after visiting the solar with the couple.

"Do you know much of the tasks of a lady's maid?" Iain asked, his intention clear to any who looked.

Agnes smiled. "I know how a woman dresses and how she washes," she said, adopting a modest manner. "And I believe I know how to follow commands, sir."

"Indeed, you do," Iain acknowledged. "Lady Leila has need of a maid, and I think you will suit well."

Lady Leila. Agnes hid her sneer with a docile smile. "Are you certain I can be spared in the kitchens, Iain?" she asked, feigning concern. "Perhaps I should begin on the morrow, after the feast."

Xavier snorted and bent his attention upon his sauce when Iain glared at him.

"That is thoughtful of you, Agnes, but I am certain Xavier can manage without you."

The cook harrumphed. "Take her," he invited. "She does not contribute that much to the effort. Perhaps we will do better without her in the way."

Iain's lips thinned. "Lady Leila has need of you now, for the handfast will be before the evening meal. Come along, Agnes, and I will present you to her."

"Of course." Agnes turned her smile upon Xavier. "I am sorry, but the onions are done."

"Half of them at best," the cook noted with disapproval. "Do not fear that I will be challenged to replace one so lazy as you. Go! And welcome to it!"

Steward and cook glared at each other, at odds in their view of Agnes as in so many other things, and Agnes considered that this change in her situation could only be an improvement.

Perhaps the whore might teach her some exotic skills, courtesy of her experience in the Orient. Perhaps she might talk in her sleep. Surely, there could only be advantage in gaining access to the solar, even if it was simply in the quality of information she could provide to Laird Stewart.

Agnes had time to feel pride in her situation before they reached the solar. Iain rapped once on the door, which was partially closed.

That was interesting. The old man had always left it wide open.

The warrior, Duncan, opened the door wider, his manner unwelcoming. He no longer had his saddlebag, a fact Agnes would not have noticed if she had not been so curious about its contents. Agnes glanced past Duncan in time to see the whore put it in the treasury, then Laird Fergus closed and locked that door. He gave the key to the infidel, who put its cord around her neck. He then passed Agnes on his way out of the solar, Duncan fast behind him.

Iain introduced her to the whore, and Agnes bowed low, as subservient and humble as ever she had pretended to be, even as her thoughts flew.

Duncan had been trusted with something of sufficient value for it to be placed in the treasury.

And the whore had the key.

Agnes was going to find out what was in that saddlebag, if it was the last thing she did.

Leila immediately disliked the girl.

The maid's gaze was too quick, her manner too furtive, her smile too smug. There was a satisfaction about Agnes that reminded Leila of a cat, content with its situation, certain of its future. She was a pretty girl, to be sure, with a long braid as dark as ebony, eyes of clear blue, and skin as fair as milk. She was slender and had a tendency to open her eyes wide, as if innocent or awed, but Leila sensed that Agnes was cunning.

Hers was an instinctive and powerful reaction, which meant that Leila would trust it. It did not hurt that she had been unobserved when the girl arrived in the doorway. Fergus had taken Duncan's saddlebag from Leila and she had turned slightly as she stepped back. She had noticed the girl after she had placed the saddlebag in the treasury, when she turned away as Fergus locked the treasury. Agnes' sly expression was gone so quickly that it might never have been, but Leila had seen it and she took it as a warning.

Leila might have to be served by an untrustworthy person, but she did not have to let the girl guess at her suspicions.

She disliked that there was one alliance at Killairic that she would not be able to make, but there was naught for it. Leila recalled Radegunde's custom of sleeping in the chamber with Lady Ysmaine, unless Gaston and Ysmaine intended to be intimate. Radegunde often joined them in the chamber once their coupling was complete, and she had herself joined Bartholomew and Anna in their chamber when they had posed as a married couple at Haynesdale. It was an advantage for a maid to sleep in the solar, which was often warmer and offered greater comfort than the kitchen or the hall. Leila did not wish to cause offense by challenging custom, but she was not going to sleep with this viper awake in the solar.

Which only meant that Agnes had to be so exhausted each night that she had no choice but to sleep, and to sleep deeply.

Leila doubted that the girl realized just how thoroughly they two were going to clean the solar—or how much of the labor she was going to be compelled to do.

Fergus sat in the hall with his father, listening to a summary of events since his departure. He was thinking, to his own surprise, about Leila.

He had been thinking about Isobel first, but it seemed that every consideration of Isobel led him to Leila. He supposed that was natural, for he had been betrothed to one and would marry the other.

What did he truly know about Isobel? She was beautiful, she smiled at his jests, she was obedient to her father's will. They both were, he supposed, for they had agreed to wed at the suggestion of their parents. They had spent time together, but mostly in the company of others, at celebrations and when riding to hunt. They had been intimate once, but that had been so furtive that he scarce recalled the details.

He could not suppress the conviction that he knew more about any of his companions on this journey than about his betrothed.

Maybe even more of Leila.

It was an interesting notion. He did not know if Isobel lingered abed in the morning or rose early. He did not know what her mood would have been after a long day riding in the rain, much less how she would have responded to a need to sleep in a stable. Or in a field. It was true that travel and its hardships unveiled all secrets.

Fergus knew far more about Leila than about Isobel, to be sure. He knew that Leila would keep her word at any price, and fulfill any promise she made. He and she held the merit of a vow in the same high esteem. He knew that she was courageous, for she had left her home over a question of principle. He knew that she was clever and resourceful, and that she accepted the challenges of travel with a tolerance that echoed his own.

And he knew that she kissed with a sweet heat that haunted him truly.

Aye, and the second one had been more scorching than the first.

Leila. Even thinking of her in his father's hall, knowing she was setting the solar to rights, knowing that they would pledge a handfast within hours, heated him to his toes. Was it simply the price of chastity?

Or would his desire for Leila linger beyond one night?

Fergus could not imagine as much. It was chastity at root, and some admiration of Leila was only natural. He doubted that his heart could be surrendered again so soon, certainly not if his beloved had been compelled to wed Stewart. His affection was more steady than that! The handfast was a compromise, an arrangement of good sense, and he would use the time to find Leila the husband she could love forevermore.

The one who would give her a son with blue eyes.

Fergus watched as the maid Agnes appeared at the base of the stairs with a bundle of linens. She strode into the bailey and returned moments later, evidently having assigned their washing to a woman in the village.

The curtains from the bed were carried out to the bailey next. Fergus could see the dust on the dark cloth even from the other side of the hall. Again, Agnes seemed to have found an ally in the village—or one more willing to ensure that the new lady's will was done. She disappeared into the kitchens once she was rid of the curtains, where laughter was heard.

Leila herself appeared, clearly seeking the girl, and went into the kitchen in pursuit of her. No words were necessary to explain her stern expression, or her finger pointing up the stairs. Agnes trudged back to the solar, and Fergus fought a smile.

It seemed that Leila's plan to win alliances at Killairic had some limitations.

Agnes descended next with the down mattresses from the great bed and carried them into the bailey. She returned quickly once more, and Fergus assumed she had again found someone to do the labor assigned to her. She climbed to the solar, looking proud of herself, then quickly reappeared, burdened with straw pallets and wearing a frown. She carried them outside, muttering under her breath with displeasure. Agnes must have been less successful in finding assistance with this task, for she was gone longer and was flushed when she entered the hall again. The pallets would have been left in the sun after being beaten, Fergus knew.

The girl then fetched a broom from the kitchens and carried it up the stairs to the solar. Fergus heard furniture being moved. No doubt, every corner of the room was being swept clean.

A disgruntled Agnes carried buckets of ash down from the braziers, and Calum cleared his throat.

"The Saracens had a fondness for cleanliness that far exceeded that of most in the west," he commented. "I remember it well. Their homes were a marvel."

"Indeed," Duncan agreed.

"Killairic will benefit from Lady Leila's inclinations," Fergus' father said with approval. "I see it now."

When next Agnes appeared, the line of her lips was mutinous and her braid was becoming undone. She was breathing more heavily as she trudged up the stairs, with a bucket brimming with water and a brush.

His father glanced after the girl. "She has not worked so hard since her arrival here," he said beneath his breath, then chuckled. "It will not harm her."

"I wonder at Leila's ability to communicate with her," Fergus said. "She speaks little Gaelic and I doubt Agnes speaks French."

"I suspect your intended is a resourceful woman," Calum said. "She has that look about her."

"As we saw, some commands can be given by gesture," Duncan contributed.

"I should ensure that all is well, just the same," Fergus said, excusing himself. "The girl looks to be vexed."

His father was clearly amused by his departure. "Cannot bear for her to be out of sight?" that man asked Duncan as Fergus left them together. "I cannot blame him. She is a beauty, to be sure. I am quite delighted by the promise of more conversation with her. Did you know that her uncle was a smith?"

Fergus climbed the stairs, moving quickly and quietly, and peeked into the solar. He wanted to see what was happening before announcing his presence. Already he could see the difference in the solar. The dust and cobwebs were gone from the corners, and the rushes had been piled outside the door. It smelled cleaner, too.

Agnes was on her knees, scrubbing the floor and casting poisonous glances at Leila at regular intervals. Leila ignored her, but he doubted she was oblivious. The bed had been stripped to the ropes that held the mattress and the wooden frame itself. Leila was unpacking the trunks of gifts he had brought for Isobel, sorting the items on table beneath one window.

There was a goodly pile of cloth of various weights and in many lengths, and Leila had arranged it by color. There were leather belts and purses, and embroidered silken shoes, and stockings so fine that they were like gossamer. Fergus was a little surprised to see it all assembled, for he had forgotten about some of the cloth.

Leila worked without expression, pausing only once in her task to glance back at Agnes, then point imperiously to a corner the girl had missed.

"It looks like a different chamber," Fergus said in French, announcing himself. Agnes hastened to her feet, wiping her hands on her skirts and curtseying to him as she smiled. He nodded at the bucket, indicating that she should continue. Her lips tightened and she dropped to her knees once more, failing to hide her resentment.

"Must you do it all in one afternoon?" he asked Leila. "Agnes will despise you."

The girl glanced up at the sound of her name, her expression revealing that she did not understand what was being said. She clearly thought she might have a reprieve. But Leila turned to her and pointed to the floor. Agnes picked up the brush once more, and Fergus saw her eyes flash before she lowered her gaze.

"I think there is little to be lost there," Leila said calmly. "There will not be fondness between us, no matter what I do."

"I thought you meant to win allies."

"She will never be one such. I will not worry about what cannot be changed."

"I could find another girl to be your maid."

"I will not be the infidel who finds this one lacking. There is a proverb, after all, about keeping those you trust close to your side and those you do not trust even closer." She cast an assessing glance at Agnes. "I will ensure that she sleeps well each night, though."

"I do not understand," Fergus said.

Leila avoided his gaze. "Surely you know that it is customary for a maid to sleep in the solar, as one of the benefits of her post. She must sleep or I will not."

Fergus thought that Leila's suspicion of Agnes was undeserved, for he did not imagine that his father would have any servant in his hall who could not be trusted. Still, he did not blame her for feeling alone in his home, and uncertain of her safety to some extent. Who would not feel vulnerable in a foreign land, not speaking the language well?

In time, she would come to trust the girl, he hoped, or they would find another maid.

In time, he knew she would learn Gaelic and her confidence would grow.

"She will sleep in the hall this night," Fergus said. "I am not so interested in additional companionship on the night of our nuptials." He savored Leila's quick smile, but her words revealed that he had not changed her thinking.

"All the same, the solar should be cleaned, and I will have it done on this day."

"On the morrow, more hands could help."

Leila turned to confront him, her hands on her hips and a glint of resolve in her eyes. "On the night of my nuptials, I will meet my husband in a clean bed, in a clean chamber," Leila said firmly. "There will be no dirt, no sweat, and no vermin."

Fergus had to acknowledge that this was only reasonable.

"Also, I think it wiser to have fewer persons in the solar at any time, and that the door should be locked in our absence." She met his gaze briefly and he knew that she was being protective of the reliquary entrusted to them.

All the same, this was wrong.

Fergus cleared his throat. "I appreciate that this is not the home you know and that you would be cautious, but if you wish to be trusted, Leila, you must trust first."

She held his gaze, unflinching. "I will trust those who earn my trust." When he frowned, she dropped her voice to a murmur. "I think it only reasonable to be cautious where such a prize is concerned. Let them blame it upon my being from afar. It will be safer that way."

Fergus respected Leila's thinking, though he knew there was only one key to the treasury and doubted the lock would be readily compromised. He also saw that her thinking would not be changed in this moment. It would take time for her to trust all at Killairic, perhaps after the reliquary had found a haven.

He did not want discord between them on the day they would take their vows, so he changed the subject.

"I did not realize I had purchased so much," he said, surveying the piles of cloth.

Leila cast him a warm smile as she opened yet another trunk, revealing even more fine cloth. "You are a generous lover, to be sure."

"Is that a criticism?"

"Of course not! It is a good trait to be generous. I simply wish the lady had returned your esteem."

Fergus leaned against the wall, wanting to watch her expression. She seemed to very mysterious to him in this moment, and he wanted to know her thoughts. "But then we should not be making a handfast this day."

Leila's dark gaze flicked to his. "We would not."

"Would you regret that?"

She put down the cloth she held, granting him her complete attention. "Of course. I told you just days ago that you are the kind of man I should like to wed. That was not a lie and it has not changed. I also appreciate that your offer ensures my security in this land."

"I would ensure that we have time for you to find a lasting match, to meet a man you can love fully," Fergus said.

Leila's gaze flicked away from his. "You are a good man, Fergus. And as a result, I regret that you had such affection for a woman who broke her vow to you and that your generosity appears to have been misplaced." He watched her brows draw together as she ran an admiring hand over the cloth.

"Then let us put it to good purpose," he said, liking that his words erased her frown. "First, choose for yourself. Which cloth will you make into a kirtle first?"

"The red, I think," Leila said, touching a length of crimson wool blended with silk. "It is a joyous color." She shook her head. "I will need assistance, though. I confess that I have little talent with a needle, and do not even know how to make the kirtles that women wear in this land." She winced. "My uncle thought it a failure that I did not try harder to sew."

"My mother despised sewing as well," Fergus confessed. "She was much happier riding to hunt."

"Truly?" Leila's eyes lit.

"Truly."

"I should have liked to have met her."

There was naught that could be said to that. "We will ask Margaret in the village to sew for you. I do not doubt that she still has the most skillful needle hereabouts and my mother was always complimentary about her talent." Fergus nodded at the array of fabric. "Choose a second. The lady of Killairic must have at least two garments of her own." Leila touched the kirtle she was wearing, and he shook his head before she could speak. "In addition to the one given to you by Radegunde," he said firmly. "It is a good serviceable garment, but not the attire of a lady."

Leila smiled and stepped back. "Then you choose."

Fergus selected two lengths of fine cotton for chemises and another length of wool in deep gold. He picked sheer fabrics to match for veils and added them to the pile. A golden circlet would replace the plain pewter one that Leila had worn since Haynesdale, and two finely crafted leather belts with detailed tooling would suit her as well. He added the stockings, a velvet purse, a heavy black wool for a cloak. "We shall find some fur to line it," he said, then frowned at the shoes and slippers. "They will all be too large for you. Let us ask Margaret what can be done."

"You are a generous lover," Leila said.

"It is *all* yours, if you desire it."

"What you have chosen is more than sufficient." Leila indicated a length of finely woven deep green wool. "Your father might be glad of a new robe, and this will be warm for him."

"An excellent suggestion. For that, you win a third kirtle, made of the wool in the hue of roses."

"Fergus!"

He grinned at her, liking that she was pleased. "And now, the gift." Fergus chose a length of blended wool and silk in a brilliant blue. He had bought it because it was the exact hue of Isobel's eyes, and he wanted rid of it. The color would not suit Leila at all and it was too fine to give to anyone else.

There was a psalter rolled within it for the journey, a small volume with delicate images that he had bought for Isobel in Venice. It was a lady's volume, but Isobel was not ardent in her prayers. Fergus had bought it because it was so beautiful, but was reluctant to give such a treasure to her now.

He would save it, for another woman might one day appreciate it. Perhaps Leila would convert, or he might be so fortunate as to love again in future.

Was that the dark cloud he had discerned? His own future without love?

Fergus refused to think about it. He set the psalter aside, recalling another trinket. There were fine needles of steel in the bottom of one trunk, the like of which he had never seen before glimpsing them in Outremer. He had bought them for Isobel, and some lengths of silk thread which would be welcome for her embroidery.

Again, the tokens had been costly, and Isobel was not diligent with her stitchery either, but Leila would never sit and embroider. She would hunt and hawk and ride with him, all of which were welcome prospects. He had seen her muck out the stalls of the horses and did not doubt she would undertake any labor she deemed practical and necessary. He doubted that embroidery would ever count. Fergus added half of the needles and thread to the blue cloth, thinking the gift was suitable. He put the remainder of the needles and thread aside for Margaret.

"Let us give these to Margaret," he suggested. "They will make you an ally, to be sure, and she will have good use of them."

"That is a fine idea."

Content with his choices for Isobel, Fergus took one of the small trunks and packed them into it.

Leila granted him a challenging glance but said nothing.

Fergus understood that she had something to say but feared to speak her thoughts. He would teach her to do as much, and he would do that without delay.

Honesty, after all, was the foundation of every good match. He would have that, even if he could not have Isobel.

CHAPTER FOUR

hat is amiss?" Fergus asked.

Leila hesitated, then spoke quietly. "Do you not think that too fine a gift to offer another man's wife?"

"It is too fine a gift to leave packed away," he replied. "The shade of this cloth does not favor you and you are unlikely to ever embroider."

"True enough, but it might be wiser to send less. She *is* wedded to another man."

"And she was betrothed to me," Fergus said stubbornly. Every time he saw this cloth he would think of her betrayal and he did not wish to dwell upon it. "I think it only reasonable that I send her a gift with my good wishes for her happiness." When she did not reply, he continued. "I will be arriving as a married man myself, Leila. Surely that will improve Stewart's view of my gesture?"

Leila arched a brow but said no more.

Fergus had a thought. "Did you desire either of these things?"

"Of course not. And since you bought the gifts, they are yours to disperse."

He ignored his sense that she had not told him all of her

thoughts. "I will ride to Dunnisbrae tomorrow to give my regards to Isobel," he continued. "Enguerrand and Yvan will remain here..."

"You mean to visit Isobel yourself?" Leila asked, her astonishment clear. "And on the morrow?"

"I cannot leave the tidings of Kerr's death to be delivered by another," Fergus said, irked that yet another person questioned his decision. "And it is not a message that should be delayed."

Leila shook her head and turned away from him, packing away the remainder of the cloth with quick gestures. Fergus could feel that Agnes was attending their discussion, but Leila said no more.

He missed both her frank counsel and the flash of her eyes. This demure Leila was far less beguiling.

"You disapprove," he said, inviting her to say more.

"It is not my place to approve or disapprove, clearly." Leila curtsied to him. "Your will is mine, my lord. Is that not how it should be between man and wife?" She moved past him to stack one trunk against the wall, only the quickness of her gestures revealing her annoyance.

"Nay! I would hear your thoughts."

"You will not *listen* to my thoughts, so I will keep them to myself."

"Leila! Tell me what concerns you." Fergus pursued her and touched her elbow when she did not turn to face him. "Leila," he said, his voice dropping low. "Let us always have honesty between us. I would hear the truth of your thinking, even if you expect it will displease me."

She stilled beneath his touch. "Truth?"

"Truth."

"Even if you will not welcome it?"

"Even so."

Leila rounded upon him, glanced at Agnes, then spoke with low heat. "It is one thing that you love her still. It is another that you wed me out of grace and kindness. But do not be such a fool as to provoke a warrior who is her husband by showing your admiration for his wife so clearly. She chose him and it is not your place to offer temptation."

As Fergus had expected, her concerns were rootless.

"You make much of little," he countered with a smile. "And assumptions of people you do not know. Isobel was my betrothed! Her nephew accompanied us by her request, and the boy died! I must tell her of his fate myself."

"You make excuses," Leila countered with flashing eyes. "You love her still, and if I can see as much, so will her husband. What else would he think, if you rush to her side the day immediately after your return? He will not be fooled by this handfast, not if he has any wits at all!"

"You would jump at shadows," Fergus said, knowing his tone was dismissive.

"Aye? What do you know of this Stewart MacEwan?"

Fergus realized that Agnes had again lifted her head. He spared her a quelling glance and she returned to her scrubbing. "That he is a warrior, perhaps twenty years older than Isobel. I do not doubt that he defends her well. She *is* beautiful."

Leila straightened. "In my experience, men who fight to gain their desires are quick to assume that others covet their prizes."

Fergus shook his head. "I have known Stewart at a distance for a long time. He will be glad of any gift that shows his wife's beauty to advantage. He will be glad of tidings from the east, as well. You will see. I will be greeted warmly."

"Even though you tell them of Kerr's death."

Fergus winced. "I expect Isobel will be dismayed. Her brother was killed, you know, and his wife wed another. Kerr was her only nephew and reminder of her brother." He knew that Isobel would be devastated by the loss of Kerr and resolved again to keep the truth of the boy's nature from her.

Leila studied him for a long moment, her eyes seeming even more dark than usual. "Do not be such a fool as to console her, at least not when her husband might see you."

"Leila! You make much of naught."

"Do I?"

"It is but the visit of a neighbor and the deliverance of news."

She eyed him, her expression inscrutable. Fergus was certain she discerned his hope that Isobel had been compelled to wed

Stewart against her own will.

When Leila's lips tightened and she turned away from him, he felt her disappointment keenly. But they had agreed to honesty, and he would not deceive her about his surrendered heart.

"I trust you are right, my lord," she said, her tone temperate once more. She worked steadily and in silence, the line of her shoulders telling him that she was yet annoyed.

The next day would prove him right about Stewart and Fergus knew it.

But in this moment, he had to regain Leila's goodwill. They were to be handfasted, after all. He turned to survey the chamber and the angle of the sun. "When you and Agnes have restored the solar to rights, would you like to bathe before the ceremony?"

Leila spun to face him and her lips parted. "I should, indeed."

"There is a wooden tub in the kitchens," Fergus said, savoring the sight of her pleasure. "I will have it brought here and ensure that all know the new lady will bathe daily in hot water."

"But Iain has much to manage this day."

Fergus smiled at her for he could clearly read her hope. "I believe he might be convinced to ensure the pleasure of the new lady of the hall. If not, I shall help to ensure that the bride has her desire."

Leila's eyes twinkled as she smiled and Fergus felt triumphant. "You are a thoughtful man. I thank you for this, Fergus." She flicked a glance at the girl, then licked her lips. "I hope you are right about this visit," she whispered. "I will pray for your safe return."

Fergus looked down at her, touched by her concern, and had to tease her a little. "I did not know that prayer was your inclination."

The corner of Leila's mouth lifted into a smile. "I was taught that Allah aids those who aid themselves, and I prefer to do what I can to ensure the goal I desire. In this case, though, my counsel has been declined. I will pray, for that is the sole course left to me, as I would prefer not to lose a spouse immediately after I gain one."

"I promise you that I will return in time for the evening meal, and that all will be as I say."

"And I will pray that you are right, my lord." Before Fergus could reply, Leila closed the distance between them with a step and stretched to kiss his cheek. He caught his breath then, unable to deny temptation, turned his face slightly so that their lips met.

Leila leaned against him, her hands landing upon his shoulders, and Fergus found himself catching her around the waist to draw her close. She was so enticing and her kiss grew more potent each time. Heat raced through Fergus as she surrendered to his kiss and he was glad that his bout of chastity would end this night.

Satisfaction would clear his thinking and ensure that he was temperate when he met Isobel again.

Though Fergus was sufficiently honest to admit that it was not Isobel who reigned in his thoughts when Leila slipped her fingers into his hair and pulled him closer.

"Gifts, gifts," Calum declared from the portal, and Leila blushed as Fergus reluctantly ended their kiss. The older man smiled as he entered the solar, and she saw that there was a length of fabric over his arm. "For you, Lady Leila, as my wife always said a bride needs a new kirtle for her nuptials."

The garment was a rich purple and gleamed with the luster of silk. There was gold embroidery upon the hem and the cuffs of the sleeves, as well as around the neckline.

Leila was surprised to be offered such a splendid garment. "Sir, I could not accept such a gift..."

"Of course, you can," Calum said, interrupting her. "I brought it from the east, almost twenty years ago, as a gift for my wife. The hue was wrong for her, or so she insisted, and has been folded away ever since." He shrugged. "I liked the purple with her hair, but she did not and ladies are always right about such matters."

Leila smiled at Fergus. "I see that you come honestly by your generosity."

Fergus laughed. "My father always lavished gifts upon my mother. We both liked to see her pleased."

Leila took the garment, then held it up to admire it. It would be a little long, but there was no time to shorten it. She reasoned that the hall had been swept and it would not be overly damaged in one night of wear.

"There is more in the trunk, of course," Calum said. "A silk chemise, along with a belt and shoes that match, but I did not think it fitting to present such garments to a lady. Send the girl for them."

"I will. Thank you so much." Leila kissed Calum's cheeks and he smiled at her. "You have made me so welcome at Killairic. I thank you for that, as well."

The older man grinned at his son. "I see the inclination of Fergus' heart and I trust his judgment in this." Leila thought it might be tactless to note that Fergus' first choice of bride had not shown his good judgment so well. Fergus himself was looking at his boots. "All I ask, Lady Leila, is that you bear a son soon."

"I shall do my best, sir." Leila curtseyed.

"And that is all any man can ask. Come, Fergus, let us leave the bride to her preparations." Calum called to Agnes and said something quick in Gaelic. The girl rose to her feet with obvious relief and followed him from the solar.

"The curtains, the mattress, the linens and the bath," Fergus said. "I will do what I can to assist, for it must all be done before the evening meal."

"Thank you, Fergus," Leila said, wishing she did not have such a dread of his visit to Isobel on the morrow. She failed to see how that journey could end well, but tried to have faith in Fergus' decision. How she wished she could protect him from a repetition of this day's unwelcome news.

In a way, she wanted to witness his meeting with Isobel yet in another, she was not certain she could trust herself to be polite in the other woman's presence.

She smiled at him, grateful for all he had done and determined to believe in their shared future. "Thank you for all of this."

Their gazes clung for a thrilling moment, then Fergus bowed and left the solar, calling for assistance in seeing her will done.

Leila would make him a good wife.

She would be the best wife possible.

And even if he did not love her fully in a year and a day, Leila would ensure that Fergus could not imagine his life without her.

She did not care what was required of her to make that so.

❧

Fergus was astonished when Leila came down to the hall in the late afternoon.

The keep had been turned upside down on this day, as if a new wind had blown through Killairic. The solar was cleaner than when it had been new, and Fergus felt a sense of new pride in the place. His father was clearly quite satisfied. The rushes on the floor of the hall had been changed and the tables had been set. The villagers had arrived and the smell from the kitchens made his belly growl. Candles and torches had been lit and there was mulled wine to be poured.

All awaited the lady herself.

When Leila appeared at the foot of the stairs, there was a collective gasp. She looked exotic and beautiful, so lovely that Fergus caught his breath. He was humbled that this woman would take him for her spouse and felt a lump in his throat as she crossed the floor to him. The purple hue suited her well, making her look like royalty, and the kirtle highlighted her delicate figure. The golden embroidery gleamed in the light, as did the circlet in her hair. The silken veil shimmered behind her, seeming to float as she walked. The villagers seemed to be struck dumb in their awe, but Leila smiled and halted before Fergus, tipping back her head to meet his gaze.

He smiled at her and took her right hand in his. The slight weight of her tiny hand made him feel protective of her in a most welcome way. Fergus took Leila's left hand in his, their hands crossing between them. She watched him with bright eyes.

"Are you certain?" he murmured in French.

Her smile was brilliant. "Aye. Are you?"

"Aye."

"Then let us not delay," she said.

His father welcomed the villagers to the hall then and spoke warmly of the inclination of his son to wed. They were all invited to stand witness to the union and they gathered in a circle around Fergus and Leila.

When it was time to pledge to each other, Fergus spoke slowly, pausing at intervals. Leila would have to repeat the vows in Gaelic so all would understand and he wanted to ensure that she made no inadvertent errors. "And so I vow to you, Leila binte Qadir lufti al-Ramm, that I will treat you with honor from this day forth, for a year and a day."

"And so I vow to you, Fergus of Killairic, that I will treat you with honor from this day forth, for a year and a day," Leila said.

"That I will hold you in my heart when we are apart and treat you well when we are together," Fergus continued.

Leila held his gaze. "That I will hold you in my heart when we are apart and treat you well when we are together."

Several of the women from the village sighed with delight and Fergus heard one sniffle.

"I will take responsibility for any child of our union, whether our vows are renewed or not," he pledged.

"I will take responsibility for any child of our union, whether our vows are renewed or not," Leila echoed.

Fergus smiled at her. "I will defend you and I will be faithful to you, and do my best to ensure our union fares well."

"I will defend you and I will be faithful to you, and do my best to ensure our union fares well," Leila said.

Fergus bent then and kissed her sweetly, not in the least surprised at the fire that was awakened by that fleeting touch. When he broke their kiss, Leila's eyes were sparkling and her cheeks were flushed. For one heady moment, she smiled up at him and they might have been alone, then his father came to congratulate them.

Calum presented a pair of rings to them, made of gold. "Your mother and I wore them," he said. "In the tradition of the Romans."

"Of course," Leila said and took the larger one.

"You know of the Romans?" Fergus asked.

"We know much of the descendants of the eastern Roman Empire, the Christians of Constantinople."

"More Franj?" he teased.

She shook her head. "Franj are from the west. Rūm are from Constantinople." She pushed the circle of gold on to Fergus' ring finger. "They taught that the vein in this finger went directly to the heart," she said.

"And does it?" Fergus asked, intrigued.

Leila smiled. "I believe all veins lead to the same destination."

"All roads to Rome, then? Or maybe Rūm?"

She laughed and Fergus was glad of her words because his mother's ring only fit on Leila's middle finger. They kissed again, a little less chastely than before, then were surrounded by those intent upon wishing them well. The men shook his hand and the women kissed his cheeks, until one impulsively kissed Leila as well. Fergus was surprised to see her delight, then she kissed that villager in return. Her subsequent laughter prompted the others to laugh as well.

"A feast!" Calum cried. "Let us all make merry, for there is much to celebrate on this night!"

The company roared approval and Fergus led Leila to the high table. The villagers clapped and hooted as he swept her into his arms and swung her around. She laughed again, looking young and most alluring, then his father rapped on the board.

Leila was seated between Fergus and his father. Duncan sat on Fergus' other side and the Templars flanked them all. The squires stood behind the knights and aided in the service, a situation that clearly pleased Hamish's aunt and uncle. Mulled wine and ale were poured, and cups raised high in a toast to the new couple. They cheered, they drank, then the roast venison was carried from the kitchen to applause. Even Xavier and Iain seemed to have found a happy accord on this night.

Fergus had to consider that though his homecoming was not what he had expected, it was better than it might have been. He had a lady by his side whom he trusted and would not ignore the merit of that.

For this night, he would ignore that persistent shadow of dread and hope it meant naught at all.

On this night, he and Leila would make their first effort to create a son, and he had to ensure that it was a joyous event.

"I shall be compelled to tell the news in French," Calum declared when the soup was being carried from the kitchen. "So that Lady Leila can learn more of her new home."

Leila was, again, the only woman at the high table. She was aware of the villagers below the salt watching her. She knew that Fergus had resolved some detail in his thoughts and wondered what it might be. He was more at ease with the compromise of their match, though she knew his regard for Isobel had not diminished so quickly as that.

Nay, the man had a scheme and she doubted he would confide it in her.

The seneschal brought a copper pot with a spout and poured mulled wine for Calum, then for Fergus and then Leila. The wine smelled of cinnamon and cloves, and a waft of steam rose from it. The scent of the spice was welcome after the bland fare they had eaten in inns since arriving in England and Leila sniffed appreciatively.

"Do you drink wine?" Calum whispered to her in sudden alarm.

"Only on an occasion such as this, when it is celebratory," Leila said.

"I thought your prophet had advised against it," the older man said, showing even more familiarity with her faith than Leila could have expected.

"And so he did, but it is not uncommon to savor wine in moderation in my homeland." It was also not uncommon for warriors and rulers to drink themselves to the point of inebriation, though Leila chose not to mention as much.

Calum nodded. "Ah, so it is drunkenness that is avoided, and this is good advice indeed."

That was not strictly so, but Leila did not wish to discuss doctrine on her first day at Killairic. She wished to blend in, not to be different, which would mean a measure of mulled wine on a celebratory occasion, such as she had savored in her uncle's home.

Calum dropped his voice to a whisper. "We seldom have wine, and this will be the last of it for a good while. A wedding is the best time for wine, I believe."

"As do I," Leila agreed and sipped of hers.

There had been wine at Aziza's wedding.

She refused to think about her cousin, not on this night, not at an occasion she would have liked to have shared with the woman as close to her as a sister.

She noticed that the villagers were served ale while those at the high table enjoyed the wine. She could only conclude that wine was expensive in this land, perhaps because the climate did not favor the growth of grapes. She would have to find out more.

Indeed, she was keenly aware that she had seldom eaten at a lord's high table, even though she had journeyed the breadth of Christendom. While disguised as a squire, she had eaten stew from a bowl. At Châmont-sur-Maine, she had eaten in the kitchens with the servants, at a long communal table, again from a wooden bowl. It was only upon returning to Haynesdale that she had eaten at the board, after abandoning her disguise as Anna's maid. No one had paid much attention to her there, and she did not doubt that she had made some errors of etiquette.

With the entire company intrigued by her, Leila was determined to have perfect manners at this meal.

Half of a loaf of flat bread sliced horizontally was placed before herself and Fergus, and Leila moved to pinch off a corner. She assumed it was the first item they should eat and she was ravenous.

Fergus stayed her with a shake of his head. "'Tis called a trencher and will act as a plate, absorbing all the sauces," he advised her in an undertone. "They will go to the dogs after the meal. You need not fear for a lack of bread. There will be smaller loaves."

"They did not use bread this way at Haynesdale."

"They had wooden trenchers there, but the notion is the same. You and I will share."

Leila nodded understanding, glad he had warned her.

"It is good you are hungry," Calum said with a smile. "We were preparing to feast for May Day, so Fergus' arrival is timely."

"As if he saw the future," Leila said, and her host laughed.

"As if he did." He smiled at his son.

"Do you still have your cook from Paris, my lord?" Duncan asked.

"I do, indeed. I do not believe any soul could dislodge Xavier from my kitchen, to my own good fortune."

Duncan winked at Leila. "At any other hall, it would be mutton stew or grilled eels, but we shall dine lavishly on this day."

Leila was glad of it. She knew she had lost weight since leaving Outremer, given long days of riding and often meager meals at taverns. The fare had been excellent at Châmont-sur-Maine but more humble since then.

A sequence of servants moved before the high table, offering each dish from the kitchen to Calum first, and she eyed the platters with anticipation. Each servant spoke, probably naming the dish, but their Gaelic was too quick for Leila. It was Fergus who translated for her. There were no olives and few legumes, but that did not surprise Leila any longer. The squires served their knights, but the others were served by those from Killairic's kitchens.

The roast venison was enormous, revealing that the deer in this land were larger than those she had known. The meat smelled wonderful and she knew she should compliment this Xavier when they met. Hamish whispered that it was Radegunde's favorite, which made Leila smile and accept a little more.

Next, there were eggs of such size that Leila doubted they were from chickens.

"Grouse eggs in mustard sauce," Fergus supplied. "While those are from pheasants and simply hard boiled. That may be parsley upon them."

"Such birds are raised here?"

"Nay. The eggs are foraged from the woods. There are geese in the village, but they will be slaughtered at the Yule. This is civet of rabbit," he said, gesturing to a dish being presented. "Which will have some wine in the sauce. The roast hare that is next will not."

Leila listened to Fergus' descriptions and indicated what she would like to taste, noting how the selections were placed on the trencher so that their sauces did not mingle. There was an onion tart and another with eels, both of which she wanted to try.

"Are the eels from the sea?"

"They are raised in the millpond."

She watched how Fergus delicately took pieces of food from the trencher with his fingers and copied his actions, noting that he left the finer portions of meat for her. This must be etiquette and

Leila mimicked him easily.

"Sweet after savory," Fergus counseled when she was certain there could not be more food. "Ensure that you can sample the next course lest Xavier be insulted."

"I thank you for the warning," Leila said.

"You said it was your intent to win allies." His eyes twinkled as he looked down at her and her heart skipped.

"And I must have one in the kitchen, to be sure."

They laughed together and continued to eat. There were no minstrels in Calum's hall during the meal as there often had been in Gaston's, but conversation was lively. The use of spice was liberal and the food was hot, the combination leaving a warm glow in Leila's belly.

Calum was the first to sit back and to take a healthy drink of the mulled wine. He smacked his lips. "And now I will tell you all what you have missed."

Duncan leaned forward, undoubtedly to hear better, and Leila felt the weight of Fergus' hand land on the back of her waist. His thigh was pressed against hers, solid and warm, and she tingled in anticipation of their first night together.

"It was April, almost exactly four years ago, that you two rode away from Killairic," Calum said. "That year passed peacefully enough—"

"Though Lady Isobel wed," Duncan murmured.

"A merry occasion," Calum agreed. "And a great feast presented by her father. The fields around Dunnisbrae were filled with tents." He sighed. "Who would have anticipated that the next year would be filled with such strife?"

"What strife?" Fergus asked.

His father raised a finger. "Gille Brigte, son of your namesake, Fergus, died early in the year, which seemed a portent of trouble."

"Surely his lands passed peacefully to his son."

"Nay, for that man is still a hostage of King Henry. Lochlann, the son of Uchtred, desired to claim his uncle's lands in Galloway, it became clear. We should have guessed in April, for there was an earthquake. It was far to the east but still felt in this very hall. As the priest said, it was a warning to us all."

"Father, you know that the earth does not grant portents..."

"As above, so below, Fergus," Calum said sternly. "And on the first of May, we were warned again for the sun disappeared in the middle of the day, swallowed by the moon, so the whole world went dark."

"An eclipse," Leila said.

Calum granted her a look. "A warning from the divine. Twice that year, Lochlann ravaged Galloway, intent upon claiming his uncle's holdings by force." His expression was grim. "We were hard-pressed to hold the border for the king."

"I wish I had been here," Fergus said.

"So did I, lad. So did I." Calum had another sip of wine. "But to our relief, Lochlann was compelled to make peace with King Henry at Carlisle in 1186. I attended the council and signed the treaty myself as did King William of Scotland. Since then, Lochlann has been William's lapdog. He even aided in putting down the revolt of the MacWilliams in Moray."

Leila saw the flash in Duncan's eyes before he dropped his gaze, but Calum carried on without noticing. "And I am glad of it. Lochlann has been occupied away from Galloway and of peaceful inclination when he returns. It is a welcome change from his past tendencies."

It seemed that violence and war had no borders. Leila supposed her new life would have some unwelcome similarities with her old one.

"And Isobel's husband?" Fergus asked. "What are his allegiances?"

His father pursed his lips. "Stewart MacEwan was a strong ally to Lochlann and fought with him in that dreadful assault upon Galloway. Perhaps he wished to have an allegiance with the Isles via Isobel." His father arched a brow. "You will have to tell them about Kerr, and such tidings cannot be delivered by a missive."

"Of course, Father. I intend to go to Dunnisbrae on the morrow."

Calum's eyes narrowed. "I would leave the news a bit, Fergus," he advised softly. "You should be calm when you confront Stewart. He is a man to seize upon any provocation."

Leila realized that she was not the only one to have noted the tension in Fergus and to disapprove of his acting upon it. It added to her growing sense that she and his father could be strong allies.

"I *am* calm," Fergus insisted, but the tightness in his tone betrayed him. "I will go on the morrow and see the task done."

Though Calum appeared to agree with Leila, he was less inclined to argue with Fergus. Perhaps her assessment of Stewart's reaction had not been unreasonable. She found her hands clenching together in her lap and tried to calm herself.

Calum lifted his brows, then turned to Leila with a glint in his eye. "And so your new spouse would leave you as quick as this."

She smiled, knowing that he tried another tactic to make his point, but had no chance to reply.

"It is not far to Stewart's abode, Father, as you well know," Fergus said firmly. "I would see the news delivered without delay."

"And your gift," Leila added quietly, then sipped of her wine as Calum studied her, his gaze assessing.

"Gift?" he echoed.

"Your son is most generous," Leila said smoothly. "Perhaps it was his father who taught him such grace."

The older man's eyes gleamed but he cleared his throat and changed the subject. "And there are more tidings, to be sure. You will likely not have heard that last year, Gudrodr, King of the Isles, died on the isle of Saint Patrick."

Leila felt Fergus' attention sharpen. "Surely one of his sons has succeeded him?"

"The islesmen chose Rognvaldr, likely because he is grown to manhood while the other sons are mere boys. But he is the son of an Irish concubine. Times change, Fergus. Both kings would prefer the crown to fall to a son born of legal marriage."

Leila stiffened at this observation, for it was contrary to what Fergus had told her. She had first to conceive a child, she reminded herself, then deliver a son, then she could worry about Calum's acceptance of him. Indeed, her marriage had not even been consummated as yet!

"Olafr svarti," Fergus supplied, evidently naming one of the king's sons. "Gudrodr erred in wedding so late, so Olafr cannot be more than a boy."

"But he has allies who are men. Rognvaldr makes his court on Mann, while he has given Olafr the isles of Lewis and Harris as his portion." Calum nodded even as Leila wondered about these places.

She also wondered about Calum's concern.

"It is a hard land," Duncan contributed. "Either rock or bog from what I hear."

"Aye," Calum agreed. "I fear there will be rebellion. Gudrodr will be interred on Iona on Whitsunday, some six weeks from now. I just had the missive on Easter. Someone from our hall should attend, but I fear I do not have the stamina for the journey."

"I will go, Father," Fergus said quickly. "And Leila can come with me." He squeezed her hand as if he wished to be with her, but his words dismissed that pleasant notion. "It will give her an opportunity to meet more of our neighbors."

And find a man. Leila's heart sank at his implication, but she smiled. "Indeed, I will be glad to see more of Scotland."

"And Iona is a most holy place," Calum told her. "Should you be inclined to convert, it would be a good place to be baptized."

"I must learn more first," Leila said, doubting this would be the last prompt that she change her faith.

"Of course, of course. Such matters take time and consideration. I have an old friend with whom you might enjoy a discussion."

"Indeed?"

"Indeed. We journeyed together to the east, but that is a tale for another time." Calum smiled. "On this night, there are nuptials to be celebrated."

"Perhaps, Enguerrand and Yvan, you might be able to linger until my return from that journey," Fergus suggested, and the Templar knights nodded agreement. Leila knew their quick assent was because of the treasure secured in the solar.

"I fear I cannot accompany you," Duncan said. "My own path lies to the north and I would depart on the morrow."

Leila smiled, liking that he was so impatient to make a home for Radegunde. "Do you have a destination?" she asked.

"I seek a man," Duncan said with resolve. "Wherever he has hidden himself is my destination."

"I will miss your companionship, but understand that you must go," Fergus said.

"Who will ride with you to Dunnisbrae in my absence?" Duncan asked.

"It is not far," Fergus said. "I will leave at dawn and return by the evening meal. Surely such new accord in the land means a man can make such a short journey unaccompanied?"

"It has been peaceful, to be sure," Calum agreed. "But should you not take Hamish with you?"

Fergus shook his head, then smiled at Leila. "I would not leave Leila without a translator when she takes command of the keep's resources."

Calum chuckled. "Indeed, indeed. I am inclined to sleep late, Lady Leila, but on the morrow, feel free to assert your authority in the hall. You are its lady now, and we both rely upon you to aid in its administration."

"I thank you," Leila said, feeling her excitement rise in anticipation of this responsibility. She knew she would enjoy it. "And thank you, Fergus, for the offer of Hamish's assistance." She thought it a poor idea for Fergus to ride alone, but did not say as much just yet. She had a suggestion to make but decided to do it in private, lest it appear that she was challenging Fergus before the entire village.

"And so it is resolved," Fergus said.

Then Calum raised a finger. "But Duncan's planned departure reminds me of my debt," he said, then rose to his feet.

"You owe me naught..." Duncan began to protest, but Calum ignored him.

He raised his voice. "Baldwin, bring the prize we discussed to me, if you please."

A sturdy man approached the high table. There was a fine crossbow balanced on his palms, the wood inlaid in a style familiar to Leila.

"It is fine, is it not?" Calum asked her with pride.

"It is, indeed," Leila said, knowing her admiration was clear.

"Was it made in the east?"

"In Constantinople. It is a noble weapon, which has awaited the right warrior." Calum winked. "He is found."

Leila smiled, liking that he was as generous as his son. This trait was why people were so loyal to Calum and would be thus to his son.

Calum lifted the crossbow in his hands as the company watched, then pivoted to present it to Duncan. "A fitting gift for a warrior who has served me so valiantly for so long. This is for you, Duncan, and if you accept it, this gift will balance the debt between us."

"I would argue that it leaves me again obligated to you," Duncan said, but Calum only laughed.

"Let us agree, for I would see you find your future happiness sooner rather than later." He gave Duncan a stern eye. "And you may have need of such a fine weapon, if you journey where I suspect you will."

"I do and you know it well."

"Just as I know you will not be turned from your goal." Calum nodded. "Take it. Let me see you well armed on this quest."

Duncan smiled, then accepted the crossbow, admiring it so openly that Leila was pleased on his behalf. "I am honored, as you well know." He dropped to one knee before Calum. "Know, sir, that you can always rely upon my alliance and friendship."

"No man could ask for more," Calum said, clasping Duncan's shoulders and lifting him to his feet. He kissed Duncan's cheeks, then the company applauded the generosity of his gift. They saluted the health of both men, then returned to their conversations as Calum took his seat again.

Some of the villagers left their places and fetched instruments. They conferred together as stray notes sounded, and evidently there would be music this night.

Leila stroked the rich garment Calum had given to her. "Will you tell me more of your journey to the east?"

The older man patted her hand. "I will, but another time. This is a night for dancing, not for tales recounted around the fire. You may be sure that there will be many nights when a tale will be more welcome than other deeds." Then he winked at her and Leila felt herself flush, for she understood his meaning well.

He anticipated that she would quickly be with child and more inclined to sit and talk.

She found herself blushing…and hoping the very same.

She was also reassured that his words implied he did see a handfast as equivalent to marriage.

Calum chuckled at her, then the music began, and Fergus urged her to her feet.

CHAPTER FIVE

ergus was entranced.

Leila danced with vigor, her eyes flashing and her feet flying, her lithe figure drawing the eye of more than one man in the hall. Though she did not know the steps of their customary dances when the music began, she learned them quickly. She laughed and her eyes shone so that Fergus was reluctant to surrender her to another partner.

They danced until they were out of breath and then they danced yet more. His father clapped, so clearly pleased with the match that Fergus would never tell him the truth of it. Even Duncan danced with Leila and the sound of her merriment made more than one person in the hall smile.

When the candles had burned low, he sent the maid Agnes to the solar to prepare it, his own anticipation rising. When Leila spun back to him, he caught her in his arms for one last dance. "Shall we retire?" he asked, aware of the quick glance she cast his way.

"I assume our traditions are the same and the match should be consummated on this night."

"I would advise it. Do you dread the coupling?"

"No," Leila said without hesitation. "I am a maiden, of course, but you are a man of great kindness. I expect that we may both be well pleased."

Her trust warmed Fergus to his toes. "I have sent Agnes to light the candles," he confided.

Leila's eyes flashed but she dropped her gaze. Instead of appreciating that she was tactful, Fergus wished again for her honesty. "Someone had to do it," he whispered.

"I think it unwise to allow any soul in that chamber alone."

"You yet have the key to the treasury," he reminded her.

She granted him a somber look. "And every lock can be broken. At Gaston's abode, there were many keys..."

"Do not be suspicious on this night," Fergus entreated. "They will all accompany us to the solar. It is tradition that the women see the bride to bed, then the men bring the husband. The priest will bless the bed, then we shall be expected to produce proof of the union in the morning."

Leila sighed and so obviously refrained from comment that Fergus whispered to her. "Remember that we promised honesty to each other," he said and she nodded. "Tell me."

"You must know that this sounds barbaric to me. Are we truly a mare and stud, meeting abed only for the conception of a child?"

"In the eyes of many, aye, we are." Fergus raised his brows and whispered to her. "But none need know that we intend to enjoy the rendering of the marital debt."

Leila laughed as the music ended. Fergus spun her to a breathless halt, then bent and kissed her fingertips. He said something in Gaelic, to much applause, and Leila understood she was to depart. She found Hamish's aunt on her one side and another stocky woman from the village on the other. That woman fingered the cloth of her kirtle with the admiration of one who knew of textiles.

"Margaret?" Leila guessed and the woman smiled at her. She mimicked the gesture of sewing as they climbed the stairs, and Margaret nodded eagerly. When they entered the solar, Leila hastened to the cloth that she and Fergus had put aside for her. She touched the sheer cotton, then the chemise she wore, then the two lengths of heavier cloth and lifted the kirtle. She made the stitching motion again then gestured to herself.

Margaret nodded her agreement, holding up the red cloth to Leila's chin and commenting. Leila caught only a few words but understood that Margaret approved of this color for her.

She showed Margaret the needles and indicated that they were a gift, and after much waving and laughing, Leila was certain she had been understood. She then lifted the hem of the kirtle she wore and grimaced at the dirt where it had dragged. Margaret clicked her tongue and dropped to her knees. She folded the hem once and held it so that Leila could see the result of turning it up that much. They both nodded in agreement that this would be an improvement.

Margaret began to undo the laces of the purple kirtle, pinching and tucking the fabric as she did so. She murmured to herself, as if committing the changes to memory. Leila turned as the woman bade her, understanding that she knew her craft. When she had shed the dress, Margaret cast the garment over her shoulder.

She pointed to Leila, made a walking motion with her fingers, then pointed out the window to the village. "Tomorrow?" she asked and Leila was glad to recognize the word.

"Tomorrow," she agreed with a smile, then continued with care. "After noon."

Margaret nodded and smiled her approval of this notion. She and Mhairi bustled Leila toward the bed, removing her shoes and stockings when she sat on the mattress. She was left in only her chemise, and one of the women took a comb to her hair. Leila noticed that Agnes, while purportedly her maid, busied herself with candles and stirring the coals in the braziers.

Mhairi touched the hem of Leila's chemise as if to lift it, then met her gaze with a questioning expression. Leila understood that most brides were left naked but her deep blush at the notion made the two women smile. They conferred and allowed Leila her chemise, which was sheer but offered some modesty.

There was a ruckus at the door, and a great company of men burst into the solar with Fergus. He was laughing and had been stripped to his braies, and once again, Leila was struck by his good looks. His hair was tousled and his eyes were sparkling, and Leila thought again that he looked his best when he was merry.

She would ensure he was so, as often as possible.

Mhairi and Margaret exchanged a glance and raised their brows. Mhairi winked at her and clutched her heart. Leila laughed, which both women seemed to appreciate. Margaret made a gesture as if she rocked a babe, and Leila nodded with enthusiasm. While the men were yet at the portal, Leila held her thumb at her own crotch as if it was a penis, then mimicking rocking a child. The two older woman laughed aloud as they nodded agreement.

Meanwhile, the men were urging Fergus into the chamber. He climbed into the bed beside her and claimed her hand in his, then bowed his head as the priest intoned a prayer. Leila bowed her head as well, seeing from the corner of her eye that Margaret was mimicking her gesture with her thumb. She bit back her laughter, knowing that she was being teased. The company sang some chorus together, led by the priest, and Leila assumed it was another prayer.

Then Fergus roared for privacy and the villagers departed, laughing and shouting what must have been friendly advice as they did so. Margaret took the purple kirtle as well as the cloth and needles, with Mhairi helping her to carry it all. Fergus left the bed and locked the portal behind them, even as the music began from the hall once again.

He leaned his back against the door, his eyes gleaming as he regarded Leila. "And so we are alone at last."

Leila could see no reason to pretend the situation was other than it was. "And yet not the wedding night you had expected."

"Nor the one you anticipated," Fergus said, crossing the floor with measured steps. He sat on the side of the mattress. "This is your last opportunity to change your thinking."

"It is too late. I would not disappoint your father."

Fergus took her hand in his. "Do you know what to expect this night?"

"Well enough." Leila closed her hand over his, seeing that he was torn. "I am not Isobel, and I never will be. I will not pretend to be. But I will try to be the best wife to you, Fergus, that I can."

"That is the most one can expect from a marriage of convenience."

"Is it?" Leila dared to challenge him a little. "Gaston and Ysmaine wed for mutual convenience, and I would argue that they found much more than a child in their union."

Fergus smiled sadly. "I would not have you aspire to what may not be, Leila. My heart is given and lost forever. Even though Isobel has wed another, she will always be my beloved. I will be as good a husband to you as I can, but that and a good home may be all I can offer to you."

Leila rose to her knees and framed his face in her hands. "The heart heals, Fergus."

"I am skeptical."

She smiled. "Then I shall have to be so beguiling that I convince you otherwise." She gave him no opportunity to argue, not this time, but leaned against him and kissed him sweetly.

Fergus caught his breath, a delicious sign of his awareness of her, then caught her around the waist. He drew her against his heat with one arm, even as he slanted his mouth over hers and deepened his kiss.

He tasted of mulled wine and Leila opened her mouth to him in capitulation, pushing her fingers into the thick waves of his hair. He eased her to her back, following her down to the mattress, and she loved the way his weight pressed her down into its softness. His hand rose to her breast and he brushed his palm across it, the fleeting touch making her ache for more. Leila gasped and arched her back, surrendering completely to him and whatever he desired of her.

He was her husband and her lord.

He was the captor of her heart.

And she would do whatever was necessary to persuade him that there was too much merit in this match to put it aside.

Fergus was awed by Leila's trust of him.

He had admired her bravery before, but on this night, it was inescapable. That she met him abed as a maiden without hesitation was as sure an indication as he could imagine of her resolve to make a home for herself in Scotland. She had said she would bear him a child and reminded him of Gaston and Ysmaine finding love in their sensible match.

Yet Fergus was aware of the differences. He was not as practical as Gaston, nor was Leila as inclined to surrender to duty as Ysmaine. That pair had found love unexpected, while Leila sought to love in marriage. Indeed, she had left everything she knew behind to seek it.

But the other difference was that he also had already fallen in love, as neither Gaston nor Ysmaine had before their marriage. His heart was no longer his to give.

The fact was that he and Leila had a handfast and he was determined to treat her with every dignity. He pushed Isobel from his thoughts. He refused to compare the two women, not on this night, and concentrated instead upon learning all he could of the lady who had put her hand in his. Fergus broke his kiss and surveyed Leila, wanting to savor every moment of their first night together.

Leila was so tiny compared to him. She was considerably shorter than he and weighed much less. All the same, she was strong, and he thought her power was buttressed by her resolve. She did nothing by half-measures and flung herself whole-heartedly into any endeavor. He had only to think of how she had defended the reliquary on their journey to be reminded of that.

She would still defend it, which he respected.

Despite the difference in their size, there was no doubt that she was a woman and not a child. Her curves were enticing, her waist tiny and her breasts full. Her lips were ripe and ruddy, and her eyes so beguilingly feminine. When she smiled at him, as she had many times this day and did again now, Fergus could not deny his desire.

He opened her chemise and bared her flesh to his view. She watched him, still smiling, content to let him explore, so confident in her trust that he was humbled. Her skin was a rich gold and her nipples were a deep rose. As he brushed his fingertips over one, the nipple hardened to a point and she caught her breath. He bent and took that peak in his mouth, teasing it so that it tightened even more, liking how she moved her hips and gasped. He reached for the hem of her chemise and slipped his hand under it, letting his palm slide up the silk of her thighs. She anticipated him, parting her legs, and his fingers slid into slick heat.

He caressed her, slowly at first, letting her become accustomed to his bold touch. She whispered his name and opened her thighs wider, her fingers knotted in his hair. He abandoned the nipple and captured her mouth again, kissing her thoroughly as his caress became more demanding. She met him touch for touch, clutching at him as she let him summon the tide within her.

Trusting him completely. Fergus was more than humbled—he was awed. He felt the race of Leila's pulse and smelled her arousal. He teased her relentlessly, wanting to ensure that she was ready for their union. She was so tiny, and he had no desire to hurt her, or much less reward her trust with pain. She tore her lips from his and whispered his name, but Fergus did not surrender. He braced himself over her and caressed her more boldly, sliding his fingertips over her as her agitation rose.

"I thought pleasure was to be savored together," she managed to say.

Fergus smiled. "On this night, you shall find yours first."

"No," she said with a flash of her eyes. "Together first. The first time as it always should be."

She was so fierce that he did not want to disappoint her.

"It is not readily done," Fergus had time to protest before she rolled to her side and closed her hand over his erection. The pressure was perfect, both gentle and unshakable, exactly like the lady herself. Fergus closed his eyes in pleasure, even as she caressed him through his braies, and rolled to his back.

Leila chuckled with satisfaction. She rose to her knees and cast off her chemise. Fergus could only stare at the sight of her beauty, so perfectly illuminated in the light of the candles. She unfastened his braies and flung the cloth aside, then landed atop him with delight. Fergus chuckled as he caught her close, then pushed a hand through her hair. It was as long as her shoulders now, and he wished he had seen it before she cut it off in Jerusalem.

"How long was it?" he asked, fingering its dark silk.

"To my hips. It had not been cut in years before that day."

"Do you regret the loss?"

She gave him an intent look, her eyes sparkling in the way that so beguiled him. "Fergus, hair will grow back. It was a small sacrifice to ensure my freedom."

"How much would you have surrendered to avoid that match?"

"Anything," she said with such fervor that he believed her. She ran a hand over his chest and her touch gave him a thrill. "I like this," she said, pushing her fingers through the patch of hair there. "Just a little, not too much." Her eyes gleamed as she closed her finger and thumb around his nipple and pinched. "Just enough," she whispered, then mimicked the way he had teased her nipple. When her teeth grazed the tight peak, Fergus found himself gasping, then felt the breath of her laughter.

"You like this," she said, her other hand caressing his erection.

"I like you," Fergus admitted, knowing it was true, and her eyes shone.

"Then take me, husband," she whispered, rising to straddle him. Her hair was disheveled, her features so alight that she was irresistible. Fergus caught her around the waist and lifted her over himself, closing his eyes in rapture when he slid inside her heat. She caught her breath a little, and he paused, his hands shaking, but she smiled down at him.

"Not so much of a twinge," she said and arched a brow, looking mischievous and delightful. "I've ridden too many horses, perhaps."

Fergus smiled, then settled her atop him, the sweet power of their union flooding his body with heat. Leila moved, rising then lowering herself again, her gaze locked upon him. Fergus felt his heart clamor and had no words for the unbearable pleasure.

"Four years," Leila whispered and moved again.

"Four years," he agreed, hearing the tension in his voice. "I fear I will disappoint you with my haste."

"Impossible," she replied, easing herself down to lie upon his chest. She kissed him, even as his hands roved over her back and locked around her waist once more. "At any rate, we have more than three hundred nights to savor each other slowly."

Fergus laughed a little. "True enough." He ran a hand over her head, drawing her near to kiss her again. He had hoped that the kiss might temper his response that he might last longer, but Leila slipped her tongue between his teeth, her hunger for him sending fire through his veins once more. His hips began to pump, and she locked her knees around him, welcoming him and drawing him ever deeper, her ardent kiss feeding his desire.

He rolled her abruptly to her side, desperate to give her the pleasure she desired, and eased his hand between them. She might have protested, but when he touched her with his fingertip, the words died on her lips. She moaned and closed her eyes, clutching at his shoulders. Fergus felt triumphant when she quickly found her release.

Her heat clenched around him in a most beguiling way. He saw the wild flutter of her pulse at her throat and swallowed her cry of exultation as she shook in his arms. Unable to resist the temptation she offered, Fergus rolled Leila to her back and buried himself inside her with a moan of rapture.

Then Leila pulled his mouth down for a heated kiss and Fergus was lost in the splendor that was his new wife.

The consummation was far more pleasurable than Leila had anticipated.

She lay back on the great bed, holding Fergus as he caught his breath. His heart was thundering and pressed against hers. She had her fingers in his hair, his weight atop her, his breath against her neck and his heat inside her. She could not imagine a better place to be.

All too soon, he heaved a sigh, then braced his weight on his elbows to look down at her. She smiled at his evident satisfaction and liked the gleam of admiration in his eyes.

"Did you find your pleasure?" he murmured and she felt the vibration of his voice against her chest.

"Can you doubt it?"

"Nay, but it seemed polite to confirm."

Leila laughed and Fergus rolled to his back, then sighed again.

She propped herself upon her elbow to stare down at him. "And you, sir?" she asked, tracing a circle around his nipple with her fingertip. He captured her hand in his, kissed her palm, and smiled at her.

"Can you doubt it?"

"It seemed polite to confirm."

They laughed together then, and Fergus rose from the bed. He fetched a cloth and the bucket of water, then helped Leila to wash. The linen with its blood stain was removed and set aside, and they worked together to put fresh linens on the bed. "I will give it to my father before I leave in the morning," Fergus said. "You do not need to be present when he shows it to the household."

Leila smiled that he understood she would find it crude. "I would prefer a more telling proof," she said lightly as she donned her chemise again.

Fergus tugged a chemise over his head, then gave her a look. "Like?"

"A child rounding my belly. That will set all concerns to rest."

He pulled back the covers, inviting her back to the bed. "Come and be warm. We will try again soon." He yawned. "I am spent for this night and you will need a day or two to recover."

"I am stronger than that," she said and Fergus smiled. When they were tucked into the bed anew, with fur pelts around them and the curtains drawn against the cold, the music from the hall seemed more clear. Leila rolled to her back to look at Fergus, not yet ready to sleep. "Were you truly chaste for four years?"

He nodded ruefully. "And counted every day and night of it."

Leila wondered if he and Isobel had been intimate before he departed, but did not truly want to ask. "I thought it might be simpler in a company of monks."

"Jerusalem was the easiest part of it, to be sure, though Wulfe was not the sole one to find pleasure with whores in Outremer."

She laced her fingers with his, liking this new intimacy enough to want more of it, yet not wanting to demand too much lest he move away.

To think of Isobel.

"I admire that you kept a vow of chastity," she said. "It is not a sacrifice that most men can manage."

"I think you know something of determination, Leila."

"Perhaps that is a trait we have in common."

He smiled at her. "Perhaps it is."

"Is it true that you can see the future?" Leila asked.

Fergus nodded. "Duncan likes to make much of it, but I see less than he imagines."

"He said you were born to the caul. What does that mean?"

"It means that part of the womb was still covering my face when I was born. It is considered a sign in these parts that the child will have the gift of foresight." He shrugged. "Also, my mother's hair was as red as a flame. In England, that is often considered an indication of otherworldly powers."

Leila saw affection light Fergus' eyes. Her aunt had said it was a good sign for a man to be fond of his mother, and that any man's treatment of his mother was a good indication of how he would treat his wife. "She was fierce in her opinions and she had a temper, to be sure, but she had no powers beyond that of a strong will."

Leila smiled in her turn, for she thought it good that she and Fergus' mother had some trait in common. "If that was all it took to make a witch, the majority of those women of my acquaintance would be found so."

Fergus laughed. "Indeed."

"What exactly do you see? Or how do you see it?"

He pursed his lips, choosing his words. Leila appreciated that he took her question seriously and did not dismiss her curiosity. It seemed he would stand by their agreement to be honest with each other, and she liked that. "It is not seeing as we do each day, as I see you here and now. It is not even like a dream, which can be clearly envisioned and follows a sequence of events. It can be like a dream, though, in that it seldom makes sense right away. And more often, it is a sense."

"A sense?"

"An awareness or a conviction. Crossing this avenue would be a mistake: step back instead and wait. Rounding this corner will change all: choose another route to the destination."

"It sounds very immediate, like a *mu'aqqib* giving you advice."

"A *mu'aqqib*?"

"An angel, charged to keep you from death until the decreed time."

"I did not know you believed in angels."

"The Qur'an says we are each guarded by two angels, one before and one behind. It says they are made of light and can take any form." Leila smiled at his obvious surprise. "Belief in angels is one of the six articles of faith of Islam."

"Truly?" His gaze was bright upon her.

"Truly. The word was delivered to the Prophet by Jibril, the angel you call Gabriel." She lifted her brows. "How could one believe the message and discredit the messenger?"

Fergus chuckled. "True enough. What are the other five articles?"

"That Allah or God is one supreme being, with no siblings or parents." Leila counted off the six on her fingers as she recited them. "That He sent his message to the prophets, which include Moses, Jesus, and Muhammad. That the gospels are His word and revelation, including the Torah, the Gospels, and the Qur'an. That there will be a resurrection and a day of judgment when we shall be judged for our deeds, good and bad. And finally, that Allah knows all, past, present, and future. All earthly life is His divine plan."

Fergus raised his brows. "It is not that different."

Leila shrugged. "There is much similarity in our core beliefs, to be sure." She knew what she had to ask, though it felt bold to do so. "Will you tell me what you see of the future?"

"For you or for me?"

"Either or both."

"I never see beyond the next instant for myself. The sense that I should step back or turn another way is the sum of my foresight, with regards to my own fate."

"But it must be useful, all the same."

He smiled. "I imagine it is responsible for my return home. More than once, I knew we had to take another route or halt an assault. Every time, if Duncan and I had continued, we would have died with others." A shadow touched his features.

"Do you blame yourself for their loss?"

He frowned. "It is impossible not to do so, yet it would be

similarly impossible to halt an army because I had a feeling it should be done."

"And what of my future? Is it rude for me to ask? Or unlucky?"

"Unusual, at the least. Many people do not want to know." He eyed her, his gaze dark. "I have seen you with a child, since we left Haynesdale," he admitted. "A babe, which I know is your babe. Indeed, you look tired in my vision, as if you had just brought the child into the world."

"Oh! I am glad to know I should survive that."

A fleeting smile touched his lips. "And you will be gladder yet that the child is a boy." He lifted his gaze to hers. "And his eyes are clear blue."

Leila was astonished. "I hope it is your son."

"As do I."

"What a wondrous vision for our first night together," she said, though Fergus did not reply. "How many children shall we have?"

Fergus laughed and shook a finger at her. "My gift is not like that. It reveals what it will, no more and no less. You will deliver of a healthy son with blue eyes. That is all I know."

"And it should be sufficient. I thank you for such a reassurance."

"You are joyous in my vision, Leila. Laughing and much enamored with the boy. He looks to be perfect, so your judgment is sound." He smiled but dropped his gaze. "It is a most pleasing vision."

Leila felt her cheeks heat and her throat tighten. She fervently hoped this vision was true and that the father was Fergus. "And Duncan?"

"I have seen a gem on his shoulder, holding his cloak. A prize and a mark of status. He stands taller in that vision, like a leader of men, but there are shadows in his eyes, perhaps because of what he has done to achieve his goal."

"Triumph can demand much of a man," Leila ceded, wondering what to make of that vision. "Is Radegunde not with him?"

"I do not know. I have dreamed of her running through a field of flowers, with two children, their hair of the same hue as her own. They laugh together, but I cannot tell the gender of the children." He frowned and rubbed his brow. "That vision is fleeting."

"Can you tell where they are?"

He shrugged. "A field in summer, beneath a clear sky." His gaze met hers and she sensed that he wished for reassurance.

"It seems a gift that raises more questions than it answers."

"It does, indeed."

"And what do you see for your father and Killairic?"

Fergus swung his legs around and rose from the bed. He went to the window and opened the shutter, the moonlight touching his silhouette as he looked over the land. Leila hesitated only a moment before following him and resting her hand upon his back. His skin was warm and smooth, his strength reassuring beneath her touch. He captured her hand in his and held it against his chest, as if they were friends instead of husband and wife.

Instead of lovers.

Leila wrapped her arms around his waist and was glad he did not push her away. He kept one hand within his own, his other arm sliding around her waist to hold her close.

She could have stood thus forever.

The hall was falling quiet below them and she heard the sounds of the villagers returning to their homes. The land seemed tranquil and quiet, different from her homeland and yet so very welcome.

Fergus looked at their hands, his brow furrowed. "I have sensed a shadow ever since we left Jerusalem, like a cloud of ill fortune that loomed ahead of us. I have expected something to go badly awry ever since we left the Temple."

"Things *have* gone awry," Leila reminded him. "Kerr died, Christina was assaulted, Duncan was hunted, and Gaston faced rebellion in his own home."

Fergus raised a hand. "Yet after each incident, the cloud became darker and more ominous, not less."

Leila swallowed. "And when you learned that Isobel had wed?"

"Darker yet," he said and shook his head. "Some dire fate lies ahead, Leila, but I cannot see more than that. I fear its import."

"The warning is a blessing," she said with a confidence she did not feel. "For it will ensure that we are prepared."

"I do not want to live with suspicion."

"We will not, but we will be slower to trust than we might have been otherwise. You must tell me what you remember of every soul in Killairic as well as what you know of your neighbors. I will watch and listen, and we will identify the threat together."

He smiled down at her. "Are you truly fearless?"

"Nay, but I refuse to sit and wait for some dire fate. I would hunt it, kill it if need be. I would act to ensure the safety of those I hold in esteem and to defend my home."

"Will Killairic be your home?"

"Aye, for I will make it so." Her words were more fiercely uttered than she intended, but Fergus did not take offense.

Indeed, he took a breath and hugged her tightly against his side. "And perhaps this is why, that day in the stables of the Temple, when I heard you and Bartholomew, I knew that I should offer you protection."

"You did?"

He nodded without hesitation. "I could see you here, in my father's garden." He met her gaze. "I do not know what lies ahead in much detail, Leila, but I hope you do not regret your choice to ride with us, much less to handfast with me."

"I do not. And I will not." She tightened her embrace, pressing herself against his heat. "Now, come, and do your part to see that blue-eyed boy come to light."

He smiled and kissed the top of her head, as if she were a child. "Not yet," he said quietly. "I must prepare for the morning." He went then to his weapons and his garb, choosing what he would wear and what he would take.

Leila bit her lip as she watched him. She sensed that he made an excuse. She wondered if he thought of Isobel, tall and fair as she was not. While she respected that he had not brought that woman to their bed the first time they coupled, she already came to resent the hold Isobel had over his heart and thoughts. Leila could not imagine that the woman was worthy of him.

If she had been, she would not have wed Stewart.

Even Calum had said as much.

Leila knew she should be patient, but it was not her inclination.

She liked to see matters set to rights, instead of letting them fester.

It seemed she would learn a new skill in this match.

She thought of telling Fergus that she felt dread at his scheme to visit Isobel and her husband, but feared he might interpret that as jealousy.

It was not her place to say more than she already had. Fergus had been good to her, better than he had reason to be, and Leila was not one to ignore her good fortune.

Much less to place it in peril.

She said nothing and returned to the bed, glad to step onto the rugs from the cold floor. She drew the curtains around the bed on three sides, then stirred the coals in the brazier before climbing on to the mattress.

"Let me come with you," she said when it seemed Fergus took overlong with his preparations. "I would like to see more of Scotland."

"I expect you would like to see Isobel," he replied lightly.

"You cannot blame me for being curious." Leila was not going to tell him that she was more curious about his reaction to the sight of Isobel than any detail about his former betrothed. "Stewart might take more kindly to your visit if you brought your wife."

"I understand and appreciate that, but you have only just arrived at Killairic." He cast her a bright glance. "Perhaps your caution is deserved and I should have someone I trust remain here," he whispered and looked at the door of the treasury before meeting her gaze again.

Leila nodded understanding, pleased that he trusted her with this responsibility, and dared to make her suggestion. "Then take Hamish with you." When he would have argued, she raised her hand. "I will manage with gestures for a day, and you should not ride alone until the shadow you discern has vanished." She smiled at him and shook a warning finger, hoping to convince him. "If you disregard the warnings of your angel, he or she may cease to keep you safe. They are willful in that way, to my understanding."

"Fair enough," Fergus said and sat down to hone his blade. "Perhaps Enguerrand might be of assistance to you tomorrow."

Leila nodded agreement. "Perhaps he might. His Gaelic seems

to be quite good, and Yvan can remain in the hall with your father, watching the stairs."

Fergus was clearly pleased. "An excellent notion, Leila. I thank you for it." He fell silent then, focusing on his task, and Leila would not pester him when he wished to think.

Even if he thought of beautiful Isobel.

She felt Fergus draw away from her, as surely as if he had left the solar. It was as if an invisible wall was being built between them, brick by brick. Would she lose him completely on the morrow? What if Isobel confessed that she wanted him still?

Leila wondered if he would return to her and Killairic, or if there would be some other reason—found by Isobel or by Fergus—for her new husband to linger at Dunnisbrae.

She was not one to sit by and wait for results. She preferred to shape events herself, and this situation reminded her of a story.

It might just be the perfect one.

Leila cleared her throat. "If you do not intend to sleep, perhaps I might tell you a tale."

Fergus spared her a glance. "I thought your expertise was with horses."

"But I like stories. My uncle liked to tell stories as he worked, at least when he was occupied with quieter tasks like those you attend on this night."

A spark of curiosity lit in Fergus' eyes. "What kind of stories did he tell?"

Leila smiled. "Stories like this one." She sat up in the bed and hugged her knees to her chest, closing her eyes and hearing her uncle's deep voice. She could see the dustmotes dancing in the sun in his smithy, smell the horses and hear them rustling in their feed. "Once upon a time, there were two brothers who were the sons of a king. They were both virtuous and handsome. When the father died, the older brother, Shahriar, became King of Persia in his father's place. The younger brother, Shahzenan, became the King of Samarkand, one of his father's other possessions. They parted with much affection when Shahzenan departed to take custody of his kingdom. Both brothers subsequently fell in love and married, each then having a beautiful and beloved queen."

Fergus smiled but did not comment.

"After ten years had passed, both kingdoms were prosperous and at peace, and Shahriar wished to see his brother again. He sent his vizier to Samarkand to invite his brother to come home for a visit. Shahzenan was delighted by the arrival of his brother's vizier and by the invitation. After greeting the vizier in his camp and sharing a meal, as well as news of Persia, Shahzenan agreed to accompany the vizier to Persia. Though he had planned to remain in the camp for the night, the prospect of his departure made him yearn for the queen's company. He wanted to share as many moments as possible with her before his departure and so he returned to the palace, late that night, and went directly to her apartment. Although he thought to surprise her, Shahzenan was the one surprised: he found a male slave making love to his own wife."

Fergus turned to look at her, but Leila continued, as if unaware that there were similarities between her tale and his situation with Isobel. "Shahzenan was outraged!" she said.

"I can imagine," Fergus noted.

"Shahzenan had not even left for Persia and his wife betrayed his trust at the first opportunity. He was so angry at her faithlessness that he drew his blade and killed both wife and slave where they lay in her bed. Bitter and angry, he left the palace and stayed in the camp until the party rode out for Persia. He felt, in fact, so betrayed that he confided in no one. Shahzenan was filled with grief when he reached Persia, although the preparations his brother had made for his arrival lightened his heart. An entire wing had been added to Shahriar's palace, just for him, with a view over his brother's private pleasure garden. It was so beautiful and his brother's warm greeting almost dismissed his disappointment in his wife. Shahriar knew his brother well and saw that something was wrong. He asked for the tale, but Shahzenan was aware of his brother's happiness in marriage. He declined to share such a tale in his palace."

Fergus nodded understanding.

"Shahriar thought to dissipate his brother's sadness with revels," Leila continued. "He arranged hunts and festivals, invited guests and ensured that every entertainment was available for Shahzenan. He did not fail to notice that his brother smiled and joined the festivities, but there was still a shadow over him. He believed his brother would confide in him in time, and he was right. For one day, Shahzenan declined to ride to the hunt and remained in his brother's palace. The hunting party had not long departed when he looked out his window and saw a door open on the other side of the palace. The queen came into the garden with her ladies. There were twenty of them and Shahzenan thought they simply took their pleasure—but when the queen clapped her hands, they cast off their veils. He was astonished..." Leila yawned then and fell silent.

"Astonished by what?" Fergus asked when Leila did not continue. "What did he see?"

"I will have to tell you tomorrow," she said, glad to see that the tale was working as she intended. She yawned again, not having to feign her exhaustion, then slid down beneath the covers and closed her eyes. It was warm and she *was* tired.

Fergus came to the side of the bed and clearly was not as sleepy as she. "But what happened?" he asked, his interest clear. "What did the queen and her attendants do?"

"I will continue the tale tomorrow night, after your return," Leila said. "It is too long a tale for so late at night." She yawned again. "We must have some sleep before the dawn." She closed her eyes. "It seems that Agnes is not the sole one tired after this day."

She felt Fergus sit on the side of the mattress. "But Leila, you cannot go to sleep yet. I am curious about the tale."

"You will have to wait to find out," she managed to murmur. She rolled over and burrowed into the warmth of the bed. Even as she dozed, she was aware of Fergus looking down at her and could sense his impatience. She could only hope that his desire for more of the tale would be sufficient to encourage him to return promptly and to join her abed the next night.

The scheme had worked for Scheherazade. Leila burrowed deeper in the bed, recalling Calum's claim that she would need a man to keep her warm at night.

And Fergus saw her with a baby boy.

With blue eyes.

The prospect left Leila's lips curved in a smile when sleep claimed her completely.

THURSDAY, APRIL 28, 1188

Feast Day of the martyrs
Saint Didymus
&
Saint Theodora

CHAPTER SIX

ergus did indeed have a guardian angel.

She was his new wife.

When he finally joined her abed, Leila did not awaken. She turned and curled against him, her move so natural and trusting that they might have been wedded for a decade. He held her close and reflected upon his good fortune to have such a sensible woman as wife. He liked that she was concerned for him, and that they spoke so honestly to each other. And yet, the passion had risen between them with rare force—and it had not been satisfied with one meeting abed.

Fergus wanted her again. Indeed, his desire was well beyond his expectation, so fierce that he did not trust it would be sated soon.

It was an appealing notion, to have enduring desire for one's spouse, and a marvel in a match wrought of good sense. Fergus savored it when he should have slept. It was good fortune, to his thinking, for a child to be conceived in affection.

He was surprised to feel his own contentment.

Ultimately, Fergus did sleep, for he awakened when the shadows were just beginning to dissipate. He left the warmth of the great bed with reluctance, knowing he had to depart soon to return by the evening meal, as he had promised. He was tempted to awaken Leila with a kiss, or a greater seduction, but feared his departure would be delayed too much. He rose in the shadows and dressed in haste, returning repeatedly to the bed to look down upon her.

Even as the sky lightened in the east, Leila slept, her lashes dark against her cheek, the sound of her breathing soft in the solar. Fergus watched the first rays of sunlight touch her features and his heart clenched in admiration. She was so delicate yet so fierce. He liked when she created a plan for them both. He admired her honesty and her clear thinking. He respected her determination to create a new home for herself and the future she wanted.

And that must lie at the root of his persistent desire. Fergus did not doubt that a glimpse of Isobel would be like a dagger plunged into his heart. He prepared himself for the sight of his beloved with another, knowing full well that he would find it wrenching, even more devastating than the news had been.

Perhaps it was wiser to feel admiration and affection for one's wife, instead of love.

Fergus bent and touched his lips to Leila's brow, savoring the softness of her skin and the little sigh of contentment that she made. He tucked the furs protectively around her, then unlocked the door of the solar. He stared at the key, then returned to Leila, sliding his hand beneath the covers to put the key to the solar in her hand. She did not awaken but her fingers closed around it instinctively. He could see the cord for the key to the treasury around her neck and imagined she would put them together when she awakened.

He knew, without doubt, that all of his treasures were safe in her care.

In the kitchens, Fergus found Agnes, sleeping on a pallet before the glowing coals on the hearth. She had to be shaken awake after her day of labor, but sat up with a jolt when she realized it was him. "My lord!"

"Shhh," Fergus said. "Do not awaken the others. I would simply ask you to take hot water to my lady wife when the sun has risen."

Agnes blinked. "She bathed last night, my lord."

"She did, but it is her custom to bathe twice daily. A bucket of hot water will suffice in the morning, then the tub at night."

Agnes wrinkled her nose but did not speak.

"Tell me what you are thinking, Agnes," Fergus said.

"But you will think me impertinent."

"Honesty is the best choice, Agnes. You should always tell the truth at Killairic."

The girl nodded and lifted her chin. "I only wonder that she would bathe twice a day, my lord. I hope such excess does not make your lady ill."

Fergus smiled, well aware that many of his fellows thought a weekly bath excessive. "I doubt it will. It has been her practice for years, and that of her people for centuries, if not more."

Agnes, it seemed, could not hide her doubt. "If you say as much, my lord."

"I will be back this evening and perhaps as glad of a bath as she." He nodded and straightened but before he could take a step toward the stables, Agnes stood up.

"Is it true, my lord, that you ride to visit Lady Isobel at Dunnisbrae?"

"It is. I will return by the evening meal, to be sure."

"Would you take a message to my brother for me, my lord? He serves the ostler at Dunnisbrae and I have not seen him for over a year."

"Of course," Fergus said.

She curtsied, her gratitude clear. "His name is Nolan, my lord, and it is said that we look alike."

"And what message would you send him?"

Agnes thought about this for a moment, her brow puckered in a frown. "Just that I missed his company at the Yule and hope to see him soon."

"It shall be done, Agnes." Fergus nodded at her. "Do not labor too hard this day," he said, his tone teasing for he guessed it would be otherwise. At the girl's grimace, he strode toward the village where he would summon Hamish, then on to the stables, Tempest, and the promise of seeing Isobel.

Duncan was not surprised to see Fergus in the stables so early, but he was disappointed. It seemed to him that a man should linger abed on the morn after his nuptials and he did not trouble to hide his disapproval.

"You will still ride north this very morning?" Fergus asked, his mood clearly merry. "Do you not take more with you than this?"

"I need little on this journey but my wits and my blade," Duncan replied. "I will break my fast in your father's hall, though, and ride out with a full belly." He gave the younger man a sharp look. "Do you not intend to break your fast with your new wife?"

"Leila is sleeping yet, and I would leave at dawn."

Duncan shook his head and could not bite his tongue. "Leaving the bed of a loyal woman to gaze upon a faithless one."

Fergus paused in grooming his destrier to turn to Duncan. "You still disapprove, but I will perform this errand today."

"I think a man should appreciate every advantage that comes to him. You are more fortunate to have Leila as your wife than you could have been with the other."

Fergus' tone cooled. "You never liked Isobel."

"I never *trusted* Isobel. I have seldom seen a woman so intent upon her own advantage, to the exclusion of all else." Duncan closed a saddlebag, tugging hard on the strap. "Her faithlessness has done you a favor, at least. You might have been wedded to her otherwise and paid a higher price than four years of chastity."

Fergus shook his head and returned to the grooming of Tempest. "That is harsh, Duncan."

"Did you never guess her faithlessness?"

"Never!"

Duncan had suspected as much but was still startled to hear Fergus say it aloud. "I thought you had eyes in your head, lad, never mind the Sight. My mother would have said that one wished for honey on both sides of her bread and more besides."

"Perhaps she deserves so much honey as that."

"Why? Because her face is pretty?" Duncan scoffed. "It is her nature that is of greater import, or should be." When Fergus did not reply, he continued. "Perhaps beauty does have a way of distracting a man from the truth of a woman's heart."

Fergus turned to eye Duncan. "You suspected all along that she would not wait?"

"I doubted she would tolerate any inconvenience to herself or her own desires," Duncan admitted. "Your absence for four years would certainly be that."

"But surely love should last a lifetime."

Duncan decided this might be his last chance to grant a measure of advice to the younger man. Who knew what awaited him in the north? He propped his hands upon his hips and confronted Fergus, his tone challenging. "Was it love that compelled her to accept your hand? Or was it advantage?"

Fergus' expression became guarded. "Speak bluntly, Duncan, if you please."

"Careful what you wish for, lad," Duncan advised with a smile. Fergus neither replied nor changed his manner. Duncan sighed and spoke his mind. "Lady Isobel is a beauty and born to a good family but not a powerful one. Her lineage will be hers forever, but beauty fades. Her father's ability to secure an alliance with her marriage would diminish every year after she began her courses."

"Four years is a long time to wait, then," Fergus mused.

Duncan chose not to add his other thought, even though he had been encouraged to speak plainly.

Fergus eyed him. "And what of your time away from Radegunde?"

"It is much the same," Duncan acknowledged, his heart squeezing a little at the mention of his beloved. "She counts the days more precisely than I do, because she desires a houseful of children. Her years to bear them are limited and I do not doubt that she will resent each day that passes without such effort on our part."

Fergus' gaze brightened. "You were going to say something else a moment ago."

"You will think it unkind."

"If it is honest, kindness is no measure. Confess it, Duncan."

Duncan pursed his lips, for he was no diplomat. "There are women of wit and wisdom whose merit as wives only increases with their age. I believe that Radegunde is one such, and I will be glad to have her hand in mine."

Fergus, of course, did not miss his implication. "But you think Isobel is not such a woman," he guessed.

Duncan winced. "I believe she might feel the passing of time more keenly, or her father would. I make no excuses for her, a broken promise is still a betrayal, but I must wonder if there were other factors she found persuasive."

"And I will wager that you think Leila of a similar ilk to Radegunde."

Duncan smiled. "Perhaps you do see clearly, after all, lad."

"Love must be of import, Duncan," Fergus insisted, and Duncan wondered who he sought to convince.

"Love might need time to blossom, as it did for Gaston and Ysmaine."

Fergus did not reply to that, and Duncan could only hope he would think upon it. Tempest was saddled and Duncan heard Hamish outside the stables with his palfrey. The younger man came to him and offered his hand. "I wish you Godspeed, Duncan, and every blessing on your journey," Fergus said. "May you find what you seek and secure a home for yourself and Radegunde."

"I thank you, lad."

"We have talked of this before, but you know you are welcome at Killairic."

"And I know that my path lies north, that my future must be built upon my past."

They embraced then, and Duncan knew he would miss the younger man's company. When Fergus spoke, his voice was husky. "One of us should be joyous in marriage, Duncan, and that task now falls to you. Ride forth and prove to me that love can conquer all."

"Do not be so quick to dismiss your chance of a good match," Duncan scolded. "You may not be able to see past the shadow of this disappointment, but I do not believe myself to be the sole one of us destined to happiness."

Fergus did not look convinced.

Yet.

He returned to Tempest and swung into the saddle, riding the beast out of the stable and speaking to Hamish. As Duncan turned back to the hall, where he would break his fast, he heard the horses canter through the village and then to run. He believed that Fergus had already found the wife he deserved, if that man would but open his eyes to see the truth.

Leila awakened with the sense that someone was nearby.

Not Fergus.

She felt the key to the solar beneath her fingers and guessed that Fergus had left the door unlocked. The hair prickled on the back of her neck, as if she was being closely watched, and she smelled straw. There was no straw in this fine bed. She smelled onions, as well. Raw ones. She opened her eyes ever so slightly to find Agnes examining the trunks and making her way to the door to the treasury.

The girl slept on a straw pallet and had likely cut onions in the kitchen.

Leila rolled to her back with a sigh, as if she moved in her sleep, but kept a wary gaze upon the girl. Agnes started and glanced toward the bed, then stepped toward the treasury door. She ran a fingertip over the lock and bit her lip, glanced back at the bed, then silently tried the latch. Leila's eyes narrowed, her resolve to limit the girl's access to anything of import redoubled.

She did not blame Fergus for his trust of those welcomed in his father's hall, but she did not share it either.

She yawned noisily and stretched, hearing Agnes hasten back to the door. When Leila opened her eyes and sat up, the girl gave every appearance of just arriving at the threshold with a bucket of steaming water. She smiled and curtsied, but Leila was not fooled.

She made sure the girl saw the lace around her neck with the key, and how she added the second key to it before she replaced it around her neck and rose from the bed.

"Good morning, my lady," Agnes said, curtseying again.

Leila decided to disguise her understanding of Gaelic. She could have replied in kind, but instead bowed her head once and answered in French. Agnes would not be the sole one with secrets in this keep.

She pointed to the door and shooed Agnes in that direction. When the girl stepped over the threshold, Leila closed and locked the door, ensuring that the girl heard the lock tumble. Then she washed and dressed alone. The laces were at the sides of the kirtle, so she did not need assistance. She swept the floor and shook out the linens, hanging the coverlets and pelts to air. She left the shutters open then unlocked the door.

Agnes was sitting upon the step, waiting for her, and quickly hid her mutinous expression. Her gaze flicked past Leila to the cleaned solar and her surprise showed. Leila gave her the bucket of water and the one of slops, then pointed down the stairs. "Today, we will clean the hall," she told the girl in French, who clearly did not understand but was leery of whatever Leila had planned.

Her lips tightened when Leila locked the solar door, and Leila held the girl's gaze as she dropped the key down the front of her chemise. She gestured then and the girl preceded her, her mood most clear.

Duncan sat alone at the board, amusement lighting his eyes when he watched Agnes stalk across the hall with her burden. Leila was glad to have the chance to speak to him before his departure and took the seat beside him. Iain brought her a piece of warm bread and some honey, and she accepted his offer of ale and an apple.

"I am glad to see you more settled," Duncan said and Leila smiled.

"Only for a year and day, Duncan. I am certain that Fergus intends to find me a husband."

"And I would hope that you intend to keep the one you have."

She smiled. "I hope to show him that I am a good wife."

"And if the lad is fool enough to cast aside the gem that has come so easily to his hand, then you must remember my offer."

Leila smiled and kissed his cheek. "I will, Duncan. Thank you."

He finished his ale and nodded, his gaze lingering upon her. "The anniversary of my handfast with Radegunde is the sixth of September. I hope to see you before then, either as I journey to collect her from Châmont-sur-Maine or as we return to Scotland together."

"You must send word," Leila said. "We could meet at Haynesdale, if it is more convenient. I am certain that Bartholomew would welcome us all."

"As am I." Duncan stood and bowed. "Until we meet again, Lady Leila, farewell."

"Journey safely, Duncan," she said, rising to take his hands and kiss his cheeks in turn. "Radegunde is relying upon you."

He smiled and touched the braid of Radegunde's hair upon his wrist briefly before donning his gloves, bowing once again, and striding away. Leila blinked back a tear, and hoped that their paths would cross again, then she sat down to finish her meal. Murdoch was in the hall and watching her once again, but she ignored the way he saluted her with his cup.

Iain paused before her, bowing low. His French was almost as careful as Calum's and certainly was more formal. "My lady, I am instructed to show you whatever you would like to see and to put myself at your disposal on this day."

"Thank you so much, Iain. I should like to see the kitchens and the stores this morning, then the garden this afternoon. I must also visit Margaret in the village after the midday meal and would ask directions to her home."

The older man nodded approval of this scheme. "We should perhaps choose a location for the dovecote while in the garden," he suggested. "I have sent word to Dumfries this morning to engage the man who builds such structures. Xavier dispatched a boy to buy fish at the morning market and it seemed a good opportunity."

"Thank you, Iain. That was an excellent notion. I know a little of the requirements of such birds, but both the weather and sunlight is different here. I remember, for example, that it was key to ensure that they had shade for part of the day, but that might not be the case here where the air is colder. Perhaps we should choose several alternatives and let the builder share his advice."

"A most excellent plan, my lady."

"Did my laird husband send word to Haynesdale?"

"He did, my lady. I sent it with the boy and bade him find a messenger in Dumfries. It should be readily done."

"Thank you, Iain." Leila set aside her napkin and rose to her feet. She beckoned to Agnes. "I should like to give Agnes the task of sweeping the hall and removing the rushes. The dogs can spend the day in the stables and the hearth can be cleaned as well."

Iain nodded and gave rapid instructions in Gaelic to Agnes.

"Would you like to meet the cook, my lady? I hope that Xavier is not in foul temper this morning..." Iain continued, taking great pains to warn Leila of the perils of the fiend who commanded the kitchens. She understood immediately that the two older men who had vied for Calum's approval for years now battled for her own.

The kitchen, to her delight, was immaculately clean. Two boys were scrubbing the wooden tables with great gusto, urged on by the dark-haired man with silver at his temples. He chided them as he chopped onions, casting them with perfect aim into a great cauldron that hung over the fire.

Iain cleared his throat pointedly.

Xavier turned, as if to shake his knife at the intruder, then he evidently saw Leila.

"This is Xavier," Iain said.

"I am most pleased to make the acquaintance of the master of this domain," Leila said, remembering that cooks often were proud. "The meal last evening was delicious."

Xavier smiled and bowed deeply, then erupted a rapid stream of French. "My lady! I am enchanted and honored by your presence in the kitchen, my small domain as you so graciously acknowledge, and would offer my felicitations upon your marriage to Laird Fergus." He bowed again. "I can only apologize that it was impossible to create your own favorite dishes for your wedding feast last evening as we knew nothing of you in advance..."

"Of course, you could not, Xavier. You had so little warning. I thought the venison was particularly marvelous."

"Ah!" Xavier's eyes lit. "But that was due to the return of your lady and his lordship, for I had no cloves before noon yesterday and they are the key to that particular sauce. You answered my dreams, my lady, and so the meal benefitted greatly from your arrival."

He bowed again, and Leila instinctively liked him. It was clear to her that his enthusiasm was bound to the creations of his kitchen and that was a trait she could both admire and encourage.

"If there is a dish I can prepare to tempt your palate, my lady, you have only to tell me of it. If there are recipes you remember and would have served in the hall, you have only to tell me of them."

Leila doubted that Xavier would have access to many of the ingredients she recalled but she appreciated the offer. "I thank you. I would not meddle in the administration of your domain, Xavier, but perhaps I can be of aid to you with the inventories."

"But of course, my lady. It is your right to approve all expenditures in the kitchen." Xavier offered a pair of keys to her, gesturing to a storeroom. Within it, there were sacks of dried peas and of flour. A small trunk was built into a wooden shelf, and the smaller key opened it. The spices were kept there, and Xavier showed her the inventory Hamish had created the day before. A quick glance proved to Leila that all was in order and she smiled to dismiss Xavier's concern.

"And you were pleased with the spices Laird Fergus brought?"

"Of course, my lady. It is only sad that we will use them so quickly."

Leila nodded. "My lord husband and I journeyed from Outremer with a company of Templars."

"So, I understand, my lady."

"One of his friends, a former Templar, now commands his father's holding in France, to the west of Paris. We stopped there on our return."

"I am told those lands are most beautiful. My own origin is in the north and east of Paris."

"I anticipate that my husband may communicate regularly with his friend in France, who might well maintain his connections with the Templars. It thus seems likely to me that when a spice is diminishing in our stores, we might be able to request the assistance of these friends in purchasing more." She smiled at Xavier. "And you might never lack for cloves again."

Xavier was clearly delighted. "This is most generous, my lady, and most kind." He frowned, thinking of this. "I wish I could devise a way to better anticipate a shortage or even the use of our last stores."

"We have an inventory made already," Leila noted. "Let us keep a record of the use of each spice. Then we shall best know how much of each is consumed by the household over time, which can inform our purchases."

"And by season!" Xavier added. "For winter meals should have more spice than summer ones, and the Yule uses the most of all." He nodded with satisfaction. "This is an improvement, to be sure."

Leila turned to Iain, who had been trying to follow the conversation and by his expression had not gleaned all of the details. She explained her intention to him more slowly and he beamed with pleasure at her. "I shall see that there is a ledger prepared for this very task, my lady. I can use the inventory compiled by Hamish and can make that the first entry." He dropped his voice. "For I should not see such wealth wasted."

Xavier glared at him, then gestured to the kitchen once more. Leila preceded him, as indicated, and raised a brow to find the two boys chatting with Agnes. The girl had evidently brought some of the rushes through the kitchen and saw fit to jest with the boys rather than complete her task.

Xavier yelled at the pair of boys and they hastened back to their labor. Agnes swept the rushes into the bailey as Xavier bellowed at her to use another portal and keep such mess from his kitchen. He swept the floor furiously in her wake, muttering curses beneath his breath as he restored all to rights.

"He does not appreciate the girl," Iain sniffed and went to the hall in search of a ledger.

Xavier glared after him. "He does not see what is before his eyes. I am glad to have that one out of my kitchen, but regret that she now is assigned to serve you, my lady." The cook dropped his voice to a confidential whisper. "Do not trust her overmuch. She came from Dunnisbrae and I cannot think any good of that holding since Laird Fergus was treated so poorly by Lady Isobel."

Leila was aware that the boys were watching, but secretly liked the cook a little more. Not only did they share a view of Agnes, but one of Isobel.

How curious that Agnes had arrived from Dunnisbrae. Was that a coincidence, or something more?

"I thank you for your counsel, Xavier," she said smoothly. "I understand that you sent to Dumfries for fish this morning. What kind of fish do you find here? And how do you intend to prepare them?"

"There will be fresh salmon at the market this morning, my lady, and Laird Calum favors the filets fried in a little butter. He tires of the eels from the millpond, no matter how I prepare them. I like to tempt his appetite, but perhaps he will eat better now that Lord Fergus is returned. Worry, as I am certain you know, my lady, is a great destroyer of the appetite." Leila nodded as the cook continued to enthuse and she had the sense that he had been waiting for a patient ear. "I thought the last of the wine could be made into a sauce for eggs..."

It was past noon when Fergus and Hamish reached Dunnisbrae and a gentle rain had begun to fall. It was not a heavy onslaught but it was persistent, and the back of Fergus' cloak was soaked through by the time the keep came into sight.

They had been compelled to take a longer route, since spring rains had washed out some of the fords and narrow bridges on the shortest path. As a result, they arrived later than Fergus had hoped. The clouds were darker in the west and he doubted their ride home would be pleasant.

He dared not linger. A mere word with Isobel, a glimpse of her beauty, a cup of ale, and a piece of bread, then he and Hamish would return to Killairic.

He noted that the keep looked less prosperous than he recalled, or perhaps it had not flourished since he had last journeyed this way. It was still a single tower, wrought of timber like the surrounding walls, but Fergus had a sense of decay. There was a fine portcullis on the gate to the bailey, though, which was a surprise. Did Isobel's father still draw breath? His own father had not said.

Dunnisbrae was to the south and west of Killairic, perched on the southernmost tip of the Mull of Galloway. The isle of Mann was to the south, Galloway and the rest of the Kingdom of the Isles to the north, the lands of the English king veiled in the mist to the south.

Hamish had been quiet on their journey, and Fergus had guessed the reason why. "There will be a fire and a cup of ale soon enough," he said to Hamish with forced cheer and the boy nodded with a semblance of enthusiasm.

"Aye, my lord."

"Are you thinking of Kerr?"

Hamish nodded and wiped the rain from his face. "He had good qualities, my lord, as well as bad."

It was a kindly concession from the one who had probably endured the greatest torment from Kerr, and Fergus took that as a measure of Hamish's character. "Which is why the truth of his nature will not be revealed by any of us," Fergus reminded him. "I think Duncan's counsel most wise in this matter."

"Aye, my lord."

"I will tell them of his death, Hamish," Fergus said and the boy's relief was obvious. "You will not need to answer questions about it."

"Thank you, my lord."

They were clearly spied and identified, for the portcullis creaked as it was raised. A man stepped into the middle of the opening. He folded his arms across his chest, braced his feet against the ground, and watched their approach.

It was Stewart himself, his posture indicating that he anticipated a challenge.

Fergus took this as an indication that Isobel had not been so willing to wed the other man. His heart skipped at the possibility that she might have been loyal to him, if she had been granted the choice.

Not that it mattered now. Duncan had been right in that. It would be a balm to his pride, though, and proof that he was a good judge of character. No more than that.

Though he had always been Fergus' senior, Stewart looked

much older now, his hair silver-gray and his expression harder than once it had been. He wore a mail hauberk with his plaid and his boots, adding to Fergus' impression that the other man was prepared for battle.

"The crusader returns," Stewart said by way of greeting, a hint of mockery in his tone. He walked toward Fergus when the arrivals paused outside the gate. His smile was cold and his gaze assessing. "I trust the Saracens have been routed from Outremer with your aid?"

"Just the opposite," Fergus acknowledged as he dismounted. He strove to keep his tone light, even friendly. "You must have heard that Jerusalem itself was lost in October."

"We did," Stewart said. His ostler came forward to take the reins of Tempest and a boy reached for those of Hamish's palfrey, but Stewart waved them both off. "I doubt my neighbor will linger," he said, surprising Fergus with such a lack of hospitality. Man and boy retreated and Fergus noted that the boy shared Agnes' striking coloring. This must be her brother, Nolan.

Stewart smirked. "I apologize for this greeting, but I will not have my lady wife disturbed."

"I have tidings I would like to give to Isobel myself," Fergus said, for he imagined she might find the news of Kerr troubling.

"But it is my obligation to defend my lady wife."

"Surely not from a friend?"

"Particularly so, when that *friend* is returned after years away," Stewart replied evenly. "Isobel is with child, again, and is in need of calm and rest during her time."

"I see."

"You may grant any message intended for her to me."

Fergus understood that he would not be permitted to see the lady himself. The realization irked him but he hid his reaction. "Of course. She had asked me to take her nephew, Kerr, in our company as a squire, and I regret that he has not returned."

Stewart arched a brow. "Did you sell him in a Saracen slave market?"

Fergus tempered his reply. "He was killed, when we were attacked by brigands west of Venice. We laid him to rest in a cemetery there.”

Stewart flicked a look at Hamish. “And yet the boy from Killairic returns with you.”

“Hamish did very well in defending himself.”

“While Kerr did not?” Stewart scoffed. “I suspect there is more to this tale than you are sharing, but Kerr is dead either way.”

“He is.”

“These are tidings that will trouble Isobel deeply,” Stewart said. “She was very fond of the boy and often has expressed concern for his welfare in distant pagan lands. It is good that I did not allow you to see her. Is that all?”

That he would push Fergus from the gates without so much as a cup of ale after such a long ride in the rain was an abomination and an insult. But Fergus could see that Stewart was trying to provoke a response, so did not give him one. “Perhaps you might give Isobel my regards, as well as this gift.”

“A gift?” Stewart asked, arching a brow. He turned to his sentries. “The returning crusader brings a gift for my lady wife. Do you think he is still smitten with her charms? Do you think he means to steal her away from me?”

The guards chuckled.

Fergus did not. He wished Leila and Duncan’s suspicions had not been proven so very right.

“A gift,” he reiterated, unlashing the small trunk from his saddle. His tone had hardened. “When I bought it, I believed Isobel to be my betrothed, waiting upon my return. I see no reason why she should not have it, even though my belief was mistaken.”

“Such generosity should not go unrewarded,” Stewart said, accepting the small chest from him. He seemed to heft its weight. “Dare I hope it is filled with gems?”

Fergus smiled tightly. “It is not.”

The other man tucked the trunk under his arm and held Fergus’ gaze, seemingly inviting him to leave with all haste.

Fergus held his ground. “I understand that you and Isobel have a son already,” he said. “I would congratulate you, belatedly, of course.”

“I thank you.” Stewart smiled.

"And her father? How does Erik fare?"

"Dead these three years, I fear." Fergus crossed himself at Stewart's admission. "A better man was never found."

"I suppose he saw your merit, in putting his daughter's hand in yours."

Stewart smiled. "I suppose he did. He saw his grandson born, at least." He stepped back. "I wish you Godspeed, of course." He gestured to the sky. "I hope the rain does not turn to snow before you reach home. It is possible, though, given the chill in the air. It would be best for you to ride out immediately."

Fergus ground his teeth, but would not give Stewart the satisfaction of reacting poorly. "You might offer me felicitations as well," he said before climbing into the saddle again.

"For returning alive against all expectation?"

"For my own handfast. I am a married man, as well." Fergus ignored Stewart's obvious interest and nodded to the boy. "Are you the brother of Agnes? Name of Nolan?"

"I am, sir," the boy said, bowing to him.

"Agnes asked that I deliver a message to you, that she regrets you were not together at the Yule and hopes to see you soon."

Did Fergus imagine the quick glance that fired between Nolan and Stewart? Could this message mean more to them than to him?

Nonsense. It was no more than two peasants sending word to each other by whatever means were available.

"I thank you, sir. I hope she is well."

"She does fare well." Fergus met Stewart's gaze steadily. "She is now maid to my lady wife."

Stewart looked skeptical. "Is it true that you are wed? To whom? And when?"

"I pledged a handfast yesterday upon my return to Killairic." Fergus granted Stewart a thin smile. "It is to be hoped that we will both have similar happiness in our matches."

"But who did you marry?" Stewart demanded, seizing Tempest's reins. "What alliance did you make?"

"None. She is a lady who journeyed in our party from Jerusalem."

Stewart laughed and stepped back again. "A whore, then? With the loss of your betrothed, you wed your whore!" His mirth seemed to overcome him and he slapped his thighs as he laughed even louder.

Fergus dismounted and closed the distance between them, seizing Stewart by his hauberk and lifting that man to his toes. "My wife is no whore," he said in a low growl. "And a clever man would not be so foolish as to suggest as much twice. Were you not always said to be clever, Stewart?"

"Perhaps more clever than you," Stewart muttered.

"Perhaps not," Fergus countered. "Perhaps one battle too many has cost you your wits."

The two men's gazes locked and held for a charged moment.

"Who is your wife?" Stewart demanded again.

"Leila binte Qadir lufti al-Ramm."

Stewart laughed again, a harsh bark that prompted Fergus to release him and step back. "A Saracen? You wed a Saracen?" The older man smiled. "And who is the witless one, Fergus? I have a beauty in my bed." He dropped his voice to a whisper. "Do you think of Isobel's pale perfection as you ride your filthy infidel?"

Fergus struck Stewart then, his reaction born of fury. The older man stumbled backward even as his nose began to spurt blood. His men drew their swords, but Stewart chuckled as he regained his balance. He wiped the blood, his gaze still fixed upon Fergus.

"Stand down," he said to his warriors. "A man with blood in his veins should have the right to express his displeasure when a lady spurns him for another man."

Fergus might have expressed more, but a woman's voice carried to his ears from within the keep. "Fergus? Fergus, is that you? Can it truly be you returned?"

Isobel.

The bottom dropped out of Fergus' stomach even as Isobel appeared in the doorway to the keep and hastened across the bailey. She was more beautiful than he recalled, her fair hair bound into a long braid, her figure tall and slender. She was as graceful as a willow, even with the slight rounding of her belly. She was dressed in a kirtle of faded blue, probably dyed with woad. She had aged a little and there was a wariness in her expression, but she had lost her father since his departure. Fergus could not imagine that marriage to Stewart would fill a woman's days with merriment.

His throat tightened at the sight of her.

Isobel.

His beloved.

Stewart's displeasure was clear, but so was his inability to stop his lady wife. "Isobel, I thought you were resting."

"Stewart, I cannot surrender the opportunity to see Fergus and hear his news!" she exclaimed.

There was something different about her, or something that Fergus saw now that he had missed all those years before. Isobel was still sufficiently lovely to steal his breath away, but he noticed an assessment in her eyes when she surveyed him. She eyed his horse and trap, his garb, then that of Hamish, and he had the sense she had put a value upon it all within a penny.

And there was no disguising the quick gleam of avarice that lit her eyes when she spied the small chest that Stewart now carried. She knew it was a gift, and one for her, and greed lit her features with such clarity that Fergus was shocked.

Then it was gone, so quickly that it might never have been.

A woman who sees to her own advantage first. That was what Duncan had said. Fergus feared his comrade had been right.

Fergus felt a fool as he had not before. Surely he had not been deceived by a lovely face. Surely he had not missed Isobel's truth. Surely life with Stewart had changed his beloved into this greedy creature.

But Fergus was not sure.

"You are home. And you are hale! Oh, Fergus!" Isobel's greeting was fulsome, but now that Fergus was listening, it did not seem heartfelt.

Fergus was surprised that he felt so little as she reached to kiss his cheeks in turn and caress his face. She smiled up at him with pleasure but he could not smile back. He could not forget that glimpse of what he believed was her truth.

Instead of the joy he had anticipated at the sight or her, he felt only disappointment—and a sense that she tempted fate by ignoring Stewart's obvious desire to keep her from seeing him.

A little bit late, Leila's advice seemed most wise, and Fergus wished he had not shown such haste in leaving his new bride.

Leila would never break her word.

And Duncan had spoken the truth. In rushing to Dunnisbrae, Fergus might have created the impression at Killairic that he did not admire his new wife.

He had erred.

"Fergus is leaving," Stewart said with resolve.

"Not yet!" Isobel cried. "He is only just arrived." She would not release Fergus from her embrace, even though Stewart looked on with a scowl. "You must come to the board and take refreshment, and tell us all of your news! Come out of this horrible rain." She made to take his hand and lead him to the gate, but Stewart stepped into her path.

"He must leave," that man said firmly. "Before the weather grows worse. You would not have Fergus ride at night in peril, would you?"

"Then he must be our guest and stay until the morrow."

"I imagine his father awaits his return."

"So he does. I would not give him cause for concern," Fergus said. "Stewart is right."

Isobel pouted, keeping his hand clasped between both of hers as she leaned against him. "Oh, Fergus. I feared for your survival so much. I am so relieved that you are hale!"

Again, Fergus heard insincerity in her words and he tried to extricate his hand. "Did you?" he asked. She was the wife of another, and Stewart was armed.

Leila had warned him and he had been too foolish to heed her counsel.

He could not resist the urge to challenge Isobel. "And you were so concerned that you forgot our pledge?"

Isobel had the grace to color. "Fergus," she whispered, resting one hand on his chest. She fluttered her lashes, looking vulnerable and lovely. She had done this before and he had always succumbed to her entreaties. In this moment, Fergus found he could only think that she had been not kept her vow. "I could not wait for you. It was too long and there was too much uncertainty..."

"I understood that you and Stewart wed within three months of my departure."

She faltered. "It was so long," she began again. "I could not wait. Fergus, I am only a woman and I am weak..."

Fergus was skeptical about that.

If her father had forced her decision, surely she would say as much?

"Then you should not have pledged to do as much in the first place," Fergus replied. "You knew I rode to Outremer. You knew I would serve two years once there. You cannot have anticipated that I would be home any sooner than this."

"If at all," Stewart interjected. "Isobel, I must insist that you return to the hall before you take a chill."

Isobel glanced at her husband before returning her attention to Fergus. "We should all go to the hall..."

"Nay, I will not." Fergus caught a glimpse of movement and saw the boy in the portal, a boy who had clearly followed Isobel.

There could be no doubt that he was Isobel's child. He had the same fair hair and blue eyes, though he was more sturdy of build.

Like Stewart.

"Ah, Gavin," Stewart said. "Here is our neighbor, Fergus."

The boy bowed and greeted Fergus formally.

Fergus had noted already that Isobel's belly was slightly round, but the way she cupped her hand protectively over its curve in this moment indicated that she ripened with child again.

Whatever had happened, whatever had changed her thinking, there was no future for Fergus with Isobel. If ever she had loved him, she did no longer.

What was of import was that Leila was now his wife.

"Stewart speaks aright," Fergus continued firmly, reaching for Tempest's reins. "We should return to Killairic with all haste, before the weather becomes worse. My best regards to both of you, and my condolences with regards to Kerr."

"Kerr?" Isobel echoed, her eyes narrowing.

"He died, Isobel," Fergus said gently. "We were attacked by bandits to the west of Venice and he was killed in the assault. He is buried there, in hallowed ground, beside a lovely chapel."

Isobel's lips parted, then she clamped them together. For a fleeting moment, Fergus thought her expression colder than a midwinter night and he wondered whether she had any heart at all. "He died?" she asked, ice in her voice. "And you left him there?"

"We were attacked by bandits, Isobel. It was not possible to bring him home from such distance..."

Isobel did not wait to hear more. She burst into loud tears and began to wail the loss of her beloved nephew. She fled back into the bailey, lamenting the boy's early death, but it seemed to Fergus that her reaction was insincere.

That glance had been chilling, sufficiently so that he found himself glad Isobel had broken their betrothal.

Stewart gave Fergus an angry glance. "This is not how I would have told her," he muttered, but Fergus was glad he had delivered the news himself. "Godspeed to you," he added, clearly meaning the opposite, and headed back through the gates with his son. The portcullis was dropped with a clang and the two sentries glared at him from the other side.

Fergus could still hear Isobel's lamentations.

He swung into the saddle, nodded at Hamish, and turned Tempest for home. His duty was done. The truth was unwelcome but delivered. He would build a future at Killairic with Leila.

The very notion encouraged him to touch his heels to Tempest's sides.

CHAPTER SEVEN

arquar did not know what to think when the laird's new wife ducked out of the rain and into his smithy. The air was thick with smoke from the forge and the rain was drumming on the roof. It hardly seemed the place for a lady, particularly one so delicate as this one, and he felt at odds in his own corner of Killairic. She put him in mind of a fine dark filly, lively and unpredictable.

How could he greet her when she did not speak Gaelic? Was he doomed to give insult? Farquar never wanted to face a reckoning from Laird Fergus, that was for certain, for that man was highly principled.

The two newly arrived horses tethered in the smithy watched with curiosity, even old Nellie's ears pricking as she watched. The plow horse had shown little interest in anything of late, so Farquar took the lady's visit as a good sign in that regard.

He stepped away from his forge, wiped his hands on his leather apron, and bowed. The lady smiled at him, pretty little creature that she was, but the smith remained uneasy at this unexpected visit.

That she was accompanied by one of the Templar knights did

little to ease his concern. That man was imposing not only due to his white tabard and chain mail hauberk but his fierce expression. He surveyed the smithy as if expecting a threat in every corner, one hand on the hilt of his blade and suspicion in his eyes.

It was clear the lady had a stalwart defender, even in Laird Fergus' absence.

To Farquar's surprise, the lady proceeded with confidence to the forge, then closed her eyes and took a deep breath, as if appreciating the distinctive smell of the smithy. He did as much each time he returned, but it was a habit he hardly expected to have in common with the laird's Saracen bride. He was intrigued, more so when she smiled again and said something to the Templar.

"Lady Leila was raised by her uncle, who was a blacksmith in Outremer," the knight explained in careful Gaelic. "She says your smithy smells like home."

Farquar grinned, for he was charmed despite himself. He invited her with a gesture to inspect his work, standing back as she did just that. She identified the best of his labors immediately, with a smile and a tap of her fingertip, her admiration revealing the truth of her claim.

The lady gestured to the horses, and Farquar recalled that she was said to have a talent with their care. Maybe Nellie sensed as much. Like a bee to honey, Lady Leila went directly to the plow horse, walked around the dapple mare as she murmured reassuringly, then bent to deftly lift the affected foot. Farquar felt his brows rise as the lady inspected the injured hoof, the surety of her movements feeding his conviction that the tale of her skill was true.

She spoke to the knight, who translated.

"She was quicked?"

"Aye." Farquar began to explain that the horse had moved just before his hammer had struck the nail, but the lady waved off his explanation. She mimed lifting a hammer then kicked her foot, clearly aware that even the most placid horse might not remain still while being shoed—and that there was no fault to the smith in that.

Farquar heaved a sigh of relief.

She frowned and touched the swelling on Nellie's hoof with a gentle fingertip. The mare snorted and stamped another foot.

She raised her dark gaze to Farquar.

He flung out his hands, hoping the knight could translate his words and that his gestures would communicate his frustration. "I cannot progress," he said. "She will not stand upon it, much less walk, and each day, it grows worse instead of better. I dare not remove the shoe and all chance of her walking, yet the inactivity gives her colic, as well." He laid a hand upon Nellie's side and leaned his ear against her belly. The loud rumble of her indigestion made the issue most clear to him and he hoped the lady understood.

Lady Leila listened to the Templar's translation, which seemed overly short to Farquar, then listened to Nellie's belly herself. She nodded and spoke briskly to the Templar.

"The lady says she can help," the Templar said. "Her uncle had a scheme that aided a horse similarly affected, but she would ask for your permission to interfere in this case."

Farquar knew his relief showed, for Nellie was important to the village and the welfare of all within it. Plus, he could not abide to see a horse suffer. He said all of this, finding himself uncharacteristically fulsome in the face of unexpected assistance, and the knight spoke to the lady.

She nodded again, then held up a two fingers before pointing back to the keep.

Farquar nodded understanding. She needed something from the hall, but would return to help Nellie. He smiled and bowed, more encouraged than he had been in days.

Leila ran, Enguerrand fast on her heels. She climbed to the solar, unlocked the door, and retrieved a flask from Fergus' belongings. Once the door was locked again, she descended to the kitchen, where Xavier opened the spice chest at her request. She raced back to the smithy with her selection, arriving out of breath.

Farquar smiled at her and she knew he would assist her. They had found common ground in their concern for the plow horse.

Enguerrand halted behind her.

"The stall must be swept out," she said to the Templar. "So that it is dry and clean beneath Nellie's feet. It is the wet and the mire that compounds the problem."

The knight translated and Farquar nodded, then beckoned to his boys. They swept out the stall, working around Nellie who regarded them with some curiosity. That, too, was a change for the better. The two palfreys that had returned from Outremer with their party also leaned over their stalls to watch and one nuzzled Leila from behind. She swatted away the nibbler, heard a playful nicker, then was nuzzled anew.

Farquar said something and Enguerrand replied before translating. "He says they trust you and I told him it was no wonder. You were the one who tended them best and anticipated their needs."

Leila and Farquar shared a smile. She gestured to Nellie's hoof. "The shoe must come off and stay off until there is improvement." She picked up Nellie's foot and braced it against her knees as her uncle had taught her. Farquar, once Enguerrand had shared her advice, brought his tools and pried the offending shoe loose. Leila liked that he was gentle and was amused that they both murmured soothing sounds to the horse. She examined the hoof and put out her hand for the hook to clean it without thinking, surprised when Farquar anticipated her request. She pointed to the swollen area and he nodded, indicating another bruise on the side. When she ran her finger along the hoof on one side, he fetched his file and they trimmed it down a little bit more.

Then Leila lifted a finger in warning. She gestured and one of the boys gave her Fergus' flask. At her indication, he opened it.

"*Eau de vie*," she said to Farquar who sniffed it and blinked. "We must hold the foot fast. This will sting her, but will cleanse the wound." Enguerrand translated, then the boys braced the horse and Farquar held Nellie's foot. Leila carefully poured a measure of the liquid over the injured foot and felt a ripple pass through the horse. Nellie snorted and stamped one of her other feet and tossed her head. Leila held the hoof until it dried. Farquar pointed to the one side, where the wound already looked less angry, and nodded approval.

"The Romans wrapped the hooves of their horses in leather," Leila said. "Nellie must walk a bit to aid her digestion, so we will do the same to keep the hoof clean. Once she returns to her stall, the air will aid more than the leather."

Farquar listened intently to Enguerrand's translation, then fetched a piece of leather and a length of narrow rope. Leila nodded approval and they encased the hoof, only letting Nellie put it down once the leather was secured. Leila stood up and brushed off her kirtle. She had a small bag of roots, ginger and turmeric, and half a dozen apples from the kitchen. She used her eating knife to cut them up into chunks, sharing quarters of apple with the two palfreys until Nellie turned in curiosity, her ears flicking. She put the remainder in a feed sack, let Nellie sniff it, then backed away.

Nellie's tail flicked. Her ears pricked. Leila held out a piece of apple and the closest palfrey nickered, stretching her neck over the stall for it. Leila gave it to her and Nellie snorted. Leila then offered another to the plow horse. Nellie exhaled, then took a step closer, putting her weight on the injured foot. She was hesitant at first, but then took another step, stretching her neck to seize the apple.

Farquar grinned and the boys would have clapped their hands, but he silenced them with a gesture. Leila backed up again, compelling Nellie to follow her. It took some time but the temptation of the treat was too much. Nellie followed her the length of the stable and back, then her belly rumbled and she farted with gusto. Leila let her have the contents of the feed bag after that effort. Nellie chewed through the ginger, turmeric, and apples, then gave a mighty belch.

By the time the boys had led her back into the stall and removed the leather from her hoof, she was touching the toe of it to the ground as she had not before. She belched three more times before Leila left the stables, then loosed another noisy fart. Leila and Farquar nodded and bowed to each other.

"Tomorrow," Leila said in Gaelic, then held up the spice bag.

"Tomorrow," Farquar agreed, his satisfaction more than clear.

"You will have no shortage of friends in this abode, Lady Leila, if you heal their only plow horse," Enguerrand said as they returned to the hall.

Leila cast him a smile. She was not thinking of allies. She was thinking of a horse being able to walk again, even a little bit, and how being in Farquar's smithy had been the closest thing to being home again.

But the Templar was right. She could and would make Killairic her abode.

Isobel had learned much since putting her hand in that of Stewart MacEwan.

She had learned the price of a hasty decision, to be sure, and the folly of impulse. More importantly, she had learned to never cultivate the suspicion of her husband—and since he was inclined to seek peril in every shadow, that was difficult to achieve.

She was pregnant again and as sick with the child as she had been with the last two. She despised the ordeal of pregnancy but Stewart had been mightily vexed with her failure to bring his second son to light. Did she dare to oust this child, as well?

Isobel might not have done as much but Fergus was returned. Fergus! And he looked even more handsome than he had four years before—as well as more prosperous. Dunnisbrae seemed poor and mean after he had ridden away, dark and dirty and desolate. Isobel hated it and her husband anew.

There had to be a way to change her situation for the better.

She knew, though, that only a fool would give any indication of such thoughts to Stewart. She returned dutifully to the hall, as if she had forgotten Fergus, and resumed her interrupted meal.

"You are forgetting your gift, Isobel," her husband said from behind her, his tone mocking. "How could you forget a present from your former betrothed?"

She was desperately curious about the gift, but would not reveal that to her jealous spouse. Stewart marched to her side and placed the trunk on the board beside her. Isobel fairly itched to open it, but she barely glanced at it.

"Are you not going to open it?" Stewart prompted.

"I have no need of a gift from another man," Isobel said. "My lord husband provides for all of my desires."

"Then perhaps one of the women in the village will welcome whatever filthy infidel trinket he has brought for you," Stewart said, so obviously trying to provoke her that Isobel had to keep her gaze downcast lest he see the flash of her eyes.

"Perhaps," she agreed.

Stewart's eyes glittered and he shoved the trunk at her. "Open it."

Isobel knew this test well enough and she steeled herself to try to succeed at it. "It smells," she said, as if repulsed by the trunk. It did smell, of spices and the salt of the sea, of foreign places and adventure, and all the things that Isobel desired. It smelled of promise and hope and far, far more than she had gained in this match.

Fergus had handfasted to an infidel.

It was the kind of gallant gesture a man like Fergus would make.

But he should be wedded to her. Surely he could be convinced to cast the infidel aside once she was wed no longer.

"Open it."

She shrugged as if her husband was tedious. "Must it be now, Stewart?"

"Open it!" Stewart commanded and, when she did not move, opened the trunk himself.

Isobel expected it to contain some trinket that she could easily find boring, but instead, the most wondrous length of blue cloth spilled into her lap as Stewart seized the trunk and dumped it. She was sitting before the fire and this cloth was illuminated by the firelight in such a way that she gasped aloud. It shone, gleaming with silken threads. It was soft and supple, woven so fine that it was a marvel beyond compare.

And it was vibrantly blue.

The same hue as her eyes.

Fergus!

"A lover's gift," Stewart snarled and seized the cloth from her lap. It was a wide piece, long enough for a kirtle even though she was tall. Maybe even enough for a short pelisse as well. Isobel cried out against her will as the cloth was snatched away and felt it slip through her fingers.

Stewart balled it up and knotted it, anger in his gestures. "A man who sends a gift like this has an expectation," he growled. "Do not be so fool, Isobel, to even think of fulfilling it." And he strode from the hall with the cloth, fury and purpose in his every step.

Isobel knew what he would do. She rose and went to the door, holding her belly as she watched Stewart stir up the blaze in the bailey that the sentries kept to warm their hands.

She closed her eyes as Stewart threw the cloth into the fire, his expression savage as it burned. She felt sickened that he should destroy her gift rather than see her happy—or elegantly garbed—and turned back to the board. It was then that she noticed that there was still something in the chest.

Needles, so fine and sharp. And silk thread for the embroidery she had never practiced much before her wedding. Isobel seized them both and tucked them away, hiding them from her husband.

Her stomach roiled and she was sick yet again in the bucket that was always close at hand. God in heaven, how she hated pregnancy. She thought of Fergus saying farewell to her, recalling how beautiful she had felt in his presence, and yearned to feel that way again.

"Do not be so foolish as to lose this one, as well," Stewart muttered from the portal. "I wed you for sons, and I will have sons. Do not deny me in this or any other matter, Isobel."

"Nay, my lord," she managed to say. "Of course not, my lord."

But rebellion had been awakened in Isobel. Aye, for with sharp needles in her possession and Fergus handfasted to a pagan, she once again had the means to see her own advantage secured.

This time, she would wed for her own benefit.

She and Fergus had lain together once, because she had begged him, but neither Fergus nor his whore knew that Isobel had not conceived before Stewart claimed her.

She could ensure that Stewart had no opportunity to share the truth.

Though the rain was merely a mist for the first hour or so, by the time Leila went to the smithy, it was falling steadily. It fell with even greater vigor when she visited Margaret, and ended any discussion of her visiting the gardens. By the evening meal, the rain was falling in sheets. It did not cease and this amazed Leila. She could hear it drumming on the roof, smell it in the air that wafted into the hall, and see the rivulets of it winding their way across the floor. No wonder the hills were so green!

The fires in the braziers smoked more and the stone of the keep radiated a chill that penetrated to her very marrow. Leila wrapped herself in a fur pelt from the bed and looked out the window of the solar into the darkness, wondering about Fergus.

He was late.

He had missed the evening meal, even though they had delayed it, and she knew he was not one to break a pledge.

The sun was gone, the clouds allowing no light from moon or stars. Did he know his way well enough to find it in such darkness? Could his horse have slipped and been injured? Could a path have been washed out?

Could Stewart MacEwan have taken exception to Fergus' visit?

Could Isobel have made a demand of Fergus that he found impossible to deny?

Only one day wedded and Leila's chest was tight with fear for their future together. She clutched at the pelt and stared into the night, worrying as she seldom had before. It was the powerlessness of her situation. There was not one thing she could do to aid Fergus. She could not even ride out in search of him, for she had only the most vague idea of the location of Dunnisbrae.

She could not help but feel that Isobel had won...something. And Leila feared the import of that.

"And so you reside in a land you must find hostile," Calum said from behind her and she jumped, startled out of her reverie. She turned to find him in the doorway of the solar and wondered how long he had stood there, watching her.

"It is very beautiful," she admitted.

"And very cold, compared to Outremer," he said, coming to stand beside her. "Have you ever seen such rain? I would wager not."

Leila shook her head. "Never."

"It is hard on the joints to be sure, but I missed it on my journey east."

"Will you tell me of your journey to the east?"

He granted her a sharp glance. "Only if you leave the window and trust in Fergus to keep his word," he said gently.

"I do, but it seems so much could have happened..."

"Or perhaps nothing more than a swollen river requiring them to take a longer route. Come down to the fire, Lady Leila, and I will tell you a tale."

She could not refuse his invitation and locked the door to the solar behind them. She took his elbow, ensuring that he did not slip on the stairs, and smiled to see that Iain had anticipated them. Two chairs were together in one corner, two braziers facing them with fires blazing in each. Leila felt pampered that so much resource should be expended on her behalf and she thanked the steward.

"I seldom speak of Outremer," Calum said as he lowered himself into one chair. "Fergus knows, of course, but I doubt he thought it of interest to you." He patted the seat opposite him. "Come and let me tell you what I remember of your homeland, then you can tell me what has changed."

"I doubt that some matters have changed at all," Leila said. There was a fur pelt on the chair and she nestled into it, welcoming its soft thickness. Fergus' father beckoned and Iain brought two more silver pelts, one for each of them. Fergus' father tucked his over his knees and sighed contentment. "A cup of mulled wine and I will feel most indulged," he said, granting a glance to the steward.

"There is only a small measure left in that cask, my lord."

"And time it is that we enjoyed it." Fergus' father waved and Iain bowed, then retreated to do his bidding.

Leila smiled as she tucked the pelt over her lap and found herself warming.

"Better?" he asked and she nodded.

"I thank you, sir."

"Sir? You will call me Calum."

"But..."

"My hall, my rules," he said firmly. His blue eyes glinted with humor even though his manner was gruff.

Leila could not take offense, not when his eyes sparkled so. "And so it shall be, Calum," she said and he smiled. "When were you in Palestine?"

"Just over twenty years ago. We answered the call, like so many others."

"We?"

"My oldest and dearest comrade, Alasdair Campbell. Our mothers were sisters and we were of an age with each other." His brows waggled. "We found trouble together, to be sure."

Leila smiled. "Like me and my cousin, but my mother was the sister of her father."

"Ah, much the same. And so it was that when Alasdair heard the summons to defend Jerusalem, he was determined to answer the call." Calum frowned. "I was wedded already and had one son."

"Fergus."

He nodded. "I was less inclined to journey so far, but Alasdair's betrothed had died of a fever before their nuptials were celebrated. I fear he blamed himself for her demise."

"But why?"

"He thought a man should love the woman he would wed, just as I loved my Eileen."

"And he did not love his betrothed?"

Calum shook his head. "She was the daughter of a powerful clansman and their marriage was to make an alliance. And to be sure, Nyssa was not the easiest woman to admire. She was prone to bouts of anger and would say much when she was riled. Alasdair is a temperate man, one who says little but means all he does say. Their match might have been good for an alliance, but their natures could not have been more different. And so it was that he felt guilt when she fell ill and died, and blamed himself for not loving her more."

"Perhaps she should have loved him more," Leila suggested.

"And learned from his manner."

"Perhaps so, but when the call came, Alasdair believed it offered him a chance to repent. He wished to journey east on crusade as an act of pilgrimage and to beg forgiveness at the Church of the Holy Sepulchre." Calum nodded. "Because he was my best friend and because I feared the result if he made such a journey alone, I agreed to go with him."

"And your wife, Eileen?"

"Oh, she thought little of the notion, to be sure. But she desired a second son, if not a third, and after Fergus was born, she had not conceived again." He winked. "It was not for a lack of effort on our part."

Leila smiled.

"So, I found merit in the notion of pilgrimage and penitence, and so, we went together." Calum sighed. "It was the spring of 1165. Fergus was three summers of age. I remember looking back to see Eileen on the top of the tower, holding him in her arms. The sun was in her hair, blazing copper it was, and he was waving with all his might. I know Eileen wept and truly, I shed a tear of my own. I had not thought until that moment that I might not see them again, and I very nearly turned back."

He fell silent then, lost in his memories, and Leila realized how dearly he had loved his lady wife. She let him remember for a few moments, content to sip her wine and watch the flames as he did, to listen to the sound of the rain and hope that she and Fergus might one day share a similar love.

"But you did not turn back," Leila prompted finally, gently drawing her companion back to his tale.

Calum cleared his throat and shook his head. "I had no real notion of how far it was to Outremer, much less how difficult a journey it would be. It took us almost a year to reach Constantinople. We finally found passage there to Caesarea, but that was where we parted."

He fell silent, staring into the fire, and Leila urged him again to continue. "But why? What happened?"

"I fell ill with a fever. I remember little of it, beyond convincing Alasdair to continue without me. I was tended there by the

Hospitalier knights, though I have no memory of those months. When I came to myself again, I was so weakened that I had to learn to walk again. There were many who aided me in their kindness, not all of them Franj or Christian. I learned more than how to walk." He granted her an intent look and Leila nodded that she understood his meaning. "And yet, in all the time it took me to heal, Alasdair did not return. I asked those pilgrims and knights going to the Holy City to look for him, but none brought me word of him. He sent no message. When I was able, I went to Jerusalem myself, but it was as if Alasdair had never existed. Perhaps he had never arrived. Perhaps he had been attacked by bandits on the road, or had fallen ill himself. I hoped that he had the opportunity to make his penitence. A year after my arrival, there was a ship returning to Constantinople. At the urging of a countryman I had met, I took passage upon it, dreading even as I did so that I had left my comrade and friend behind." Calum frowned and fell silent once more.

"But you spoke of him earlier as if he yet lived."

"He does!" the older man said. "He does indeed, but when I think of those days and that choice, I believe that I failed him as a friend."

"Does he believe as much?"

"Nay, but let me continue. It was a long journey home and in my weakened state, I might not have survived without the aid of that countryman. His name was Murdoch Olafson."

"The warrior in your hall?"

"The very one, but more of that later. I returned here to Killairic, almost six years after my departure, only to learn that many believed me to be dead. Eileen was to be compelled to wed another by my brother. Only her stubborn nature and a measure of luck had ensured that she remained in command of Killairic with Fergus. My return was welcomed with much joy."

"Even by your brother?"

Calum chuckled. "I think he was glad to see his dispute with Eileen ended. It was Gille Brigte who wished to ensure the defense of Killairic, and truly, if it had been more important, Eileen's resolve would not have made the difference. My brother ensured that the holding was safe, but Gille Brigte wished for a greater guarantee. With my return, he had it and all was well."

"Did you have more sons?"

Calum shook his head. "Naught changed in that matter, at least not for the better. They told me in Caesaria that the fever would affect my ability to father children, and indeed, they were visibly relieved to learn that I already had one son. I did not believe their prognosis, but as the years passed, it became clear that they were right." He shrugged. "Saracen medical knowledge."

Leila was touched by his sadness. "Your wife must have been disappointed."

Calum nodded slowly. "It was the one argument we had, and we only had it once. She did not blame me for choosing to journey to the east, but she was bitter about the results. She called it my Saracen fever, and believed the Saracens had cheated her of more sons." He smiled a little. "If she could have seen past your faith, though, I think she would have liked you."

"That might have been a considerable challenge."

"But one that would have been good for her." Calum pursed his lips. "It is too easy to hate those we have never encountered, to see the differences between us instead of the similarities. Why do we shed so much blood in Outremer? Because we all believe Jerusalem to be a holy city. We all could worship there, but instead of tolerating each other's needs, we fight for suzerainty over a place that should be above such battles. I witnessed such kindness there, at the same time as there was ruthless slaughter."

"My uncle says our best and worst are both revealed there."

"And he is right in this, to be sure." Calum lifted a finger. "But to continue with the tale, Murdoch went home from here only to discover that his father and brother had been killed in battle, and that he had no home any longer. He has lived here ever since, and at my invitation."

"Duncan said he was a good warrior and loyal."

"He is, and his presence makes me miss Duncan a little less." Calum smiled. "Fergus was twelve summers of age when we had another guest at the gates. It was none other than my comrade, Alasdair, finally returned from Outremer. He was welcomed, of course, though I saw a new sadness in him."

"What had happened to him?"

"He had gone to Jerusalem, and he had prayed in the Church of the Holy Sepulchre. He prayed there daily for many months, both for his own forgiveness and for my recovery. So it was that he came to know several of the Knights Templar who lived there. He came to trust them and to admire them. When he sent word to Caesaria and was told that I was no longer there, he pledged himself to the Templar cause instead of returning home alone. He was an excellent swordsman and a valiant fighter, but more importantly, he was a man who could find a solution in any muddle. I have no doubt that they were glad of his skills in those times. He eventually helped to administer justice in the towns left by King Godfroi to the Church of the Holy Sepulchre."

Leila nodded understanding. She had been born in one of those villages and she saw from Calum's quick glance that he had guessed as much.

"Alasdair served several years, until three of the villages were raided and razed. He said he felt he had worked for naught at all, for he saw war returning to the region, a tide of fury as relentless as ever. Amalric of Jerusalem had led five campaigns to Egypt, but by 1169, that land was claimed by Saladin. Alasdair knew the Saracen leader would not halt until he held Jerusalem itself. It was the end of Alasdair's sworn commitment to the Templars, and so he returned home, alone. He came here first."

"Saladin conquered Jerusalem last October."

"And so they will call for another crusade," Calum said wearily. "I have heard rumors of it already. I am glad my son is home and would have him remain so."

"What of your friend? Did he return to his home and marry?"

Calum shook his head. "Not Alasdair. War changed him in another way. He lost his hope. He lives in solitude on the islands and I think he makes his peace with the past."

"Like a holy man," Leila said.

"But one who refuses to pledge to any one religion," Calum said, which was intriguing. "Service with the Templars showed him more of your kind even than I saw, and taught him a tolerance that is enviable." He pushed to his feet and went to a trunk on the far side of the hall. He opened it and removed a small rolled rug, then returned to his chair. "Alasdair brought this home with him, a gift from a man who was pleased with a solution Alasdair found to an old dispute," he said, setting it upon his knees. "He gave it to Eileen for Killairic's chapel. While she was polite in his presence, she refused to have a Saracen rug in the chapel. She said it was an insult to God to pollute a holy place with something made by an infidel." Calum shook his head then unfurled the rug, putting it on the stone floor between their chairs.

Leila caught her breath at its beauty. It was small and the colors were rich. The design was intricate and she even caught a whiff of the east snared in the fiber. She stretched out a hand in admiration and caressed the wool. "It is beautiful," she said, her voice husky.

"It is," Calum agreed. "I don't believe there can be wickedness in an item of such beauty, made with such care, and intended to allow someone to honor the divine." He bent and rolled up the rug, then offered it to Leila.

"I cannot accept such a gift."

"Whyever not? I would wager that you will welcome it beneath your knees when you say your prayers. That is its intent, and now, it has found the person to use it best." Calum urged it toward her. "Take it, Leila. Please. Take it as a wedding gift from me to you and use it in good health."

Leila accepted the gift, her chest tight. She fingered its fringe. "I thank you."

"It is so gently used that it might yet be new." Calum nodded with satisfaction. "I like that it was here, waiting for you, as if you needed a sign that this could be your home." He smiled at her. "*Inshallah.*"

As God wills it.

Leila blinked back unexpected tears. She had not expected to hear Arabic again, not so long as she was in Scotland.

"*Inshallah,*" Leila repeated softly, finding it easy to believe that she was meant to be at Killairic. She stroked the softness of the rug and inhaled deeply of the scent of the souk it still carried.

"Alasdair always comes to celebrate the Yule with us," Calum said, sipping his wine. "You can ask him more about the rug and his days in Outremer then."

The Yule. Eight months away. Leila could only hope she was still at Killairic.

Nay. She would *ensure* she would be at Killairic for the Yule. She would conceive Fergus' son by then and continue to progress in making this place her home. Surely events of this day had shown her that it could be done.

It was a miserable ride.

The weather was foul and the land was slick from the rain.

Fergus felt as if every force conspired against him and was vexed that it should be thus when he was so intent upon returning home to Leila. He wanted to show his newfound appreciation, but the elements kept him from Killairic.

His thoughts were consumed with Leila and what he had noticed this day about Isobel. It seemed he had surrendered his heart in error, and he had to acknowledge that he was relieved to not have Isobel as his wife. Those quick glances had been chilling and Fergus realized he shared Leila's view that he would sleep better when he trusted all those in the solar.

He had been wrong.

To be sure, Fergus had expected little of marriage before riding to the east. Pleasure abed. Sons. Some measure of companionship. He had assumed that the admiration and interest he felt for Isobel was the love that the troubadours sang about. He had believed their future happiness together was assured. He had thought the matter simple.

But it was not nearly so simple as that. On his journey, Fergus had seen his friends and comrades touched by a much greater passion and devotion. He knew their futures were changed by it. Though Gaston had made a marriage of convenience with Ysmaine, by the time they reached Paris, it had been clear to all but those two that their hearts were bound together forevermore.

The spark between Bartholomew and Anna had been tangible, if not hot enough to scorch a man. Fergus had not needed second sight to anticipate that they would make a match, for they challenged each other's expectations and filled each other's dreams.

Duncan, it was evident to Fergus, would do any deed to ensure that his beloved Radegunde smiled. The maid's conquest of the warrior's reluctant heart had made the man-at-arms seem twenty years younger.

Even Wulfe, a man whom Fergus had originally believed to possess no heart at all, had been smitten with Christina and ultimately had won both her hand in marriage and been named as his father's heir.

It seemed that love, a true abiding love, made marriage all the merrier. Yet having such love between man and wife might not be that common a situation, and certainly not one gained without active cultivation. Leila was not only right in yearning for it in her marriage, but offered Fergus the chance to gain it himself.

She was honest. She was honorable. He would commit himself to her and their marriage anew and strive to create the marriage she desired above all else. If she wished to wed another, Fergus would let her go for the sake of her happiness, but on this night, he wanted to win Leila's love for himself.

He also wanted to hear what the king with the faithless wife had seen in the garden.

Despite his desire for haste, their progress was slow. Fergus could not believe the quantity of mud, much less the amount the rivers and streams had swollen in the rain of this day. He and Hamish retraced their footsteps a dozen times to continue on higher ground if they did as much once. As it grew darker and the rain became more chilling, he began to wonder if they would ever arrive home again.

A warm fire was beginning to sound like a taste of paradise.

When the sun sank below the horizon and the last of the light was gone, he and Hamish urged the horses to stumble onward. They finally reached a place where the water ran shallow and Fergus nearly shouted in relief.

"Give me your reins," he said to Hamish.

"Just in case more goes awry," the boy agreed, then sneezed mightily as he followed instruction. "Truly, my lord, I cannot recall a journey of such challenge."

"Nor I."

The boy sneezed again. "Nor of such relentless cold."

"It is a far cry from the scorching heat of Jerusalem," Fergus agreed as Tempest picked his way down the bank to the stream. He let the horse choose his own path, for it was safer thus. Even so, Tempest slid several times in the mud before he stepped into the shallow water. The stallion shook his head and snorted, clearly disliking the temperature of the water. Fergus eased him on with a touch of his heel.

"When we were there, I thought I might never be cold again," Hamish said with a smile. "Now I wonder the very opposite." The boy clutched the neck of his palfrey, following Fergus' choice and trusting the pair of horses to negotiate the running water. There was an abundance of stones on the river bed and Tempest proceeded with caution. It seemed to take a thousand years to cross, but Fergus knew it was his own impatience to be home at root.

Would Leila be concerned for him? He could only imagine so. His father certainly would be, though he believed that Leila would reassure the older man. He imagined them sitting together, and Leila coaxing tales from his father, distracting Calum from the passing hours. The notion made him smile despite his discomfort.

At the deepest part of the river, the water was almost to the horse's knees, though Fergus would have wagered it had been hoof-deep that morning. Tempest balked and snorted, probably at the chill of the water, then, evidently encouraged by the proximity of the other bank, took another step.

The rocks the stallion stepped upon loosed themselves and rolled. Tempest whinnied, tossing his head as he spooked to find naught beneath his hoof. No doubt the darkness did not assist. The destrier stepped backward before Fergus could soothe him and the palfrey took exception to the proximity of the stallion's rump to her nose.

She nipped his flank, seemingly impatient with his pace. Tempest neighed in protest and bolted forward, leaping onto the shore. Fergus released the palfrey's reins as soon as he realized what the stallion was doing, but it was too late. The palfrey was compelled to step forward and stumbled in her turn, stepping into the same hole that Tempest had created. The palfrey stumbled to her knees, whinnying in indignation, and Hamish fell into the river with a splash.

Tempest spooked at the sound and galloped onward a dozen steps. Fergus leaped from the saddle and cast the reins over the destrier's head. The palfrey, much less easily disconcerted than the stallion, regained her footing, marched across the remainder of the river and climbed to the shore. She gave the destrier's flank another nip, as if to chide him for his folly. Tempest whinnied and stamped again but he did not flee.

There was some mercy, after all.

Fergus was already striding into the river, He seized Hamish, who was not injured but was struggling to get to his feet in the cold water. The boy's cloak and clothing were sodden and heavy with the weight of the water. It took some effort for even Fergus to haul him to his feet. They were both soaked by the time they reached the shore, and breathing heavily. The weight of his own wet woolen cloak made Fergus feel a handspan shorter. He removed one boot and then the other, draining the water from them, and Hamish followed suit.

"An exercise in futility," Fergus muttered, considering how wet his boots and feet were.

"We will not need a bath when we reach Killairic, sir," the boy said in an attempt at humor.

Fergus chuckled and urged him toward the horses. The pair stood with their heads down and their ears folded back, evidently also dejected by their wet state.

"On the contrary, we will be in dire need of a hot soak to drive out this chill." Fergus helped the boy into his saddle, then swung into his own. "At least we are finally on the right side of this cursed river." He looked about himself, knowing they were far uphill of the road he would have preferred, and his heart sank.

"There is a good path, sir, unless I remember incorrectly. Just there on the left."

To Fergus' delight, Hamish was right. It was not a sufficiently wide path for them to ride abreast, but it would hasten their return to Killairic. Fergus knew that they all needed to be warmed soon. "Our fortune changes for the better, Hamish," he said with cheer. "Let us ride for home with all haste."

"Aye, my lord."

"You ahead of me," Fergus instructed. "Your palfrey shows good sense so Tempest can follow her. Let her set her own pace."

As soon as they were on the path, the palfrey lifted her head. She seemed to catch the scent of home and a warm stable, for she began to canter with purpose. Tempest followed her, his nostrils flaring, and it was not long before Fergus smelled a fire.

The horses broke into a gallop just after Fergus recognized the shape of the land surrounding Killairic, then to his relief, the silhouette of the keep appeared in the distance before them. Golden light gleamed from the windows and smoke rose from the village.

"Home!" he cried.

"Home!" Hamish echoed and laughed aloud as they galloped for the gates.

CHAPTER EIGHT

he sound of the horses' hooves echoed loudly in the night. The pair splashed through puddles and flung mud with their hooves, and Fergus was certain he had never been so wet and filthy in his life.

The sentries gave a cry of welcome when they approached the gates and immediately opened one portal to them. The horses trotted through, tossing their heads with impatience and casting rain water in every direction.

"We feared you would not return this night, sir," the porter said.

"I am late, to be sure, but would not let my wife and father worry until the dawn." Fergus did not need to urge Tempest to trot toward the stables, for the stallion knew where to find food and shelter.

"The smith will have a tale for you of your wife, sir," the porter cried merrily and Fergus looked back in curiosity. He did not slow Tempest, though, who was resolved to reach the stable as soon as possible. The ostler met them at the door, his chemise hanging loose as if he had tumbled from his bed to tend the steed.

"Hamish! Here, boy!" a man shouted, and Fergus saw Farquar

waving to Hamish from outside the smithy.

"Go then, and let us all be dry as soon as possible," Fergus said to the boy. "I thank you for your company this day. I will have some hot stew sent from the kitchens for you and your aunt and uncle."

"Thank you, my lord." Hamish bowed his head and rode on to the smithy.

Fergus saw Farquar seize the palfrey's reins and lead her into the smithy, then heard his rumble of concern.

"Such a night!" Stephen declared as he guided the stallion into the middle of the stable. "And such mud! My lord, you look to have ridden through an untilled field." He divested Tempest quickly of his saddle and blanket, putting them both aside and beginning to rub down the horse. "Every item soaked beyond compare. It will take a week to see it dry!"

"It was less than an ideal day for this journey, to be sure, but my obligation is completed now," Fergus acknowledged. At a minute sound, he pivoted and caught a glimpse of a woman peering out from the stairs to the loft.

It looked like Agnes.

But the ostler had a wife. Had he imagined that face in the shadows?

When Fergus looked more closely, the maid was gone, if she had ever been there in the first place. "Are you alone this night, Stephen?"

The ostler gave Fergus a quick look. "Of course, sir. I waited for your return before going home."

Fergus frowned, for he sensed an untruth, but he said no more. He reached for a brush, but Stephen waved him off. "Go the hall, my lord, and see yourself warmed. I can manage this one well enough." Tempest tossed his head and whinnied, as if in agreement, and Fergus headed for the kitchens.

In truth, he was most intent upon seeing Leila, though there were responsibilities to be tended first. Fergus was met in the kitchens by Xavier, who chided him for taking such a risk with his health. He requested that a pot of hot venison stew be sent to the home of Hamish's aunt and uncle.

The boy should have a sip of *eau-de-vie* as well, Fergus reasoned, then continued into the hall. He smiled to see his father and Leila sitting by the fire, their heads bent together. His heart glowed that Leila had done just as he had envisioned and he was reassured to see his father at ease.

Then Leila rose to her feet, her delight clear. "Fergus!"

"Tell me you did not fear for me," he said, but she ran toward him, her concern more than clear. He caught her in his arms and held her tightly, feeling that she was trembling. "Did you not remember that I promised," he whispered into her hair.

"You promised that you would return for the evening meal," she chided, pulling back from him a bit. "Which was completed hours ago." She dropped her voice to a whisper and he saw her relief in her eyes. "I was most concerned."

"I thank you for sitting with my father, so he did not dwell upon my delay."

"He invited me to join him. He is a delight." Leila held his gaze for a moment. "And your quest?" she asked with care.

"My obligation is served," Fergus said firmly. "And I was most vexed that I could not return to hearth and wife with greater speed."

"You just wish to know what the King of Samarkand saw in his brother's garden," she teased and Fergus laughed.

"I did, indeed, though we have another matter to attend first." He bent and kissed her, intending to reassure her, and heat flared within him when she surrendered to his touch.

"Aye, I see the reason for your return!" his father teased and they ended their embrace with reluctance. Leila's eyes were sparkling in her relief, and Fergus resolved in that moment to spend the night showing her the extent of his regard for her.

She plucked at his cloak, disapproval replacing her fear. "You are wet to your very marrow, sir." She turned and clapped her hands. "Iain, my lord must have a very hot bath, if you please," she said slowly, her Gaelic perfect, and Iain nodded agreement.

"Thank goodness you yet have a measure of *eau-de-vie*," she continued in French to Fergus. "It will drive away the chill."

"My thoughts, exactly," he agreed. "They are sending venison stew for Hamish, and he should have a measure as well."

"Of course," Leila agreed. "Go and sit with your father by the fire. I shall manage it all."

"Thank you."

Leila smiled then hastened up the stairs to fetch his flask. Fergus watched her, liking her reliability as much as her practicality, then joined his father. The fire was wonderfully warm and after embracing his father, he stretched out his hands to the blaze.

"There is more than one way for a man to warm himself," his father teased.

"You will have your grandson soon enough, Father."

"I am old," his father complained good-naturedly. "I have earned the right to be impatient."

They chuckled together as Leila came back down the stairs. She poured Fergus a cup of *eau-de-vie*, then carried the flask to the kitchens after insisting upon Fergus remaining where he was. She orchestrated all exactly as he would have done, and he liked that their thoughts were as one.

He sipped of the liquid and it sent a welcome heat through him. Indeed, he caught his breath at the vigor of it, then recalled Leila's words.

"What does she mean, I yet have measure of *eau-de-vie*?" he asked his father, belatedly realizing what she had said. "Have you been indulging in it?"

"Nay, not me." Calum grinned that Fergus was mystified. "By all accounts, Lady Leila encouraged Nellie to walk again today and has won the avid support of Farquar in so doing."

"And what has that to do with my *eau-de-vie*?"

"I believe it was part of the solution."

Fergus pursed his lips. "They say it has the power to raise the dead."

His father scoffed. "Not that. It merely proves if a man is dead. If he fails to cough or respond when that is poured down his throat, there is no point in wasting more. Nay, Lady Leila used it to clean the hoof of the plow horse, from what I am told."

"They do use it in medicines in the east," Fergus recalled.

"Aye, and she seems to know much of it. Your wife has been busy this day, my son." Calum nodded with approval, drinking the last mouthful of wine. "I like her well, Fergus. You could have done much worse."

"Indeed," Fergus agreed.

"How fares Isobel?"

"She is married and pregnant," Fergus replied. "And perhaps less than I remembered her to be."

"Perhaps less than you wanted her to be." Their gazes met for a moment of understanding. "Do not blame yourself. I thought she had more merit in those days, as well. There was no one more shocked than me when we heard of the wedding." His father patted his arm just as Leila reappeared, then directed the boys who carried buckets of steaming water to the solar. "Do not sacrifice the gem in pursuit of the glimmer, Fergus."

"Nay, I will not be such a fool as that." Fergus smiled and clasped his father's hand tightly. "My father, you see, taught me what is of import in this life."

Calum chuckled contentedly and pointed to the solar above. Fergus laughed at his teasing, but he rose and bade his father good night. He took the stairs three at a time, determined to show Leila his newfound appreciation of her and her charms.

There was something different about Fergus. Leila noted immediately the glow in his eyes and tasted the heat in his kiss. She could not name the cause, but she cared less for the reason than the change itself. He regarded her as if she was a marvel, as if she was the sole woman he desired, and his expression made her heart thunder.

What had happened this day? Perhaps they had defeated some peril on their journey, one that had made his return all the sweeter. Leila wondered if he would ever confide it in her. She scarcely dared to hope that Isobel had proven herself to be unworthy. Nay, Fergus would love a woman forever once his heart was surrendered.

Leila was desperately curious, but she reminded herself sternly to accept what she was granted and not be greedy for more.

To have Fergus intent upon her had been her dream. Demanding the reason for his newfound attention might dismiss it, and Leila did not intend to risk that.

He followed her to the solar much sooner than she had anticipated, and the boys hurried to fill the tub. A steaming bowl of stew and a cup of ale had been brought from the kitchens for Fergus and awaited him. Leila was still lighting candles and coaxing the coals in the brazier to burn with greater enthusiasm when her husband appeared.

Though her mouth went dry at the sight of him in the portal, she spoke quickly. "I fear all is not yet prepared, my lord."

"Where is Agnes?"

"She was overly tired today, so I dismissed her after the evening meal."

"She is not in the kitchens."

Leila flicked a glance at the boys and they departed with their empty buckets. "I am not her keeper, Fergus."

He laughed. "Nay, only her tormentor. I found it curious that she would have left the hall on such a night as this."

"Perhaps she sleeps in some corner."

Fergus sobered. "I thought I saw her, actually. At the stables."

"Truly?" Leila could make no sense of that. "Why would she be there?"

"I do not know. Perhaps I was mistaken." He smiled again and came to her, his gaze warm upon her. "Neither of us wish to talk about Agnes," he said quietly and Leila smiled.

"I am glad to find that we are in agreement, my lord."

"You owe me more of that tale," Fergus reminded her. "The one of the queen in the garden," he added. "But it will have to wait."

"Indeed?"

"Indeed." Fergus lifted a hand to Leila's cheek, his caress making her tingle. He let his fingertips trail down her throat, then arched a brow when he found the cord with the two keys. "I have had good advice that we should lock the portal," he whispered, bending to kiss her beneath her ear.

Leila closed her eyes and sighed contentment at the touch of his lips upon her skin. "An excellent idea," she murmured in agreement.

Fergus slid his fingers into her hair and cupped her nape, tipping her face up to his so that her circlet and veil fell away. Leila did not care, for his mouth closed over hers in a most satisfactory way. He deepened his kiss as he had not in the hall and she leaned against him, welcoming his touch. His kiss was both languid and fiery, as if he had all the time in the world to sample her and coax her passion. There was a new demand in it, and Leila was fiercely glad.

Whatever had happened to cause the change.

When Fergus lifted his head, her heart was pounding and his eyes were shining. She raised her fingertips to the pulse at his throat and he captured her hand, then kissed her palm, never breaking his gaze. "My beautiful wife," he murmured and Leila's heart fluttered. "I hear you made a conquest of Farquar the smith this day."

She smiled at the recollection. "He was most concerned about Nellie, the plow horse, and her injured hoof. I was lucky that my uncle's solutions worked as well as they did, but of course, I will check upon her on the morrow."

"You might sleep late on the morrow," Fergus murmured, his lips tracing a beguiling path over her cheek. Leila nodded, knowing it was a distinct possibility if her husband was amorous.

Fergus lifted the cord with the keys over Leila's head, brushed his lips across hers, then strode across the chamber to lock the door. She missed the heat of his presence immediately, but the look he cast her from the portal sent new fire through her.

Leila caught her breath, for the solar felt smaller and more intimate, simply because the door was locked. "You should bathe before the water cools," she said, hearing the tension in her own voice.

"I would bathe with you."

"I am sure the tub is not large enough."

"I am sure it is. You are tiny, after all." Fergus smiled and held her gaze as he shed his boots. He stood them by one brazier. His cloak had been cast over a bench in the hall, and Leila knew she should help him to disrobe. Instead she found herself watching as each increment of flesh was revealed. His leather jerkin was the first to be removed, though it was dark with water as well. He unbuckled his belt and laid it aside, then unwound the length of wet plaid. She made to take it from him, even as she admired his legs, but Fergus waved her off.

"It is too heavy in this wet state," he said and spread it upon the clean floor. His chemise was cast aside next, and he wrung it out with a grimace before leaving it with the plaid. Leila watched the muscles ripple in his arms and shoulders as he moved, and felt her mouth go dry. His braies were abandoned then and he stood nude before her. His tan was fading, she noted, but he looked no less vital than he had when first she had met him.

And no less alluring, to be sure.

He smiled slowly and took a step closer. "I wanted you to know how I missed you," he murmured. "And what prospect sustained me on this day."

"I thought you would bathe to drive the chill away."

Fergus chuckled. "There is more than one way to do that."

There was a twinkle lurking in his eyes and she glanced down, blushing a little at the sign of his enthusiasm for their night together. He came to her then, kissing her cheek as he untied the sides of her kirtle with gentle fingers. The garment was quickly discarded and her chemise after it, a little growl of pleasure emitted by Fergus as he locked his hands around her waist and lifted her for his kiss. He held her fast against his chest, teasing and tasting her, keeping her captive to his salute, and Leila flung her arms around his neck, wanting only more. She liked the feel of his chest hair against her breasts and the strength of his grip upon her. She liked the new hunger in his kiss best of all, and the feel of his erection against her belly.

She thought when he took a step that he would go to the bath, but instead, she found herself cast atop the furs on the bed. Fergus laughed at her surprise, then claimed one of her ankles. "You cannot bathe in your stockings," he chided, casting away her shoe. He bent and untied the garter with his teeth, his eyes gleaming and his breath sending delicious shivers over her thigh. Leila shivered as he slowly smoothed the stocking down with one hand. His palm was warm against her skin and he followed the stocking's course with a row of kisses.

He removed the other with the same attention to detail and Leila was certain they would then savor the bath. Instead, Fergus eased atop her, his shoulders between her knees, and caught her hands in his own. He laced their fingers together, smiled with such purpose that Leila wondered at his intent, then bent to kiss that most intimate spot.

She gasped in pleasure and surprise.

He chuckled, then caressed her with his tongue. He teased her, moving so slowly that Leila feared she would die of anticipation. The furs were soft beneath her, Fergus was warm and strong atop her, and the pleasure he conjured from deep within her was more intoxicating than *eau-de-vie*. She heard herself moan in pleasure as she never had before, but he was relentless in his assault. He coaxed her passion steadily, making her want him more with every passing moment, ensuring that she murmured incoherently and clutched at his hands. But two nights in his bed and she was convinced that no man ever would love her with such diligence as Fergus.

She cried out his name when the pleasure erupted, locking her legs around him and holding his hands so tightly that her nails dug into his flesh. Her heart was racing as if she had run a league, but Fergus smiled down at her, evidently as satisfied as she was.

"You cannot have thought all day of doing that," she charged and he laughed.

"You think not?" He kissed one of her palms then placed her hand upon his shoulder. He did the same with the other, easing himself atop her so slowly that she smiled in anticipation.

"You thought of this, perhaps," she teased, then gasped as he eased inside her.

"I thought of both," Fergus admitted. He wiped his mouth, then bent to kiss her ear, carefully holding his weight above her. "I thought of my lady wife crying out my name as she found her pleasure," he whispered. "And I schemed how I might best convince her to do as much."

"Your plan succeeded, and did so very well."

Fergus shook his head, slowly moving deeper. Leila arched her back to welcome him. "I think it a scheme that should be tested again to prove its merit," he rumbled and she laughed despite herself.

"How many times?"

"A dozen," he said, looking into her eyes. He looked content and confident, his eyes gleaming. Leila thought of a predator making his claim and was more than glad to be the object of his affections and attentions.

She shook her head. "That will not be sufficient to gauge its reliability," she said solemnly and was rewarded by the flash of his smile.

"Nightly?"

"Perhaps daily, as well."

He chuckled, then moved so deliberately within her that she gasped in pleasure. Her reaction clearly pleased him for he repeated his movement and Leila allowed herself to moan. "I love that sound, Leila," he said, his voice turning rough. "I vow to make you moan nightly for the duration of our handfast."

Leila ignored the mention of the end of their time together and smiled at him instead. Indeed, she made good progress at capturing his attention and in this moment, could only hope for the best. "And what if I seek a similar sound from you?"

"It would only be gracious to allow you the opportunity," he acknowledged.

Leila laughed. She rose against him and urged him to his back, straddling him as she sat atop him. She smiled at him as she reached down to caress him, then moved with exquisite slowness. She managed three strokes before Fergus closed his eyes and moaned, the sound seeming to come from the depths of his soul.

Then he seized her waist, urging her to move more quickly. She leaned over him, liking how his strength rubbed against her, and caught his face in her hands. She captured his mouth beneath her own and kissed him, showing the same enthusiasm as he in their recent kisses. Fergus growled with pleasure, and Leila felt her own passion rising again. She felt the beat of his heart against her own and the heat emanating from his skin. She kissed him as if she might never have another chance to do as much, nearly devouring him as he drove her to the height of pleasure again.

They cried out in unison as Leila found her release. She realized that she was shaking in the wake of the tumult they had summoned.

Fergus exhaled unsteadily and held her close, his heart thundering beneath her cheek and his fingers threaded into her hair. Leila felt treasured and cherished, and could scarce draw a breath that all seemed to come aright so soon.

"Welcome home, Fergus," she whispered, and he chuckled.

"Aye, this is home," he said with satisfaction. He kissed her temple, then stood, lifting her into his arms as he abandoned the bed. "And now, that bath seems a most welcome notion."

"I fear it has cooled," Leila said.

Fergus held her against his chest, and stepped over the lip of the tub with ease. "It is perfect," he said, then lowered himself and Leila into the water. She ended up seated in his lap, the water around their shoulders. A little of it did slosh over the side of the tub, but Fergus did not seem to care. He smiled down into her eyes as he claimed the cloth and the soap, then kissed her once again before they set to washing each other.

Leila was thrilled that unlike the night before, her husband did not turn away once he had had his satisfaction. Indeed, Fergus gave her his undivided attention and she could desire naught more.

"And now the tale," Fergus invited, when they were nestled together in the great bed. He was clean and tired and warm. His wife was curled beside him and his belly was full. He had not known such contentment in a long time.

"Where were we?" Leila asked.

He pressed a kiss to Leila's temple. "Shahzenan had looked out of his window to see the queen enter the garden with her ladies to take their pleasure. The queen had clapped her hands and they had cast off their veils." He gave her a look. "And he was astonished..."

Leila smiled, evidently pleased that he remembered her tale so clearly. "And he was astonished to see that half of the attendants were men in disguise."

Fergus feigned shock. "She had not hidden men in her harem?"

"She had!" Leila said, laughing at him merrily. "Shahzenan was even more shaken to see how the queen and her ladies took their pleasure in the garden. 'At least I am not alone in being so betrayed,' he said to himself, and wondered if he should tell his brother."

"Of course, he should," Fergus said without hesitation. "A man should know when he has been deceived." Was this the point of her tale? To make him aware that Isobel had deceived him? If so, the lesson was learned already, but still, he would listen.

Leila nodded. "That night, after the two kings had dined and shared tales of the hunt, Shahriar again asked for the reason for Shahzenan's sadness. This time, Shahzenan confided in him, and the brothers commiserated over the faithlessness of Shahzenan's queen. 'Gladly, I am not so unfortunate,' declared Shahriar. 'And you can take hope in the good conduct of my queen.' Shahzenan frowned instead of agreeing. His brother asked for an explanation and Shahzenan told him what he had seen that day. In truth, he was relieved to have the opportunity, for he did not wish to have secrets between them. Shahriar did not believe the tale and insisted that Shahzenan had misinterpreted what he had seen. He defended his wife most vigorously and Shahzenan offered to show him the truth. They resolved upon a plan to prove the queen's guilt or innocence: the next day, they would ride out with the hunting party but return to the palace in disguise and see what the queen did in the garden."

"Do you mean to teach me that all women are faithless, Leila?"

"Only that trust can be misplaced," she said, casting a glance at him.

Fergus smiled, liking that she tried to warn him. "And what did they see?"

"And so, the two brothers followed their scheme. They rode out with the hunting party, but then turned back and entered the city alone together and in disguise. They returned to the wing of the palace built for Shahzenan and went to the same window. No sooner had they arrived then the queen appeared in the garden with her ladies. As the day before, they were twenty in all. As the day before, the queen clapped and all cast off their veils. As the day before, half of the party were revealed to be men in disguise. The queen laughed and beckoned to one man, just as she had the day before, and took her pleasure in the garden while her husband was away."

"Did he execute her, as his brother had killed his own wife?" Did she expect him to avenge himself upon Isobel with such violence?

"He did," Leila agreed. "He called for the guards and he condemned his wife for her faithlessness. He confronted them all in the garden, so they had no time to hide their deeds. The guards killed the ladies and the men, but the king himself executed his queen with his own sword. He grieved her loss as much as her betrayal, for he had loved her completely, never guessing her treachery."

Fergus nodded understanding of that. "He felt like a fool."

"I would wager that he did. In fact, Shahriar did not sleep after his brother returned to his kingdom. He strove to derive a scheme for his own satisfaction and one sleepless night, he did just that. His vizier was summoned the following morning and informed that Shahriar would never be betrayed by a wife again. He had resolved to marry a virgin each day, savor her that night, and have her executed with the dawn. The vizier noted that this would turn the people against him but the king was adamant that his will would be done. Shahriar married the first virgin that very day, but any hope that he might recant his plan was lost when she was executed at his command the following dawn."

"Surely this did not continue," Fergus said, wondering at the import of this story.

"Surely, it did, though the vizier found it troubling indeed. That man was even more troubled when there were no more virgins to be found in the city, for the king had married and killed each and every one. The vizier was at a loss as to what to do, but the eldest of his own daughters suggested a solution. Her name was Scheherazade and she was both lovely and clever. Though he had two daughters, Scheherazade was the light of his life, so he was appalled when she offered to wed the king next. The vizier argued with his beloved daughter, for he knew that he should be the one compelled to order her execution. She was adamant, though, and in frustration, he cried 'Your folly will take you to your ruin! I fear that your fate will be like that of the donkey, who did not appreciate what it had.' Scheherazade asked what had happened to the donkey, so her father, the vizier, told her the tale."

Fergus smiled and settled back to listen.

"Once, there was a merchant who had the gift of understanding the language of all creatures. The sole caveat was that he was forbidden to reveal to others what he had heard. The price for him doing as much was his own death." Leila took a breath. "And so it was that one day, he was in his own stables, where he had a donkey and an ox. He heard the ox say to the donkey 'I wish I had your good fortune! All that is ever required of you is to carry our master on short journeys and not every day. If he stayed at home, you would have a life of leisure. I, on the other hand, must labor hard, each and every day. I am harnessed to the plow at dawn, beaten while I work all day, return here only when darkness falls, am fed dry beans and left to sleep in dirty straw.'"

"Did the donkey give him advice?"

"Indeed, he did. The donkey chided his companion and gave him advice. 'You are used thus because you allow it to be so. You have horns! Nature has given you the means to gain respect, but you do not use them. The master has need of you to till the fields. It is only reasonable that you demand the respect you deserve. When they give you beans, do not eat them. I predict your situation will change with speed if you take my advice.' The ox thought upon this and thanked the donkey for his counsel. The pair then fell silent and the merchant retired to his bed."

"I will wager that matters were different the next day," Fergus said.

"Indeed!" Leila agreed. "The ox was difficult all the day long, as the plowman complained to the merchant. The ox even charged the plowman once, then refused to eat the beans he was given. The plowman told the merchant all of this, and was much vexed with the creature. The merchant, though, saw that the ox followed the advice he had been given by the donkey. He advised the plowman to leave the ox in his stall the following day and give him better fare, for the beast might be ill. He suggested that the plowman hitch the donkey to the plow instead."

Fergus laughed.

"And so the donkey was tethered to the plow and compelled to work hard all the day long. He was beaten when he slowed down. He finally returned to the stable when it was dark and he was exhausted. He was also furious that he had been so treated. The ox, meanwhile, had rested all the day long and was much pleased with the situation. That night, he thanked the donkey for his suggestions."

"Did the merchant hear their conversation?" Fergus asked.

"He did. You are right. I omitted to say that he had gone to the stable, specifically to hear their exchange. He heard the ox thank the donkey. The donkey then asked the ox what he intended to do the following day, and the ox said he would continue to do as the donkey had instructed. 'I would advise you otherwise,' the donkey said. 'For this night, I heard the master say that if the ox was ill, he was of no use. He advised the plowman to send you to the butcher if you were not hale in the morning.' The ox was much gratified to hear of this plan and vowed that he would be both robust and cooperative in the morning, as if he had healed completely from whatever ailed him."

"Clever donkey," Fergus said.

"Not so clever as that, for his day of labor had left him half-dead from exhaustion."

"For he did not appreciate his own good fortune," Fergus said, pulling her a little closer. "Whereas I do."

Leila's smile was brilliant. "The merchant reasoned that both ox and donkey had learned their lessons, and all continued as it should have done. The vizier, upon concluding his tale, said again that his daughter was like the donkey and failed to see the advantages of her life."

"And so Shahriar was vexed?"

"Nay, nay. Scheherazade was unswayed by her father's tale. In fact, she even appealed to the king himself that he should take her as his wife—and once Shahriar saw her beauty and grace, he had to possess her. The king reminded the vizier that if he married Scheherazade, she would be killed in the morning, and vowed that if the vizier failed in this duty, he would be killed himself. The vizier wept, but Scheherazade married the king with a smile."

Leila paused.

"And?" Fergus invited.

"And they married, and they retired to the king's chambers, and Shahriar possessed his new wife with great pleasure. Yet when he would have slept, Scheherazade asked if she could see her sister one last time before she died. The king could not deny her such a request, and so, the younger daughter of the vizier, Dinarzade, was summoned to the king's chambers. When she arrived and the sisters embraced, Dinarzade asked Scheherazade to tell a story. 'For you tell stories better than anyone I ever have known, and this will be my very last chance to enjoy your talent.' Scheherazade appealed to the king, who was intrigued, then with his permission, she began."

Fergus could have listened to Leila all night long. This Scheherazade was not the sole one with a talent for telling stories.

"Once, she said, there was a rich merchant who undertook a long journey across the desert to another city. He packed some dates and water for his trip, and reached his destination without incident. He concluded his business, then made similar preparations for his return. On the third day of his ride toward home, he stopped to eat and refresh himself. He ate his allotment of dates, and flung the stones into the desert. He had a sip of water, then he washed himself and knelt to pray. He was not yet done his prayers when an enormous djinn appeared before him. The djinn had a flowing white beard, rage in his eyes, and he brandished a sword. 'Rise up!' he roared. 'For I must take your life in exchange for that of my son.'"

"His son?"

"The merchant was as mystified as you, Fergus. He protested that he had killed no one, but the djinn insisted otherwise. He said that he did not know the djinn's son so could not have killed him. The djinn asked if he had thrown date stones into the desert, and the merchant had to admit that he had. 'One of those stones hit my son in the eye and he died of it,' the djinn charged. 'Stand up that I may kill you in exchange.' The merchant begged forgiveness and pleaded for mercy. He offered to do whatever the djinn wished in exchange, but the djinn would accept nothing less than his death. The djinn raised his blade and the merchant closed his eyes."

Leila fell silent and Fergus touched her hand. "But what happened?"

"Ah, Scheherazade saw that the sky was turning pink so she ceased her tale. Her sister begged her to continue, but she indicated the rising sun and said that the time had come for her to be executed. 'But he cannot have died, alone in the desert with a djinn,' Dinarzade protested. Scheherazade agreed that would have been unjust and smiled a little. 'Indeed, the story is a marvel of his cleverness,' she said, casting down her gaze in acceptance of her fate. 'I regret that there is no time to tell you of it.' Dinarzade then appealed to the king, imploring him to let Scheherazade live another night that they might hear the end of the tale. Shahriar was similarly intrigued, so he agreed."

"And so she had a reprieve. How clever," Fergus said.

"The vizier had been awake all the night long, fearful of his daughter's fate. To his relief, the king never gave the order for Scheherazade's execution, but conducted his business that day as was customary. The couple retired that night to the king's chambers again, and after their intimacy, Scheherazade again asked to enjoy her sister's company one last time. Dinarzade did not have to ask for more of the story, for Shahriar himself demanded that Scheherazade finish the tale of the merchant and the djinn as soon as Dinarzade was seated. And so she continued, that the djinn had lifted his blade to execute the merchant when the merchant cried out."

Leila bit her lip and ceased her tale again.

Fergus smiled down at her. "Is this your ploy?" he asked. "To enchant me with a tale each night?"

"You came back from Dunnisbrae," she said.

"Surely, you did not fear otherwise?" He saw in her eyes,

though, that she had doubted his return. He touched his lips to her brow, knowing he must ensure that she never had such fears again. "And yet you leave another tale unfinished. You cannot expect me to have you executed at dawn?" he asked, his tone teasing.

Leila laughed. "I should hope not," she said with a smile. "For then you would not know how the merchant escaped the djinn's wrath." Her eyes sparkled, then she rolled over, cuddled against him and fell asleep.

Fergus grinned, knowing full well that Leila's concerns were unfounded. He was not like the donkey, for he appreciated the blessings that had come to his hand. He had the better part of a year to convince Leila that he was the best husband for her. He pulled up the covers and settled down to sleep, certain they had made a very good start.

FRIDAY, APRIL 29, 1188

Feast Day of
Saint Hugh of Cluny

Claire Delacroix

CHAPTER NINE

ergus dreamed of a storm of uncommon ferocity. Dark clouds tumbled across the night sky toward Killairic, lightning bolts erupting from their bellies as the wind rose to a tempest. He cried out a warning, but his words were snatched away, just as the pennant at the summit of Killairic's tower was ripped free.

The cloud descended with fury upon the keep, the rain hammering upon its roof. The moat was flooded by the onslaught and he saw both children and animals swept away. The mill was deluged and the nets containing the eels were broken. Buildings and roofs collapsed, and stores of grain were claimed by the river that was consuming the keep. All the wealth of Killairic was flowing down to the firth and there was nothing Fergus could do to stop it. It seemed that he alone was left to stand fast against the storm.

Horses shrieked as lightning struck the high tower and the roof burst into flame even as the sound of the thunder made the ground shake beneath his feet. He saw the glow of the fire descending into the tower, doubtless igniting the stairs and the floors as it journeyed to the heart of the keep.

He heard the screams of those trapped within the keep, caught between fire and water, but he could only watch the destruction of all his father had built. He raced through the village, seizing one child or another, each one torn from his grasp. He tried to dam the flow of the water, but the raging stream leaped every barrier he created. He tried to reach those in the keep, but water kept him from them.

Where was Leila?

Where was his father?

Where was the reliquary he had vowed to defend?

It was a horrific nightmare and Fergus knew in his heart that this was the threat he had dreaded since Jerusalem. The complete loss of his home and his legacy, his wife and his family, never mind his own inability to save any of it, was his worst fear come true. He felt powerless and was infuriated by his own failure to defend what mattered most to him.

He roared in his fury and tried again to reach the portal to the keep. The dark cold waters rolled over him and drove him beneath the surface. When he rose sputtering, he had been swept downstream and the water was carrying him onward. He could not even touch the bottom, and he could not swim in the deluge. He was flung against some obstacle with such vigor that the breath was forced from him, then he took a mouthful of river water. Someone hauled him to the shore, someone with a fierce grip. He shook the water out of his eyes to find Isobel bending over him, her eyes shining with triumph.

"Mine," she said with force, then opened her mouth. He saw her tongue become an asp and she laughed at his horror. She gestured to the sky and another bolt of lightning struck distant Killairic, setting the protective wall afire before Fergus' eyes.

"A man can only love once," she told him, her eyes shining in a way he did not trust. "And you swore to love *me*."

Then she kissed him, her mouth locking over his as if she would claim his very soul. Fergus fought against her unholy grip and flung her aside, astonished that he could have erred so greatly.

"Isobel!" he shouted in anguish, wishing he could change the past.

He awakened, cold sweat on his back and his heart racing, the linens clenched in his fists.

"Fergus," Leila whispered, her small hands upon his shoulders. She shook him. "Fergus! You are safe."

She was right.

Fergus exhaled. He was in the solar at Killairic, safe and warm, the candles gutted and the fires in the braziers burning low. The rain pattered lightly on the roof, the fury of the earlier storm passed, and he took a steadying breath.

And his wife was beside him, concern in her eyes. Fergus took Leila's hand in his and kissed her knuckles, willing his heart to slow. "It was only a dream," he said with relief. "I am sorry I awakened you."

Leila smiled and said that it was naught. Still shaken, Fergus drew her against his warmth and nestled them both beneath the covers and pelts, savoring the sweet curve of her against him. He remembered his dream with perfect clarity and wondered what it meant. How could Isobel put Killairic at risk? She was no sorceress and he could not dispel the image of the snake.

His dream—or perhaps his guardian angel—was telling him that Isobel was untrustworthy and Fergus knew better than to ignore a warning such as that.

Leila could not sleep after Fergus' dream. She lay with him, his arm around her waist, listening as his breathing slowed.

Isobel.

He had called out for Isobel.

Which meant that Leila had hoped for too much too soon. She thought Fergus had changed his thinking about his former betrothed, that his journey to Dunnisbrae had strengthened his resolve to make their handfast a success. She assumed that Isobel was happy in her match, or that she had spurned him, or that something had occurred to dismiss Fergus' regard for the other woman upon seeing her again.

But still Isobel claimed his dreams.

Perhaps his passion this night had been fueled by the sight of his beloved and was not prompted by Leila. The notion was a disturbing one, as was the possibility that she was mistaken in her understanding of her husband. She felt in the darkness of the night that she had wedded a stranger and cast her life down a path fraught with uncertainties.

Sleep was impossible. Leila recalled every observation, every word, every gesture, seeking a solution to the riddle of winning her husband's heart. What was the root of Fergus' terror? That he would lose his beloved forever? Leila could not bear to think about it, and yet she could not cease to think of it. It seemed that her efforts to gain allies at Killairic and make a new home in this place were doomed to failure, if Fergus could not see her merit.

Would she win the loyalty of his father, of his smith, of those in his village, but not his own regard? It was an unreasonable possibility. What if she was already with child? Leila considered her future and did not care for the view.

Leila had never been one overly inclined to prayer and certainly she had been remiss in her routine on the journey from Jerusalem. But she had to believe that Calum's gift had been a timely reminder. She would continue to fight for her desire and to take steps toward its achievement, but she had need of strength for the battle.

When the sky began to lighten in the east, she slipped from the bed. She washed and dressed, quickly and in silence, then took the small rug Calum had given to her and left the solar. She hesitated a moment, then locked the door behind herself, reasoning that she would be back before Fergus awakened.

She was glad of her choice, for she saw Agnes sleeping on a pallet in the kitchens. She continued to the garden, where the plants were lush and wet after the rain.

There was a stone bench there, aligned with the rising sun. Leila spread her small rug over it and kneeled to pray. With all her heart, she hoped that her husband would come to love her, though on this morning, it seemed that a miracle would be required for that to occur.

Fergus awakened to a knocking upon the solar door. Leila was gone and he was alone in the great bed.

"My lady?" Agnes said from the other side of the door. "Would you like to bathe, my lady?"

Fergus swung out of bed and dug in his baggage for fresh braies. "Agnes?" he asked as he went to the door.

"Aye, my lord. I am sorry for I did not mean to disturb you..."

Fergus tried the latch but the door was locked.

Of course. He sighed and pushed a hand through his hair. "My lady has taken the key with her, Agnes. Could you find her, please?"

"Of course, my lord. Right away, my lord."

Fergus leaned back against the door as Agnes' steps sounded on the stairs. He appreciated that Leila was protective of the reliquary, but they were home, not forced to take shelter in an inn where they knew none of the other occupants. Even so, it was locked securely in the treasury, so there was little need for the solar to be locked as well.

He had seen Leila's resolve, though, and wanted her to have time to gain confidence in those who lived at Killairic. Doubtless, she was winning hearts already this morn, while he lingered abed. Had he ever met a woman of such determination? Fergus smiled, knowing he had not and feeling blessed that Leila was his wife. He would have the silversmith copy the keys this very day and surrender one to his father's care.

Leila should find that acceptable.

In the meantime, he yawned mightily and returned to bed. It was too early to rise after his ride of the day before, so Fergus burrowed beneath the pelts and covers. He thought fleetingly of his nightmare, but then he smelled the scent of Leila's pleasure, smiled and fell asleep with contentment.

Leila.

By the time she finished her prayers, Leila was aware that she was no longer alone.

She stood and rolled up the small rug, before turning. It was Murdoch who leaned against the wall of the keep, his gaze bright and watchful. He stepped out of the shadows and bowed, clearly not wishing to surprise her.

But surprise her, he did, for he addressed her in Arabic.

"Good morning, Lady Leila."

Leila was struck by a bout of yearning for her uncle's home that nearly took her to her knees again. She straightened and returned the warrior's greeting, reminding herself that Killairic would now be her home.

She stifled her doubts.

"At the risk of impertinence, I would suggest you turn a little more to the right. Mecca is further south than you seem to believe."

Leila blinked, then remembered Calum's story. "You journeyed from Palestine with my lord husband's father."

"I did, though I was there many more years than he." His expression lightened but he did not exactly smile. "Long enough to learn your tongue."

"You speak it well."

"And yet I fear I have forgotten much. I beg your indulgence."

"You have it, surely." Leila made to return to the keep, but Murdoch stepped forward. Her gaze flew to his face, though she found his expression inscrutable.

"In truth, I sought the opportunity to speak with you."

Leila had a moment to realize that they were alone, that no one knew her location and that she knew little of this man before Murdoch cleared his throat and continued.

"Calum is a good man and a better laird," he said quietly. "But his health is not what it was."

"I would not think of his demise," Leila said. "He has been good to me, and I like him well."

"As do many, yet his passing will come. I do not wish for it, either, but I would have you know the challenge before you."

"Challenge?" Leila did not understand.

"What do you believe will happen to Killairic when Calum leaves this world?"

Leila frowned. "Surely it is the legacy of my lord husband..." She fell silent when Murdoch shook his head, his gaze unswerving.

"Killairic was granted to Calum by the king."

"And now it is his, surely?"

"It is the king's," Murdoch said, his expression intent.

"Then it is not my husband's legacy?"

"It might be, or it might not." The warrior looked over the hills to the firth and England beyond, his eyes narrowed. "Is it true that Jerusalem is fallen?"

"Saladin reclaimed it, aye."

"And the King of England would call for a crusade to retrieve it?"

"We heard that rumor in France and England as well. The French king means to join him in that effort, by all accounts."

Murdoch nodded. "Do you think it likely that a king who called for a crusade to evict the infidels from Jerusalem would entrust a holding upon his borders..."

"To a man wedded to the enemy," Leila finished, then sat down upon the bench. She knotted her hands together in her lap, hating that she could be the obstacle to Fergus keeping his home.

"I do not," Murdoch said softly.

"Nor do I," Leila agreed.

She watched him look past her to the village, his gaze sharpening on something there. She twisted on the bench and saw the priest outside the chapel, sweeping the steps free of the debris that must have gathered there in the storm. The sunlight seemed to touch the cross on the roof of the building as she watched the priest and Leila made up her mind.

She turned back to Murdoch, who appeared to be waiting for her decision. "I was born and raised in one of the villages claimed by King Godfroi and surrendered to the command of the Holy Sepulchre after his death. More importantly, I grew up in a household much concerned with tolerance. There were Christians serving in my uncle's household."

"Rūm not Franj," Murdoch guessed.

"Aye, their kin were from Constantinople and Antioch. The wife of one told stories that were common to both faiths, like the Seven Sleepers, to my cousin and me. My uncle was much enamored of the works of Abū Alī ibn Sīnā, both in matters of medicine and the nature of the soul."

"They call him Avicenna here. His works are known in some circles."

"I understand that it would be of aid to Fergus if I changed faith," Leila said with care. "But I would not imperil my immortal soul without understanding fully what I do." She gestured to the priest. "It is unlikely that I can speak to this man, or understand him with sufficient accuracy to discuss such matters."

Murdoch bowed. "I would be delighted to be your servant in this, my lady. Though I am not a religious man myself, I believe I could translate for you."

"This is what you came to propose to me," Leila guessed, seeing that he was not surprised.

Murdoch nodded and the barest smile curved his lips. "I would see the succession of Killairic assured, my lady. It is possible that you will soon conceive a child, which would be good, but I would not have such a detail put all at risk."

Leila nodded. "I thank you, Murdoch. Yours is good counsel and I appreciate that you dared to offer it, though I cannot say what the result will be. Not yet."

He bowed again. "*Inshallah*," he said and Leila smiled.

"*Inshallah*," she agreed. She hastened back to the solar then, intent upon leaving her rug there and greeting her husband.

There was no doubt that Fergus had married well.

Everywhere he went that day in the village, praise of his lady was in the air. The smith, Farquar, was uncharacteristically fulsome in his admiration and showed Fergus how the dapple plow horse, Nellie, already improved her gait. Leila had evidently been there before Fergus to check on her charge, as well, a circumstance that impressed Farquar as much as the lady's knowledge.

He had the keys copied by the silversmith, lingering with that man while a mold was made and the metal poured. He chatted with the silversmith, who had always possessed an excellent memory, and caught up on births, deaths, and gossip in the village. The miller had died after the marriage of his son, and the silversmith hinted that the younger man was overwhelmed with his responsibilities. His wife had borne a son and was with child again, and the silversmith noted the demands of infants. Fergus resolved to send Hamish to assist him, under the guise of learning more about the milling of grain.

He then made a visit to Margaret, only to hear more praise of his wife. Margaret was very happy with the needles and thanked him for his gift. Margaret and her girls were busily sewing and he was pleased to see the cloth he had brought home being so expertly shaped into garments for Leila. They agreed upon the suitability of the colors and how they would flatter his wife, and Margaret reminded him that the old midwife had died in his absence.

"I would wager, my lord, that you might wish to find another before the winter," Margaret said, keeping her gaze fixed upon her work. Fergus knew she felt she was speaking out of turn.

"Because my lady may conceive?" he asked gently.

Margaret nodded. "She is such a wee thing, my lord, and so kind. I would not see her welfare at risk."

"Nor would I."

"I beg your pardon, my lord, for speaking so boldly, but men do not always think of these matters."

"You are right, Margaret, and your counsel is welcome. Do you have any notion of where a midwife of skill might be found?"

"There are two in Dumfries, my lord, the younger being the daughter and apprentice of the older. She might welcome the opportunity to leave her mother's tutelage."

"So long as she knows all she must."

Margaret scoffed. "At thirty summers, I doubt she will learn much more. She was to wed, my lord, and have a family of her own, but her betrothed died before the nuptials were celebrated."

"Tell me her name, Margaret, and where she might be found. I will seek her out when next I am in Dumfries."

"I think that would be wise, my lord. Some folk need time to make such a choice as this."

From there, Fergus visited the mill and admired the children of the miller's son. He asked if the younger man might offer some tutelage to Hamish, as a favor, and the offer was gratefully accepted. He collected the finished keys from the silversmith then, feeling that his morning had been well spent. Fergus was returning to the hall for the midday meal, thinking that he should hunt this week to ensure there was sufficient meat, when he saw Leila and Murdoch leaving the chapel together.

They were unexpected companions, to his thinking, but Leila smiled and hurried to his side. He bent to kiss her, knowing that many eyes watched them. "I begin my lessons with the priest," she said, her words falling in a rush. "Murdoch aids in the translation of more subtle notions."

"I could assist you in the same way."

"But you have obligations, Fergus," Leila said, smiling up at him. "And Murdoch has offered most kindly to do this for me."

"Are you sure it is not too much of a burden, Murdoch?" Fergus asked the warrior, who he would have named the most unlikely assistant for any studying matters of faith.

Murdoch smiled, his gaze flicking to Leila with admiration. "I would aid my lady to find her footing in this land, sir. It is not a simple task she has undertaken, and I would see her succeed."

"It is most appreciated," Fergus said, wondering if he saw too much in this new union. He had no reason to be suspicious of Leila, and little more to doubt Murdoch's intent. He did not like how openly the warrior admired his wife.

Still, he felt uneasy but could see no elegant way to change the arrangement. Leila was clearly pleased with it and he did not wish to tamper her enthusiasm. Matters would be much simpler if she changed faith, but he knew it was a delicate matter. He was glad she had embarked on the quest of learning more, and that without his prompting, and reasoned that Murdoch's assistance was a compromise he would tolerate.

Just as Leila would tolerate the duplication of the keys. Fergus had learned from his parents that marriage was challenged by differences of opinion and the trick lay in negotiating a balance between both views.

He would not criticize her scheme.

They reached the hall to find his father still in his chamber. Enguerrand and Yvan were playing chess in one corner while Iain arranged the midday meal.

"I will take the duplicated keys to my father," Fergus said to Leila, showing her that they were already upon a lace. He surrendered the original to her once more, noting how her fingers closed over them protectively. Her lips tightened, but he smiled at her. "There must be a second set," he whispered. "And I saw the silversmith destroy the mold."

She nodded reluctant agreement.

"My father will not surrender them to any other."

Leila nodded again. "If he is tired from our vigil last night, I could take a meal to him."

Fergus smiled down at her, appreciating how she cared for his father. "He might prefer that. I will ask him." He kissed her again. "Thank you, Leila," he murmured for her ears alone. "We make a good beginning together."

Fire lit in her eyes. "We shall build a future, Fergus," she said with familiar ferocity. "One day at a time."

"And each night there will be another increment of a tale, if I join you abed," he teased. She flushed a little but did not deny it. "You will see how readily I am taught to do just that, my lady," he whispered and she could not hide her pleasure. "Ride with me this day. I will show you the land of Killairic and perhaps we will hunt a bit."

"I would like that well," she said, her pleasure clear.

"I will send word to Stephen. Tempest can take his leisure today, and we will ride palfreys. Some of the men may come with us. It will be good to check the level of the rivers, as well, after that rain and ensure that the bridges are in good repair."

Hamish was surprised to find himself regarded with a kind of awe in Killairic village. The situation was so vastly different from the time before his departure that he could scarce believe it. Was it simply because he had journeyed so far?

It was his aunt who made the reason clear to him, when he finally had the opportunity to linger at home for a day. Laird Fergus had released him from service for the day after their return from Dunnisbrae, and Hamish was glad of it.

His uncle Rodney's cottage was smaller and darker than he

recalled, and his aunt was more plump, but the smell of her rabbit stew was achingly familiar. It made his mouth water just as it always had.

"I suppose you have had much finer fare on your journey," Mhairi said when she was serving the stew into bowls.

"I have missed your cooking," Hamish confessed. "I have often wished for such good hearty fare as this."

"And fine fare it is," Rodney agreed. "There are many less fortunate than ourselves, to be sure." As was his wont, he bowed his head and they prayed together for a moment.

"The bread is from yesterday, I fear," Mhairi began but her husband interrupted her.

"You have no need to apologize, Mhairi," he said. "Our fortunes are what they are and we offer our best. Hamish can have no complaint." He arched a brow. "Or if he does, he can eat in Killairic's hall."

"I have no complaint," Hamish said quickly. "There were nights we had naught to eat at all, and nights that what we had was not palatable."

"Not palatable?" Rodney echoed with a grin. "The boy has become a diplomat, Mhairi."

They laughed easily together and ate in silence for a few moments. Mhairi's eyes shone with pleasure when Hamish requested a bit more of the stew.

"You must tell us of your adventures," his uncle invited.

"I do not know where to begin. Outremer is so different, and yet, so much the same."

"How so?"

"It is hot and dry, dusty. The food is different, and then there are all the languages to be heard. The Temple was a refuge, for it was tranquil and orderly, and most there spoke French."

"And it was a sanctuary in a troubled land," Rodney contributed.

Hamish nodded. "True. I always was relieved when we passed through its gates, and slept well in that place. It was a fortress, to be sure." He eyed the last of his stew as a realization struck him. "It has fallen now and is in the hands of the Saracens. That refuge is no more." His throat was tight as he recalled their near escape and the men he had known who might not draw breath any longer.

His uncle put a hand over his. "But you are home and safe here, lad," he said gently.

Hamish took a breath and nodded.

"Praise be," his aunt said. "I feared for your survival day and night, Hamish, and thought my heart would burst when I saw you returned."

"It is remarkable that only one of your party did not return," Rodney said. "Given all the woe in that part of the world."

Mhairi sniffed and rose to clean the table. "I doubt any will miss Kerr overmuch," she said, then poured ale for them all.

"Mhairi..." her husband warned, as Hamish often recalled him doing.

His aunt ignored the warning, which he also remembered well.

"Can I not speak the truth in my own home?" she demanded. "That boy was not one to turn your back upon. In truth, I feared him more than the Saracens when Hamish rode out. Like all those linked to Lady Isobel, he could not be trusted."

Hamish said naught.

His aunt fixed him with a look. "And if ever there was a soul less likely to come to the aid of others against a party of bandits, Kerr it was."

"Mhairi!"

"Hamish does not have to reply. I know the truth in my own heart." Mhairi raised her cup. "And so we should drink to the health of Laird Fergus, whose heart is so good that he sees only the merit in others. Bless him for his kindness in concealing whatever truth there was about Kerr. There is naught to be gained in sharing a man's wickedness once he is dead."

They drank the toast in silence, which Hamish supposed was a good indication that they all agreed.

"But a Saracen bride? Now that is not a matter that will pass unchallenged," Mhairi said once she had drained her cup.

"Why should any challenge it?" Hamish asked. "Surely Laird Fergus can take whoever he desires to wife?"

"Surely he can, but the king must invest him with the seal when the old laird passes," Rodney said.

"Do you truly believe that when kings call for a crusade against the Saracens that they will suffer an infidel to be wedded to one of their lords?" Mhairi shook her head and filled the cups again. "I think not."

"But Leila is good and kind."

Mhairi pursed her lips. "She seemed pleasant enough on her wedding night, but I suppose any woman would be glad to wed Laird Fergus. So tiny." She raised her brows. "So brown!"

"She is said to be his whore, but would a man find such as she alluring?" Rodney asked.

"Leila is no whore!" Hamish said hotly. "She was our companion and friend. I am glad that Fergus has ensured she could remain here."

His aunt and uncle exchanged a glance.

"For a year and a day," Mhairi noted gently.

"I heard that Murdoch is aiding her in taking lessons from Father Gregory," Hamish said. "She wishes to learn before she changes her faith."

"There is no harm in that," Rodney acknowledged.

"I would trust Leila with my life," Hamish continued. "Indeed, I have done so."

Mhairi flicked a look at him. "Even though she is an infidel?"

"At the Temple, I was taught that there is good and bad in every kind, believer or infidel, and in truth, there are many areas of common belief between our faiths..."

"Which is why men slaughter each other in Jerusalem," Rodney said wryly.

"In Outremer, in many places, people of different faiths live together in harmony," Hamish argued. "It is the knights from France and England who provoke war there. Those who live there only defend themselves and their property."

His uncle raised his brows.

His aunt took a deep breath. "And so you think the Holy City should be surrendered to infidels?"

"They also hold it as a place of worship. Lord Gaston, the leader of our party, tried to negotiate peace. He said both claims had merit and should be respected."

"And infidels respected this?" Rodney's skepticism was clear.

"I am sorry to say this, uncle, but they were more likely to respect it than Christian kings and knights." Hamish shook his head. "I have seen things to make me doubt the merit of my own kind."

There was a moment of quiet in which Hamish looked at the table and his aunt and uncle studied him. He knew he was defying their convictions and was aware that he had never done as much before. He felt that he had erred, for he was now a guest in their home, and wished he could take back the words—even though he yet believed them. He had not intended to give offense.

Finally, Rodney cleared his throat. "You are not the sole one to think well of the lady. Farquar said the Lady Leila has helped old Nellie. He said she shows the surety of a good ostler and her care already makes a difference."

Hamish looked up. "What is wrong with Nellie?"

"She is lamed and refuses to put one foot down. We have been plowing the fields without her and it is heavy labor." Rodney shook his head. "You know how Farquar cannot bear to see a horse suffer and can anticipate how he would argue with those who suggest Nellie's time should come to an end. He was most impressed by Lady Leila's efforts yesterday."

"She has a talent with horses, to be sure," Hamish agreed. "That was how we knew her. She came to the Temple, disguised as a boy, to aid in their care. She was friends with Bartholomew, the squire of the knight Gaston I mentioned earlier. He served almost twenty years with the Temple, and Bartholomew was his squire all the while. It turns out that Bartholomew is the lost heir to Haynesdale, and now he is lord there."

"Well, well, Mhairi, our Hamish has gathered powerful friends in his time away!"

"And how did Lady Leila come to be in your party, then?" Mhairi asked.

"Her uncle had betrothed her to a man she distrusted and would not listen to her protests. She fled and asked for our protection. Laird Fergus took her as his squire, saying he had bought so much for Lady Isobel that he had need of another squire. We called her Laurent, and I did not know she was a lady until several weeks ago."

Rodney chuckled at that. "It is no good thing to be adept at disguise, lad."

"She defended my lord's belongings and his welfare more than once," Hamish said with ferocity. "I would trust Leila as well as Laird Fergus, in any situation."

"Well, there is an endorsement for you, Mhairi," Rodney said. "And a potent one as well. The boy has found his voice on his journey, to be sure."

"An honorable nature is all well and good, and truly I am glad to hear of hers," Mhairi said. "But there will be trouble yet over her faith, upon that you can rely."

His uncle nodded sagely. "Killairic is prosperous and Laird Calum is aged. We had best brace ourselves for assault."

Hamish disliked this forecast and knew his feelings showed, for his uncle gave him a nudge. "What is it, lad?"

"I had thought all was different here. I had thought we rode home to peace."

"Perhaps that is one trait men hold in common, a desire for whatsoever belongs to another. We have seen our share of war and pillage in your absence." Rodney was philosophical. "I am glad to hear that my lord Fergus has taken a good woman to wife, though. That is reassuring, whatever her faith."

"Aye, for he could have wed Lady Isobel." Mhairi grimaced.

"Mhairi..."

Mhairi shook a finger at her husband. "We have not seen the last of that one, not since Laird Fergus came home, hale and handsome, with riches besides. I would wager that old Stewart MacEwan is not looking so alluring on this night."

Hamish guessed from what he had witnessed the day before that his aunt was right.

"Mark my words, she will try to find a way to return to Laird Fergus' affections. I hope this time he is wiser about the truth of her nature."

"What is the truth of her nature, Aunt?"

"Mhairi..."

Yet again, Mhairi ignored her husband's warning. "She is one who sees to her own advantage alone. She wed Stewart because he admired her and offered her a home. In absence, Laird Fergus lost his appeal to that one. It is a measure of her nature that she could not keep a pledge and that her love was so thin that it could not sustain her while she awaited his return. And now, she will wish to leap from one to the other, for her spouse is older and perhaps harsher. Nay, we have not seen the last of her."

"Mhairi, you see shadows in every corner."

"Usually, because they are there. It will be that little maid who aids in the matter, to be sure."

"Which maid?" Hamish asked, though he already guessed his aunt must mean Agnes. Pretty Agnes, who smiled at him so sweetly and whose attention made his heart pound.

"The one come from Dunnisbrae, that one with the fair face and the dark heart."

"Agnes," Rodney contributed. "The orphan."

"Who is cut of the same cloth as Lady Isobel, to be sure. It is no wonder they could not abide in the same hall and no coincidence that she came from Dunnisbrae to Killairic, purportedly in search of labor. Nay, she came to watch for Laird Fergus and her loyalty is to Dunnisbrae if not her own self. To be sure, Laird Fergus comes by his kindness of heart honestly, for his father shares it." Mhairi gave Hamish a hard look. "Do not be fooled by that one with her twitching skirts, lad."

"Of course not, Aunt," Hamish said stoutly, though he very nearly had been so tricked. "Tell me what else is new in the village."

"Well," Rodney said, his manner becoming expansive as they returned to topics of greater comfort to him. "Gavin at the mill there, he finally married young Inge. It took no small resolve on the part of both fathers, given that she was out there on the isles, but they are happy, to be sure."

"Two sets of twins she has born to him in four years," Mhairi contributed. "And you never saw such handsome children."

"You think all children are handsome, Aunt," Hamish teased

and the older couple laughed.

His aunt leaned toward him with sparkling eyes. "I will tell you this, Hamish. There will never be a babe more beautiful than the first one you sire."

Hamish found his neck heating. "I am too young to wed, Aunt."

"Nonsense! You have been across the width of Christendom, served with the Templars and are pledged to Laird Fergus. Your future is as secure as ever it will be." His aunt raised a brow and Hamish nodded agreement.

He had not considered marriage, not yet, although he had thought of intimacy with Agnes. Perhaps one day, he would find a woman of merit, just as the knights in their company had done. If naught else, he would help Leila to find allies at Killairic, for defending a lady was what a man of any measure should do.

Hamish smiled because he had learned that from his uncle, long before he had journeyed to Outremer.

CHAPTER TEN

Agnes was not one to miss an opportunity.

She knew that time was of the essence.

Fergus' whore was clearly determined to earn the goodwill of those at Killairic and to do so with haste. It was astonishing to Agnes that the infidel had made so much progress in only one day—by the end of their handfast, it might not be possible to be rid of her.

Already, it was becoming impossible to avoid the sound of some fool singing the praises of Lady Leila. Laird Fergus was the worst of them all—he looked to be besotted with her since his return the night before, his gaze trailing after her every step. The old laird scarce showed less esteem. Agnes could not make sense of their acceptance of a woman with such dark skin. From the sounds that had carried from the solar the night before, Laird Fergus showed great enthusiasm for the task of fathering a son.

Agnes knew she could see to her laird's pleasure better than any infidel whore. A notion had occurred to her and had steadily grown in appeal. What if Agnes were to replace the whore in the young laird's affections? What if she were to bear the son who would inherit Killairic? The old man already liked her, and she made every effort to feed his affection. When she had a moment to spare from the witch's commands, she saw to his comfort. She knew what he liked. A sweet from the kitchens in the afternoon. A warm cup of goat milk in the evening. A little assistance on the stairs and a flirtatious comment about his vigor. Agnes knew it all.

She also knew that the whore did not remove the lace from her neck with the keys. This was vexing and gave Agnes a challenge. What had they secured in the treasury? Could she use knowledge of it to be rid of the whore? Agnes had to oust the whore soon if it was to be done and she was convinced that the item in Duncan's saddlebag would assist in that quest.

It could be stolen and the whore blamed.

On the day after his return from Dunnisbrae, Laird Fergus had a second set of keys made. He might have heard Agnes' wish and she had to hide her delight at the tidings. When he climbed the stairs to give the newly made set to his father, Agnes' plan was made.

Only two sets of keys, and no one would blame the old laird for the loss of any item from his own treasury.

Agnes waited until midday meal had been served, and the whore had assisted the old laird with his stew. She waited until Laird Fergus and his whore rode out, waited until she could hear the hoofbeats no longer, then waited some more.

She tapped on the door to the old laird's chamber, though it was standing open. He was dozing and the keys gleamed on the lace around his neck. She was tempted but waited for the right moment.

"Agnes!" he said, pushing himself up to a more seated position.

"I thought your knees might be troubling you, my lord," she said demurely. "It is oft so after the rain."

"And so it is on this day. It is kind of you to ask, Agnes."

"Let me rub some of the liniment into them, my lord. It always gives you relief."

"Thank you, Agnes!"

"Would you like a cup of warm milk as well? It seems a day to linger abed, especially after such a late night."

"Indeed, indeed. You are thoughtful, Agnes." He smiled at her and she bowed, hastening down the stairs to gather liniment and milk. Her palms were damp for she stood on the threshold of opportunity but she dared not give herself away.

She wished she had a bit of valerian to put in the milk, but there was no midwife in Killairic any longer. The hut of the former one had been left untouched after her death, but Agnes could not have identified the right herb by herself. She knew better than to guess. The old midwife would not have granted it to her, either for she had distrusted Agnes.

When Agnes had delivered a son to Fergus, the villagers would know better than to disdain her.

She returned to the old laird with the liniment and the milk. He thanked her effusively. She helped him to his chair, positioned in the sunlight by the window, and tucked pelts around him. Then she knelt before him and rubbed his favored liniment into his knees, striving to appear fascinated as he recounted the same stories that he had told her a hundred times. She exclaimed in all the right places and encouraged him, watching as he sipped the warm milk.

"Surely, you did not need to abandon the solar, my lord," she said. "I am certain Laird Fergus would wish for you to be comfortable."

"I like the view here, Agnes, and this room is more cozy. The wind is diminished here." He leaned back his head and yawned mightily. She saw the cord around his neck and looked down as if disinterested. "Stir up the coals on the brazier, if you please, Agnes."

"Of course, my lord. Would you like more milk?"

"Nay, but I thank you." He yawned, doubtless because the room was so warm, then waved her away. "Leave me sleep, Agnes, but do not let me miss the evening meal. Tell Iain that I must be awakened when Fergus and Leila return, for I would hear of their day."

"Of course, my lord," Agnes agreed, but his lids were already drooping. She waited, watching and listening, still rubbing his knees but with diminishing force. The old laird slipped into a deep sleep, his head drooping and his hands slack. Agnes waited a little longer, scarcely daring to breathe.

She heard Xavier and Iain arguing in the kitchens. She knew the Templars played chess in the hall. No one came up the stairs. The sounds of the village seemed remote.

Laird Calum began to snore.

Agnes held her breath as she stood. She waited, then stepped closer to his shoulder. She reached and slowly lifted the knot on the cord away from his skin. She did not even dare to breathe. He murmured to himself in his sleep and she froze, waiting until his snoring began again.

Slowly, carefully, she untied the knot. The keys fell into her palm with a soft tinkle and she caught her breath, fearing she would be caught.

But Laird Calum slept on.

Agnes left the cord around his neck. She retreated with care, closing the door behind herself, and stopped to listen while she stood on the stairs. No one was near.

This was her chance.

She hastened up the stairs on silent feet, unlocking the door of the solar as quietly as she could. She breathed a sigh of relief that the key worked, then ducked inside.

She closed the door quietly behind herself, then locked it again so she could not be discovered at the worst moment. Her heart was racing. She crossed the solar, avoiding the floorboards that creaked. Her hands shook a little as she unlocked the treasury, and she feared that the saddlebag had been removed.

But it was there, on the floor just inside the door, just as it had been from Laird Fergus' return. There were also chests of coins and one of documents, but this was the bag that intrigued Agnes.

She listened, but there were no indications that anyone climbed to the solar or sought her. She crouched down and unlocked the buckles, threw back the flap. There was a wrapped bundle within the bag. It smelled faintly of manure, which surprised her, but she lifted it out of the bag and carried it to the window.

Agnes set the bundle on the table beneath the window and studied the way it was wrapped. She took careful note of the details so that she could return it with the appearance that it had been untouched. Then she opened the bundle. There was a great deal of cloth wrapped around whatever was inside, as if it might be fragile. It was round and of a goodly size. Agnes thought she felt metal and could not make sense of it.

Until the last length of cloth was removed and the sunlight fell upon the golden reliquary in her hands. Agnes' mouth fell open in astonishment. The treasure was gold, gleaming gold and studded with gems, marked with inscriptions and crosses.

Agnes could not read the inscription but she knew this was a prize, a treasure beyond price. She traced a cross engraved in the surface with a shaking fingertip. This explained the presence of the Templars. They guarded this marvel and were yet in the keep. She licked her lips, wondering how best to use this treasure to see the whore discredited.

The answer was clear. Of course, an infidel would not hold such an item sacred. An infidel might steal it, perhaps to finance her journey home. Agnes smiled. She would steal the reliquary and make it look as if the whore had taken it. Laird Fergus would challenge the whore, she would deny that she had done anything amiss—as one would expect—and he would cast her out.

Leaving his bed cold and his father yet in need of an heir.

The scheme was simple, yet flawless.

Perhaps Agnes would be rewarded for restoring the prize, when all seemed to be lost.

Certainly, she could grant Laird Fergus all he needed.

Agnes lifted the reliquary out of its protective wrappings and rolled it instead in one of the whore's dirty chemises. She left the saddlebag splayed open in the treasury, and placed the wrapping in the bag, but in disarray. It looked as if someone had hastened to seize it and not cared that its absence would be obvious.

Well pleased with herself, Agnes locked the door to the treasury again. She ensured that there was no sign of her presence, then left and locked the door from outside the solar. She hugged the treasure as she descended the stairs, praying that she would not be spotted.

The bucket for slops was outside the old man's door. It was empty but only Agnes knew that. She put the bundle in the bucket, replaced the lid, then took a deep breath. She eased into the old man's chamber, where he still snored, and placed the keys back on the cord. Her hands were still trembling, but her excitement rose as she neared success. She knotted the cord again, holding her breath all the while, and worked both cord and knot beneath his chemise. When she was certain he slept uninterrupted, she backed slowly out of the chamber.

The bucket was just as she had left it. Agnes hefted it to descend the stairs.

Iain had come into the hall. She smiled at him, noting that one Templar was playing chess with Murdoch while the other looked on. That second one spoke while gesturing to the board, apparently giving advice, and Murdoch snorted.

Disdaining it, no doubt.

"Laird Calum is asleep but wishes to be awakened for the evening meal," she said to Iain and the steward nodded.

His gaze dropped to the bucket with a frown. "My lord does not usually evacuate at this hour of the day."

"And so he did not," Agnes said, concocting a lie. "But I forgot that I was to take his bucket this morning. I am sorry."

Iain was stern. "See that you do not make such an oversight again, Agnes. His lordship should not have to endure the smell for a moment longer than necessary, and the hall must be kept clean, by request of her ladyship."

"Of course, Iain. I apologize again." Agnes bowed and apologized and said whatever was necessary to convince the old busybody to look the other way. Finally, she was able to leave the hall. She took measured steps to the stream on the far side of the keep where the sewage was dumped.

Instead of emptying the bucket, though, she placed it on the ground. She looked back but could see no one. She tipped off the lid and seized the treasure. Agnes jumped the wall and crossed the stream, clutching her prize. She ran for a hiding place she knew well.

The reliquary would be safe there until she could give it to Laird Stewart.

How soon could she convince someone to look for the

reliquary to ensure that the whore was condemned for its loss? Agnes was not certain who knew about the prize and doubted that Laird Fergus would hear a word against the infidel in his bed.

She would have to watch and listen and seek her chance.

Laird Calum might provide the opportunity she sought.

It had been a fine day and one that gave Leila much hope for the future. She and Fergus had ridden the perimeter of Killairic and he had shown her the bounty of the holding he called his home. She had been much impressed by Killairic's beauty and more so by Fergus' affection for the people and the land.

Even better, they had talked of those in the village and she had seen his talent for taking responsibility without meddling. They discussed how best to aid the miller's son, and he had shared his scheme to send Hamish to help.

He had told her about the midwife who had passed away in his absence and had conferred with her about seeking out a new healer for the village. They had discussed the possibility of tempting one to move from Dumfries and what inducement such a woman might find appealing.

Leila liked that Fergus was concerned not only with her own welfare, should she conceive, but with that of the other women in the village. They had agreed that Radegunde could test the knowledge of whoever they chose, for Fergus expected she would pass through Killairic either with Duncan or in search of him by the fall.

They spoke of Hamish and his future, the possibility of him training for his spurs at Haynesdale, and agreed that the boy might be glad of the opportunity. This, too, Fergus resolved to discuss with Hamish.

Their conversation was easy and companionable, and she liked the glances that Fergus cast her way. He asked for her advice on the administration of the keep itself, and they considered who should accompany them on the journey to Iona.

The sun was setting when they rode back into the village. Farquar beckoned to them to share Nellie's progress and it appeared the mare would be well enough to pull the plow within a week or two. The priest smiled and waved at them, and Leila agreed to meet him the next morning for more lessons.

All went aright.

Calum was coming down the stairs when Leila and Fergus climbed to the solar. They were muddy from their ride and both meant to change their garb for the evening meal. Fergus changed course and accompanied his father to the hall, tactfully ensuring that the older man did not fall, while Leila continued to the solar.

She was unlocking the portal when she smelled manure.

She had crossed the threshold when she smelled Agnes. The girl was not as clean as Leila might have preferred in a maid, but she knew better than to give that one counsel. And truly, it was not all bad for Agnes to have a distinct scent, since Leila did not trust her.

Agnes smelled of perspiration, and faintly of sexual pleasure, as well as onions. Undoubtedly, she had peeled vegetables for Xavier before her change of post though Leila wondered who the girl's lover could be. It was somewhat disgusting that she had washed so little in two days.

Leila thought at first that the girl's scent lingered from earlier in the day, but it was stronger in the middle of the solar.

It was strongest yet by the window with the trunk beneath it.

Had Agnes been in the solar in their absence?

But how?

There were more keys, just as at Châmont-sur-Maine.

Leila felt cold.

She saw then that the soiled chemise she had left for the girl to wash was gone, though the other laundry was not. Fergus' plaid was still stretched out to dry and his chemise from the day before had not been moved.

She was frowning at the door to the treasury when Fergus entered the solar.

"What is amiss?" he asked immediately and she indicated that he should close the door. He locked it before coming to her side, his eyes alight with curiosity.

"There is another key," Leila said quietly. "Agnes has been in this chamber in our absence."

"How can you tell?"

Leila touched her nose and Fergus nodded.

"Alone?"

"If not, her companion is cleaner than she."

They both looked at the door to the treasury as one.

Fergus put out his hand even as Leila drew the cord with the keys over her neck. She handed the keys to him, fearful of what he would find yet having a curious conviction of it all the same. He opened the door to the treasury as her heart pounded in fear and she knew immediately that her suspicion had been right. His posture changed, his shoulders drooping, then he glanced back at her, his lips a hard line.

"It is gone," he said softly.

"As is my chemise."

Fergus nodded. "Whoever took it meant for you to appear to be the villain."

Leila watched him, wondering what he would decide. He closed the door and locked it again, then he came to her. His eyes were dark, his expression solemn. "I will keep the keys now, as that will cast doubt on any accusation."

Leila nodded, feeling that her position was precarious.

Fergus slid his arm around her shoulders and drew her close. "Do not look so fearful. I know that you have defended the prize with your life. I know your innocence. But what scheme does our villain have? Agnes is yet in the hall, so if you are right—"

"I am right. I know her scent."

"Then she has not gone far to hide it. That means it can be found." Fergus smiled down at Leila. "Let us say naught and let her provoke the display of the reliquary. There must be some plan to reveal your supposed theft."

"And we may find the treasure before that," Leila concluded.

"I will ask Hamish to follow Agnes and see if he can find it, but we will confide in no one else." Fergus raised his brows. "Certainly not our guests, the Templars."

Certainly not.

Leila was clearly shaken by the theft of the reliquary. Indeed,

Fergus was worried about it, as well, but he strove to appear more confident than he felt in order to reassure his wife. He guessed that Leila feared she would be blamed and did not doubt that she was right.

He had to find the reliquary first.

He spoke to Hamish after the evening meal, striding to Rodney's abode to speak to the boy in confidence. Hamish was thrilled to be entrusted with the responsibility of watching Agnes and Fergus knew the boy would do whatever was necessary to aid Leila. His loyalty was indisputable. Fergus chose to wait a few days before sending Hamish to aid the miller, and asked instead what Hamish thought of journeying to Haynesdale to train for his spurs.

Hamish's shout of joy brought Rodney and Mhairi and offered a suitable guise for Fergus' mission.

"It was Leila's idea," Fergus said. "She was the one who guessed your ambitions."

Hamish's eyes glowed and his aunt and uncle were most grateful.

Fergus returned to the hall to find Leila laughing with Calum beside the fire. Agnes was cleaning the board without enthusiasm and he wondered where she might have hidden the reliquary. He recalled that glimpse he thought he had of her in the stables and resolved to look there the next morning.

At this hour, though, he wanted naught more than his wife's companionship.

And truth be told, he wanted to give Agnes a surprise.

Fergus caught Leila's eye and smiled at her, glad that she smiled warmly in return. He pulled the keys from his purse and let them swing on their cord, catching the light. Agnes stared at him. "You have the keys, my lord?"

"Aye, Agnes. After my lady locked me in the solar the other day, I vowed that would not occur again."

The girl flushed and stammered an incoherent reply, then glared at Leila before she returned to her cleaning. Fergus thought she deserved no less, for it was clear to him that she meant to let Leila be blamed for the loss of the reliquary.

Leila's distrust had been deserved, after all.

He could only hope that Agnes would soon lead Hamish to her hiding spot.

In the meantime, Leila spoke to his father, who rose to his feet and the pair crossed the hall to Fergus.

"You will not have a protest from me when you summon your lady wife to bed," his father jested and they climbed the stairs together. Calum retired, Iain coming to assist him, and Fergus escorted Leila to the solar. "Since I have the keys," he said. "I would serve as your maid this night."

Leila smiled. "I would wager that you wish for a boon from me for your trouble."

"Of course. I have waited all day to learn whether the merchant escaped the djinn or not."

She laughed aloud. "You could have asked me during our ride."

"I could have, but our discussion was so lively."

They entered the solar and Fergus locked the door behind them, even as Leila lit some of the candles. The chamber was chilly and Fergus lit the braziers, then drew the curtains around the bed.

"If you recall, the djinn had lifted his sword, intending to behead the unfortunate merchant," Leila said as she sat on the edge of the bed. She slipped off her shoes and began to untie the laces of her kirtle.

Fergus shed his own garb with haste, then came nude to the bed.

She spared him a glance and a smile. "It is cold for such enthusiasm," she said.

Fergus laughed. "Then hasten yourself, woman, and warm me."

Leila laughed again, and Fergus helped her with her stockings. He coaxed her out of her kirtle and chemise, then tugged her beneath the coverlet and pelts.

She licked her lips, her eyes shining, and continued the tale. "Just before the djinn made his blow, the merchant cried out. He asked the djinn to delay his execution, so that he could return home and say farewell to his family. The djinn was not inclined to do as much, but the merchant noted that he had not yet made a will and that his affairs had to be left in order. He begged the djinn to let him see that his property was divided and his family provided for—and he vowed to return when all was done. The djinn was skeptical that the merchant would return, but he swore an oath that he would return in exactly a year and a day, to the very spot, to accept his fate. They agreed and the djinn disappeared."

Fergus did not fail to note that the term was that same as that of their handfast.

"The merchant raced for home, both glad he had escaped a dire fate and fearful of his future. He knew he could not break his word, yet he was not ready to die. His family greeted him with great joy, but his wife noticed that he did not share their jubilant mood. Husband and wife were much in love and knew each other very well..."

"All the couples in your tales are much in love," Fergus noted, even as his hand slid from Leila's breast to her stomach.

Leila smiled. "Why should stories not mirror the most ideal of marriages?"

"I will guess that the merchant confided the truth in his wife." He held her gaze as his fingers slid ever lower and he smiled when she flushed a little. He touched her gently and she gasped, then parted her thighs to welcome his caress.

"Of course!" she said, her voice a little more husky than was usual. "And she was much distressed, though she could not find a solution either. The merchant then began to arrange his affairs. He made his will and paid his debts. He set his slaves at liberty and divided his property amongst his children. He appointed guardians for those who were young and saw his eligible daughters married well. There was much to do, but to him, the day that he had to depart to keep his appointment with the djinn arrived all too soon. His wife wished to accompany him but he could not bear for her to see him so struck down. He embraced her and took his leave, his heart heavy with the knowledge that he would not return."

"Let us consider for a moment as to how they might have spent that last night together," Fergus said, then bent and kissed Leila.

She sighed, winding her hands into his hair, and arched against him, her tongue slipping between his teeth to tease him. "Like this, I would think," she whispered when he gave her a chance, then caught his nape to pull his head down again. "Since they must have believed they would never meet again."

Fergus gave her a long and languid kiss. "But did they?" He kissed her ear, her throat, and the hollow of her shoulder.

Leila sighed. "I cannot tell you the end of the story before the middle."

"I come to think this story has no end," he complained and she laughed. He caressed her slowly and any reply died on her lips. She whispered his name and Fergus liked the breathless sound very well. "Aye, she must have begged him to please her," he said and Leila did the very same. "She must have tried to convince him to remain."

"But no woman of merit would truly want to convince the man she loved to break his word," Leila protested. She rolled suddenly atop Fergus, and he was content to be her captive. The covers fell away and the light from candles and braziers made her skin look even more golden than it was. "Perhaps she held him down and took her pleasure from him," she whispered, her eyes sparkling.

"Perhaps he willingly surrendered to her," Fergus replied. "For he wanted naught more than to see her delight."

"Perhaps you do not truly wish to hear the tale."

"Perhaps I would be satisfied first," Fergus replied. Leila laughed, then knelt above him and he was surprised to realize how prepared she was to welcome him. He had intended to pleasure her first but she sat upon him, the sweet heat of her making him dizzy. She moved slowly, casting a spell of her own, and Fergus knew he never wished to be freed of this enchantment.

"I would wager they did not sleep at all that night," he murmured and she smiled. "After all, they believed it to be their last night together."

"Is it possible to love more than once or even twice a night?" Leila asked and Fergus grinned.

"Aye," he said, pulling her down for a thorough kiss. "Let me show you."

Thrice Fergus seduced her before they doused the candles to sleep. When the solar was dark, save for the burning coals in the brazier, he gave Leila a squeeze. "Do not go to sleep before you tell me the merchant's fate," he growled and she smiled in the darkness.

"Well, after a sweet farewell from his wife, he left his home to keep his word to the djinn."

"Of course, he did, for he was a man of honor."

"Of course. That was why his wife loved him so well," Leila agreed. "The merchant arrived at the designated spot and sat down to await the arrival of the djinn. While he sat there alone, he saw an old man came into view, leading a hind. The old man halted in surprise when he noted the merchant. He warned the merchant immediately to leave the area, for he said it was infested with evil djinn and a dangerous place to rest. The merchant confessed that it was too late and told the old man his tale. The old man lamented with him and admired his honor in keeping his word. He asked if he might remain to witness the merchant's meeting with the djinn. The merchant thought the old man might be able to take word to his family of his fate, so he agreed."

"That seems a sensible arrangement," Fergus murmured.

"The pair sat together until they saw a huge cloud of dust rise in the distance. It swirled into a tall column and spun to the spot right before them. The djinn with the white beard appeared in the midst of the dust and made to seize the merchant. 'Wait!' cried the old man with the hind. He threw himself at the djinn's feet and begged for him to show mercy to the merchant. 'He has kept his oath and shows himself to be of more merit than most.' The djinn agreed with that, but refused to surrender his right to take the merchant's life in retaliation for the loss of his own son."

Leila lifted a finger. "But the old man indicated the hind and asked the djinn why he thought he kept it with him. The djinn did not know why any man would keep a deer, and the merchant quickly saw that the old man had caught the djinn's attention. 'I will tell you the tale,' offered the old man. 'If you will consider releasing this merchant if you find my tale to be wonderful.' The djinn considered this offer, then agreed and seated himself to listen."

Fergus chuckled. "Another tale nested with the tale. I tell you this saga knows no end."

Leila ignored him. "The old man then began his tale. He confided that the hind was not truly a hind, that it was his wife and she had been enchanted. The djinn was clearly intrigued by this detail and begged the old man to explain. He confessed that he had married his wife when she was very young and that he had fallen deeply in love with her."

"More loving couples," Fergus teased and Leila smiled before she continued.

"They were married for thirty years without her bearing a child, which gave them both considerable grief. Because he had need of an heir, the old man bought a female slave, and she soon bore to him a son, just as he had hoped. The boy was clever and handsome, and the old man was glad to have an heir. His wife, though, was unhappy in her jealousy and feared that her husband would prefer the slave over herself. She hid her fears well, though, so well that the old man had no awareness of them. When the boy was ten summers of age, the old man had been obliged to undertake a journey and leave his family behind. He knew he would be gone for a year. He left both slave and son in the custody of his wife, entreating her to take care of them both, then he departed."

"I will guess that all went awry," Fergus said. "I think you mean to teach me a lesson about spurned women and their jealousy."

Leila did not reply to that. She had not considered how well these tales echoed the truth they were living. "The wife had spent those years studying the arts of magic. Soon after the old man had departed on his journey, she cast a spell upon the son, turning him into a calf. She gave the creature to the steward, as if she had bought it in the market. Her jealousy was not sated by this, though. Next, she turned the slave into a cow, which she also surrendered to the care of the steward. When the old man finally returned home, his wife pretended to be contrite. She told him that his slave had died and that his son had disappeared. The old man was much troubled by this, for not only was he without an heir, but he had loved both slave and son dearly."

"A liar, though she was beloved," Fergus murmured. "How interesting."

"He knew his duty, though, and called for a celebration of his return. In this place and time, it was customary to sacrifice a cow for such a feast, and the wife ensured that the enchanted slave was the cow so chosen. The old man himself was to make the sacrifice, but the cow wept at the sight of him and made a mournful sound. He found this so curious that he could not strike the killing blow. His wife chastised him for his whimsy and he tried again, but again failed to complete the deed. His wife had much to say about this and the shame that would come upon the house if the guests were given no meat. The old man asked his steward to perform the sacrifice. It was done, but the cow did not have sufficient meat for the feast when she was skinned and prepared. Though she had looked fat, in truth, she had not been."

"Not all is as it appears," Fergus noted.

"The wife insisted they had need of more meat, and commanded the steward to bring the calf that was the enchanted son. This calf, too, acted most oddly, weeping before the old man and putting its head upon the old man's feet. He thought it also meant to entreat him to spare it and again found he could not strike the blow. Once more, his wife chastised him, but the old man would not be swayed. He bade the cook add dishes for the guests that were without meat and sent the calf back to the stables. The wife was livid, and finally, he agreed that the steward could kill the calf the next day."

Fergus was drawing little circles upon her belly but Leila continued, despite the distraction he offered. "When the steward led the calf back into the stables, his daughter was there. She laughed at the sight of the calf, then burst into tears. He thought this a most curious reaction so asked her to explain. The daughter had some skill with magic herself and told her father that the calf was the enchanted son of the master who had just returned, just as the cow that had been sacrificed had been the enchanted slave who was the son's mother. She named the wife as the one responsible for the spells, and the steward was so astonished that he immediately told the master about this. The master came to the stable and asked the girl to tell the tale herself. He wept that his faithful slave and mother of his son had been killed."

"For he had been deceived," Fergus said.

"Then he asked the daughter if she could break the spell upon his son. She said she would, but in exchange, she wished to marry the son and that her sorcery required that the wife be punished for her deed. The master gladly agreed. The daughter then took a bucket of water and murmured some words neither master nor steward could hear, then cast the water over the calf. The son was restored to his usual form and embraced his father with joy. He professed himself pleased to marry the daughter of the steward, and there was much merriment. Before their vows were exchanged, though, the daughter cast a spell upon the wife, turning her into the hind. 'It has been many years since these events, and my son was widowed,' the old man concluded. 'He left our home to travel with his sons and it is long since I have had word of them. I left in my turn to seek him out, and thought it proper to take my wife with me.' The old man smiled at the djinn and the merchant watched with hope. 'Do you not think this a most remarkable tale?' The djinn nodded agreement, thanked the old man for sharing his tale and patted the hind. He forgave the merchant, then disappeared in a swirl of white dust. The merchant was most thankful and embraced the old man, inviting him to journey home with him and enjoy the hospitality of his family, for they would rejoice that he was returned."

"One tale ends, at least," Fergus noted.

"The king, Shahriar, applauded the conclusion of Scheherazade's tale, but Dinarzade shook her head. 'It was a fine tale,' she told her sister. 'But not my favorite of the ones you recount so beautifully. Do you not think, my lord king, that the tale of the fisherman and the djinn is a better one?' Shahriar was compelled to admit that he did not know the tale of the fisherman and the djinn and entreated his new wife to tell it. Scheherazade, though, gestured to the pink in the morning sky, and apologized that there would not be sufficient time to share the tale before she was to be executed. The king fingered his beard, considering the matter, then promised Dinarzade that her sister could live another day, if only to share the tale of the fisherman and the djinn."

Fergus laughed. "I will wager that it was not recounted in a single night," he said.

"I could not spoil the tale by admitting any such detail," Leila said, then yawned. "Do you not wish to sleep this night?"

"How long did Scheherazade beguile the king with her stories?"

"The story is called the *Hazar Afsan*, or the thousand stories. Scheherazade entertained the king for a thousand and one nights, until he could not bear to be without her. In some versions, they have a son by then, while in others, they have two."

"And what is your design in telling me this story."

"To tempt you to return to this bed each night."

"I need no further temptation than you, Leila," Fergus said, kissing her most thoroughly.

Leila was reassured, even though she wished for even more. She had only three hundred and sixty-three nights to win Fergus' heart, but his words made her dare to hope that she might succeed.

TUESDAY, MAY 3, 1188

*Feast Day of
Saint James the Less*

220

CHAPTER ELEVEN

t happened again.

Leila was awakened in the night by Fergus' agitation. As every night thus far, they had loved sweetly and afterward she had told him more of Scheherazade's tale. As had happened once before, he had shouted Isobel's name in the darkness.

On this occasion, he turned away from her when she would have consoled him. His action left Leila awake and filled with dread. Did his gesture reveal the truth of his heart? She could not say.

She rose early and said her prayers in the garden, striving to keep from making much of little. Like every other day thus far, she went to her lesson with the priest afterward, Murdoch by her side. When she returned to the hall, Fergus was breaking his fast with his father. His mood was good and she wondered if he even recalled his dream of Isobel.

Or if it pleased him to so dream of her.

The notion was like a knife twisted in a wound and added to Leila's sense of discontent. It irked her that Hamish had not yet found the reliquary and began to fear it would be lost forever.

What if Agnes had somehow sent it away?

Fergus had sent Hamish to the miller's son after two days of the boy watching Agnes, for it seemed that the girl grew suspicious. She had challenged Hamish about his interest in her after mass on the Sunday, so Fergus had bidden Hamish to be more subtle.

The lack of resolution troubled Leila beyond all else. She feared the reliquary might be journeying ever farther away from Killairic and worried about the repercussions of its loss. That could be the meaning of Fergus's sense of doom. She had no doubt that as an infidel, she would be blamed for the reliquary's loss, no matter what Fergus said in her defense. The Templars had no greater fondness for women than for Muslims. She wanted to solve the riddle, lock the reliquary where it belonged, and be rid of the scheming Agnes—and she wished to do it immediately. Fergus had more patience than she.

Leila forced a smile as Fergus surrendered the key to the solar to her, then continued up the stairs to put the rug away. Murdoch remained in the hall.

She opened the shutters on the windows before leaving the solar, for the wind was crisp this morning and the sun was already warming the air in a most pleasant way. She took a deep breath of the scent of growth and greenery, then went to the last window. This one faced away from the village, to the north and west of the keep, and she was not certain she should open it. The wind from this direction was often chilly, though she supposed it might offer some relief in summer.

Leila could not wait to feel the sun's heat again. She had just moved the shutter an increment when she spied a movement in the forest below. Some instinct encouraged her to freeze and watch.

It was Agnes. She carried a bucket of slops, presumably to dump it in the river on the quiet side of the keep. Leila was surprised to find the girl actually performing her labor in a timely manner, but perhaps Iain had chided her. She was about to open the shutter all the way, when Agnes did the most curious thing. She put down the bucket on the bank of the river, then looked up at the keep.

As if she feared to be observed.

Leila could not imagine why the girl would be afraid to be seen dumping slops, which was one of her tasks. She remained motionless and watched.

Apparently reassured, Agnes abandoned the bucket. She crossed the river on a number of stones, then leaped to the opposite bank. Leila caught only a glimpse of her running through the forest, for the trees were coming into leaf and obscured Agnes from view.

She waited, watching and counting steadily. She reached eighty-two before the maid reappeared.

Agnes carried nothing, though again, she spared a glance at the keep.

Had she been checking on her prize?

Leila intended to find out. She left the solar in haste, locking it quickly, and fleeing down the stairs so that she could appear to have been there all along when Agnes returned to the hall. She took her place beside Fergus who spared her a questioning glance. She smiled at him and took his half-eaten piece of bread, feigning it was her own just as Agnes appeared in the portal.

The girl seemed to check that all were present before continuing up the stairs with the empty bucket.

"I believe she visited her prize," Leila murmured to Fergus.

"Indeed." He took the bread back from her with a smile and gave her another, as well as a comb of honey.

"I saw her from the window. She went to empty the slops, but left the bucket. She crossed the river and ran into the forest. I counted to eighty-six before she returned."

"At what speed?"

"The speed of my heart." Leila tapped her rhythm on his thigh, her hand hidden from view, and he nodded.

"I will speak to Hamish," he vowed. "Let us put an end to this." He kissed her brow and left her at the board.

Leila ate her breakfast with leisure, hoping against hope that Hamish would find the reliquary. She realized that she wished even more for Agnes to be shown for what she was. The girl reappeared at the base of the stairs in search of a broom and Leila ignored her, speaking instead to Calum, as if she were more calm than she felt.

A storm was brewing, to be sure, and she could only hope that she could outwit the maid.

Hamish had used the days since Laird Fergus' assignment to make preparations to hide the reliquary again once it was found. His scheme gave him great pride. Recalling how Lady Ysmaine had made a substitution for the prize on their journey, he had devised a means of doing much the same. He had found a block of wood at the carpenter's shop of suitable size and shape, then purchased a half sack of barley from the miller. This last he left hidden beneath his own bed at his aunt and uncle's home.

It was vexing that he had not been able to find the reliquary, though. He had learned that Agnes spent many an evening with the ostler in the stables when Stephen's wife awaited him at home. He had learned that Agnes was inclined to chat instead of do her labor. If naught else, he had no illusions about her nature and thought her to have more in common with Lady Isobel than might have been expected.

Indeed, he held the miller's wife, Inge, in higher esteem than Agnes or Isobel. She reminded him of Lady Ysmaine, of Radegunde, and of Leila. He knew what manner of woman he would take to wife, when the time came.

When Laird Fergus told him of Leila's observation, Hamish shared his scheme with his knight.

"That is clever," Fergus said with approval. "Now, let us see if we can retrieve the prize."

Hamish set off to find the place where Agnes dumped the slops, carrying a sack with the block of wood. He paused outside the kitchens of the keep and quickly discerned a path that led around the back of the keep. He knew the slops were dumped on this side of the hall, but had never gone to do it himself. Those from his aunt and uncle's house were dumped downriver of the village, as were those from the stables.

Hamish was stealthy for he feared to be spied where he did not belong. He found the spot in question—there could be no mistaking the smell—and glanced up. Sure enough, he could see a single window high on the tower of the keep, though the shutters were closed over it. There were stones at reasonable gaps in the water, and he used them to cross the river, needing to make one last leap to the other shore. Fortunately, it was not as muddy as it had been and his boots left no visible impression.

He broke into a run, counting in a rhythm as Laird Fergus had shared with him, and following what looked to be a path. He halted at thirty-five, pausing to look about himself. There was a footstep in the dirt ahead of him and it looked to be fresh. It also looked to be the right size for Agnes' foot and was deep as if she had hit the ground hard. The next one was at a long interval, as if she had been running. Hamish walked in the brush to one side of her path, ensuring that his own boots left no mark.

Agnes' trail ended at a large old tree. It was split and charred, as if it had been struck by lightning years before. Only a part of it was coming into leaf and there was a hollow within its trunk.

Hamish considered the situation for a few moments, for he wished to leave no hint of his presence. He found a bough of evergreen, recalling how Duncan had hidden their path at Haynesdale, and laid boughs to the hollow of the tree so they would cushion his steps.

Once there, he reached within the dark space and smiled when he felt a familiar round shape. The reliquary was wrapped in a chemise. Hamish noted the way it was bundled and its position, then carefully replaced the reliquary with the wooden block.

He ensured that there was no hint that he had been there, and returned to the village by another route. Once at his aunt's cottage, he retrieved the sack of barley and pushed the reliquary deep into the grain so it could not be seen.

He then took it to his aunt's kitchen.

"And what have you there, lad?"

Hamish did not like to tell a fiction to his aunt and uncle, but in this situation, there was no choice. Laird Fergus had insisted upon secrecy. "I had a commission from Laird Fergus that had to fulfilled with all speed."

"Is that why he sought you out so early? And what task would he grant you on this day?"

Hamish put the sack on the table and lowered his voice, aware that both uncle and aunt listened avidly. "The laird has had a dream."

"Aye, he was born to the caul," Mhairi acknowledged. "A dream of what? And how can it involve you?"

"He dreamed of famine coming to Killairic, because the crops failed in the rain."

"It has been a wet spring, to be sure."

Hamish patted the sack. "So, he asked me to hide a sack of barley somewhere safe, and tell no one of it. I had to go to the mill to fetch it, for he was most insistent it be done this day."

"In secret?" Mhairi echoed.

"When there is famine, there is theft of seed, Mhairi, and you know it as well as I do," Rodney contributed. "Lock it into your stores. No one will know it is there but we three, and no one can steal it when you hold the only key."

"That is a fine idea, Uncle." Hamish was relieved that it would be locked away.

"I trust it is good barley and not wet from the rain," Mhairi said then and he feared she would dump the sack. "It achieves little to save grain that is going to rot."

"The boy has learned a thing or two, Mhairi."

His aunt was not reassured by this. She propped her hands on her hips and Hamish untied the top of the sack, glad he had pushed the reliquary down so far. His heart nearly stopped when Mhairi pushed her hand into the grain.

She lifted out a handful of barley and let it slide through her fingers with satisfaction. Hamish thought his knees might give out.

"It is good and dry," she announced with a nod, then lifted the key from her belt. "Come along then and lock it away. We will not question the laird's whimsy, not when he seeks to ensure the welfare of all."

"It will not go to waste, even if he is wrong," Rodney said.

"Indeed," his wife agreed. "Though you may have stewed barley thrice a day after the harvest, given the size of that sack." They laughed together as the sack was locked away and Hamish was relieved when it was done.

"I must tell him that the task is fulfilled," he said.

"Indeed, you must," Rodney agreed. "A laird must know who he can rely upon."

"Of course, he can rely upon our Hamish," Mhairi said, smiling he departed. "What a good boy he is," Hamish heard her say. "Do you think Laird Fergus truly will see him trained for knighthood?"

"If the laird sees sufficient promise in our Hamish, he will do as much," Rodney said, winking at Hamish. "I have no doubt he will ensure the boy's future in one way or another. He is a man of merit in that way." He gestured to Hamish. "Now, go, and prove to him that you can be relied upon."

Hamish needed no further encouragement to do just that.

The theft had not been discovered, and Agnes grew impatient. What manner of person did not verify the safety of his prize? Especially such a treasure of such value as this one? She had been twice to her hiding place to confirm that it had not been removed.

It showed a trust in the world that Agnes did not share.

She was skeptical of all who surrounded her. She had even thought that Hamish might have been following her until mass on Sunday, but his interest had proven to be more personal. Once she had commented on his apparent infatuation and teased him about his youth, he had abandoned his pursuit.

Agnes could not understand why the Templars did not wish to see the treasure she assumed they defended, but they played chess as if there was naught else to be done.

It was time she provoked someone's curiosity and prompted a search.

The Templars were playing chess in the hall again that afternoon, while the laird and his whore had gone to the garden with Iain and the man from Dumfries who would build the dovecote. Agnes was left to sweep the hall, which she did without enthusiasm. The old laird was watching the chess game and dozing a little by the fire. Murdoch had joined the party in the gardens.

This was her chance.

Agnes swept toward the table where the knights bent over their game. They spoke seldom and usually in French, but she knew the taller one understood Gaelic. Enguerrand was his name and he had a great hooked nose as well as a piercing stare.

He glared at her when she swept beside him. "Must you do that now?" he demanded. "We are at our leisure."

"I have been told to do it, sir, and I must follow my lady's commands."

Enguerrand made a comment to his fellow, who smiled, then returned to his game. The old laird stirred himself and spoke to her. "I hope there will soon be matters of greater interest to attend than a dirty floor, Agnes."

"Indeed, my lord?"

His smile broadened. "Perhaps Fergus will share tidings of a babe soon."

Agnes bit her lip, thinking of the abomination of a brown son standing heir to Killairic. She also thought it best to keep from commenting upon Laird Fergus' enthusiasm for his wife each night. "I hope the tidings are as you hope, my lord, and delivered as soon as you desire."

His gaze landed upon her, his expression knowing. "It is not evil to be different, Agnes," he said gently and she was startled that he had any inclination of her thoughts. "You will learn that there is good in every kind. Lady Leila has a good heart, and that is of the greatest import of all."

"Of course, my lord." Agnes took a breath and dared to say more. "I only hope your trust and generosity is returned in kind, sir." She was proud that she let a little doubt color her tone. It had been perfectly uttered, to her thinking, and she knew she was right when Enguerrand turned his head slightly to listen to her.

The old laird's gaze brightened. "What do you imply, Agnes?" he asked.

"Naught, my lord. I simply found it curious that the lady had the key to the treasury upon their arrival and not my lord Fergus."

The old laird fingered the keys on the cord about his neck. "Indeed?"

"Indeed, my lord. Laird Fergus is your son and heir, as well, while Lady Leila is newly arrived." She was aware that Enguerrand watched her closely, and shrugged. "I wish I had your capacity for trust, my lord. But then, it is not for me to know what is sheltered in your treasury. Perhaps there is little of value there." She smiled and bobbed her head, turning back to her sweeping. Her heart was thundering and she hoped that her hint would be acted upon.

Agnes was not to be disappointed.

Enguerrand made a sharp demand in French, but the old laird shook his head. He closed his hand over the keys upon the cord and resolve lit his eyes.

Of course, he would defend the infidel.

But the Templars were not so inclined to trust as their host.

The second muttered something but Enguerrand snapped at him, saying something fast in French. Agnes guessed that one of them would pay if the treasure was gone, probably Enguerrand.

"What have you seen?" he demanded of Agnes, his manner so fierce that she did not have to pretend to be afraid of him.

She retreated hastily. "Naught, sir. I only wonder, though it is not my place to do so."

Both Templars got to their feet in unison, moving so abruptly that the chess pieces were toppled. Enguerrand's fists were clenched. "What have you seen, girl?" he repeated.

"I dare not make a false accusation," Agnes said, dropping her gaze as if she were demure. "Although it seemed most odd to me that my lady left her chamber in such haste that morning, with a burden I could not see. It was only natural to wonder what it might be."

The old laird inhaled sharply.

"A bundle?" echoed Enguerrand.

Agnes described a shape with her hands, of about the size of the reliquary. "It looked to be dirty linens, but that could not be." She strove to appear mystified as to what it might be.

"Why not?"

"My lady did not have so much garb until Margaret completed her new kirtles. And, if it was but laundry, sir, why be secretive about its removal from the solar?"

The Templar caught his breath. "What morning?" he demanded.

"The one after my laird swore his handfast to her. I had

completed my labor in the solar and was taking out the slops, sir." It was remarkable how easy it was to fashion a lie and have it believed. Agnes thrilled at her easy triumph.

"That was the day Fergus rode to Dunnisbrae," muttered the Templar.

"Before he had the second keys made," Agnes noted and the old laird gave her a hard look.

The other Templar said something about "Saracen," which was perfect, in Agnes' view. The old laird took exception to the comment, which indicated that it had not been kind, and they argued briefly in French. Agnes returned to her sweeping, hoping for the result she desired.

"Where did she go?" Enguerrand asked Agnes, his eyes flashing.

"I regret, sir, that I do not know." Agnes looked Enguerrand right in the eye. "I had duties to attend and was not at liberty to follow my lady." She bowed her head. "Nor would I show such disrespect as to question her, sir."

"You question her now," the old laird noted.

"And rightly so," whispered Enguerrand. He studied Agnes for a long moment, then his lips thinned. He turned to the old laird and made a demand. The old laird appeared to be vexed by whatever Enguerrand asked him and did not relinquish his grip upon his keys. The pair exchanged a few harsh words in French, and it was evident the old laird would defend the infidel to the last.

Enguerrand barked a command to his comrade, then marched out of the hall. The Templar set a course for the garden, and Agnes resumed her sweeping, well content with the results of a few well-chosen words.

"Agnes, Agnes," the old laird murmured, his tone chiding. "What have you done?"

"I, my lord? Naught at all." Agnes held his gaze, striving to look as innocent as might be. "Laird Fergus says it is best to always tell the truth, sir."

"Indeed," the old laird said, then his lips tightened. He toyed with the keys, his expression troubled, and Agnes let him fret about the fate of the infidel.

She would get what she deserved, in Agnes' view, and soon Laird Fergus would be in need of another wife. Laird Stewart had not arrived at the gates, nor had he sent Nolan to learn what she knew, so evidently he had neither the wits nor the desire to respond to her message. More fool him. Agnes had repaid her debt to Laird Stewart, in her estimation, and was thus released from any obligation.

At any rate, she liked the look of Laird Fergus much more than that of Laird Stewart. Let Lady Isobel keep her husband. Agnes had chosen another finer one.

She could scarce hold her pace steady as she swept the floor, for anticipation made her heart pound. But an appearance of innocence and honesty was key to the success of her scheme.

Agnes even managed to look startled when Laird Fergus and Enguerrand appeared in the hall and hastened past her to the stairs. She stumbled a little and Laird Fergus caught her elbow, ensuring that she had found her balance, before he charged toward the solar with the Templar, the second trailing behind them.

She smiled, pleased by his attention, and felt the weight of the old laird's assessing gaze upon her. It mattered little what he thought of her now.

Indeed, his opinion might not be of import for much longer. Laird Calum was aged and feeble. If he defended the infidel whore too much, Agnes might be compelled to hasten his demise.

It would be in pursuit of a good cause, after all.

In a way, Leila was glad to have the truth revealed.

Enguerrand and Yvan appeared suddenly in the garden, and Enguerrand was intent upon interrupting the discussion about the dovecote. Fergus squeezed her hand, then took the Templars aside. Iain meanwhile, escorted the mason to the gates, finalizing the arrangement for the construction of the dovecote.

"I must see the prize entrusted to us!" Enguerrand declared, making no effort to keep his voice down. "I must verify its safety." The Templar's demand to be given the key to the treasury was clearly heard by all, for both Iain and the mason glanced back from the other end of the garden.

Murdoch folded his arms across his chest and watched.

Leila hoped they did not all understand French.

She feared otherwise.

The men conferred more quietly for a moment. Then, Enguerrand marched back into the keep with Fergus and she knew they would ascend the stairs, unlock both doors, and find the reliquary missing.

And she would be blamed.

Praise be that Hamish had found the reliquary and ensured its safety.

She sank down to that stone bench, feeling the urge to pray all the same.

What if Agnes had guessed the location and stolen it again?

"What is amiss, my lady?" Murdoch asked from her side, but Leila did not reply. In this moment, she was uncertain who to trust fully and chose to trust no one. She intended to be a good wife to Fergus, because she loved him, but as the cries of outrage rose from within the hall, Leila realized that being a good wife might not prove sufficient.

When she was forbidden to climb to the solar, she feared the worst. She returned to the stone bench and reminded herself to trust Fergus in this matter.

But there was no disguising the fact that Leila felt very much alone.

Fergus hated that he had to let Leila appear to be guilty in order to keep the reliquary safe. Enguerrand was furious about the apparent loss but probably more concerned with his own status. For that reason, Fergus did not confide in him.

He had a lingering sense of malaise this morning, as if the dark cloud drew closer. He feared that he had said something in his sleep, for Leila had been less happy this morning than was her inclination.

Could it be that more than the reliquary was in peril?

In the solar, Enguerrand raged about the folly of letting Fergus take custody of the treasure and spewed hatred about Saracens and women that set Fergus' teeth on edge.

"She did not steal it," he said finally. "Think of what you are saying."

"Of course, she stole it!" Enguerrand raged. "A priceless relic stolen when a Saracen held the sole key to its hiding place! What else could have happened?"

"My father has a key as well."

"To his own treasury. How could he not?" Enguerrand shook a finger at Fergus. "And he did not have a key on the day you rode to Dunnisbrae."

"What has that to do with it?"

"That is the day it was stolen!"

"How do you know?"

"Because there was a witness," Enguerrand insisted.

"Ask the witness who took it."

"She—that person will not say." Enguerrand paced the width of the solar. "Your father did not take it, that old man. Why would he steal it? It was in his possession already!"

"And why would Leila steal it, after she had defended it from thieves all the way from Jerusalem?"

"She had a scheme. They all have schemes..."

"Why would she want to steal it?"

Enguerrand rounded upon him with flashing eyes.

"Saint Euphemia is not sacred in their tradition. The relic has no power for her. She meant to sell it," the Templar hissed. "It was for the coin that she wished to have it."

"Then why would she not have stolen it in Venice or in Paris, where such a prize could be more readily sold?" Fergus argued. "There are no buyers with fat purses in Galloway in search of relics, and if there was one, he or she would not buy from a Saracen woman." He shook his head. "There is no reason for my wife to have taken the reliquary."

"Yet she did. She had the keys!" Enguerrand snapped his fingers. "Perhaps she intended to extort coin from us!"

"You have no coin," Fergus pointed out. "Being sworn to poverty and chastity."

"But the order is wealthy beyond compare," the Templar said with fury. "This must be her scheme. Summon your infidel wife and demand her price!"

"Have you not considered that someone else might have wished to blacken Leila's reputation by making it appear that she had taken it?"

"She is an infidel," Enguerrand said. "What reputation has she to defend."

It was difficult for Fergus to keep his temper. "Yet she is my wife and has some authority by dint of that."

"Who would care?"

"I have an idea, but I would like to be sure." Fergus arched a brow. "What of your witness?"

"I care little for treachery in your household. I care more for the relic entrusted to me." Enguerrand pounded his fist upon a table. "Where is the prize?"

Fergus heard a tap upon the door. He opened it to find his father in the portal, his expression grim. He gestured for that man to enter, then closed the door again.

"What is missing from the treasury?" his father asked and Enguerrand started. "It is evident from Agnes' comments in the hall that you expected some prize to be secured here, and your expression now reveals that it is missing. What was it?"

Enguerrand said naught.

"The reliquary of St. Euphemia," Fergus told his father. "We were entrusted with it at the Temple in Jerusalem, and I was charged to bring it here for safekeeping."

"Yet is it not safe!" Enguerrand said.

"Ah!" Calum said, taking a seat and nodding at Enguerrand and Yvan. "Now I understand your presence in the company."

"On the contrary, the reliquary is quite safe," Fergus said, much to the knights' astonishment and his father's interest. "We discovered the theft soon after it occurred, and later the hiding place of the prize. The reliquary has been moved to a new location."

"Where?" Enguerrand asked.

"It is safer if no one else knows." Fergus bowed to his father. "I apologize, Father, for not confiding in you sooner..."

"It is of no matter, my boy," that man said calmly. "A secret is better defended if fewer know it."

"This is outrageous..." Enguerrand sputtered but father and son ignored him.

"The girl provoked him to search for it," Calum said. "And knew its dimensions." He raised his gaze to that of Fergus. "Which means she knew your secret."

"Aye. We believe she stole it on the day I showed Leila the holding."

"But she said she saw her lady with it the day before," Yvan declared.

"A lie. Leila had the sole key to the treasury that day."

"Until you had the silversmith copy them and gave a set to me," Calum said.

"And when we returned from that ride, Leila smelled the girl in the solar."

His father chuckled. "Saracens and their sharp noses!"

"But how could that be?" Enguerrand asked. "If you and your father had the sole keys, only you could have entered the solar and the treasury then."

Calum wagged a finger at him. "But the knot in the cord of mine was retied that day, for it was different when I awakened from my nap. I wondered at it at the time, but saw no reason why it should be so until now."

"But still, any soul could have taken it..."

"The girl was particularly attentive that day. I wondered at that at the time, as well, but was content to let her serve me."

"She wanted the key," Fergus concluded.

"Alas, it is not my attention she covets," Calum said.

Fergus did not understand. "What do you mean?"

"I would wager that she has a scheme to better her position, by ousting Leila from your marriage and stepping into the vacancy herself."

"What madness is this?" Fergus demanded.

His father chuckled. "I have seen her watch you when she thinks herself unobserved. That one never planned to labor all her days, and if you would wed a Saracen, why would you not wed a peasant?"

Fergus swore. Enguerrand looked shaken and Yvan hid a smile behind his hand. Calum looked most pleased with himself. "And what is your scheme now?"

"We shall pretend to fall for her ploy," Fergus said. "Enguerrand and Yvan can search the solar and we will ensure that Leila is believed to be guilty so that Agnes reveals the fullness of her plan..."

His father raised a hand to silence him. "I have a better idea, one that will not discredit your wife in the least."

"I should be glad to hear it," Fergus said, and the older man dropped his voice to a whisper. The Templars and Fergus leaned close to hear his suggestion, which was a vast improvement, indeed.

Calum knew he was going to enjoy this feat. Agnes had tricked him and he was not a man to let such an insult pass. That she meant to discredit Leila, the lady she served and the wife of the laird, was a breach of everything Calum held dear. The scheming girl would be taught a lesson and soon.

He had a wager with Fergus that Agnes would flee and he intended to win it.

"It must be here!" Enguerrand roared from the solar above him, then audibly tipped a chest to its back.

"My wife is innocent," Fergus shouted back. There was a great sound of a scuffle in the laird's chamber, one loud enough to draw the attention of all in the hall. Furniture was tipped and Calum had no doubt that the contents of the various chests were scattered. He made his way down the stairs to the hall, pretending that the task was more difficult than it was.

Of course, there was a small cluster of souls awaiting him at the foot of the stairs. Iain was there, but Calum raised a hand to halt him from climbing to the solar. "I would have a cup of hot milk, Iain, if you please," he said firmly. "Lady Leila, your husband would speak with you in solitude."

Leila nodded and climbed the stairs quickly.

Agnes smirked, turning away to hide her expression as she returned to her sweeping.

Enguerrand and Yvan passed him, noisily demanding a search of the entire keep. "To the smithy!" cried Enguerrand. "She must have hidden it there!"

In truth, they were going to make their way toward Agnes' hiding spot to ensure she could not retrieve what she believed was the relic.

Enguerrand paused on the threshold of the hall and turned back, fixing his glare upon Agnes. "You!" he cried and the girl looked up. "Do not even think of leaving this hall before I speak to you again."

"Of course, sir." Agnes curtsied, her satisfaction with this most clear. She evidently thought she would have the opportunity to condemn Leila, but Calum would help her to see otherwise.

Calum returned to his abandoned seat and sat down heavily, passing a hand over his eyes as if he were more tired than he was. He considered the chess pieces on the floor and bent with painful slowness to pick up a pawn, drawing her to him like a fish on a line.

"My lord, let me assist you in that," Agnes said, easing him back to his seat before she bent to gather the errant pieces. In truth, if she were as dutiful as she would have him believe, she would have picked them up already.

Calum sniffed. She did smell like onions.

"Thank you, Agnes," he said, as if exhausted beyond compare. "I shall miss you, to be sure."

"Miss me, my lord?" She smiled at him. "Why would you miss me? I have no plan to leave Killairic. It is a most fine keep."

"I fear I have been unable to defend you in this matter." Calum shook his head. "It is most unjust, but then, such matters usually are." He sighed.

"What is unjust, my lord? What matter?"

"The matter of the missing Templar prize, of course," Calum admitted heavily. "You were right to tell them of what you saw, but they are not inclined to sense. It is Enguerrand's conviction that Lady Leila must have had an accomplice."

"But why?"

"How else could she sell the prize, knowing so little of Scotland

and of Gaelic?" Calum shook his head. "Nay, by their thinking, she worked with another to ensure her success. They seek that accomplice now."

Agnes paled and licked her lips. "Surely she might have made such an acquaintance on her journey north?"

"But someone must have hidden the treasure for her. How else could she fulfill her obligations of that day, as well as hide the treasure? And given her activities of the day, it must have been someone within the hall."

"Must it have been, sir?"

"Of course!" He ticked off events on his fingers, watching the girl's fear grow. "On her first morning here, Lady Leila broke her fast early at this very board, with Duncan. Iain saw them both, for he told me of their farewell when I rose."

"Perhaps she gave it to Duncan."

"Nay, Iain said Xavier packed provisions for him and that Duncan took naught else from the hall."

Agnes sat down.

"Iain told me also that Lady Leila was subsequently with Xavier in the kitchens, reviewing inventories and making plans. She went then to the smithy, where she aided poor Nellie, and all the village knew of that. The rain was such that she could not have gone any farther without being in a more foul state. Then we two sat together, here by the fire, awaiting Fergus." Calum shook his head. "Nay, if she is the culprit, she had an accomplice, and you can be certain that the accomplice will be the one to bear the burden of the blame."

"What is this?" the girl cried.

"My son will hear no criticism of his lady wife! He believes her innocent. Nay, Agnes, the sole person who could have aided her in this hall, by Enguerrand's reasoning, is you, and I wager that he will not be silent until he has seen you tortured and tried for the crime."

The girl rose to her feet. "Me, sir?"

"You, Agnes. There is no other person who could have so aided Lady Leila." He held her gaze for a moment, letting her see his conviction. "I fear for you, Agnes, which is why I tell you of this." He dropped his voice to a whisper. "Is there a place you might find sanctuary? For once the Templars return to the hall, your fate will be sealed, and even I will not be able to speak for you."

Agnes surveyed the hall, her panic clear. "Dunnisbrae," she whispered. "My brother is there."

"Then flee, Agnes," Calum advised. "Flee now while there is a chance. It will not endure long, so do not delay."

"I will not, my lord. Thank you for this!" She kissed his hand, then walked quickly from the hall. Calum sat back in his chair, not doubting that she broke into a run as soon as she was out of sight.

He wondered how much she would steal on her departure and could not help but think that any loss was worth the price of being rid of Agnes and her schemes.

Leila could not believe that Fergus had convinced the Templars to take her side. She stood at the window of the solar with him, the same one from which she had watched Agnes visit her prize.

Fergus was at the opposite window, both of them ensuring that they remained out of the light. "My father has done as he suggested. She is running to the stables."

"But she has no horse."

"Hamish thinks Stephen is her lover."

That would explain the girl's scent. Leila gripped the sill, watching. She had a glimpse of Enguerrand and one of Yvan. The pair had separated in the forest and their mail had shone briefly in the sunlight. She guessed that they had both closed their cloaks for she could not see them any longer. There was no motion below at all.

Fergus muttered a curse. "And so she steals one of my palfreys," he muttered. "I suppose I should not be surprised."

Leila turned to him as the sound of the hoof beats echoed in the village. "Will she go to back to Dunnisbrae?" she asked and he shrugged.

"I do not care where she goes, so long as the reliquary remains safe and we are rid of her." He came to Leila's side and they watched together. Soon enough, Agnes and a palfrey came into view. She had arrived so quickly that she could not have stopped at the hut of Hamish's aunt and uncle, even if she had divined the new location of the reliquary. She hesitated at the point where the road curved toward the forest.

"Let us send her on her way," Fergus muttered. "Wherever she is going." He leaned out the window then, pointing at her. "There!" he cried. "There is the thief!"

There was a hue and cry from the walls, but the Templars did not reveal themselves. Agnes turned the horse and gave it her heels, urging it to a gallop. She fled down the road that led to Galloway and Leila had never been so glad to see the back of another.

Fergus pulled her into his arms again and held her tightly. "Shall we find you another maid?"

Leila smiled. "Not until the shadow you sense has been dispersed. Is it gone?"

Fergus winced and shook his head. "Perhaps on the morrow."

But perhaps not. Leila held tightly to his hands, glad beyond all that he trusted her, and hoping they would survive whatever threat he sensed.

Would his portent hang over them for all time?

Was it caused by her presence at his side?

What if only her departure would see Killairic safe?

WEDNESDAY, MAY 4, 1188

*Feast Day of the virgin
Saint Walburga*

CHAPTER TWELVE

Châmont-sur-Maine

The messenger assumed he would be spotted quickly.

He had no certainty of how protective a former Templar might be of his holding, and also no desire to be killed before delivering his message. The messenger dismounted while still under the protective cover of the forest and surveyed the village and keep. It was late afternoon and the gates to the village were still open.

To ensure he was not regarded as a threat, he led his horse out of the forest and walked the last increment to the village. He knew the moment he was spotted and was not surprised to see two armed sentries step into the opening of the gate. He drew no weapon and made no quick moves, but continued to walk steadily closer to their watchful figures. His steed, a fine and fast mare, tossed her head, content to walk beside him after their long journey.

The messenger paused outside the gates, knowing he was within range of any archer, and held out the missive in his gloved hand. He spoke in French, knowing that his accent would betray him as a foreigner, but then, his garb probably had done as much already.

"I have a message from Outremer for Lord Gaston de Châmont-sur-Maine," he cried.

The sentries exchanged a glance, then one stepped forward. "From the Temple?"

The messenger shook his head. "The Temple has fallen," he said, for it was a fact. His choice of words did not reveal his own alliance. "This message is from a man who begs the assistance of Lord Gaston."

The sentry offered his hand. "Give me the message and I will see it delivered. You can wait here for any reply."

"Nay." The messenger raised the missive to his chest, his hand closed around it, and took a step back. "I swore to put it into his hand myself." He was aware of the peasants who had gathered to watch the exchange and wondered what they whispered to each other. The local dialect was almost incomprehensible to him and he feared that by entering the village—if he were invited to do so—he might be stepping into a trap. A trickle of cold sweat slid down his back, but he held his ground.

The sentries conferred quietly but only for a moment. "You will leave your horse and your sword here, and Raoul will escort you to the gate of the keep. It will be Lord Gaston's choice to meet you or not."

The messenger bowed, a lump in his throat. "I thank you for this courtesy," he said, hoping that all was as it appeared. Would he die suddenly and so far from home? He hoped not, but there was little choice. He had to deliver the missive. He left his mare with the quiet sentry and surrendered his sword before he followed the first. He never looked back, for he knew that a man's posture could decide his fate. He was uneasy crossing the bridge to the keep, but spared only a single glance to its towering height.

As he crossed the threshold of the keep, he prayed that Lord Gaston was as thoughtful a man as he was reputed to be, and that his own life would not end this day.

Gaston was surprised, as he seldom was.

He did not know the man who stood before him, but he knew

his kind. The visitor had seen perhaps fifty summers and had worked hard for most of those years. He was sturdy and undoubtedly strong, a man with a lined face and grim manner that revealed his trade as a warrior. He had removed his gloves and shoved them into his belt, and Gaston saw his history in his hands. The visitor's garb was plain, his boots and gloves sturdy and well-worn. His armor was repaired but in good care. He traveled without a squire, and a fading tan revealed that he had been in warmer climes of late. His eyes were narrowed and his lips were thin, and Gaston recognized that he was a man who had done what needed to be done.

Gaston was reminded of Duncan and dozens of other men who earned their way with their blades. He was glad that the sentries had taken the sword of this one, but was certain this man carried several more knives.

He would be fast in their use.

Gaston looked the messenger in the eye as that man approached. The messenger dropped to one knee and offered a scroll graced with a seal Gaston did not recognize. The writing that Gaston could see was Arabic.

"Who sent you?" Gaston asked in Arabic. His speech was less fluid than it had been in Outremer, but he knew he was understood.

The man's gaze flicked in surprise. "A friend to me and a stranger to you," he replied. "The message provides the introduction."

Mindful of the possibility of poison, Gaston tugged on his gloves. He accepted the scroll and retreated to the window. He turned it in the sunlight, finding nothing unusual about it. Who would send him a message? The expense of dispatching the messenger over such a distance would have been considerable, and Gaston could not think of what appeal to him would merit the cost.

He broke the seal and opened the missive, unfurling it with care. There was no powder within it or other unpleasant surprise, just a few lines of Arabic script.

It began with compliments about his reputation for honor and trustworthiness, then continued with an entreaty that he direct the messenger to Leila binte Qadir lufti al-Ramm, if Gaston knew her location, or to dispatch the messenger to someone who did know her whereabouts. In the event that Gaston did not know Leila or her location, the sender asked for that information to be sent as a reply.

This must be the full name of Leila, the girl who had been disguised as the squire Laurent, and had left Jerusalem under the protection of Gaston's small party. He ran his fingertip over the signature. "Hakim ben Yasir lufi al-Ramm," he read, then glanced back to the messenger.

That man bowed his head. "He sent me."

"Do you know the contents of this missive?"

The messenger smiled a little. "I have had time to think about it," he admitted. He made to reach beneath his tabard, but Gaston cleared his throat and he froze. One of Gaston's men stepped forward and the messenger raised his hands. "There is a second scroll in a pouch hung around my neck," he supplied in halting French.

Gaston's man retrieved the scroll, then brought it to Gaston.

It was addressed to "Little Flower" with a tiny illustration of a flower beside the words.

Gaston raised his gaze to the messenger.

"His niece," that man supplied. "She disappeared, and he believes you know where she is. He wishes to find her."

To what purpose? Gaston did not know precisely why Leila had been determined to leave Outremer. He had not been aware of her gender when she joined their party in disguise but truly, her choice indicated a certain desperation. Would the uncle's intentions be clear from his missive? Or would he attempt to deceive Leila to encourage her return? Gaston considered the question for only a moment before he broke the seal on the message to Leila.

The messenger gasped, but Gaston ignored him. He saw at a glance that this message was much longer and would take him time to understand fully. "See that the visitor is fed and offered refreshment in the hall," he commanded. "I will have a reply for him shortly."

He gave his seneschal a hard look and knew that the messenger would be guarded and kept from seeing too much of the keep's interior. He climbed the stairs to the solar where his lady's counsel could be sought.

Radegunde, Gaston recalled, had been friendly with Leila. Perhaps his wife's maid would make more sense of this missive than he could. Undoubtedly, she would know more of Leila's reason for fleeing her home. He would not imperil Leila now, but the endearment and the tiny flower made him wonder if she was missed.

It was not within Gaston to be cruel, and he felt the weight of responsibility in making the right choice for the fugitive Saracen.

He wished only to make the right choice.

FRIDAY, MAY 20, 1188

Feast Day of
Saint Ethelbert of East Anglia
& Saint Alucin of York

CHAPTER THIRTEEN

ergus awakened abruptly, his heart beating rather too quickly. He felt agitated and threatened, but was relieved to find himself in the solar. He was alone in the bed and sat up quickly, wondering where Leila was. She was watching him from a short distance away, her brows drawn together in concern. She was already dressed, and he wondered at that, for it was still early enough for there to be shadows in the corners.

He had had the nightmare again. He knew it.

What had he said in his sleep?

"Is something amiss?" he asked.

"Why do you dream of her?" Leila asked, showing her usual inclination to be outspoken.

"Who?"

"Isobel, of course. You shout her name in the night."

"I do?" Fergus knew he had experienced the nightmare of Isobel three times, but he had chosen not to speak to Leila about it. He did not wish her to fear for her future at Killairic and had kept its details to himself, but he saw on this morning that he might not have a choice.

In a way, it was a relief.

"You do." Leila began to pace the width of the solar. "You take your pleasure with me, then you call out for her." She spared him a hot glance. "It is most unsettling."

Fergus rose and pushed a hand through his hair. Before he could find a way to explain, Leila continued. "I did not expect love to blossom between us quickly, especially when your heart was already surrendered. But I do expect some effort on your part, Fergus, and perhaps I am a fool, but I should prefer fidelity."

"I have been with no woman but you, and so it shall be until the end of our handfast. I gave you my word."

She flung out a hand and he found himself intrigued that she was so passionate. "Then why cry her name with such anguish? It is as if your heart is wretched." Her voice turned husky. "If you wish so greatly to be with her, then we should part and you should go to her. I will not stand in the path of your happiness, Fergus. Go and be with your beloved."

Fergus was surprised. "You suggest that we part because of a dream?"

She spun to face him. "It is in dreams that we cannot hide our true desires."

"What of nightmares?"

Leila frowned, clearly not understanding his words.

Fergus crossed the floor to her and caught her shoulders in his hands. She was trembling and again, he was surprised by the intensity of her feelings. On the other hand, though, she had risked much and was reliant upon him. He looked down into her eyes, hoping she would believe the truth. "I am haunted by Isobel but not in the way you believe," he explained. "She has appeared to me in a recurring nightmare, one in which I see Killairic destroyed because of her efforts."

"Which efforts?"

"I do not know. It is a dream, so it makes little sense."

"Your angel is warning you," Leila said and Fergus nodded.

"As my wife has done before. Isobel's tongue is a snake in this dream, and Killairic is consumed in flames. I cannot find you." He heard his voice drop lower as the terror of his dream assailed him in daylight. His voice was hoarse when he continued. "I cannot protect you and Killairic itself is lost." He shuddered involuntarily, aware that she watched him closely. "All is lost, and it is devastating."

Leila leaned against his chest and her arms slid around his waist. "It might not mean that. It might be symbolic. If so, the dream could mean many things."

"It could," he acknowledged, drawing her closer.

"It could mean that Isobel lies."

"That was my first notion. Snakes are often symbolic of deceit."

"Or of healing," Leila suggested. "Perhaps her words will reveal a dark truth that must be faced."

"Perhaps. I should have told you," he admitted, then kissed her temple. "I did not wish to concern you with what might be whimsy."

"I told you before that if you do not heed your guardian angel, he may abandon you," she chided, then pulled back from his embrace to look up at him. He saw unexpected concern in her expression. "What if your dream warns you that you could lose Killairic because of me?"

"What? That is nonsense!"

"Is it?" Leila demanded, abandoning him to pace again. "Murdoch says Killairic must be bestowed upon you by the king, in the event of your father's demise."

"Aye, but there is tradition..."

Leila met his gaze, her tone urgent. "What king will call for a war in one moment, then grant a key holding to a man who is wed to the enemy?"

Fergus would have liked to have believed that the king would make an exception for him, but he saw immediately that Leila did not share his view. "This is why you talk to the priest."

She nodded. "I will ask to be baptized on Iona. I think it will be best for there to be many witnesses of my choice, and also that this matter be resolved sooner rather than later. Your father, as fond as I am of him, weakens."

Fergus was humbled by her choice. "Are you certain, Leila?"

She lifted her chin, looking fierce. "I vowed to be the best wife that I could be, Fergus. It would hardly be fitting for you to lose your legacy because of me."

He smiled at her, closing the distance between them to cup her chin in his hand. "And what do I give you, Leila, that merits such choices on your part?"

"A home," she replied immediately. "A sanctuary." She sighed. "What of the prize? Do you think it still safe where it is hidden?"

"I do. I suspect it is safer there than it was in the treasury."

"We must find a better place for it, a permanent place," Leila said, her worry clear. "Do you think Agnes went to Dunnisbrae?"

Fergus pursed his lips. "Perhaps. She fled in that direction but Enguerrand turned back once he thought her unlikely to return to Killairic. He is likely right that her exact destination is of little concern."

It was evident that Leila did not share his conviction. "She will make trouble for me, no matter where she goes," she said softly.

"Even if she told Stewart of the reliquary, he would have the wits to be skeptical of any tale Agnes might tell. She came from there, which hints to me that she might have been cast out."

"Because he knew her nature," Leila murmured, appearing to be slightly reassured.

Fergus smiled. "We do need to find a better place for it. Enguerrand and Yvan will not depart until they are convinced it is secure."

"Perhaps there will be a bishop at Iona to take it into his care."

"Perhaps the Templars would not approve of that." Fergus frowned. "I have been wondering if we should undertake a journey to Edinburgh, purportedly so you can meet my mother's kin. There are Templar houses near there, and perhaps the prize will find sanctuary with them."

"Another journey," Leila said. "I would see your dream banished before we depart. Do you still sense that threat?"

He nodded. "It grows more ominous every day."

"This is not reassuring."

Fergus could only agree. "Perhaps Gaston will send word soon of any plans for the prize."

Leila nodded. "Surely Duncan will halt here when he rides to retrieve Radegunde or after he weds her."

Fergus hoped the warrior managed to do both. "I have not thus far given you a haven, Leila."

"But you have given me a home." She lifted a finger. "With a dovecote."

"The birds should arrive soon."

Leila smiled a little. "And then perhaps you will give me a child with blue eyes."

Fergus slid his fingers beneath her veil, caressing the softness of her skin, for he was awed once again by the tiny lioness he had taken to wife. "Must you hasten to the hall?" he murmured, then bent and touched his lips to hers. Leila sighed and leaned against him, her small hands landing upon his chest. "I would endeavor to create that child if my lady would linger a little longer."

She lifted her mouth to his, her surrender as sweet and hot as ever. She was so trusting. She gave so much. She planned for his success and tried to remove every obstacle. On this morn, Fergus would ensure that Leila understood that no other woman ever intruded upon his thoughts when he was with her.

A curse upon Isobel for even giving his loyal wife a doubt.

Isobel had not been surprised when she finally bled.

In fact, she had been relieved, even triumphant. Once again, she had compelled her body to support her own desires. She had secretly bumped her belly into furniture and prayed for deliverance from her misfortune. She had exerted herself overmuch and had been impressed that a babe could be so hard to dislodge even when so young.

She hated pregnancy, the uneasy stomach, the bulge in her figure, and the physical discomfort that resulted from the growing burden. She had felt clumsy and unattractive while carrying Gavin, though she had known it was her duty to do so. Her distaste had been naught compared to the actual delivery of her son, which had been a hell of seeming eternity. Isobel was determined to never again endure such torment.

Stewart should have been content with one son. Gavin was such a robust boy that there was no chance of him being lost to illness. Isobel had done her duty, in her view, but in this matter, as in all others, Stewart was greedy for more. Isobel could not keep her legal husband from her bed or deny him the marital debt, but she had no intention of destroying her life—and risking it—by bearing child after child after child.

She had thought she might bear one more, but the return of Fergus had dismissed that notion.

And time was of the essence. It could not be long before a man like Fergus found a willing and suitable bride, yet Isobel could not appeal to him with Stewart's babe in her belly. Her previously successful tactics had not worked quickly enough, but Isobel had not been daunted.

In desperation, she had consumed herbs that were said to oust babes from the womb. This felt daring and bold and a part of her feared that she went too far, but all ended as Isobel desired. When this child abandoned her womb, just like the last, she wept for the sake of appearances but within her heart, Isobel was glad.

So very glad.

Stewart was significantly less so.

He raged at the injustice. He was foul of temper with every soul at Dunnisbrae and impossible to please in any matter. He shouted at her and might have struck her, if he had not so desperately desired another son.

His greed was Isobel's salvation.

It was only days before he joined her abed and his efforts began anew. Each night, as he thrust atop her in pursuit of his pleasure, Isobel hated him a little more. Each morning, when she awakened to the feel of his hand between her thighs, she kept her eyes closed and despised him. Stewart thought she had not noticed the pretty maid return to labor in the hall, the one Isobel had not seen in years, the one so willing to do whatever Stewart demanded of her. Isobel had seen and hated Stewart even more for welcoming a whore.

She knew she might not have loathed Stewart quite so much if Fergus had not returned. If Fergus had not been so handsome, or so affluent, she might have accepted the truth of her marriage more readily. She knew Fergus to be gentle but firm, a fair man and a good lover. Isobel knew that her life would be vastly improved with Fergus as spouse instead of Stewart.

Especially if she ensured she never ever conceived again.

She would never forget the shape and smell of that herb, to be sure.

Isobel's plan was made. She would leave Stewart and throw herself at the mercy of Fergus. She would tell him a tale, one that he would believe, and she would have her way. She lingered only a week at Dunnisbrae after the loss of her child, only a week to ensure that she could endure the ride to Killairic.

She feared discovery with every moment, but Stewart, livid about the loss of another child, was not attentive to nuance. All the same, Isobel scarcely slept the night before her planned departure. She reviewed her preparations endlessly, certain that Stewart would somehow foil her scheme.

But, on that chosen morning, Stewart did precisely as she had anticipated. He awakened with his usual morning erection. He rolled over and used her for his pleasure, grunting like a rutting pig, indifferent as to whether she was even awake herself. Her anger simmered along with her sense that justice would be served. His hands ran over her, and Isobel hated that this was the extent of his appreciation for her. She had brought him a holding and given him a son, but Stewart always wanted more.

Isobel's hatred sharpened. Even as her husband labored for his release, she reached beneath the bed and retrieved one of the needles Fergus had given to her, hiding it in her hand. Stewart found his pleasure with a shout, then collapsed on his back, panting as his eyes closed again.

It was yet early. The villagers were only beginning to stir. He usually slept an hour, maybe more, after relieving himself.

This day would be different.

Isobel rolled over and looked down at her husband, at the silver in his beard and his hair, at the lines on his face and the harsh line of his mouth. She saw him for the hard warrior he was, the older man whom she would survive. There was no tenderness in her heart in this moment for this man. She saw only what he had cost her, what he had taken, how he had used her for his own gain.

She saw only that he was less of a man than Fergus and hated him for that.

Stewart's hand slipped from her hip as he dozed and his mouth slackened. She waited, watching, heart racing, until his breath slowed.

He would never forget this day, to be sure.

Isobel licked her lips and steeled her resolve.

She lifted the needle with its sharp point.

And she drove it into his eye with all of her might.

She would have done the same to the other, but Stewart roared in pain and seized her wrist. She bit him so that he released her, then pulled out the needle. He snatched at her but she kicked him in the groin, stumbling from the bed. He lunged after her and swore, one hand upon his bleeding eye and the other at his crotch.

His man had already raced up the stairs and flung open the door. "What is amiss?" he demanded, his gaze darting between Stewart and Isobel.

"I do not know. I welcomed him as ever, but then he cried out."

"Bitch!" Stewart bellowed. "Deceitful, wicked bitch!"

She dropped her voice to a whisper. "Perhaps a fit or fury," she said to Stewart's comrade. She lowered her gaze demurely. "I regret that he did not find his pleasure."

"Ah!" said the guard.

Stewart began to swear more vehemently. He stumbled across the chamber, blood streaming down his cheek from beneath his fist, and tried to snatch at Isobel.

"He would finish what was left undone," she whispered even as he roared.

His guard swore in astonishment. "Blood runs from his eyes!"

"God in Heaven! What has he done to himself?" Isobel whispered in mock horror. "I will get old Helga from the village!"

"Do!" the guard insisted. "Make haste, my lady." He moved then to seize Stewart and forcibly guide him back to the bed. "My lord, you must be still."

"Seize that witch..."

"My lord, I beg of you, show a care for your own welfare..."

Isobel ran, but she did not run to Helga in the village. She raced down the stairs and seized Gavin, carrying the sleepy boy. She spat on the girl, Agnes, when that whore might have tripped her and shoved her aside. Stewart was welcome to her charms!

Isobel fled to the stables and to the stall of the horse she had saddled the night before, after the ostler had retired. All her preparations had been made. She donned the kirtle left there and the boots. She seized the packed saddlebag she had left in the stall, then flung on the cloak folded beside it. She leaped into the saddle, hiding her son beneath the cloak, and holding him fast against her side.

"Hush, Gavin," she said and he obeyed, curling his heat against her and closing his eyes. She raced the palfrey toward the gate. "My husband is stricken!" she cried to the sentries. "I must fetch help with all haste!"

The guards opened the portcullis, fools that they were, and Isobel galloped out of Dunnisbrae at speed. She took a breath of precious freedom, not caring how much she had left behind. Fergus would buy her more garments, and Killairic was far more prosperous that Dunnisbrae had become. Her father had oft said that good fortune must be claimed not waited upon. The sound of Stewart's rage carried to them even at a distance and Isobel shivered.

She was rid of him, for good.

"Mother?" Gavin whispered. "What is wrong with Father?"

"Naught more than he deserves."

"Then why are we leaving?"

Isobel kissed the top of her son's head. She loved him more dearly on this morning than she had yet, for he was the key to the success of her scheme. "We ride to Killairic."

"But why?"

"To meet some friends, Gavin."

"But Father..."

"Is only angry this morn. He will be fine by the time he breaks his fast."

"But..."

"Hush, Gavin. All will be well." Isobel touched her heels to the horse's flanks, smiling at the prospect of success.

It was the only possible outcome, after all, with a scheme so infallible as this.

It was late afternoon when Fergus noted some agitation at the village gates. A woman shouted and it looked as if a palfrey had arrived. It was unusual for a horse to arrive alone, particularly ridden by a woman, and Fergus headed for the gates to investigate. The sentry argued with the woman and though Fergus could not discern their words, he feared he recognized the woman's voice.

Had his vexation with Isobel summoned her to Killairic? It seemed as much. He feared that Leila might imagine it were so. He quickened his pace, hoping he was wrong.

He was not. It *was* Isobel. She wore a heavy cloak and a plain kirtle and her voice was raised in anger. Her hair was loose and her manner imperious.

"Of course, Laird Fergus will see me," she insisted. "You must escort me to the hall. I must speak with him immediately..."

"Then do as much," Fergus invited, knowing his annoyance showed. How would her arrival at his gates alone be construed? He doubted Stewart would approve and suspected that man might blame him for Isobel's choice. Fergus needed no new friction with Stewart, to be sure. Leila might be concerned, given his own nightmare. "There must be good cause for you to have ridden so far without escort."

Relief lit Isobel's features. "Fergus! Stewart had a fit this morn and I feared for my life!" A murmur passed through the company of those who had gathered in curiosity and Fergus wondered if Isobel had desired to start the tale. She leaped from the saddle and reached up to lower her son to the ground. The boy looked uncertain, and rightly so. "I feared for both myself and Gavin and fled, knowing you would offer us sanctuary."

It was a risky matter to offer a haven to another man's wife, especially the wife of a warrior like Stewart. Fergus did not appreciate that Isobel embroiled him in her troubles and wondered if she meant to make this a habit.

He would halt the inclination now.

Fergus folded his arms across his chest. "A fit?" he echoed. "That does not sound like Stewart. I thought him a temperate man. Are you certain you did not provoke him?"

If Stewart had not threatened Isobel before this day, Fergus wagered there was some detail omitted from her tale. Her quick sidelong glance at his query confirmed his suspicions.

It was odd that after four years apart, he found her so much less enticing than once had been the case. In fact, Fergus wondered how he had missed Isobel's quick expressions, the ones she tried to hide, the ones that revealed her words might not be the fullness of the truth. Even without the warning of his dream, he distrusted her.

What had she done this morn?

"Temperate?" she repeated with a laugh. "His is harsh beyond belief, cruel even." She cast herself at Fergus, an entreaty in her eyes. "I was in despair, Fergus, until your return. I knew that if I left Stewart, you would stand by our betrothal. Let us wed this very day that I might have sanctuary at Killairic. You have a priest, do you not?"

Fergus frowned and stepped back, extricating himself from her embrace. "What madness is this, Isobel? You are wedded to Stewart..."

"I have left him!"

"You exchanged your vows before a bishop. You have borne his son." He gestured to the boy, who simply watched. He looked pale, to Fergus' thinking, and had to be in need of a hot meal. "Have you eaten this day?"

"Nay, of course not. I fled for my life!"

Fergus scanned the gathered company and spotted the smith. "Farquar, would you take Gavin to the kitchens for me, please? Tell Xavier that the lad has not eaten all day."

"Certainly, my lord."

Intriguingly, Gavin did not look to his mother for her approval but simply followed instruction. Doubtless the boy was starving.

"What madness is this, Isobel, that you would not ensure the boy was fed?" Fergus demanded of her.

Isobel's expression turned sly and she clutched at his arm.

"Fergus, we must speak in private. There is much you do not know."

"I know all I need to know," Fergus corrected. "You chose to forget our betrothal and wed Stewart instead. What is done cannot be undone."

"You would conclude differently, if you knew the whole of the truth," Isobel said, her tone challenging.

"I doubt as much. I have a wife, Isobel, and I will not put Leila aside to better suit your convenience."

"A wife?" Isobel scoffed. "Is that what you call an infidel who meets you abed?"

"We have a handfast."

"A handfast is no firm bond, Fergus, and you know it well."

"My word is my bond, and I have given it to Leila."

She lifted her chin, her eyes flashing. "You gave it to me first."

"And you disregarded it, thus freeing me from any commitment to you." Fergus sighed. "Go home, Isobel. Go home to Dunnisbrae. Make amends with Stewart for whatever you have done and be content with your lot."

Fury flashed in her eyes before she dropped her gaze. "Content," she muttered so softly that only Fergus could have heard her. "Why should I be content with less than my father chose for me?"

Fergus leaned close to her. "Because you already chose to abandon his arrangement."

Isobel licked her lips, spared a glance at the villagers, then laid her hand upon Fergus' chest. "Have mercy, Fergus. I have journeyed all this way to speak with you. Will you not hear me out and offer me a measure of hospitality?"

Fergus did not point out that her husband had failed to offer him and Hamish such courtesy. It was too late for her to ride back to Dunnisbrae before dark, and he would not be to blame for any crime befalling her in darkness. Gavin had to eat, and he supposed that he would have to offer Isobel a meal, as well.

She could ride to Dunnisbrae in the morning.

He turned and pointed. "The midwife's hut stands empty. You and the boy can sleep there this night. I will welcome you to the board for the evening meal." Fergus knew his lack of enthusiasm showed, but was surprised by the rage that shone briefly in her eyes.

Then Isobel laughed, as if he made a jest, but there was no merriment in her eyes. "A hut? Fergus, you tease me! I will stay in the keep itself, of course, as befits my birthright..."

"There is no room," Fergus said, interrupting her. "And it would not be fitting for you to sleep in the hall with warriors."

Isobel's tone was sweet, too sweet. "As I recall, there are two chambers in Killairic's keep."

"One occupied by my wife and me, and the other by my father." Fergus held her gaze. "I will oust neither for a neighbor who arrives uninvited."

Isobel inhaled sharply but bowed her head so quickly that only Fergus guessed her wrath. "As you wish, my lord," she said with a sweetness that had to be feigned. "I look forward to seeing you at the board."

Fergus returned to the hall, knowing that he had made the best possible compromise but distrusting Isobel's intent all the same. He could not dismiss the memory of his dream or the fact that his dread had redoubled when Isobel entered Killairic's gates.

Even though Fergus had warned her about their guest, Leila was startled when she came into the hall and found Isobel there.

The tall, slender beauty with hair of gold could be no other than Fergus' former betrothed. She spoke to a young boy, as flaxen-haired as she, her expression so sweet and serene that Leila was reminded of a Madonna she had glimpsed in a church on their journey north. She thought it might have been in the chapel adjacent to the cemetery where they had buried Kerr.

She distrusted the other woman and disliked that she had arrived at Killairic's gates unannounced and uninvited. Even without the warning of Fergus' dream, Leila would have disliked how readily Isobel could anger Fergus. She had a power over him yet, and one Leila would have preferred to have seen dispelled.

Isobel glanced up at Leila and her smile was cool. Then she stepped gracefully across the hall. Leila noted that the other woman was almost as tall as Fergus and felt at a disadvantage. Isobel's manner in greeting Leila was such that she might have been lady of the keep herself, which only increased Leila's determination to conquer Gaelic. Leila was certain that her suspicions about the other woman's malicious intent were correct, but she smiled politely all the same.

"It must be so strange for you in Scotland, Leila," Isobel said, omitting any form of address. Leila knew it was no accident. She spoke slowly, evidently intent upon being understood. "Fergus' stray Saracen, so far from home."

"Fergus' wife," Leila replied. "In her new home."

Isobel laughed, as if with pity. "But I understood you made only a handfast."

"Surely the pledge of a man like Fergus has merit."

Isobel shook her head. "Surely men are the same in all the world, Leila, especially in the matter of their pleasure. Why, Fergus pledged himself to me before his departure to the east. I doubt he was chaste."

"I believe he was."

Isobel laughed again. "Proving only that you believe men's lies while I have learned my lesson. I should never have surrendered my maidenhead to Fergus, but four years ago, I was still trusting."

Leila supposed that she should not have been surprised that a betrothed couple had been intimate, especially before one of them departed on a long journey. She could not think what to say, but Isobel gave her little chance.

She turned an adoring smile upon her son. "Gavin so resembles his father, does he not?"

"I could not say," Leila admitted in some confusion. "I have not met Stewart MacEwan."

Isobel laughed merrily at this, as if Leila jested with her. "You must see it, Leila," she said in a confidential tone. Her eyes shone. "You must *know*."

If Isobel meant to imply that Gavin was Fergus' son, Leila would wait for her to say it aloud. She held the other woman's gaze, fairly daring her to do it.

Isobel did. "Gavin is three years and three months of age," she whispered, her eyes gleaming. "I married for the sake of Fergus' son. I was with child and had no defender. Until Fergus returned to Killairic. I left Stewart this morning for the sake of Gavin. A son should be raised by his blood father and no other. Do you not agree that would be best?"

"Not for me," Leila said, referring both to the notion of Gavin remaining at Killairic and her own childhood in her uncle's home.

Isobel's lips twisted. "Nay, the sole course best for you would be your immediate return to the lands of your own kind." Fergus appeared at the base of the stairs, and Isobel continued in a quick whisper. "You will never be accepted as one of us. Your insistence upon remaining can only destroy Fergus and the regard that others have for him here. I know he acts with honor: give him the opportunity to do as much for his own son. If you care for him, surely you care for his advantage."

Isobel was a viper to be sure, a viper who spewed venom with very word. Leila did not respond but went to Fergus to ask him some detail about the meal. He surveyed her and concern lit his eyes as he perceived that she was disturbed. His gaze flicked to Isobel as his lips tightened.

"Sit between my father and me," he said tersely and Leila nodded agreement.

Calum descended the stairs in that moment, his features brightening at the sight of her, and Leila escorted him to the board. The older man spared their guest only a quick greeting, then continued to speak French to Leila as he took his place.

She did not miss the warning in the other woman's eyes, and knew this matter was not yet put to rest. To Leila's thinking, Isobel could not leave Killairic soon enough.

Isobel's allure was diminishing so rapidly that Fergus could not imagine he had ever seen any merit in her. When he had changed and descended to the hall, he knew at a glance that Leila was upset. Her features were composed and her manner quiet, her thoughts hidden so surely that he knew something had gone awry.

Isobel looked pleased with herself, which meant she had said something to his lady wife. Fergus doubted it had been true, but could scarce discover the truth as the company sat down to the evening meal. He kissed Leila as if they had been parted for longer than had been the case and felt a little tremor in her response. He hoped his touch reassured her and kept his hand upon the back of her waist. He seated himself between the two women, certain this would simplify matters. He also invited Murdoch to sit by his father, so that the two warriors could share a trencher while he shared with Leila.

Isobel took this in poor humor, clearly having believed that she would share with Fergus instead of her son.

All the same, Fergus' plan was ill-fated. Isobel pressed herself against him and talked ceaselessly to him. He thought she scarce took a breath, for fear that he might glance at his wife. He knew that she spoke in quick Gaelic, thick with dialect, deliberately so that Leila could not follow her words. She said little of import, merely reminding him of some event in their shared past or spoke of some mutual friend, but clearly intended to demonstrate that they shared a history that Leila did not.

Leila ignored Isobel, turning her attention to Calum. As much as Fergus admired her grace and good manners, he disliked that Isobel would so insult Leila in their home. He could not utter more than a word, though, and his temper rose steadily during the meal.

By the time the trenchers were cast to the dogs, he was furious with Isobel.

When she entreated him to accompany her to the healer's hut, lest she become lost on the way, Fergus ceded to her request immediately. He had more than sufficient to say to his former betrothed.

He begged the indulgence of Leila, noting how she scanned his features before she nodded, then seized Isobel's elbow and marched her from the hall. The boy ran behind them.

"Fergus!" Isobel said with pleasure. "I had no notion that you were so intent upon being alone with me."

"How else should I chastise you for your rudeness?" he demanded. "What ails you that you would insult my lady wife in our hall? What seizes your wits that you would touch me as a lover in the company of my wife?"

Isobel smiled up at him coyly. "You would rather I wait until we are alone?"

"I would rather you recall that you are Stewart's wife."

"Stewart!" Isobel made a dismissive gesture, even as they reached the door to the healer's hut. Fergus opened the portal, urged her inside, and left the door open while he lit a lantern. Isobel wrinkled her nose at the simplicity of the place, but Fergus did not care about her pleasure.

The boy was less insulted than his mother. Indeed, he was already eyeing the pallet with such yearning that Fergus guessed he was exhausted.

Fergus gestured to the pallet with clean bedding upon it. "You will be sufficiently comfortable here until your departure in the morning. There is oil in the lantern and you will not need a fire on so mild a night. They will give you bread to break your fast in the kitchens." He inclined his head and bowed slightly. "I wish you a good journey to Dunnisbrae, for I doubt I will see you again."

Isobel's dismay was clear. "You cannot believe that I will leave Killairic for Dunnisbrae?"

"Of course, you will, and you will do as much before noon on the morrow." Fergus smiled thinly. "I would not have you be without shelter when night falls and it is a long ride." He nodded to Gavin, then turned to leave.

Isobel pursued him, snatching at his sleeve. "Fergus! I left Stewart to come to you! I have no plan to return to Dunnisbrae, and truly, Stewart might not have me back."

"He is your husband. Of course, he will welcome your return."

Isobel's expression was sly for a moment, then she appealed to him again, looking feminine and vulnerable. "But he beats me, Fergus. I cannot bear to stay with him."

Fergus glanced to the boy, who was visibly listening. "Then you must appeal to the king for sanctuary and to the bishop to have your match annulled."

"I thought you would aid me."

"You were wrong."

Anger simmered in her gaze, but Fergus did not care. He

stepped out of the hut, pausing to turn back and meet the fury in Isobel's eyes. "Even if I were inclined to assist an old friend, your rudeness to my wife since your arrival would kill that impulse. Farewell, Isobel."

"Farewell!" she echoed in outrage. "Your wife?" She lunged after him and drew him to a halt, her words falling in an angry torrent. "Just because you have a Saracen whore in your bed does not mean that your obligations to me are done. We were betrothed, Fergus."

"And you chose to wed another. That is an effective means of ending a betrothal." He shook off her grip. "Godspeed to you, Isobel. Do not be so fool as to return again without your husband."

"And what of my son?" she cried. "What of our son?"

Fergus turned to look at her in confusion.

Isobel smiled. "Oh, aye, Gavin is our son, Fergus. He is *your* son."

"We laid together but once..."

"And it was sufficient, to be sure. The proof accompanied me this day!"

"Gavin is Stewart's son. I see his father in him."

"You are deceived!" Isobel retorted. "We were intimate. I conceived. You were gone! What was I to do, a woman with a rounding belly but no husband? My father would have been outraged. I seduced Stewart and ensured that we were discovered, then my father insisted upon the match. I told Stewart that I bore his son, and he believed me." She was triumphant, which said much of her nature. Fergus could not believe that any person of merit would take such pride in a deception of such magnitude.

She was also lying.

"But you wed Stewart three months after my departure. Surely he noted that the boy was born three months too soon?" he asked quietly, knowing this was not the least of the issue with her tale.

The boy watched with wide eyes, clearly uncertain what to think. Fergus hoped he did not understand it all.

"I lied, for the safety of both of us," Isobel said. "I went to my cousin on the isles and gave birth to the boy there. He was born at the Yule. I lingered for the winter, then returned to Dunnisbrae, and told Stewart the boy was younger than he was." She sneered. "He knew naught of babes and their size, and he trusted me."

Fergus thought that said more good of Stewart than of Isobel. "Whether this tale is true or yet another lie, it matters little. Gavin cannot be my son."

"I say he is!"

"And you lie, Isobel," Fergus said, his recurring dream at the forefront of his thoughts. "All children in my family are born with red hair." He glanced back at the yawning boy, even as Isobel's lips parted in dismay. "Stewart is your father, Gavin. Never doubt it."

"Aye, sir."

"Fergus! Even if that is true, you cannot compel me to return to Dunnisbrae..."

"I can and I will. Farewell, Isobel." Fergus left the hut then, ignoring the way she shouted after him, and strode back to the keep with purpose. He told Stephen to have Isobel's palfrey saddled at first light. He spoke to Xavier about the morning, ensuring that it was understood that Isobel and Gavin could break their fast in the kitchens.

Enguerrand and Yvan were bent over their chess board and his father was reminiscing with Murdoch. Fergus wished them all a good night and climbed the stairs to the solar, to Leila, and to a misunderstanding that had to be put right.

SATURDAY, MAY 21, 1188

Feast Day of Saint Helena

CHAPTER FOURTEEN

sobel was outraged.

She was accustomed to having her way, and to ensuring it by whatever means were necessary. How dare Fergus choose his dirty little infidel over her? How dare Fergus insist that she lied about Gavin?

And how dare he send her back to Dunnisbrae? Stewart never had beaten her, but she feared he might do as much after events of this day. She could not return to the keep that had been her father's holding.

It was unjust!

She had to compel Fergus to let her remain at Killairic. He could not be so indifferent to her fate as he would have her believe. She needed only a few more days to wear down his resistance and gain her sole desire.

But how? He was gone and she was left in this barren hut for the night, with only her son for company. Even the comforts of the hall were denied to her, and this travesty added to her indignation.

Isobel marched around the small hut in a tight circle, thinking furiously as Gavin watched her with uncertainty. How could she set all to rights? That was when she noticed the array of dried plants hanging from the beams of the roof. They were brown and dusty, but the sight reminded her that this had been the healer's hut.

Herbs! They had been key to the success of the first part of her plan.

Isobel flung open the cupboard that stood in one corner and rummaged through its contents. She would make herself ill. She would ingest some herb or root that would void her stomach. She would be pale and weak, and Fergus would not be able to cast her out. Indeed, he might insist that she be moved to the hall. If he set his whore to tending her, she could tell the other woman more lies, perhaps even encourage her to leave of her own volition.

Aye, it was the perfect scheme.

Its weakness lay in Isobel's limited knowledge of herbs and healing plants. She sniffed at the various leaves, but doubted any would be strong enough. She could not find the one she had used just weeks before. She had need of a root, for that was where the potency of the plant was concentrated. She found two different ones, stored separately and with a care that indicated their power. She sniffed them both and chose the largest rhizome of the one with the sharpest scent. She then pivoted to meet Gavin's gaze.

"Run to the keep," she instructed him. "Tell Laird Fergus that I am taken ill."

"But you are not, Mother."

"Aye, Gavin. I am." Isobel bit the root and chewed it, grimacing at its bitter taste. She managed to swallow that mouthful and take another bite before the convulsion seized her, barely giving her time to realize that she had made a terrible mistake.

Leila was sitting on the side of the bed, her innards in turmoil. Could it be true? Could Gavin be Fergus' son? She knew he had been chaste in Outremer, or even since leaving Killairic, but what about before that? Had his betrothal to Isobel been celebrated in a most earthy way? It might well have been.

What were the ramifications for her if Fergus acknowledged Gavin as his son? Leila doubted that her position would be secure, even if she did bear a son to Fergus, for hers would be the younger and thus not the heir.

She rose from the bed to pace, restless in her uncertainty. She felt the situation more keenly because her own courses were a week late. Was it simply the change in diet and situation, or had she conceived?

If Fergus welcomed Isobel's return and acknowledged Gavin as his own blood, Leila doubted that she would even be permitted to remain at Killairic. Where would she go, especially if she had a babe in her belly?

Haynesdale, she decided, liking the notion as soon as it occurred to her. Bartholomew had been her friend for many years. He and Anna would give her shelter. Aye, she would ride to Haynesdale. It would take her less than a week, and she was certain she could manage the journey without incident. Perhaps Murdoch would escort her...

"What did she say?" Fergus demanded from behind her.

Leila spun to find him standing in the portal, waiting on the threshold as if he were uncertain of her reaction.

She took a breath. "That the boy is yours."

Fergus shook his head and stepped into the room, closing the door behind himself. "The same nonsense she said to me." He came directly to her and took her hands within his own. His gaze was piercing. "You know it is a lie, do you not?"

Leila shook her head. "I do not. You might have been intimate with her before your departure. I cannot fault you for that."

"I was, at her insistence, though I spilled my seed on the linens out of concern for this very result."

"That is scarcely a guarantee."

Fergus smiled and tugged his own hair. "The red cannot be disguised, Leila. Every child in my mother's family is born with red hair. Mine was almost as bright as that of Hamish when I was a boy."

"Every one of them?"

"Every single one." Fergus smiled down at her. "Gavin is not my son. He cannot be. This tale of him being born nine months after my departure sounds like a lie, one contrived because Isobel finds Killairic more alluring than Dunnisbrae. I do not think Stewart could be so readily deceived in such a matter, either. I fear that Duncan saw her truth, that she thinks solely of her own comfort and not that of any other.”

“I feel sorry for the boy.”

“As do I.” Fergus sighed and shed his boots. “She gave no consideration to the fact that he stood there, that he could hear her words. When they arrived, she did not spare a thought to his discomfort or his hunger.” He shook his head. “Her disinterest in the welfare of her own son is most troubling.” He unbuckled his belt and unwound his plaid, granting her a smile that warmed her to her toes. “I am sorry for her words this day, Leila, but she will be gone in the morning at least.”

“I doubt her claim will be dismissed that easily,” Leila could not help but say. Fergus granted her an enquiring glance. “I wonder what she said to Stewart when she left. Will he welcome her back to Dunnisbrae?”

“If he does not, it has been her own doing.” He shed his chemise and came to take her in his arms. His caress was welcome and his touch warm. He touched his lips to her temple in that gentle way that awakened the heat within Leila, and drew her against himself. He speared his fingers into her hair and tipped her head back, smiling down at her. “Matters could have gone much further awry this night,” he murmured. “Yet we defeated her scheme for we worked together.”

“Do you ask if I mean to welcome you abed this night, my lord?” Leila asked with a smile.

“I do, my lady.”

“You are always welcome in my bed, Fergus.”

“And you, Leila, are always welcome in mine.” Fergus bent to capture her lips with his own and Leila stretched to her toes to welcome him. Just before their lips touched, someone hammered on the solar door.

“My lord!” Murdoch said in his familiar growl. “My lord, you must come. It is Lady Isobel!”

“I will not tolerate any interruption from her,” Fergus said firmly and did not relinquish his grip upon Leila.

"But, sir, she sent the boy to say that she was ill. He seems most upset."

"God in Heaven," Fergus whispered. "Is there no limit to her disregard for the child?"

They both seized their cloaks and boots. Fergus raced down the stairs, calling for aid, and Leila followed as quickly as she could, wondering what Isobel had done.

Perhaps the portent of Fergus' nightmare had not been dispelled, after all.

Isobel was not ill: she was dead.

Fergus and Leila entered the hut, Murdoch and the Templars close behind. Gavin was kept at the portal by the knights, but Fergus knew he had already seen the worst. Fergus crouched beside Isobel's body, noting her grimace and the contortion of her posture. He wondered that she had made a choice that led to a death of such pain.

Leila was at the far wall, surveying the midwife's herbs. Fergus did not recall that they had been in such disarray when he had been in the hut earlier.

There was something clasped in Isobel's hand. He uncurled her fingers to reveal the root there. Clearly, she had bitten part of it. Leila bent to sniff it, then looked at Fergus.

"Do you know what it is?" he asked.

"The scent is familiar, I think." She gestured and Fergus sniffed the root himself, then sat back on his heels again.

"Monkshood?" he guessed.

Leila nodded. "I believe so."

"How strange that she and Kerr would be felled by the same toxin."

"Not so strange as that, for it is a poison of high repute and grows in most climes." Leila glanced around the hut. "I would wager that every healer across the breadth of Christendom and all the way to China has monkshood amongst his or her collection."

"Why would Isobel kill herself? And why in such a painful manner?" Fergus shook his head. "I cannot understand it. She did not seem so troubled when I left her."

"What was her mood?"

"She was angry because I denied her desire to remain in the hall, and because I refused to acknowledge Gavin as my son. Her will had been denied." He raised his gaze to that of his wife. "I would have expected her to do injury to me, or even to you, but not to herself."

Leila bit her lip as she thought. "Was she learned in the use of herbs?"

"Not when I left these parts but it has been four years. She would not be the first woman to find an interest in the healing arts after bearing a child."

"Nay, she would not." Leila looked skeptical, and Fergus thought it unlikely that Isobel would have shown the patience to study any art. He could not think of a way to say as much without speaking ill of the dead, but he had always found her attention to be short-lived.

With the exception of her interest in him.

Unless, her interest in him had been short-lived and then reborn upon his return. He frowned, not liking Isobel's death even though he had found her irksome. It seemed to Fergus that even their dispute was no cause for her to wish to die.

"You should ask the boy what she did at the end," Leila counseled quietly.

Fergus met her gaze. "You think you know."

"I merely guess." His wife straightened, her thoughts hidden from him once more. Fergus wondered in that moment what it would take for Leila to open herself to him fully. He wished he knew, for he would do it. "The boy may know more than he realizes," she added gently.

"I will take her to Dunnisbrae at first light," Fergus rose to his feet as he spoke to the Templars. He heard Leila swiftly inhale, but her gaze was averted. "She must be laid to rest with her kin, Leila. Surely you see as much. Dunnisbrae was her father's holding and that of his father before him. Her brother is laid to rest there, as well."

"Of course. You must show every consideration to Lady Isobel."

There was a curious note in Leila's tone. Was she jealous? Fergus hoped she was, for he would be glad to see their relationship deepen beyond affection into love. He could not see her features, for she was drawing a cloak over Isobel's face. He wished there was time to discuss all the details with her, but that would have to wait until his return.

In this moment, there were obligations to be fulfilled. He addressed the Templars. "We depart for Dunnisbrae at first light. See that no one enters the hut until then."

"Aye, my lord," agreed Yvan.

"We?" repeated Enguerrand, his gaze flicking to Leila. She stood a little straighter but pretended not to have noted his comment. "I must remain at Killairic. As you can surely guess, this disruption to the routine offers opportunities."

Fergus sighed. "Then you must remain, of course, Enguerrand."

Leila was again inscrutable and had stepped back into the shadows to watch and listen. Fergus changed to Gaelic to address the boy, ensuring that he blocked the view of the corpse. "Gavin, can you tell me if your mother said anything after my departure?" he asked. Gavin swallowed, his gaze clinging to his mother's body. He seemed to have been struck dumb. Fergus guided him outside of the hut and crouched down before him there, repeating his question.

"She told me to run to the keep and tell you that she was sick," Gavin provided. "But she was not sick. I said so, and she said I was wrong. She ate it." His face crumpled as he fought tears. "Then she *was* sick."

"The root in her hand?"

The boy nodded.

Fergus recalled well enough the speed with which monkshood did its deadly business. "Where did she get it?"

"She smelled the herbs after you left and found it there."

"Was your mother a healer?"

The boy shook his head, his eyes wide. "Nay, sir. It is Helga at Dunnisbrae who tends the sick."

"Did your mother name the root she ate?"

The boy shook his head again.

Was it possible that Isobel had chosen a root on a whim and had the misfortune to choose the most toxic one? Or had she been intent upon destroying Fergus' happiness, because he had denied her? He could not say, but the shadow of dream seemed very dark in this moment. He sent the boy to the kitchens with Murdoch, for he knew he would be treated with care there. Fergus stood outside the hut, considering his course, then Leila joined him. He told her what the boy had said.

Leila nodded. "Was she sufficiently angry to kill herself in order to cause you trouble?"

"Who can say?"

"I did not know her, but she did not strike me as a woman who would willingly endure such torment. There were other herbs that would have been more kind."

"What else was there?"

"There was the milk of poppies, which surprised me. I know it well from home. It offers a gentle death. One sleeps deeply and, with sufficient dosage, never awakens."

"She might not have known it." Fergus nodded. "I will ask this Helga, the healer of Dunnisbrae, when I take Isobel's body home."

Leila frowned. "Are you certain you must take her there yourself?"

"I would rather not, but I fear that Stewart may be insulted if I do otherwise."

"I suspect he may be insulted either way," Leila said, her manner pragmatic. "His wife is dead, after she fled to you."

"And after I brought her a rich gift." Fergus grimaced. "I should have taken your advice, Leila, and forgone the gift. I fear it encouraged Isobel to believe that more was possible between us than could be. I thought only to be kind, and to show her the respect to tell her of Kerr myself. He was under my protection, after all."

Leila nodded. "You are kind, Fergus, but there are others who are not. I understand why you would take Lady Isobel home, but I fear for your reception. Will you take as many men as possible with you as escort?"

"You think Stewart will assault me?" Fergus considered what he knew of his neighbor and had to admit that it was a possibility. "I will take your advice this time, Leila, though I hope that you are mistaken. I will take Yvan and Murdoch with me, as well as Hamish."

Leila's lips thinned but she said no more.

"Tell me," Fergus prompted.

"I know you think it prudent to show such courtesy to your former betrothed." Leila's dark eyes flashed. "But you cannot be surprised if there are those who imagine me to be your whore and little more."

"What did Isobel say to you?"

"That a handfast suited a man's convenience, just as I suspected." Leila shook her head. "I am not certain that I can make a home here, Fergus, though perhaps I am simply tired in this moment." She turned away and he sensed that she hid some detail from him. Then she spoke and he guessed that she was shy. "Perhaps you should stay in the hall this night. My courses have begun and I cannot welcome you abed."

Fergus thought there was more to sharing a bed than the efforts to create a child, but bit back his words. He thought Leila looked smaller than was her wont. More fragile and in need of his protection.

"I am sorry."

"As am I," she said softly.

Had Leila found another man who could claim her heart? Fergus hoped it was not so, but he had noted how much time she spent with Murdoch.

Would she request a release from their handfast now that there was no chance of a child to bind them together? Fergus hoped not but he sensed her withdrawal and wished to speak to her.

Yet, he would not decline her request.

If she loved another, he would release her so that she could be happy.

Fergus was vexed that he had duties to attend the next day and resolved to do whatever was necessary to hear all of her doubts and fears upon his return.

"As you wish," he ceded, hoping his agreement would please Leila but she gave no indication of her thoughts. "We will ride out before the dawn and return as quickly as possible. I pray it will be just after midday."

Leila nodded, but her concern was clear. "Do you see the shadow yet?"

"I do," Fergus admitted, though he did not tell her that it had become much darker. They would each keep their secrets, though he regretted the change. "But do not tell my father of it. I hope it will dissipate when Isobel is home forever."

"As do I, Fergus," Leila murmured. "As do I."

He claimed her hand in his and kissed her fingertips, holding her gaze. "When I return, Leila, we must talk of our present and our future. You must tell me your hopes and fears, and I vow I will see that all evolves as you desire."

She stared into his eyes for a long moment, but he could not guess her thoughts. "Aye, you will," she agreed quietly. "For you are a man who keeps his vow, regardless of the cost."

"Will you tell me about your home in Jerusalem?" Fergus asked, not wanting to be spent the night apart. Leila cast a glance at him that made her look vulnerable. "You never have. I did not wish to prompt sad memories, but I would like to hear of it."

Leila considered this for a moment, then nodded. "If you desire, my lord."

"I will come to you after I have arranged all for the morning."

She shook her head with a resolve he recognized. "You will need your rest before you depart. I will tell you after you return."

It was a rebuff and one that stung.

With a nod, Leila turned and left him there. Fergus watched her go, his gaze clinging to her small figure, unable to fight the sense that something precious slipped through his fingers.

Leila did not sleep.

It was not solely because she had lied to Fergus. She felt as if her tale about her courses planted a stake between them, the beginning of a barrier that could quickly become an insurmountable wall.

She felt as if she had erred in beginning the construction of that obstacle.

On the other hand, she tired of his persistent consideration for beautiful Isobel. Even in death, the other woman drew his attention and his time. Leila suspected Fergus did not understand how difficult it had been for her to try to make allies in a strange land, with unfamiliar customs, where people spoke a language in which she was not fluent. She missed having a friend or a confidante, and though she had hoped that might be Fergus, it seemed that it was only abed that they had a perfect union.

The fact was that she would have done as much as she had done already and more besides, simply for the promise of winning his heart. Her determination faltered because she began to fear that his heart would never again be his to surrender.

Isobel had died with it securely in her grasp.

She knew from Radegunde that it had taken Duncan twenty years to dare to love again after the death of his beloved. Leila knew she was not so patient as that.

Did she desire too much too fast? Was she overly impatient? Perhaps her dutiful attempts to be the wife Fergus needed were not sufficient to win him truly.

Perhaps they never could be.

She would never be tall, beautiful or blond, after all. Aye, as Leila stared at the canopy overhead, her doubts redoubled and redoubled again. Should she tell him that she had conceived? She did not know. She was not even certain herself. She feared that Fergus would make theirs a marriage in truth, then, but for the sake of the child's legitimacy, not out of any affection for her.

And she would be trapped in this land, trapped with a man who forever yearned for another, trapped amongst strangers.

Alone.

It was unlike Leila to be indecisive, but when it came to the matter of Fergus, she was torn. Could he ever come to love her? She was not interested in half-measures and she did not need his complete commitment immediately—what she did need was hope. She wanted her husband to be Fergus, and for Fergus to love her as completely as she loved him. She wanted their children to be conceived in love and raised in a loving household. She wanted all of him and was prepared to surrender all of herself. But though she made progress with others at Killairic, she felt that Fergus still regarded her as a comrade.

Was it true about the babes in his family all having red hair? Or had Fergus denied Gavin to avoid a confrontation with Stewart? Leila wished she knew. Could there be more to the matter than that? There might well be a custom of which she was ignorant.

She rolled over, vexed with her own endless questions.

Had Fergus lied to her about the import of the handfast? Leila doubted as much, but after Isobel's words, she wondered. It was likely the other woman had intended to cause dissent, but that did not mean there was no truth to her words.

Leila exhaled mightily. The truth was that she was prepared to accept less for herself, in the hope of the future bringing more, but she was not willing to compromise the future of her child. She might be second-best, a substitute for the dead Isobel, but her child would not stand second to Gavin. She would leave Killairic, Scotland, and Fergus before she let her child grow up with the conviction that he or she was not good enough.

The possibility that she had conceived changed all for her.

Was that selfish? Did she make too emotional a choice? Leila's thoughts spun and she knew it was because she had no anchor, no friend, no one to hear her worst fears and dispel them, either with laughter or practicality. She had no one in whom she could confide, no one she trusted fully, no one who would tell her when she was wrong.

She ached to see Aziza again, to talk to her just once, to pour out her worries and have her cousin laugh at her, then help her to see the solution.

Leila's heart clenched and she closed her eyes against unwelcome tears, refusing to recall her parting from Aziza. She would think of her cousin's life on this day instead.

It was yet dark here, but the first tinge of the sun was on the horizon. It would be morning at home by now and Leila envisioned her cousin there. Aziza would be in the kitchen, where the sun shone brightly in the morning, warming the room. Leila's uncle would be in the adjacent smithy, greeting his neighbors and starting the fire in his forge. There would be the sound of horses being brought to the smithy, and those stabled there being fed by the two boys who worked for her uncle.

Karayan would be telling the woman who helped in the house what to do, though Noura knew her labor well enough. Noura would roll her eyes at his bossiness even as she complied. Aziza and Noura would have started the bread already and the house would be filled with the scent of it. Aziza would be playing with her son, Kamal, in the sunlight, and Noura would halt her tasks to admire the baby at such frequent intervals that Karayan would chide her for her laziness. They would bicker, as familiar with each other as a married couple, though in truth they were not.

Leila smiled, able to perfectly envision the house.

Kamal had been a new babe when Leila had touched her lips to his soft brow in farewell, the dark tangle of his baby hair tickling her face. He had chortled at her, his dark eyes wide, not understanding that they parted forever.

Kamal would be crawling by now, chubby with Aziza's good care, strong and tall for his age. He had been a long baby, and even then, the cousins had agreed that Kamal would take after his father, Husain.

A handsome man and a hard worker, Husain was soft spoken and kind, as well as honorable. His eyes shone when he entered Aziza's presence, and Leila's cousin always smiled at the sight of her husband. The love between them had been so strong from the outset that it was clear they had been meant for each other.

How much would Kamal have grown by now? How much more silver was in Noura's hair? Had Aziza conceived again? What of Husain? Was his business thriving? He had wanted to put his olive press in the house, a matter of great contention with Leila's uncle, though Hakim well understood the urge to keep one's eye upon one's trade. She wondered if those two had found a solution. Aziza had been adamant that she would not move from her father's home to her own. Perhaps Hakim had built that small addition to the back of the kitchens, as Karayan had quietly suggested one night as a compromise.

If only Hakim could have chosen such a good man for Leila as he had selected for his own daughter.

If only the cousins' dreams of raising their children together could have come true.

But it was not to be, and Leila would not mourn what could not be hers. She was more pragmatic than that. As the sun brightened the sky, she thought of the donkey in the tale and smiled. She recalled all that was good about her life, instead of dwelling upon the lack. She was handfasted to Fergus, a good and honorable man who treated her well, and resided in his home. She reminded herself that the smith thought well of her, as did Hamish and Murdoch. She, Hamish and Fergus had ensured the safety of the reliquary, and Calum was kind to her. She had been in Scotland a mere month.

Instead of reassuring her, that fact made her realize that she might have only eleven more months with Fergus as her husband.

Still, she did not know whether to tell him about the child. She might be wrong, after all, and she would not raise his hopes. Perhaps, she should wait until she missed a second bleeding, to be certain.

It felt like a deception, another post in that barrier—though it was an omission and not a lie. Still, it seemed like splitting hairs to note the difference.

Leila heard horses and rose from the bed, standing at the window but ensuring that she was hidden by the shutter. She caught her breath when Fergus glanced up as he mounted Tempest. The sight of him, she feared, would always have the power to stir her. She watched as they made their preparations.

The small party rode through the gates just as the sun slipped over the horizon. Fergus rode Tempest, Hamish rode a palfrey, Yvan rode his destrier and Murdoch rode another palfrey. A third palfrey pulled a wagon with a shrouded bundle in the back, and Gavin sat alongside the villager who rode in the wagon. Was it the young miller? Leila thought as much but could not be certain.

Leila watched the party until it was out of sight, still snared in indecision. Then she shook her head and decided to act rather than fret. She bathed in the cooled water from the night before, then dressed. She picked up her small rug, hoping the day ended with more promise than it had begun.

It should do so, for Fergus would be returned.

It was late morning when Fergus and his party reached Dunnisbrae.

Stewart came to the gates himself to meet them. He was dressed for battle, as seemed to be his custom, and there was now a patch over his right eye. His expression was grim. "Where is she?" he demanded, then his gaze fell upon the bundle in the cart and he paled.

Fergus knew then that Stewart had cared for Isobel.

Gavin jumped from the wagon as soon as it stopped and ran to his father, who swept him up immediately. "She is dead, Father. She died!"

"What is this?" Stewart demanded. "Where? When?" He came to the side of the cart, and held the boy's head against his shoulder, then flicked a finger. The miller's son pulled back the shroud so he could see Isobel's face and Stewart's jaw clenched. He crossed himself and stepped back, obviously shaken.

"She came to Killairic yesterday," Fergus said, choosing his words with care. "She said you had had a disagreement but I bade her to return home to resolve matters with you. It was too late for her to complete the journey before darkness fell, so she was to sleep in an empty hut in the village, then ride out this morning."

"Not in the hall?" Stewart demanded.

"Not in the hall," Fergus confirmed.

The other man winced. "Whatever killed her was not kind."

"She ate a root," Gavin said.

"What manner of root?" Stewart asked and the boy shrugged.

"I believe it was monkshood," Fergus said. "My question is whether she knew the healing plants. Did she err in choosing this one, or did she select it apurpose?"

"You infer that my wife sinned and took her own life by choice? How dare you say as much!" Stewart's voice rose. "Of course, she erred! What manner of hut did she occupy that such a root was even there?"

"It was the abode of the former healer of Killairic, and the sole one empty," Fergus said with growing impatience. "I sought to give her shelter, naught more, Stewart, and to ensure that she was not riding during the night, when ill could befall her."

Stewart took a deep breath and stepped back. "Of course, Fergus. I would ask your forgiveness for my sharp words." He ran a hand over his head and looked almost lost. "This is a most unwelcome surprise."

Although Fergus could appreciate the sentiment, it seemed most odd for it to have been expressed by Stewart. That man had not shown any such sensitivity or tact in the past, but he dared to hope that there was a change. It was clear that he was distraught by the loss of Isobel, which indicated that he had loved her. Perhaps there was more to his neighbor than he had glimpsed in the past. At Stewart's gesture, Fergus' company rode through the gates, where the villagers came to their doors to watch their passage.

"My lady Isobel is dead," Stewart cried and the tale was repeated, the news spreading through the village. "I ask you all to name her in your prayers. She will be buried on the morrow." He indicated the chapel ahead to Fergus. "Let us take her there, that the candles can be lit for the vigil. Summon the priest!" he called and a boy ran to do his bidding.

The little party followed his direction and dismounted before the chapel. The miller's son halted the cart and Hamish helped him to lift Isobel. All were silent and the villagers crossed themselves solemnly. Together, Hamish and the miller's son moved Isobel on to a board. Murdoch and Yvan aided them to carry her into the shadowed darkness of the chapel. Fergus followed out of respect.

The chapel had no windows and there was only a beam of light from the open door to illuminate the interior. The sole piece of furniture within it was the table that served as an altar. The cup and plate must have been locked away, for the table was bare. It was cool inside the chapel, and the floor was of beaten earth. They were lowering Isobel's corpse before the alter when the chapel was plunged into sudden darkness.

All five of them started and spun. No doubt they each believed, as Fergus had, that the door had swung shut. Then Fergus heard a bar drop and knew otherwise. He lunged for the door but by the time he reached it, it was too late. The heavy wooden portal was secured from the outside, and he could not wrench it open.

"Stewart! Open the door!"

"Never!" that man said, his tone more characteristic. "You have taken what was mine, Fergus. Now I will take what is yours to see my vengeance served."

"Stewart!" Fergus roared, but he realized the other man had moved away. Stewart shouted for horses, and Fergus heard Tempest whinny in fear. There was a sound of racing hoofbeats, then Stewart's voice again.

"We ride to assault and seize Killairic!" He shouted and Fergus heard the clatter of arms and horses, as well as the stamping boots of soldiers. "My lady will be avenged upon those who saw her dead—and may the Lady of Killairic be prepared to welcome me." He laughed. "Take your leisure this day, Fergus. I will have a tale of conquest to share with you upon my return."

Leila!

"Stewart!" Fergus bellowed and shook at the door. He hammered upon it, to no avail, and even with the aid of the others, could not force it open. "He will kill Leila to settle the score," he whispered. "And I have left her undefended."

His father would protect Leila but was scarcely at his greatest strength. Fergus could not be certain that Enguerrand would defend her, given that man's lingering suspicions that Leila had stolen the reliquary.

Fergus turned to the others in appeal, even as the sound of Stewart's forces riding out carried to their ears.

They must have been preparing to do as much before Fergus' arrival.

Stewart must have concluded that Isobel had gone to Killairic and had already planned his assault. If he had not done the noble deed and brought Isobel home to rest, he would have been at Killairic to defend it.

Did Agnes have any part in this?

"We must escape this chapel with all haste!" His eyes had adjusted to the darkness, but he could see that there was little in the chapel that could be used to their advantage.

"We must aid Lady Leila," Hamish agreed.

"But the walls are sturdy and the portal is barred," Murdoch said.

"There is not a single window," Yvan agreed. "Only a dove hole in the roof."

They all tipped their heads back to consider the dove hole that Yvan had noticed. It was covered, for it was not Whitsunday, but it gave Fergus an idea.

"And naught that can be used to batter the door," Murdoch agreed. "We are trapped." The miller's son looked fearful at this and glanced toward the shrouded Isobel.

"But it is all timber," Fergus said and the others turned to face him. "We must uncover the dove hole, then light a fire. The smoke will escape while we burn a hole in the walls to aid our own escape."

Yvan and the miller's son moved the table so that it was beneath the covered hold. Murdoch stood atop it, then helped Hamish to climb to his shoulders. The boy's fingertips brushed the underside of the roof and Fergus feared he might be too short. But Hamish jumped a little and managed to poke at the cover so that it was dislodged. Sunlight came through the hole and the sense of triumph was tangible.

"Who has a flint?" Fergus demanded.

The miller's son grinned and removed a flint from his purse. "I never am without one, my lord."

Fergus grinned in turn and accepted the flint, then chose a corner to begin their fire. "To the right of the altar," he decided. "It faces south and will be the driest. It also faces away from the village. Those remaining may not notice it as soon."

Hamish took his knife and began to make shavings from the interior of the walls. The miller's son watched, then did the same. The Templar grimaced, then took his knife to the legs of the table that served as an altar. Murdoch joined the task. Within moments, Fergus had a pile of tinder against that corner. When the flint sparked and the tinder lit, he hoped they would reach Killairic in time.

CHAPTER FIFTEEN

It was midday and Leila was in the solar, hoping for some hint of Fergus' return. He was not the only one who felt a portent of doom on this day.

Yet the horizon remained tranquil and devoid of any riders. She turned away from the window and busied herself with tidying the chamber.

Perhaps she looked too soon.

Perhaps she had need of a task to occupy her.

"There is smoke!" someone cried from outside the hall and Leila ran back to the window to look. It was true. A thin dark plume of smoke rose in the southwest, though at considerable distance.

Was it at Dunnisbrae?

Had Fergus set the fire or was he in peril?

She clutched the sill and watched as the smoke grew in volume, until it billowed into the sky in a dark plume that terrified her.

She was more terrified by the movement on the distant hills. The dark cloud of a company approached, all of them on horseback. They rode with haste, dust rising behind them and Leila did not believe their appearance to be a good sign.

"Look!" She ran to the summit of the stairs and called to Enguerrand. "A company approaches!"

He hastened up the stairs and his expression turned grim as he looked upon them. "They ride to Killairic. Is this company from Dunnisbrae?"

"I could not say."

"I do not think Laird Fergus is amongst them," the Templar said. "I would recognize his horse."

"And that of Yvan."

"There is not a knight amongst them."

"But still they can do damage.

"Indeed." Enguerrand left her side and leaped down the stairs. Leila heard him shouting orders to close the gates and see the hall defended, but she was thinking of Fergus' dream.

Surely Killairic would not be burned in his absence?

Enguerrand returned to her side and they stood together in terse silence, watching the company draw near. Leila caught her breath when she spied the two riders who had pulled ahead of the others. A girl led on a palfrey, her dark hair loose behind her.

"Agnes," she whispered.

The man following behind rode a larger heavier steed, and the sunlight glinted on his armor. "And I will guess Laird Stewart," the Templar added.

Leila eyed their course and guessed their destination. "They mean to retrieve the reliquary from her hiding spot," she said and knew the knight agreed. She pressed the key to the solar into his hand. "I must stop them from continuing to the keep."

The knight frowned. "But you cannot go alone. And I must remain to lead the defense of the keep in Laird Fergus' absence."

"I must go," Leila insisted. "If he seeks to avenge his wife, only my death will suffice."

"My lady!" Enguerrand roared, but Leila was already running down the stairs. If the price of saving Killairic was her life, she would gladly pay it.

For Fergus and his future happiness was the only matter of import now.

Agnes was certain of the success of her new scheme.

Laird Stewart had been disinterested in whatever tidings she brought from Killairic, though he had allowed her to remain at Dunnisbrae with Nolan. Agnes had despaired of retrieving the treasure and putting it to use, but the flight of Lady Isobel had changed all. Laird Stewart had mustered his troops all day and made provisions to attack Killairic immediately to reclaim his wife and son.

He had heeded her tale of the reliquary the night before, though found little merit in her suggestion of negotiating with it to take Killairic without striking a blow. The man yearned for vengeance and only the shedding of blood would suffice.

That impulse had visibly multiplied when Lady Isobel's corpse was brought to Dunnisbrae. She was in the crowd of villagers when Laird Fergus arrived and ducked low to keep from being recognized. Lady Isobel dead? It was one more crime to place at the feet of the whore. She was thrilled when Stewart locked all those arrived from Killairic into the chapel, insisting that justice be done.

His quest for vengeance began at Dunnisbrae.

And without Laird Fergus to defend her, the infidel would finally get the fate she deserved.

Agnes' own fate had to improve, as well. She knew it when Laird Stewart summoned her to ride to Killairic with the host, the better for her to point out the location of the prize. Nolan had saddled the palfrey she had stolen from Killairic with Stephen's aid, undoubtedly guessing his laird's intent in advance.

Laird Stewart would claim both treasure and Killairic, and he was without a wife. The obvious reward to grant Agnes was to make her lady of all.

They rode hard that morning, pushing the horses toward Killairic. Agnes smiled when Stewart roared at her to lead him to the prize, and she pulled away from the company, liking that she was part of a great scheme. Nolan granted her a wave and the ragged company continued toward Killairic. They would surround the keep, by Stewart's command, but remain out of range of those on the walls.

"It is here!" she said to Stewart, slowing her palfrey just inside the patch of forest and slipping from the saddle. She led Stewart toward her hiding place. The warrior's boots left deep imprints in the soil, but it no longer mattered. Agnes would have no further need of the sanctuary and her prize would be moved this very day.

She reached the hollow tree and reached into its interior, her heart in her mouth. She smiled when her fingers brushed the soft cloth of the chemise and she felt the bulk of the reliquary.

"And what is it again?" Stewart asked.

"I do not know. It is gold and covered with letters, as well as large gems," Agnes said, cradling the bundle in her arms. "They called it a reliquary."

"A holy relic and a treasure then," he said, his eyes gleaming.

"One beyond compare," Agnes agreed and offered the bundle to him.

Stewart did not take the burden, but only brushed aside the cloth, leaving the weight of it Agnes' grip. He unveiled the prize with haste, then he frowned. Agnes felt her mouth drop open, for she held a rounded piece of wood.

She stared down at it, unable to explain how the gold had changed to wood.

Before she could speak, Stewart struck her. The back of his gloved hand landed so hard upon her cheek that Agnes staggered backward. She dropped the wood and scrambled to pick it up, even knowing it had no value.

"Stupid wench," Stewart snarled and kicked the wood aside. He raised his hand again and Agnes cowered. "To think that I believed you, a lying, deceitful peasant..."

"But it was here. It was gold. It was beautiful." Agnes stammered incoherently, even as she realized why the whore had not been punished. "She took it!" she cried, right before Stewart struck her again.

"As if I would believe another lie," he snarled and spat upon her, then turned to return to his horse.

"You should," a woman said in heavily accented Gaelic. "For, this time, Agnes tells the truth."

The whore! Agnes spun to look and found the whore standing

in the shadows of the forest, closer to the river. Her arms were folded across her chest and her expression was guarded.

Stewart took a step toward her. "Who are you?"

"She is the Saracen whore Laird Fergus handfasted," Agnes supplied.

Stewart smiled a little as he surveyed her. "I can see why. Though she is swarthy, she has an allure. Perhaps I will have her next." He stepped toward the infidel and her eyes narrowed.

"You must speak slowly," Agnes said. "She scarce speaks Gaelic."

"And what truth do you claim Agnes tells?" Stewart asked, doing just that.

"Agnes stole the treasure," the whore said. "I stole it back." She smiled, looking cunning and confident in Agnes' view. "If you desire it, we must bargain."

"I do not need to bargain with an infidel," Stewart snarled and seized the whore by the arm. She was clearly too small to defend herself against him, for she stumbled and could not shake free of his grip. He flung her to the ground and stood over her, his pose threatening. When she spared him only a scathing glance, he seized a fistful of her hair and drew her to her knees. "Here is my offer, infidel." Stewart bit off his words slowly. "You will surrender the treasure to me now and I might let you live."

She parted her lips, no doubt to negotiate, but he struck her so hard across the face that she fell to the ground, stunned.

"Understand that I am not inclined to let Fergus keep his pleasure when he has cost me mine," Stewart smiled coldly. "Surrender the treasure and I might let you live."

The whore looked up at him, assessment in her dark eyes. "She said Gavin was the son of Fergus."

"He is not!" Stewart roared and struck her again. Her lip was swelling as was one eye. Agnes was glad at the limited extent of her own injuries. The infidel did not cede, though, but spat at Stewart in disdain. He grasped the whore's hair again and forced her to her feet. "I might have need of a whore, but let us see how well you please me first. Give it to me."

"It is not here," she said, her manner still defiant.

"Then take me to it!" He flung her ahead of himself with such force that she barely kept her footing, then turned back to Agnes. "Do not imagine that you will remain behind to tell another of this. Mount your horse. The whore will ride with me, the better to ensure that she remembers where she had left the prize." His eyes narrowed to slits. "You will follow and do as I say, or I will hunt you down, Agnes. You will regret your choice, but not for long."

Agnes swallowed and nodded, for Stewart frightened her mightily. She would not have been the infidel for any price in this moment, but she also had the wits to ensure she did not draw his wrath.

It was only a matter of time before he had his fill of the whore. Agnes would not be next.

Indeed, her scheme to become Stewart's wife showed a decided flaw now that she had witnessed his truth.

What she had to do this day was survive.

Enguerrand remained hidden in the forest until the sound of Stewart's departure had faded. He did not like leaving the defense of the keep in the old laird's care, but his primary obligation was to the Temple and thus to its treasures.

He no longer could guess whether Leila truly knew the location of the reliquary, but he was charged to defend it. He would follow, at a distance, and intervene to possess it, if possible.

He would also leave a trail that Yvan and Fergus would know how to follow.

And if Stewart strove to kill the lady Leila, Enguerrand would intervene to ensure the secret of the reliquary's location was not lost forever.

Their horses were gone.

Fergus swore with a savagery that clearly astonished his fellows, but he did not care for their opinion. They had kicked out the back of the chapel after starting the fire, and their sudden appearance had startled those few who remained. Several villagers were trying to put out the fire at the chapel, but Fergus did not care if all of Dunnisbrae burned. There was not a steed in Dunnisbrae's village.

Indeed, there was not a man in the village or the keep. Stewart had assembled an army of peasants and laborers, but if they were sufficiently intent upon their prize, Fergus knew they might win.

Killairic, after all, was thinly defended in his absence.

The few women remaining there retreated into their huts with haste. Fergus seized the sleeve of one woman who was evidently terrified of his intent.

"What of the horses?" he demanded. "Did the laird take them all?"

She nodded and he released her with a curse, then strode to the gates. The sole sign of Stewart's raiding party was a cloud of dust in the distance.

"We shall never reach Killairic in time to be of aid to anyone," Yvan said grimly from beside him.

Clearly, this had been Stewart's plan.

In frustration, Fergus whistled for Tempest.

"Silence," Hamish said, despondent beside him.

Fergus heaved a sigh and began to walk. His long strides took him ahead of the others and the miller's son trailed behind them all. He whistled again, with less expectation of success.

He straightened when there was an answering nicker.

To Fergus' astonishment, Tempest cantered into view, his reins trailing and his step high. The stallion was agitated and fighting the bit, but he came to Fergus.

"I wager he threw whoever was fool enough to try to ride him," Hamish said, his tone much brighter.

"I wager he did," Fergus said. It took him a few moments to settle the stallion sufficiently that he could swing into the saddle, and by then, Yvan's stallion had appeared as well. That horse was just as skittish and had the bleeding mark of a lash upon his rump. Yvan's lips thinned and Fergus guessed that if he ever knew who had struck his horse with such savage fury, he might well return the favor.

The palfreys did not appear and Fergus could only conclude that they had been taken by Stewart's party. He was torn between defending the others and riding to Leila's aid, but Murdoch scoffed at him. "Go, lad!" he cried. "We can walk back in time to hear of your triumph."

"They can defend themselves better than your lady wife," Yvan muttered, and Fergus was not so certain the Templar was right.

"Leila is more resourceful than you believe," he said, but gave Tempest his heels and raced toward Killairic.

If Leila had been harmed, he would ensure that Stewart rued this day forevermore.

Leila had no good scheme beyond compelling Stewart to leave Killairic. He did not bring his company with them, though she would have preferred otherwise, and he was inclined to be rough, which she admired yet less. Leila had been shoved onto the horse before Stewart and he held her captive there. He smelled like wood smoke, meat, and perspiration, a combination which made her stomach churn at such proximity. Agnes rode with them, while those who supported Stewart remained around the walls of Killairic.

Leila doubted they would wait very long for Stewart's command to attack.

She hoped that some soul saw her situation from the tower, but did not rely upon it. They would be busy, following Enguerrand's command to defend both village and keep. The smoke she had seen in the distance had dissipated so that fire must have been extinguished. She wondered where it had been, but knew she had more immediate concerns.

When Stewart would have turned his horse toward Killairic's gates, Leila shook her head adamantly. She directed Stewart away from Killairic and down toward the firth, remembering the day that Fergus had shown her the boundaries of the holding. There had been a stone wall, an old one that had tumbled down in places. Fergus had talked about seeing to its repair after the crops were sown. She would insist that the reliquary was hidden there and pretend to have forgotten the exact place. It could only be better to delay longer, though she had no plan for the inevitable moment when Stewart realized she was lying.

"But it must be in the hall or the village," Agnes insisted, and Leila took great satisfaction in pretending to be unable to understand the girl. "Treasure!" Agnes shouted. "You take us to it!"

"Treasure!" Leila nodded and pointed down the hill. "Hidden," she said, then nodded. "Safe."

Agnes winced. "I thought it *was* safe."

Leila laughed, delighting in vexing the girl. She shook her head. "*Now* safe."

Agnes gave her a furious look and Leila laughed again.

"Enough," Stewart roared. "Guide me to it."

Leila pointed away from Killairic and he slapped the rump of his horse. The beast galloped away from the keep, the palfrey following fast behind.

It took them an hour to reach the wall that Leila recalled, then she insisted upon walking alongside the crumbled wall as she pretended to seek the spot. She touched distinctive stones, and gave the appearance of counting, then looked into more than one gap in the wall, first with hope then with disappointment. Stewart's impatience rose with every false location, but the sun made steady progress across the sky as Leila stalled him.

"It is not so safe if you cannot find it," Agnes snapped.

Leila held up a finger as if recognizing the spot and hastened to a deep breach in the wall. She climbed into the gap and moved several stones as if they obstructed her access. She pretended to be unable to move a larger one and shook her head in vexation. Stewart swore and dismounted, flinging down the reins as he strode to her side. He moved the stone with a grunt and peered beneath it. There was naught but a small snake that slithered into the grass.

He seized Leila's arm and lifted her to her toes. "You lie," he said, undoubtedly speaking slowly to ensure that she understood. "The treasure is not here."

Leila heard the sound of racing hoofbeats.

A destrier.

Fast approaching.

She could guess which one it was. She held Stewart's gaze and smiled.

His eyes flashed in warning, then he cuffed her once again. Her eye was already swelling but this time, his ring cut the skin. Leila cried out and fell, tripping over the loose stones of the wall.

"I will take what is his. I will have vengeance," he muttered, lifting his hauberk and unlacing his chausses. Leila scrambled backward but he stepped upon the hem of her kirtle, trapping her. Leila tried to tear the cloth without success.

"God in Heaven!" Agnes cried in obvious horror. "You cannot couple with a filthy infidel!"

"I will take whatever she can give to me." Stewart freed himself, his gaze locked upon Leila. His intent needed no translation. The cloth of her kirtle finally tore and Leila made to flee, but Stewart seized her wrist and held her captive. His grip was bruising and she bent to bite him, but was struck again. She fell from the wall to the grass on Killairic's side and knew her ankle had been twisted in the fall.

She could not run.

And Stewart knew it. He smiled as he jumped down from the wall and strode toward her. Leila scrambled backward, knowing she was doomed. The hoofbeats had fallen silent, which meant she had erred.

He would kill her and no one would intervene.

Stewart loomed over Leila and she instinctively cupped her belly with one hand, realizing only too late what she had communicated to him.

For Stewart smiled coldly. "Rise, whore," he said with malice. "I will take something else from Fergus this day." He laced his chausses again and Leila got to her feet, fearing his intent. She had to stand on one foot, able to only brace herself with the toe of the injured one. "You are a whore, no more than that," Stewart said, speaking slowly and deliberately. "He has sheltered you for the sake of his child, but once it is gone, he will treat you like the offal that you are." He spat. "Whore!" he reminded her.

Resistance rose in Leila but she had no chance to argue, for Stewart raised his fist and punched her in the belly. Leila took a step backward at the force of impact, then heard a whistling sound. She was amazed that Stewart had not hit her harder than he had, then she saw the blood, the knife in his throat and the wide stare of his eyes. He fell atop her, his weight taking her to the ground and his warm blood flowing over her. Leila screamed and heard Agnes' palfrey gallop away. She was inundated by the filthy smell of Stewart, pinned beneath his weight and rapidly being covered with his blood. She panicked as she seldom did but could make no difference in her situation, which terrified her.

Until Stewart's weight was abruptly hauled away, and Fergus lifted her in his arms. Leila fell against him and wept in relief, though his features might have been carved in stone. He was furious and she could feel the thrum of anger deep within him, but she did not have the audacity to ask him what precisely had provoked his response.

She could not be just a whore to him, could she?

But then, why had Fergus not trusted her with the location of the reliquary?

She could not be of value only for the child she bore, could she?

It was not like Leila to have doubts but she had them aplenty in this moment. Indeed, she wanted to weep, which was not characteristic of her in the least. She closed her eyes, hating her own weakness and surrendered to the pain Stewart had inflicted.

Would her child die?

Would her child live but be damaged forever?

A tear slipped from beneath her lashes and Leila prayed silently, even as she feared all would be as it would be.

Inshallah.

Fergus sent Enguerrand after Agnes, for he had no desire to leave Leila. She seemed to be broken as she never had been before, without her customary force of will. He feared that she would die of grief, if not of her injuries.

That Leila had been struck with such force infuriated him beyond any anger he had felt before. Her swollen face, that cut upon her cheek, the sight of Stewart striking her in the belly, all sickened Fergus beyond compare.

She had tried to lead the villain away from Killairic and had paid a high price for defending his holding.

He felt that he had failed her, though she made no such accusation.

He wrapped Leila in his cloak and set her gently in the saddle on Tempest. She sat there without speaking while he and Yvan flung Stewart's corpse over that man's own saddle. Fergus would have liked to have left Stewart's body to be desecrated by predators but he knew the sight of it would scatter the invading army from Dunnisbrae.

Let them take the villain home to be buried alongside his faithless wife.

He led the horse away from the wall, then saw Enguerrand returning with Agnes. The maid had her hands bound and was trussed to the saddle of her palfrey. She swore with sufficient fury to make any man blush.

"She bit me," Enguerrand said with disgust, displaying the mark of her teeth upon his forearm.

"I would do more than that to you," Agnes muttered, continuing her diatribe as Fergus mounted his steed and drew Leila into his embrace. She did not speak, did not so much as utter his name, and she did not look into his eyes.

They returned slowly to Killairic, for Fergus did not wish to jostle Leila too much. He knew she had to be badly hurt. When they reached the party that surrounded the keep, it was just as Fergus had anticipated. One glimpse of Stewart and their ranks melted away from the gates, horror in their expressions.

"Bring a cart!" Fergus cried. "Bring a cart and take this offal back to Dunnisbrae to be buried. I would not have our cemetery polluted by one so wicked as this."

Gazes flicked from Stewart to Leila, covered in his blood and clearly bruised. The people crossed themselves, and Fergus did not wait to see his word done. He rode into the bailey and dismounted. The ostler hastened to take Tempest. The smith came to gaze upon Leila with a worried frown. Margaret came from her hut to cluck and Hamish's aunt joined her.

"Poor lamb," Mhairi said.

"She will desire a bath," Fergus said. "Iain! Can you see that hot water is brought to the solar?"

"It is being heated already, my lord," that man replied. His gaze flew to Agnes.

"She is too filthy to ever be scrubbed clean," that girl spat.

"Agnes will be placed in the dungeon. When next there is a court, she will be tried for conspiring against the laird and his kin, and for theft."

"The dungeon!" that girl echoed with horror. "There are rats there."

"Indeed, the rats are the least of it." Fergus gave her a cold glance even as he lifted Leila into his arms. "I beg your forgiveness now, as it may be at least a month before we have a court day. There is so much else to be done." He walked into the hall as Agnes swore thoroughly, cursing him and all his kind.

"Leila!" His father exclaimed, rising to his feet. She spared the older man a wan smile, which only made Fergus wish all the more that she would bestow a similar one upon him.

"Leila will keep to the solar for now, Father," he said. "Would you ensure that all who rode with me today have the hospitality of the hall?"

"Of course, of course!"

"I believe Margaret and Mhairi might be glad to assist Leila in her bath." Fergus held her a little more tightly. "If that is acceptable, Leila? You will need someone to tend to your injuries." She nodded agreement, but still said naught. He sensed that she did not particularly care, which worried him deeply. He made for the stairs, then recalled another detail.

"Ensure that Gavin is sent here from Dunnisbrae," he said to his father, feeling Leila stiffen slightly. He reasoned that she was in pain and hastened to the solar. "Perhaps the healer from Dumfries might be persuaded to come to Killairic sooner rather than later," he called and barely heard his father's agreement.

Leila sank into the hot water of the bath, glad to be rid of Stewart's blood and the mire of this day. Her ankle hurt. Her cheek was cut. Her face was bruised and her eye was swollen shut.

But she did not bleed.

At least, not yet.

Margaret and Mhairi spoke quietly to each other, and their presence was unexpectedly soothing. There was kindness in their voices and their eyes, and they were gentle as they helped her from the bath and eventually into bed. It was just time for the evening meal, and Leila could hear activity in the hall below. She wanted only to sleep, to forget, to heal, and maybe to dream.

She did not hear the two women leave, and she did not hear Fergus come into the solar much later. She did not hear his sigh or feel the kiss he placed upon her cheek, the one that was not bruised. She did not feel his weight as he sat on the side of the bed, nor the weight of his gaze as he watched her all the night long.

She did not even know he had been there, for when she awakened, Leila was alone.

Just as she feared she would always be.

Fergus had not even come for the next increment of Scheherazade's story.

And he had summoned Gavin to live at Killairic.

The combination was disheartening. She had tried to win his heart and she had failed. Though he said Gavin was not his son and that he did not love Isobel, his actions spoke louder than his words. Like Duncan, his heart was lost and would be so for more than what remained of their year and a day.

Leila stared at the ceiling, choosing her course.

She would stay, until she knew Radegunde's fate, until her friend stopped at Killairic. She anticipated that would be before September. If Leila carried Fergus' child, she would bear him the babe. If she did not, or if she lost the child now, she would no longer welcome him abed. *Inshallah.* If there was no child now, she would not strive to make one.

She would continue to act as his wife and complete her scheme with the pigeons, but there would be no more tales.

No more intimacy.

When Radegunde arrived, Leila would accept Duncan's offer of a home. The choice was made, but the timing relied solely upon the presence of a child in her womb.

Either way, Killairic would not be her home.

Leila rolled over and buried her face in the linens, allowing herself to cry as she never had before. She had tried but she had failed, and she knew better than to give more when there was no hope of success.

"She has been injured," Calum said in the hall below, but Fergus shook his head.

"It is more than that. I sense it."

His father shook his head. "She has been beaten," he reminded Fergus. "And doubtless was frightened. Let her sleep and all will be better in the morn."

Fergus shook his head and drummed his fingers on the board. "I do not think so."

"You could be wrong, boy."

"It is not like Leila," Fergus insisted. "She does not sulk and she does not weep. She shares her thoughts and is honest above all." He shrugged. "I feel that she has hidden herself from me, that there is an obstacle between us."

He did not tell his father that even though his nightmare of Isobel had very nearly come true, his sense of impending doom had not lifted. It was unsettling and he tired of it. He wanted all to be resolved and happily. He wanted Leila to decide to stay, whether she chose to be baptized or not. He wanted to hear more of her stories. He wanted to make love to her.

Most of all, he wanted her to open her eyes and look fully into his own.

But he sensed that she did not desire his company on this night and feared that unhappy situation might last.

"Then there is some detail she does not wish to share," his father said easily.

"Something changed on this day," Fergus said, shaking his head. "Stewart said something to her, or Agnes did, something that changed her thinking." He sighed. "I hope the healer comes with all haste. The bruises upon her face must hurt."

"She is stronger than you guess, Fergus. She will heal."

But Leila had chosen and Fergus knew it. Was it because he had left her undefended on this day? He feared he had failed her and knew she would never accuse him outright.

But if she did not confide in him, how could he reassure her?

He would do as much with his deeds, Fergus decided. He would make every effort to let Leila know that she was welcome and that he did not wish her to leave.

Because he did not, and he was startled by the vigor of his conviction. He had long admired Leila but as Fergus sat in the hall with his father, he realized that he loved her. He loved Leila as he had never loved Isobel, and the prospect of losing her—even of being denied her companionship—was devastating.

Yet all the same, he would not hold her captive at Killairic, not if she desired to be elsewhere. He wanted her to have whatever she desired, whatever it was.

Whoever it was.

"We will not go to Iona," he said to his father. "For I fear she might not be strong enough to make the journey, and I will not hasten her conversion."

"Let her choose in her own time," Calum agreed. "That is more kind." He patted Fergus' shoulder. "Let us send Murdoch. He can gather such tidings as are to be heard there."

Fergus nodded agreement, more interested in how he might regain the trust and goodwill of his lady wife.

If she desired time, he would give it to her. Eleven months remained of their handfast and though he was impatient to see matters resolved between them, he would give Leila all the time she needed, in the hope she would choose to stay.

SUNDAY, JUNE 4, 1188

Feast Day of Saint Optatus

308

CHAPTER SIXTEEN

ergus was frustrated by the time the rider appeared.

Leila had continued to be subdued and Fergus could not doubt that there was a new reserve between them. He had tried to talk to her several times, but she said only that she needed to rest. He sensed her concern but could not persuade her to share it with him. If ever she had been mysterious, now she was more so. He felt that all was at stake, though that made little sense, and he disliked that the easy camaraderie that had once been between them was gone.

What had Stewart said to her? She would not speak of it.

Fergus was sleeping each night in the hall, a courtesy to his lady wife that made him keenly aware of how much he missed her company. It was more than the tales she had shared with him. His sense of doom lingered, though he could not explain it. Killairic was safe. His father was well. There was no peril he could discern. Gavin appeared to be happy to be helping the miller's son, and Fergus hoped there would be word of a relation who would take the boy when Murdoch returned from Iona.

Leila had told him of her home in Jerusalem, at his request, but he sensed that the tale was thin, as if she did not wish to confide in him. He felt that he was told the version any stranger might hear. He offered to help her to learn more Gaelic and her acceptance was less than enthused. She was certain he had more important matters to attend. He asked her to teach him Arabic and she demurred.

Murdoch had gone to Iona in his stead, as planned, and Fergus thought he had made the right choice in that, at least. He knew that Leila had ceased her lessons with the priest, though she still went to the smithy every day. He had no desire to force her to convert, though he did wonder why she had abandoned the plan when she had been so intent upon it.

It must mean that she reconsidered her plan to stay.

The birds had arrived from Carlisle and the dovecote had been completed. Leila took them beneath her care and gave them much attention, but said naught about them being her nuptial gift. He had visited the dovecote at her invitation and tried to share her pleasure that they had laid eggs.

He could not, for her smile did not reach her eyes.

Fergus was pacing in frustration when he was summoned by the guard on watch. He studied the approaching figure, wondering at his arrival. The horse had the slender grace of the horses bred by the Arabs, which troubled Fergus. Such beasts were uncommon even in Paris and virtually unknown in Scotland. Something about the rider's trap and his garb made Fergus recall the dust and sun of Outremer, and he wondered that this arrival wore no insignia.

He could not think of any incident that would prompt a man to pursue him all the way from Palestine.

Surely Leila had not expected to be pursued? Was this man's arrival what she awaited?

Fergus could not wait for the man to reach the gates. He strode out to meet him on the road, well beyond the gates. The wind was up and Fergus knew there would be rain by the evening. He supposed this man would be their guest, though he balked at that.

The arrival was dressed in the Frankish fashion, but his garb did not look quite right, as if he mimicked a style he had seen but was himself accustomed to dressing otherwise. His skin was tanned and his eyes were green, his features lined, and his gaze sharp.

The man eyed him warily, then dismounted, his gaze falling to the signet ring on Fergus' finger. "I seek Fergus of Killairic," he said, his French slow and accented.

"And you have found him," Fergus replied, propping his hands on his hips. He supposed he did not look very welcoming, and he did not care. "Why do you seek me?"

The man raised his hands. "I bring a missive. It was read first by Gaston de Châmont-sur-Maine, for he was the one to direct me here."

Fergus frowned in his surprise. Gaston had sent the man here? "Where is it?"

"In a pouch beneath my tabard."

"Where are you from?"

"Jerusalem."

Fergus nodded understanding, even though he was mystified. He could not imagine why Gaston would have granted directions to anyone, and thought of the safety of the reliquary. He pulled his knife from its sheath, thinking it made sense to be wary, even though he sensed no threat from the visitor. "Move slowly. If you deceive me in this, it will be your last living deed."

The man nodded. He eased one hand beneath his tabard then removed a leather pouch from beneath his clothing. He opened it slowly to reveal a furled scroll. When he freed it from the pouch, Fergus saw that its original seal had been broken. Fergus did not recognize that mark, but there was a new one of red wax with Gaston's insignia alongside it.

He told no lie about Gaston, at least.

Fergus frowned at the script, which was familiar to him but also illegible. "This cannot be intended for me. I do not read Arabic."

"It is addressed to Leila binte Qadir lufti al-Ramm and is a message from her uncle. Lord Gaston implied that you might know her location. I am charged to deliver this to her with my own hand so would appreciate your assistance."

Fergus hesitated. Was this from the uncle who had arranged Leila's marriage? He doubted any other relative would have troubled to send a message so far. Could it be good tidings? Or was it a threat? Could it be a deception, meant to lure her back against her own better judgment?

What should he do? He wanted to protect Leila, but accepting the missive would reveal that he knew her location—or even indicate that she was hidden here at Killairic. On the other hand, he did not want to deny her any contact with her family.

"Karayan," Leila said from behind him, and Fergus realized that she had not only followed him but recognized the visitor. He spun around to see her approaching quickly, then turned back to find the messenger had dropped to one knee.

"How is it that you are here, so far from home?" she asked the man in French, then switched to Arabic. Fergus assumed she said the same thing and watched the messenger's hardened features melt into an affectionate smile.

He replied to her and she hesitated only for a moment before plucking the scroll from his rough hands. She frowned at Gaston's seal, then met Fergus' gaze. "Lord Gaston gave him directions?"

"Apparently so." He watched her think about this for a moment, her gaze lingering on the broken seal.

Then she nodded briskly and Fergus was pleased at even this short glimpse of her former manner. "Might I request that Karayan be shown hospitality?" she asked. "I will read this message. He is charged to wait for a reply and I will give him one by the morning. He will be a guest at Killairic for only one night and only if you find that acceptable."

Karayan looked between the two of them, clearly attempting to guess her meaning.

Fergus eyed her, unable to guess her thoughts when she spoke with such purpose. Had she expected the message or the messenger? Did she know the contents of the missive? He had the sense that she had already chosen her reply, which made no sense.

He also understood that she was not inclined to confide in him.

"He is known to you, so, of course, he is welcome in our home," Fergus said, noting how her gaze flicked to his when he said 'our.' "I must ask, though, that he surrender his horse and all of his weapons." He could not even think about Leila departing with this man, but also could not imagine why else he had come so far.

But if it was her heart's desire to return to Outremer, he would not stop her.

No matter what the cost to himself.

Leila spoke quickly to the messenger, who nodded. At the gates, he began to divest himself of his weapons. Fergus beckoned to a pair of guards, one of whom took custody of the horse while the other accepted the messenger's weapons.

"She will be cold," Leila called after the one who led the horse away. "Please put her in the stall at the left end, for it is warmer, and find a blanket for her."

"Aye, my lady."

She spoke again rapidly and the messenger shook his head. She glanced up at Fergus, her grip tight on the scroll. "Neither of them have any illnesses, but I suspect both are more hungry than they prefer to admit."

"They will both have our best hospitality." He held her gaze for a long moment. "You are lady here, after all."

She smiled then, tears shining in her eyes as she closed both hands around the scroll. "Thank you, Fergus," she said quietly, then turned and strode to the gardens with purpose, her head down.

She looked so unhappy that Fergus' heart clenched tightly.

And it was in that moment, as he watched her walk away, that Fergus truly realized the threat he had sensed for so long. The peril before him was the risk of losing Leila. She could depart with this messenger, because of whatever word he had brought her or despite it, and Fergus would never see her again.

He could not bear the thought.

Yet at the same time, if leaving Scotland would restore her smile, he would not obstruct her departure. He loved Leila, but he loved her sufficiently to want her happiness more than anything else. Her sadness of late had been almost too much to bear. If she wanted to return home that badly, he would not stand in her way.

"Leila binte Qadir lufti al-Ramm," Karayan said with satisfaction and nodded once.

"The choice will be hers to make," Fergus informed the other man in French. "And I will defend it with all the power I can muster."

He held the messenger's gaze, waiting until that man nodded understanding and agreement. Then he indicated the hall. "Come. Our fare is simple but it is plentiful. You are welcome at Killairic, Karayan. I hope our hospitality suits you well."

The older man bowed. "It cannot fail to do so." He raised a fist to his chest. "It lifts my heart to see Leila well. All else is simply more blessings."

It was against all expectation.

A missive from her uncle.

Leila sat on the stone bench beside the dovecote and listened to the cooing of the birds. She stroked the parchment and failed to swallow the lump in her throat. She recognized her uncle's script and there could be no disputing the little flower he always drew after her name. She ran her fingertip over the ink, smiling a little in memory of his protectiveness. The arranged marriage aside, he had always been kind to her.

Hakim had not needed to take her in. He had not been required to raise her alongside his own daughter. He had been a good father.

She hesitated to open the missive, to break that seal, for she feared its contents. Was Aziza well? What of little Kamal? Surely her flight had not caused repercussions for her family? Leila was not certain what tidings Karayan brought, and she did not want to be surprised if they made her weep. She took a breath, then broke Gaston's seal, knowing that knight must have been convinced of the merit of both message and messenger to have confessed her location.

Leila swallowed then unfurled the scroll. There was a dark stain on one side, about the size of her uncle's thumbprint, and she bent to smell it, smiling a little at the familiar scent of ash. She could close her eyes and see the smithy again, the hot sun on the roof, the smell of steel and fire and leather.

Leila tried to read the missive slowly, wanting to savor this unexpected gift, but her gaze danced over the message. When she was relieved that it brought no bad news, she read it again.

My dear Leila, beloved flower and blessing of our house—

This missive carries both an apology and an entreaty, and I hope it finds you well. In fact, I am greedy with my wishes. I would not only have my message delivered into your hands, but I would have you sufficiently well to read it. I would have your heart still open to my words despite our disagreement. I would have Karayan find you promptly, and also return to me with a message from you—if not with you yourself by his side. I wish for much, more than perhaps is my due, but I cannot stop the wishing all the same.

I fear for your fate and for my own part in driving you from the safety of my home. I cannot blame you for making your choice, given my refusal to consider your view of Ahmed. I can only hope that the price you have been compelled to pay for fleeing with the Franj has not been too high. I know much of these men, more than I would wish to know, though truly, few men will show themselves to be honorable when a young beauty begs for their aid. I fear that you may have paid for your escape in the oldest of ways.

And so I write to you, not only to apologize, but to remind you that you are as my own daughter. You are welcome in my home now, as ever you were, and you are welcome regardless of what you have done or what has been done to you. You think, perhaps, that I will be shamed if you were to return unmarried and with a child fathered by a Franj. You might not believe any protest I might make in my own defense, so I will tell you this, a story that proves the intention of my heart.

Many years ago, your mother came to me when she knew she carried a child fathered by a Franj. He was a warrior, defending the claim of the Franj to our village, al-Ramm. He took far more than was his right, though I did not know of his wickedness in time. Indeed, I thought him to be a man of honor. It was the blue of his eyes, so steadfast, that tricked me into trusting when I should not have done. This man abandoned your mother after taking her innocence and planting his seed. She argued always to his merit, but he seized what he should not have touched and he left no provision for my sister or her child.

For you.

That is not the choice of the man of honor I had believed him to be.

I welcomed my sister into my home and I refused to see her as shamed. She bore you and died in the delivery of you, leaving you alone in the world. I believe her heart was broken, for she faded during her pregnancy when she should have blossomed. After her death, we contrived a story that her husband had been killed in battle and that she had been a widow. This was the true reason why we left al-Ramm and came to Jerusalem, so that few would question the tale. It was true that there were raids and that the village was less safe than once it had been, but we began again to give you a life. I saw you raised in my house as if you were my own child, and the secret was kept between your aunt and me. We were determined to make right from wrong and to give you the upbringing you deserved. I bought a new shop, I found new clients and established my name again, and we made a new life in Jerusalem. It was not easily done but I do not regret it.

Now your aunt is gone, her wisdom lost to me, and I am the sole keeper of the secret. I owe it to you, Leila, to tell you the truth of your parentage before there is no one left who knows it. You are half-Franj, and though I know the name of your father, I swore before your birth that it would never cross my lips again. I hope he is dead, denied by his own family, in justice for what he did to the mother of his own child. I pray he did not know of you, for then his heart would be darker and he would still be your father.

Then you fled, and I feared that my scheme to keep the past secret had led you into peril. You could only have escaped with the Franj, and I hope that my error has not put you in peril. I hope you have not paid too high a price.

And so I send Karayan in pursuit of you, though I would have preferred to go myself. As a Rūm, if not a Franj, he is more likely to pass without notice than I ever could. I pray daily that he finds you, and thank Allah that a man of such valor and dedication serves our family.

If your mother's fate has been your own, please do not fear my wrath. You are my sister's daughter, the blood of my heart, as dear to me as if you were my own child. I would hear your laughter again. I would see your smile. I would know you to be safe and well. Aziza believes that you can do any deed and perhaps her faith is justified. I know too much of men, though, little flower, and I am afraid that you are alone, impoverished, and with child. I fear a repetition of the past.

Let me help you.

Let me offer her a haven.

Please send word with Karayan that you forgive me for believing in the match I arranged. Please send word that you are well—or better yet, return home under Karayan's protection. You know he can be relied upon. Aziza misses you. We all miss you, but mostly, we want you to be well and happy. Please let me know that you are so.

Leila blinked back her tears and clutched the missive. She stared unseeingly at the garden she had come to love so well. The bees were working in the flowers and the pigeons cooed over their nests. The hills rolled before her to the firth, which shone in the late afternoon light. The sky was streaked with gold and red as the sun dipped low, and some clouds were gathering overhead. The first raindrops began to fall, making the air look as if it was filled with silver. Leila did not move, merely tucked the missive into her sleeve to protect it. She loved it at Killairic, and if Fergus had been inclined to surrender his heart to her, she might have happily stayed.

As it was, her uncle's offer was not without appeal. Leila could go back to everything she knew and everyone she loved. She could play with Aziza's baby and maybe find a husband to give her children of her own. It was tempting to slip back into the life she had known—although Leila knew that she had changed and that there might always be a yearning in her heart for what she left behind.

Or whom.

Her father had been Franj. She wished she knew more about him, then wished his nature had not been as her uncle described. She supposed she had been of two places even before she left Jerusalem.

Half Franj.

Half Christian.

Was that why this land appealed to her so powerfully? Was that why she had had a sense from the outset that she could make a home here, with the right impetus?

But she did not have that impetus. Fergus had said he did not love Isobel, yet Isobel's son was at home in this hall. Would Gavin be named heir of Killairic because his lineage was pure?

Still she was torn. She had not bled but it was too soon to know if she would miss her courses a second time.

If she carried a child, would it be born hale after Stewart's blow?

If she carried a child, would life be better for her child in Jerusalem than here?

Was it important that Fergus had decided they would not travel to Iona together, when they had resolved she would be baptized there?

Leila did not know and she hated this new indecisiveness in herself. She read the missive again, shielding it from the rain, then rolled it carefully and tucked it into her sleeve again. Her heart in her throat, she stood and turned to return to the hall. She would find out what was happening in Palestine from Karayan. It would not make a difference to her choice, but the gathering of information could only be sensible.

Leila realized that Fergus was watching her from the doorway to the kitchens. She lowered her own gaze, feeling as if she had been caught, and felt herself flush. How long had he watched her? Her innards clenched and she wondered what he was thinking.

She made to step past him, her heart thumping, but Fergus laid a hand upon her arm. "Is it bad news?"

Leila shook her head. "My uncle apologizes and invites me home."

She felt Fergus stiffen. "Home," he echoed and Leila nodded.

She had no words and it appeared Fergus had none either. She eased from beneath the weight of his hand, and swallowed the lump in her throat. She would not make this difficult for him. He had been kind. "I would speak to Karayan and learn what has changed," she said, and continued to the hall.

Fergus did not pursue her, though she felt his gaze upon her.

Well aware that Fergus' father was watching her progress, she went to sit beside Karayan.

He smiled at her, his gaze searching. "The news is good?"

"You did not read it?"

"It was forbidden for me to do so. I gave my pledge."

Leila placed her hand over his and smiled. "You are a good man, Karayan. Thank you for undertaking this journey. It must have been long and difficult."

He shrugged. "You are here yourself, so you know how long it is." Again, he surveyed her and she knew he would ask her a question.

"It is almost a year since I left Jerusalem," Leila said, speaking before Karayan could. "Tell me what has happened there."

He exhaled and sat back, drumming his fingers on the board as he thought. "So much," he murmured. "I am not certain where to begin."

"Jerusalem was besieged," Leila suggested and that proved to be all the encouragement Karayan needed.

Fergus did not know what to do.

He did not want to interfere, but he itched to know what message had been brought to Leila from Outremer. He was fiercely jealous that she sat with Karayan and spoke with him, that they were apparently oblivious to everyone else in the hall. Her laughter and the quick sound of her Arabic made him realize how much she had left behind, how much she had surrendered in handfasting to him.

Too much? Fergus suspected it might be so.

He sat with his father, but did not hear his father's words. He ate, but did not taste his meal. He consulted with those who came to seek his advice—about the harvest, about the pasturage, about the courts, about the next day's meal—but could not have told anyone what matters had been discussed by the time they were all gone. He sipped his ale, but did not taste it, and watched Leila with a hunger he had not realized he possessed.

"Tell her," his father advised softly, when Leila took her leave of the messenger. She stood and the messenger dropped to one knee, and Fergus loved how delicate and beautiful she was. "He leaves in the morning," Calum continued. "Should you not ensure that you have made every possible argument in your own favor?"

"I would have her make the choice that will guarantee her own happiness."

Calum lifted a brow. "I think what you have not yet told her might affect the outcome."

"How do you know what I have not yet told her?"

His father smiled. "She hesitates, though I would wager that she is by nature decisive. This indicates that she hopes rather than knows, and there is only one detail that might change all if she knew." He nodded. "I wonder if she is with child."

Fergus knew his surprise showed.

"It changes much," Calum said sagely. "Your mother was more inclined to weep when she was with child than was otherwise her nature. Perhaps Leila is more inclined to doubt than is her usual manner."

"Doubt? But what can she doubt?"

"What she does not know, of course. The future." Calum gave Fergus a fierce look. "Tell her, while you can."

"And if you are wrong?"

"She will leave anyway, and you will never see her again. If I am wrong, you will have risked very little in the end." He nodded. "If I am right and you do not take my advice, you will have lost all when you could have claimed it."

Fergus rose at that warning and strode to Leila's side, touching her elbow with his fingertips. She looked up at him, her dark eyes full of questions, and he smiled despite the turmoil inside himself. "I know you make a choice," he said, his voice husky. "And I would not impede that." He swallowed. "But there is one detail I would tell you before you choose."

"Only one?" she asked and he nodded.

"There is only one detail of import that I have not confessed to you." He gestured. "Will you walk in the garden with me?"

Leila nodded and preceded him, her quick pace making him wonder if she wanted to see his impulse set to rest and forgotten. They reached the garden and the air was sweet with the scent of ripening fruit. The rain was more like a mist, though Leila did not seem to mind. They walked toward the finished dovecote, and the cooing of the birds within could be heard.

She did not prompt him, which Fergus refused to take as a bad sign. "You said your uncle invited you back to Jerusalem," he said.

"Aye."

"And you called it *home.*"

She glanced up at him, then averted her gaze.

"I had hoped that Killairic might become your home."

"Did you?" her voice was as soft as a whisper, but he heard the tremor in her words.

"If returning to Jerusalem is your desire, I will not impede your departure, not with the escort of this man you clearly know." Fergus lowered his voice. "Though I offered before to take you there."

"You could not truly have meant it, though it was kindly offered," she said. "You were betrothed to Isobel then."

"Who showed the worth of her pledge clearly enough." Fergus pushed a hand through his hair and frowned. "You trust this man?"

"Karayan is a Rūm who has served my uncle for as long as I can remember. He is a servant but has lived with the family so long that he might be part of it."

"Ah! The one who Iain reminded you of," Fergus guessed and she nodded.

"He is a good man, a loyal man, and if I journeyed with him, he would defend me with his life."

"And will you?"

"I am not certain."

"You must miss your cousin."

"I do." Leila smiled sadly. "I would like to eat olives and figs again. I would like to see my cousin's son. I would love to sit with Aziza and talk, about everything and nothing." She fell silent and frowned.

"But?"

"But once there, I will miss here. I love the bounty of Scotland, and the beauty of Killairic. I like the mist in the wind and the brilliant green of the hills. I would miss the view from the solar window if I could not open a shutter and see it again." She raised a hand. "I would miss this garden, and the smithy, and the chance to see my pigeons raise their chicks."

"But you cannot have both."

She shook her head and a tear loosed itself. It fell sparkling and was lost on the ground. "Nay. And in the absence of the one thing that would make either place a home, I am compelled to choose, though neither place will suffice."

"What one thing?"

She looked up at him, her eyes glowing. "There is only one thing that makes any place a home, Fergus. Killairic is your home because you love it so, because you love your father, because it has claimed a piece of your heart."

"And Jerusalem is not thus for you?"

She shook her head. "It does not hold my heart." She swallowed. "No one there does, and I know that no one there ever will."

"How can you know such a thing? Can you see the future?"

Leila laughed a little, making a sound beneath her breath. "I do not need to see the future to know that my heart is already claimed, that it has been claimed for a long time. The question is what do I do since my regard is not returned? Do I stay in one place, with the person who holds my heart but does not love me? Or do I return to another place, only to be denied even a glimpse of him? Which is kinder? Which is crueler?"

Who was the person? Fergus wanted to know but could not bring himself to ask. Surely not Murdoch? "Which will make you happy?" he asked instead.

"Neither," she said with finality. "And so I wonder if it matters where I am. I might as well be useful if I cannot be happy. My cousin is married and has a son. My uncle is a widower, with no one to keep his house. My cousin does this now, but if she has more children, perhaps I would be of more assistance there."

She wandered away from him, sadness in the droop of her shoulders, and he could not bear to see her so unhappy. "Perhaps we have more in common than I had realized, Fergus. Perhaps you, too, are denied the company of your beloved."

"I will be, if you return to Outremer," he dared to say.

Leila spun to face him, her eyes wide. He saw a welcome spark of hope in her eyes and dared to be encouraged. "How so? You love Isobel. She has died with your heart in her possession as surely as Duncan's wife died with his."

Fergus shook his head. "I thought I loved Isobel. I was convinced of it for four years, but in truth, I loved the notion of Isobel. In my dreams, she changed to become a woman I admired much more in memory than in truth."

"But you cried out her name in your sleep."

"When I dreamed that she cost me Killairic."

Leila folded her arms across her chest. "You shelter her son as if he is your own. She said he was your own."

Fergus shook his head. "And I told you that it could not be so. The boy must be raised by someone and there is no one at Dunnisbrae any more. I have asked Murdoch to seek out Isobel and Stewart's kin at Iona. When he returns, I hope he brings news that one of them will take the boy."

"You did not tell me this."

Fergus arched a brow. "You have not been conferring with me."

Leila blushed and dropped her gaze.

"And when I tried to speak with you, you kept our conversations short and formal." Fergus took a step toward her. "I feared these past weeks that Isobel had cost me something of greater import than Killairic." He took a deep breath when Leila did not reply. "I feared that Isobel had destroyed any chance of you loving me."

"Impossible!" Leila said, her eyes flashing with welcome and familiar vigor. "She could never have done as much, no matter how many lies she told me."

Fergus smiled in his relief, then took Leila's hand within his own. "I love you, Leila. Will you stay at Killairic and exchange wedding vows with me before a priest? I would have you be my legal wife, for what God has put together, no man shall put asunder."

Her features lit with a joy he could not mistake. "Fergus!" Leila cried and he caught her in a tight embrace. She stretched up and kissed him with the passion he had missed.

"You have not given a reply," he teased and she laughed at him. "Is it because you do not wish to be baptized?"

"I will be baptized and I will wed you," she said with resolve. "I will gladly be your wife, Fergus. If you love me, that is all the reason I need to stay. Killairic will be my home in truth."

He kissed her with satisfaction, loving how she surrendered to his touch with such enthusiasm. It began to rain with greater vigor, though Fergus chose to ignore it for the pleasure of his lady's kiss. When they parted, breathless, he sheltered her from the rain as they returned to the keep, then stared down into her shining eyes.

"I thought when you decided not to go to Iona, that you did not want me to be baptized," she said.

"I did not want you to be compelled to take a long journey after Stewart's abuse. I thought you needed to rest."

Her answering smile was glorious. "It is too bad, though, as your father said Iona was a good place to be baptized."

"But it would be more fitting for you to be baptized here," Fergus replied. "What of the morrow? We can visit the reliquary and have the blessing of Saint Euphemia upon our match."

"You would reveal it?"

"Nay, I would not invite attention. Perhaps we shall have a blessing of the grain on the morrow."

Leila laughed.

"But the fact is that Karayan followed me to Gaston's abode and thence to here," Fergus noted. "That means any other soul might do the same. We will undertake the blessing of the reliquary, then a more secure home must be found for it."

"But where?"

Fergus smiled. "If the reliquary is to be hidden longer than it has been thus far, I have an idea. I will send a missive to Gaston with Karayan and seek his counsel."

"What idea is this?"

"Do you recall how Lady Ysmaine hid the relic on our journey?"

"Of course!"

"I have not yet had word from Duncan, but it seems that if Radegunde is to join him on the anniversary of their handfast, she might do the same."

Leila's eyes lit. "She would be glad to do as much. I know it well."

"And it would be safe wherever they make their abode, for none spoke of Duncan as a member of the party."

"That is most clever," Leila said and granted him another kiss. "You mean to teach me the price of having no discussion with you," she teased. "You tell me so many interesting things this day."

Fergus put a fingertip on her lips. "Aye, and there is more."

Leila laughed. "What else do you scheme?"

"Solely to ensure the happiness of my lady wife."

"I believe you have done as much."

"Not to my own satisfaction. I have a suggestion for you, one that Karayan can take back to the east."

Leila regarded him, her eyes bright with curiosity. "What manner of suggestion?"

"What if we were to make an arrangement with your cousin and her husband, to meet them at a designated time and place?"

"When and where?"

"Some city where Franj and Saracen can meet, between here and Jerusalem."

"Venice, perhaps, or Constantinople," Leila suggested, her excitement clear. "But she has a young son. She cannot leave him, and she will not."

"I hope that soon we will have a young son, as well."

Leila flushed in a most becoming way. "I am not sure," she confessed softly and Fergus wanted to lift her in his arms and protect her from every breath of wind.

"Truly?"

"I missed my courses once," she whispered. "But then Stewart struck me in the belly." Anger thrummed through Fergus at the import of the other man's choice. Leila's brow puckered. "I know so little of these matters and have no one to ask..."

"Then I shall add to that missive to Gaston and ensure that Radegunde visits here with all haste."

Leila smiled at him. "Thank you." She ran her hand over his chest. "I hope there will be more than one son, Fergus."

"As do I. We could choose a date, perhaps ten years from now, and we agree that we shall be at the selected city, all of us. You could see Aziza and talk to her to your heart's content and share your tidings."

"Fergus! I would be so glad of such a chance!" Leila bit her lip. "Do you truly think it could be done?"

"Any deed can be done if people have sufficient desire to do it." Fergus watched her, knowing he would move the stars and the moon to see her happy. A journey to the east was a small effort in comparison. He had only to look at the resolve she had shown in making a new life for herself.

"And you would make this journey for me?"

"I could do no less," he said, smiling down at her. "I told you before that I would take you east at your request."

"And so you did. I like this scheme better, to travel together and both return to Killairic."

"You have surrendered all that you know to be with me, Leila. I will surrender anything to see you happy." He caught her close once more. "I would even have let you ride away with Karayan, never to see you again, if it would have given you joy."

"Fergus! I can only truly be happy with you."

He found her in his embrace again, a situation that suited him very well. "And I can only be happy with you, though it need not be at Killairic."

"Of course, we must be here," Leila chided, her eyes dancing. "I cannot imagine a place more perfect."

"And I cannot imagine a wife more perfect," Fergus concluded, capturing her lips beneath his own once more. His heart thundered when she rose to her toes and returned his kiss with the enticing heat he had long associated with her.

He had nearly lost the prize of his heart, but Fergus would never put it at risk again.

FRIDAY, AUGUST 26, 1188

*Feast Day of Saint Zephryinus
& Saint Bregwin of Canterbury*

CHAPTER SEVENTEEN

hey arrive!" Leila cried when she spied the party approaching Killairic. She had remained in the solar that morning, simply to watch the road. "Fergus, they arrive!" she called again from the top of the stairs. She managed to take only three before he was before her, having run up the stairs from the foyer.

"Do not rush on the stairs," he said sternly, then swept her into his arms to carry her down to the great hall.

"You fuss too much," she chided him.

"We shall ask Radegunde about that," he replied, then gave her a quick kiss. Leila had not bled once since arriving at Killairic. Her belly was rounding so that more than Margaret noticed the change—that woman had commented upon the change when fitting Leila's new red kirtle with its fine embroidery. Leila felt like a queen when she wore it and she felt hale with the child. Calum was delighted by the promise of a baby, but Leila wanted Radegunde's conclusions before she would be at ease.

There had been much activity at Killairic over the summer. A distant cousin of Isobel's had returned from Iona with Murdoch and had taken Gavin back to the isles to be raised with his kin. Their family had a number of children and Gavin had been pleased to go with his relation. Gavin had learned a great deal while helping the miller which impressed his relation, too. The harvest was in and it was bountiful. Killairic did indeed seem like a paradise as well as a home.

Bartholomew had sent word that he had a missive from Duncan, and that Gaston and Ysmaine would escort Radegunde north to rejoin Duncan. They intended to halt at Killairic, and Leila could not wait to see her friend again.

Given the flurry of messages that had been exchanged over the summer, she anticipated that her plan with the pigeons would be well received. She was excited by the prospect of sharing that, as well.

The Templar knights, Enguerrand and Yvan, had returned to Paris, after escorting Karayan back to Châmont-sur-Maine. It was only under protest that Enguerrand agreed to pretend the relic in his custody had been lost, and Leila hoped that Lord Gaston, with his experience of diplomacy, had been more persuasive. Fergus thought that knight would write to the Master of the Temple in Paris to ensure that the two knights did not believe they had failed in their duty. She hoped the party brought tidings of the Grand Master's plan for the reliquary.

Bartholomew and Anna had arrived at Killairic the day before and they were already in the bailey by the time Leila and Fergus reached it. Lord Gaston shouted from the gates, waving from the back of his destrier, and Fergus cried a welcome in return. Leila wished she were taller and could see better over the crowd of villagers come to greet the arrivals.

Lady Ysmaine followed her husband through the gates on a mount of her own. Radegunde's brother, Michel, was in the small party, which surprised Leila, then she saw Radegunde and shouted a welcome of her own. She ran and the two met in the middle of the village, each embracing the other with force.

Then Radegunde pulled back, her eyes wide. "You are with child!" she declared then hugged Leila again, but more gently. "Since when? You must tell me all."

Leila smiled, anticipating the kind of discussion she had missed so much. "Since the end of April, I think. Fergus and I swore a handfast as soon as we arrived."

"And when does your year and a day conclude?"

Leila smiled. "It matters little, for we were wed in June."

Radegunde congratulated her, then kissed her cheeks in succession. Leila looked up to find Gaston smiling at the pair of them.

"I did not tell her," he whispered with a wink. "Though Karayan told me."

Radegunde gasped in outrage and Lady Ysmaine chuckled. "Gaston! How cruel!"

"How is a welcome surprise unkind?" that man protested. "It is Leila's news and should be hers to share." He shook a finger. "If she had sent a missive to Radegunde, that would be another matter."

"I apologize that I did not," Leila said, but Radegunde was not distressed. "And how can you speak of surprises, when you have planned one for Duncan?"

Radegunde smiled and blushed, her anticipation of their reunion clear. "How was he when last you saw him?"

"Missing you." Leila seized her friend's hand. "Come to the garden with me. I have a surprise for you all."

"Before they even have a cup of ale?" Bartholomew said.

"It is not that far from Dumfries, which is undoubtedly where they halted for the night," Fergus noted, his eyes twinkling at Leila. He knew her scheme, of course, for he had helped her in ensuring all was ready.

"Fergus is right in that," Gaston acknowledged. "And I confess to be curious."

Once in the garden, they all turned naturally to the dovecote. It was as if they guessed its import, though they still did not know why they were there. "I saw yesterday that you raised birds," Bartholomew said. "Doves?"

"Pigeons," Leila corrected, taking one of the adults from the dovecote into her hands.

"Ah!" said Lord Gaston and smiled, evidence that he had

guessed.

Lady Ysmaine looked from her husband to Leila, clearly mystified. "Is there a reason why?"

"I will wager that they are homing pigeons," Lord Gaston said.

Leila nodded. "They are. And I intend to give each of you a mating pair."

"But why?" Anna asked, looking as if the last thing she desired was a pair of birds.

"Leila intends to share some wisdom from the east with us," Lord Gaston said.

The others looked at her in confusion.

"It took some time for us to discern how the Saracens knew of our military actions, and did so faster than any man could ride to tell them," Lord Gaston said. He took the bird from Leila's hands gently, then showed its leg to his wife. Leila had tied a red cord upon it. "Red for Killairic?" he asked and she nodded.

"I do not understand, Gaston," Lady Ysmaine said and the others concurred. The former Templar nodded at Leila.

"The homing pigeon is distinct in that it will always return to the place it was born. The distance does not appear to matter. They do not fail in this marvel, and so, they are used to send messages in Palestine and Syria."

"How can that be?" Bartholomew asked. "If you release this bird, will it not return to the dovecote there?"

"Aye, it will," Leila agreed. She showed the baskets that Fergus had ordered to be made. "But if I give it to you along with its mate and you take them to Haynesdale with you, when you release it, it will return here."

"And you can tie a message to its leg when you do," Fergus added.

"And the ones born at Haynesdale will return from here to there," Leila said. "So, I thought that we could breed homing pigeons at all of our abodes and tie cords to their legs to indicate where they were born. When we visit each other, we can bring the birds."

"And in between," Fergus concluded. "We can send messages to each other as needed." He smiled at Radegunde. "You can send us word when you rejoin Duncan."

"I will help you write the missive," Lady Ysmaine said gently to her maid, which pleased Radegunde.

"It is a scheme that is clever beyond compare," Lord Gaston said with satisfaction, stroking the bird's breast before returning it to Leila's care. "Just think of how we could have conferred about Karayan before I revealed your location to him." He lowered his voice. "I was right in that, was I not?"

"Aye, and thank you," Leila said. The others had broken out into chatter, discussing how they could house the birds and how many they would need to breed. "Take two pair each when you depart," Leila said. "Two for Haynesdale and two for Radegunde to take north. I have more breeding and will send two more pair to Haynesdale that you might take a pair to Châmont-sur-Maine upon your return, as well as a pair for Altesburg."

"We will choose a color for each holding," Fergus said. "And be able to share tidings."

"This is a marvel of an idea," Bartholomew said and all congratulated Leila on the notion.

Lord Gaston raised a hand. "I must tell you that we just had word from Wulfe. Christina bore twin sons at the end of May. Their names are Bertrand and Konrad. He waited until they were thriving until he sent word of the good news."

"Twins," Radegunde murmured with a shake of her head. "They can be so fragile."

Lord Gaston smiled. "I sense that Wulfe is a protective father."

"You mean Ulric and Juliana," Lady Ysmaine corrected and Lord Gaston shook his head.

"They will always be Wulfe and Christina to me."

"To me, as well," Bartholomew agreed and the others laughed. Neither Bartholomew nor Fergus knew of the births, so they vowed to send congratulations. Leila was pleased to hear the news, as well. She was glad that Wulfe had found both the love and the home he desired—just as she had.

Fergus winked at her and claimed her hand. "Now, come to the hall and meet my father," he said, ushering them back inside. "I wish to hear more of this missive you have had from Duncan and your plans for this journey."

"Shall we go to the solar?" Radegunde asked Leila in a whisper. "I would put your fears at ease with all haste."

"Thank you!" Leila said and embraced her friend once more. She caught Fergus' gaze and nodded. "Perhaps you should keep your cloak tight around yourself," she counseled Radegunde in an undertone. "As you will appear to be in similar state by the time we join the others in the hall."

"I had forgotten," Radegunde said, then smiled. "Your suggestion was most clever."

"It was you and Lady Ysmaine who thought of it first," Leila replied, as the two friends climbed to the solar together. The others had gone on to the hall, but Fergus lingered at the bottom of the stairs.

"Not too fast!" he cried and Leila smiled.

"He fusses so," she whispered to Radegunde.

"For he loves you," that maid replied. "And there is no better fate for any of us than that."

THURSDAY, DECEMBER 22, 1188

*Feast Day of the martyr
Saint Ischyrion*

EPILOGUE

eila was looking forward to her first celebration of the Yule. She liked the celebratory mood that had seized both Killairic's village and hall. The air was cool but not so very cold during the daylight hours—and she had Fergus to keep her warm each night. Her belly grew rounder and the new midwife from Dumfries declared herself pleased with the progress of Leila's pregnancy. Radegunde had advised her not to worry and she tried not to do as much. They expected the child in the new year, although all was already prepared.

Leila walked a little more slowly and tired a little more quickly, but those were small prices to pay when she knew the child—boy or girl—would make her husband and his father so happy. She still feared that Stewart's savagery might have left a mark, but the midwife assured her that the babe was vigorous and seemingly hale. Would the babe have blue eyes as Fergus had once foretold? She could not imagine how the babe would have red hair, but Leila could not wait to know for certain.

Ever since Karayan's departure, Fergus had returned to the solar to sleep each night. They made love or cuddled and she continued to tell him Scheherazade's tales. Leila could not imagine a greater contentment than living by this man's side.

She was leaving the chapel after discussing the arrangements for Christmas Eve and making her way back to the hall when she noticed the visitor enter the village gates. He was older and dressed warmly but simply. Indeed, he looked to have walked, for he had no steed, but only a great heavy walking stick. He glanced up when she passed and Leila smiled at him, assuming he was a friend or relation of someone in the village. No doubt she would be introduced to him over the holidays. At this moment, she was late for the midday meal.

Instead of smiling in return, his mouth dropped open and he paled. "Saffirah?" he whispered, his tone incredulous.

Leila halted and looked at the new arrival, puzzled by his address. How could he know her mother's name?

"I beg your pardon?" she said, thinking she must have heard him incorrectly.

He apologized as he approached, his gaze roving over her face as if he could not believe his eyes. "I am sorry, my lady, for my eyes must deceive me. You remind me greatly of a lady I once knew, but she would be many years your senior by now." His smile was sad. "It has been a long time."

"A woman named Saffirah?" Leila said with care. "I did not know there were any so named here."

"It was not here." The man ran a hand over his brow and looked suddenly fatigued. "So many years," he whispered, then seemed to recover himself. He inclined his head. "I am Alasdair Campbell, the comrade of Laird Calum. I hope he is yet sufficiently hale to greet an old friend." His gaze sharpened, and she noticed the vivid blue of his eyes. "Unless I am mistaken, you are far from home."

Leila did not return his smile. Could it be? Her heart fluttered. She could not bear to think that the Franj who had broken her mother's heart stood beside her now, speaking her mother's name with such ease. "Nay, sir, I am at home. Calum's son, Fergus, is my husband and now is Laird of Killairic."

"Ah!" Alasdair said. "And so the details come together. Fergus was due to return from Outremer, and Calum hoped for his appearance last Yule."

"Our party arrived in the spring, sir."

Alasdair nodded approval. "He is wed, then, and wed well, I would wager." He indicated her belly. "For it cannot be long before your child is born."

She had to ask. "You then are the comrade who journeyed to Jerusalem with Calum," she said, recalling every word of her uncle's missive. It seemed unlikely that this kindly man would use a woman as Hakim had declared the knight had mistreated her mother.

Perhaps he had repented of his former ways.

"I am, though I lingered there longer than he did."

"Why?" Her question was too sharp and Leila knew it.

"I was in love," Alasdair said. "I suppose there is no cause to hide it. I was assigned to a post in one of the villages granted by King Godfroi to the care of the Holy Sepulchre..."

"Al-Ramm," Leila said, her heart in her throat.

Alasdair stared at her. "How could you guess that?"

"I would ask you to continue your tale first, sir."

His features softened. "Al-Ramm. That is where I met my Saffirah. She was the sister of the blacksmith there and talented with the administration of herbs. Both she and her brother admired the work of Ibn Sīnā, she for the pursuit of healing in people and he for the healing of horses."

"You were in their home?"

"Nay, never. I was struck with affection for Saffirah when first we met and was astonished to find my admiration returned. We met secretly, only to talk, though I would have wed her in a heartbeat. She insisted that such a match could not survive, and truly, we saw the hatred between our kinds each and every day. She told me of her family, as I told her of mine, so I knew much of Hakim though I only met him briefly." He swallowed and shook his head. "The day came that I was released from my post and another man sent to take my place. I would have stayed. She told me to go." His voice turned husky. "I might have defied her command if I had not loved her so."

This was a vastly different version of the tale than her uncle had shared with Leila and she hoped it was true. She could find no hint in Alasdair's manner that he deceived her and wondered if it had been another Franj who had violated her mother.

"And you were never intimate, despite this love?" she dared to ask.

He smiled, taking her elbow for the steps to the keep. "So, you might well ask, for passion is so often taken as the full expression of love. I was concerned for her future, should we be intimate, for if we were not to wed, I would not have wished for her to be shamed. Much less to be left with a child. I was stalwart, until our last night together. We were more amorous than we had been yet, for we knew we should never see each other again." He frowned. "I was weak, though she insisted that we enchanted each other. It was marvelous. As perfect as she was."

He seemed to be overcome for a long moment, but then finally cleared his throat. "I hated to leave. She practically cast me out. I begged her to send me word if she had need of me, but she wept and kissed my cheeks, telling me that her heart was mine forever but that we should not see each other again. I have prayed for many years that she found good fortune, that she wed a good man, that she had many children and a long life." He sighed and Leila saw how it grieved him. "I will never know."

Alasdair would have continued to the hall, but Leila laid a hand upon his arm to halt him. "There is a reason I resemble the Saffirah you loved so well," she said softly. "And I can tell you that she had one child, a daughter."

He stared at her, aghast. "She did wed, then..."

"Nay, she did not. She told her brother that she had been abandoned by her lover, no doubt to win his mercy. He took her into his home but she died in the bearing of her child."

Alasdair crossed himself, obviously struck with grief.

"Hakim moved us all to Jerusalem. He raised me along with his own daughter and called me his little flower."

Alasdair was clearly astonished. "Saffirah," he whispered.

"She never wed," Leila said with a smile. "She told Hakim that my father would hold her heart forever, but I was never told that man's name."

Their gazes locked and held, so much joy and hope in the eyes of Alasdair that Leila could scarce take a breath. "You did not tell me your name, little flower."

"Leila. Leila binte Qadir lufti al-Ramm."

"Leila. Lady Leila." Alasdair wiped a tear, then bowed low over her hand. He kissed her knuckles and she felt him tremble. "And so God's mercy is shown to an old man in his winter years. I wish you every joy, my daughter."

"And I am slow in offering you hospitality, my father," she said with a smile. "Come, come into the hall, for Calum will be glad of these tidings."

"Perhaps not," Alasdair acknowledged with a laugh. "For he will see far more of me now, and have competition to dote upon that child you carry."

They laughed together and entered the hall arm in arm, Leila's heart full with the unexpected joy the older man's arrival had brought. Fergus glanced up from a discussion with his father and smiled at her, the sight of her beloved making Leila feel that she was fortunate indeed.

Then she felt a contraction, a hard wrench of her womb, and caught her breath. Alasdair seized her arm to steady her and Fergus hastened to her side. It was only a few moments before she felt the pain again, and she gripped Fergus' sleeve. "I believe, sir, that there may be a babe in hall for the Yule," she said, trying to make a jest.

Fergus' eyes lit and he swept her into his arms, carrying her to the solar even as he shouted for the midwife.

"It will not come so quickly as that," Leila chided, but Fergus would not heed her.

"The babe will come when it chooses, but we shall be prepared," he said with resolve. "And if there is so much time, you can tell me how you made old Alasdair smile."

By the time Leila's water had broken and the midwife arrived, she had done just that and could not fail to see how the tale satisfied her husband.

Her cry at the next powerful contraction, however, did not.

It was just as he had dreamed.

Fergus sat in the solar late that night, holding the tiny miracle that was his son. Leila's labor had been short and fierce, and though the midwife had warned him that it might be thus, he had been terrified by her ordeal. In truth, he could not have endured it much longer and he marveled at her strength.

She slept as he rocked the babe, and he was glad that they were once again alone in the solar. The candles burned low and the coals glowed in the braziers. The shutters were closed tightly against the chill of the night, though Fergus had liked that the night was clear and the sky filled with stars. The keep had fallen silent at this hour, particularly after the excitement of the heir's arrival.

The babe stirred and fussed a little, and Leila seemed to sense it. She awakened in almost the same moment and sat up. Her hair had grown longer this year and spilled over her shoulders, though her smile was as warm as ever. "Let me try to coax the milk again," she said and lifted her hands.

"He is so tiny," Fergus said as he laid the precious burden in Leila's arms. She smiled and nestled the babe close, offering her breast to him.

Fergus smiled at the sight of the babe's dark auburn hair. The color had only been discernible once his hair dried, but proved Fergus' forecast true. The boy's skin was palest gold, lighter than Leila's and darker than Fergus' own. He watched, wondering how many other traits he would notice over the coming years, in which the boy took a bit from Leila and a bit from him to make his own way.

The babe caught the nipple in his mouth and sucked with such vigor that Leila caught her breath, then she smiled at Fergus.

"And he is strong. I was so afraid that Stewart had damaged him."

"He is perfect." Fergus sat beside her, putting his arm around her shoulders. This was the scheme he had envisioned so long ago, Leila nursing a child. The boy opened his eyes and they were of clear blue, as vivid a hue as those of Alasdair. "Which grandfather is more proud, do you think?"

Leila laughed. "It is impossible to say." Her eyes were shining, as if lit by stars in the way that he found most enticing. "I think his father is most smitten of all, though."

"If only because his lady wife is hale," Fergus said and kissed her brow. "I see how he makes you happy."

Leila nodded. "I would adore him even if you did not need an heir. We should have another."

"And a daughter," Fergus agreed. "I would like to see if she, too, would resemble Saffirah." He sobered then. "I wish she had been here to see your joy, and your cousin, too."

"Aziza will see it in Venice, when we meet, and I am certain that Karayan has been compelled to tell her of Killairic over and over again." Leila smiled. "As for my mother, I felt her presence this day, as if she meant to aid me."

"A guardian angel on your shoulder?"

"A loving one," Leila said, her voice husky. "Who will never be forgotten."

Fergus held her tightly, and eased away her tears. "I have a gift for you this Yule, but would give it to you now, when we are alone together."

"It is a little soon for that manner of gift, husband," Leila teased.

Fergus chuckled and retrieved the parcel. As she was holding their son, he had to unwrap it for her. It was the psalter he had bought, with no clear idea at the time of why. "It was not intended for Isobel," he said before she could ask. "I knew she would not value it. But I thought it so pretty and I could envision it in a lady's delicate hands as she made her prayers."

Leila smiled up at him. "Any particular hands?"

"These ones," he said and lifted one to his lips. He kissed Leila then and they sat in silence, admiring their son as he dozed. Fergus could imagine no finer way to spend this night. "He has need of a name, this son of ours," he murmured finally to Leila and was relieved when she smiled again.

"You must have a family name to bestow."

"My family will bestow much upon him, including the tradition of his mother choosing his name."

"Truly?"

"Truly. The decision is yours."

Leila stared down that the boy, her finger caressing his cheek. "Then I would name him for his guardian angels, his grandfathers both by blood and by honor."

"One on the left and one on the right." Fergus smiled, for he thought it a perfect tribute. "In what order?"

Leila considered it, then chose. "Alasdair Calum Hakim," she said. "It sounds best that way."

"And so it shall be thus," Fergus agreed and kissed his wife again. The shadow of doom was dispelled, the future was assured and he was happier than he had ever imagined he might be.

And it was all because Leila had put her hand in his. He would spend the rest of his days and nights ensuring that she never regretted her choice.

He would spend the rest of his life ensuring that Killairic was the home she had been determined to make her own. "Are you too tired to tell me a story, Leila?" he asked as he tucked himself into the bed beside her. "I believe that last night you were telling me a tale of three apples."

"Indeed, I was," Leila agreed, then smiled up at him. "And what shall you do when I reach the end of Scheherazade's tales?"

"What did Shahriar do?"

"He confessed that she had won his heart and his admiration, and he revoked his law to have his queen executed in the morning. He asked her to be his queen in truth and she agreed." Leila's eyes danced. "I believe they lived happily ever after."

"But you are already my lady and my wife, for my heart and my admiration are both conquered," Fergus said, pretending to consider this as a puzzle. "Perhaps, you could start at the beginning again and tell Scheherazade's tales to our children. Alasdair will be old enough to listen after another eight hundred nights or so."

Leila laughed with a merriment that made Fergus smile. "I think that might ensure that we *all* lived happily ever after," she said, and Fergus could not argue with that.

ABOUT THE AUTHOR

Bestselling and award-winning author Deborah Cooke has published over fifty novels and novellas, including historical romances, fantasy romances, fantasy novels with romantic elements, paranormal romances, contemporary romances, urban fantasy romances, time travel romances and paranormal young adult novels. She writes as herself, Deborah Cooke, as Claire Delacroix, and has written as Claire Cross. Her Claire Delacroix medieval romance, *The Beauty*, was her first book to land on the New York Times List of Bestselling Books.

Deborah was the writer-in-residence at the Toronto Public Library in 2009, the first time TPL hosted a residency focused on the romance genre, and she was honored to receive the Romance Writers of America PRO Mentor of the Year Award in 2012. She's a member of Romance Writers of America, and is on the RWA Honor Roll. She lives in Canada with her family.

To learn more about Deborah's books, please visit her websites at:
http://deborahcooke.com
http://www.delacroix.net

www.ingramcontent.com/pod-product-compliance
Lightning Source LLC
Chambersburg PA
CBHW051207190726
48288CB00006B/1851